FRESH KILLS

CAROLYN WHEAT

BERKLEY PRIME CRIME, NEW YORK

For Mom, my first editor
For Dad, my first opposing counsel

A Berkley Prime Crime Book
Published by The Berkley Publishing Group
200 Madison Avenue, New York, New York 10016

Copyright © 1995 by Carolyn Wheat.

The lines from "when faces called flowers float out of the ground,"
"in Just-," "all ignorance toboggans into know," and "pity this busy
monster, mankind," are reprinted from *Complete Poems, 1904–1962*, by
E. E. Cummings, Edited by George J. Firmage, by permission of
Liveright Publishing Corporation. Copyright © 1923, 1944, 1950, 1951,
1972, 1978, 1991 by the Trustees for the E. E. Cummings Trust.
Copyright © 1976, 1979 by George James Firmage.

Excerpt from "The Goose-Girl" by Edna St. Vincent Millay from
Collected Poems, HarperCollins. Copyright 1923, 1951 by Edna St.
Vincent Millay and Norma Millay Ellis. Reprinted by permission of
Elizabeth Barnett, literary executor.

First edition: June 1995

Library of Congress Cataloging-in-Publication Data
Wheat, Carolyn.
    Fresh kills / by Carolyn Wheat.
        p.   cm.
    ISBN 0-425-14785-1 (hardcover)
    ISBN 0-425-14920-X (trade paperback)
    I. Title.
PS3573.H35F74   1995
813'.54—dc20   94-40140
                                                                      CIP

Printed in the United States of America

10   9   8   7   6   5   4   3   2   1

PROLOGUE

Little Fresh Kill. The name rolled around in my head as I trudged through the long grass, eyes intent on the boggy, soggy ground underfoot. I thought about what we were looking for and shivered.

I was part of an army of searchers. Men in red checked hunting jackets, cops in blue windbreakers, teenaged boys in leather jackets. I was one of a few women, plodding behind the men's longer strides, feeling like a camp follower.

Staten Island is full of kills, narrow inlets that were once the despair of captains maneuvering wooden ships around the island toward the bustling harbor of Manhattan. The word comes from the Dutch, meaning creek. Nothing sinister. Or so the old Staten Islander who walked next to me said. Now the tall ships were gone, and the swampland we trudged along lay between the Con Edison plant and the sanitation landfill.

Ecological types have taken to calling places like these

"wetlands"—and the name was apt; I was up to my ankles in chilly water hidden beneath tall reeds—but to me it was still a swamp. Full of secrets. Capable of sucking people into the marshy ground, never to be seen again. An obstacle course in brown and gray.

It was a great place to dump a body.

It was getting late: dark and cold and raw. The calendar said April; this particular evening would have felt at home in November. My denim jacket, even with a wool sweater underneath, wasn't warm enough. My feet, in sneakers, had been soaked for hours. But it wasn't just the cold that froze my heart.

Every muscle ached as I plodded through the spongy, overgrown swamp, pushing aside brown, feather-topped grass. But I couldn't stop, couldn't knock off and call it a night the way some of the other searchers were beginning to do.

In the distance I heard the frantic barking of police dogs. The cop next to me broke into a run. I stumbled as I tried keeping pace with him, damp cold stabbing my lungs. As I ran on frozen feet toward whatever the dogs had discovered, my shins cried out in pain with each ragged step. Reeds whipped my face; I no longer bothered to push them out of the way before rushing toward the place where the dogs bayed.

As I tripped over hillocks of sphagnum moss, my sneakers sinking into the boggy ground, I prayed to the God I didn't believe in that the dogs had found a dead rabbit.

They hadn't.

Little Fresh Kill clung to its dead tenaciously, moss and weeds grasping at the girl's body as though pulling her into a watery underworld.

It was my fault. I stood on the bank watching the Emergency Services cops lowering ropes, knowing I should leave and knowing that I couldn't. That my punishment was to watch my client being pulled from the swamp like a discarded boot.

She was so small. Not a child, not yet the adult she'd tried to be. Long, blonde hair weed-tangled, face bleached white. A Staten Island Ophelia, with foam coming out of her open mouth. Her hands were clenched; had she grasped in death at the reeds, trying to pull herself out of the watery grave?

Around me the voices of the civilian volunteers who'd combed the area for the last several hours began to swell with speculation.

"Poor kid must've drowned herself," a man with a pipe in his mouth said, shaking his head.

"But what was she doing here?" a heavyset woman in an Army fatigue jacket wanted to know. "I thought she was staying at that place in New Springville."

"What place?"

"Home for unwed mothers. Didn't you hear the story on the news?" Fatigue Jacket's eager face proclaimed her ready to provide an update for anyone who'd missed the story.

"Didn't know there were any unwed mothers anymore," the pipe smoker replied, "what with abortion and all."

I moved away from the crowd, away from the cops trying in vain to keep the volunteers from turning into ghoulish rubberneckers. Turned toward—what? The stand of misshapen dwarf trees? The willow in the distance, head bowed as if weeping? The acres of swamp turned from wasteland into a wildlife refuge big enough to hide a hundred bodies?

The sun was setting, blood-red spilling into all the watery lanes of the kills. The sky was streaked with improbable colors, creams and lilacs and pinks as artificial-looking as a paint-by-number landscape. I kept walking, head bent, legs moving like pistons, aching like hell.

She was dead. Amber was dead.

I wasn't feeling too good myself.

The truth stabbed through me like the ice-cold swamp air: It was my fault. It was all my fault.

I wasn't the only one who thought so. Squishing footsteps behind me made me turn, fear jumping into my throat. "What the hell—"

It was Detective Aronson. The last guy in the world I wanted to see.

He grabbed my arm. It hurt, but he wasn't going to know that.

"Where do you think you're going, Ms. Jameson?" The voice was as smooth as the hand was rough. Aronson could play good cop/bad cop all by himself.

"I don't know. I—" I grabbed a deep breath and looked the detective in the eye. I had to know the worst. "Any sign of the baby?" I asked, my voice a dry croak.

"You hoping for a perfect score, Counselor? Two for two?"

"That's not fair," I protested. Yet even as I spoke, I felt a perverse comfort in the fact that Aronson knew it was my fault. At least I wasn't on a self-blame trip for nothing.

"All I did was represent her in court. I'm not responsible for what she—" My voice broke. I turned away. If I wasn't responsible, who was?

Detective Milt Aronson released my arm and sighed. "No sign of the baby. We're going to keep looking."

I nodded. When I was able to speak again, I said, "I'll go back with the others and help search."

The look he gave me was ninety percent contempt and ten percent pity. "Don't you think you've done enough?"

He turned on his heel and walked back toward the clumps of searchers.

I marched like a zombie toward the place where I'd left the car. Once I tripped over a hillock of moss and sank to my knees in cold water. It was hard getting up; I felt as if I deserved to lie in the stinking, freezing muck that had claimed Amber's life.

I'd known girls like Amber existed. I'd known there were people in the world who sold babies, others who bought them, and lawyers who did the deals.

I just hadn't known I'd be one of them.

CHAPTER ONE

I was number eighty-four on the calendar, a one-case lawyer with nothing to do but wait. If I'd been in Criminal, I'd have had other courtrooms to cover, clients to greet, calendars to answer. But here on the Civil side, I was a stranger, as out of place as a Wall Street corporado in Brooklyn night court.

Other lawyers milled around, calling out names, looking for clients or opponents. "Anyone here on *Thompson v. Powell?*" a stoop-shouldered man with a bald spot asked everyone who came through the door.

"Who's here for the Transit Authority?" a woman in a size-four black suit asked in a tiny voice.

"Who'd admit working for the Transit Authority?" the lawyer sitting next to me said under his breath. He was a young, upwardly mobile type with a Land's End briefcase and a supercilious smile. Clearly the Brooklyn Supreme Court motion part was a comedown in his professional career.

It was oddly soothing, the lazily expectant atmosphere of the motion part. There was bustle; there were brisk clerks hauling tons of official paper; there were the Service "girls" who answered motions for absent attorneys. There were deals in the hallways, slaps on the back. Typical lawyer stuff. With one difference from my daily fare in criminal court. No one was here because she'd drowned her children in three feet of scalding water.

"Anyone here a notary?" The voice was unmistakable, though it had been a while since I'd heard it. East Bronx Irish, loud enough to cut through the din of legal chitchat but not so loud as to render the speaker unladylike.

Marla Hennessey. Sometime friend, sometime rival, sometime bitch. Which of her multiple personalities would be out today?

Before Marla got her answer, the bailiff called out, "All rise," and the judge took the bench. Sixty lawyers stood, then flopped back down on the benches. Somehow, during the thirty seconds we were up, Marla substituted herself for the Land's End briefcase.

"No, I'm not a notary," I whispered, as the calendar call began. "How are you? Haven't seen you in ages," I went on, doing the Greeting Old Law School Friend number as though there had never been any bad blood between us.

"Can you come out in the hall for a minute?" Marla's green eyes had a calculating look I knew all too well.

"I don't dare miss the first call," I whispered back. "I'll be in this damned courtroom for the rest of my natural life as it is."

As the clerk droned out the names on the calendar, lawyers jumped up and said, "Ready For," "Ready in Op," or as an occasional variation on a theme, "For the Motion."

"Cass, don't bullshit me." Marla was one of the few people I knew who could shout in a whisper. "I checked the calendar. You're number eighty-four. It'll take two minutes to explain, you say yes or no. The worst thing that happens is you're second-called.''

Second call is the civil court equivalent of the Chinese water torture. It meant waiting until at least noon. But such was the force of Marla's personality—or the depth of my curiosity—that I followed her into the hall.

Once there, she lit a cigarette and began waving it in her hand, her huge hammered-silver bracelet riding up and down on her wrist.

She'd put on weight. She'd colored and cut her hair, wearing it in a platinum pageboy that fitted her head like a cap. Her clothes were silver and mauve, flowing garments that gave an illusion of soft femininity. As I listened, I reminded myself that it was only an illusion. Marla was as armored as if her clothes and hair were made of stainless steel.

I was so busy studying her that it took me a minute to realize she was talking about adoptions. About me handling an adoption, to be exact. I shook my head and started to protest.

"I don't know anything about—"

"Cass, I'm telling you. It's no big deal." My neck stiffened. Whatever Marla Hennessey was selling this time, I was determined not to buy. Everything in life that was hard for me—getting through law school, finding and then losing boyfriends, starting my own law practice—came under Marla's heading of "no big deal."

"I've never handled an adoption before." I said it flatly, as though that were the only problem.

"Adoptions are easy, Cass. A piece of cake." Life to Marla was just one plate of angel food after another.

"It's exactly the same as a closing," Marla went on, her nicotine voice rasping, "except that instead of a three-bedroom co-op in Park Slope, you're transferring title to a bouncing baby boy."

Why were baby boys always bouncing? And when had Marla learned to reduce human life to "transferring title"?

"Jesus, Marla, that's a humane way of putting it."

"Well, that's all adoption is. Legally speaking."

Legally speaking. Our first day at NYU Law School came back to me in living color. The Torts professor handed around a yellow legal pad for us to sign in on. By the time it got to me, it contained more three-named individuals than a library of Victorian novels. Good old Sam the hippie had transformed himself into Samuel Lionel Ripnick. Ed Franklin, who still had acne on his chin, blossomed into E. Harrison Franklin III. And Marla listed herself as Marla Hennessey Schomberg, thus raising from the emotional dead her despised ex-husband. Anything for those elegant three names that spelled "Partner" to white-shoe law firms.

Except me. *Cass Jameson*, I wrote in bold black strokes, forgoing the middle name I've never liked anyway. Integrity above all. I was very young.

The funny thing was, nearly twenty years later, the three-piece suits with the three-name handles were doing pretty well, while I was always behind in the mortgage payments on my brownstone office-home. I doubted whether repainting the office window to read "Cassandra Louise Jameson" would help, but . . .

Could adoptions be all that difficult?

Could they be harder than standing before a judge and representing a woman who'd listened too long to the devils in her head and plunged two toddlers and an infant into near-boiling water?

What would it be like to handle a case with a real, live, unhurt baby? A baby with no cigarette burns on its legs, a baby who smiled at a kind world? Rojean Glover's children had never known a kind world, even before their fatal bathtime.

"Tell me how easy," I said with a sigh. Resisting Marla Hennessey in full thrust had never been easy. And part of me, a very strong part, wanted to atone for Rojean.

How can you represent those people?

It's a question I've been answering in one form or another for all the years I've practiced criminal law. How can you represent a rapist? What if you know for a fact your client is guilty? What if your client told you point-blank she was going to lie on the witness stand?

The last one is easy; you get off the case. Guilty is one thing, perjury another. Try explaining that fine ethical distinction at a cocktail party.

If you're going to practice in the criminal courts, you work out a philosophy that lets you answer the other questions. Answers like: I don't *know* he's guilty; I wasn't there, was I? Answers like: The Constitution requires a fair trial, with lawyers on both sides doing their best; by defending my client, guilty or not, I maintain the integrity of the criminal justice system.

Good answers. Most of the time.

But they didn't work when it came to Rojean.

I didn't know, I told myself.

How could I know?

You should have known. The answer pounded at me, woke me up at two A.M. *You should have known.* Her Family Court history was right there; she'd been charged with abuse four times. Each time, the judge returned the kids after a few months of foster care. And then the cycle of poverty, frustration, and ignorance would start again. Tonetta had a broken arm; she must have fallen out of her high chair. Todd cut his head open when he stumbled against the radiator. Trudine fractured her leg on the monkey bars in the playground. Always an answer, always an excuse.

I represented Rojean Glover on a charge of endangering the welfare of her children by leaving them alone for two days while she struggled to get back on public assistance so she could feed them. Six-year-old Tonetta, the oldest, was left in charge. When a neighbor called the Bureau of Child Welfare, the children were found hungry, dirty, and scared, and were taken away—"put in protective custody," in the bureaucratese of BCW. Shoved into foster homes, where at least they had more to eat than one box of Cap'n Crunch cereal with no milk.

It was a triumph of legal representation. I commissioned my own social work study to compete with the official probation report and convinced the judge that if Rojean went into a special parenting program and saw a counselor once a week, she could learn the parenting skills she'd never gotten from her own junkie mother. Not that Rojean was an addict—she'd seen enough of drugs in her childhood to keep her clean—but she'd never seen a healthy family, so how could she possibly raise one?

How can you represent those people?

By understanding them. By seeing them as people, not monsters, no matter what they've done. By finding the whole story, the one that appears between the lines of the official records. By listening instead of talking.

So why, two months into her counseling program, did Rojean listen to the voices that told her the kids were possessed by the devil and had to be cleansed in a scalding bath so they could enter the kingdom of heaven?

And why didn't I know it was going to happen? Why didn't I see the schizophrenia as well as the poverty and ignorance? Why didn't I prevent it?

The newspapers blamed the judge. A few mentioned my name in the last paragraph of the story. But the truth was that if a less conscientious lawyer had represented Rojean, those kids would be alive. In a foster home, but alive.

How can you represent those people?

I didn't have any more good answers.

I came back to attention, realizing I'd drifted away while Marla outlined the ridiculous ease with which I could handle an adoption.

"I've got a horny white teenager about to pup. I've also got a desperate older couple who'd like to have a kid before they get their first Social Security check. So they've decided to bypass the adoption agency crap. They're paying the girl's medical expenses and a reasonable legal fee."

FRESH KILLS • 11

"Where do I come in?" Marla wasn't the only lawyer taking a smoke break. The air was blue and thick; I wanted this conversation over.

"Judge Feinberg—a real pain in the ass—says the girl needs her own lawyer. That it's a conflict of interest for me to represent both the kid and the parents. As though every lawyer in the city hasn't done it that way since God was a teenager. So," she went on, exhaling a stream of smoke that matched her silver silk, "I need someone to meet with the girl, get her consent, and file the papers in court. Easy, no?"

"Sounds easy enough," I conceded. I thought back to the one or two things I knew about adoptions. "What if the girl changes her mind? Doesn't she have—what, thirty days?"

"God, Cass." A drag on another cigarette was exhaled in an elaborate sigh. "Talk about looking gift horses in the mouth. The last time we had lunch all you could talk about was that broad who killed her babies, and now you want to open Pandora's box on this adoption before you even take the case. Trust me, this girl's not changing her mind."

The holding pens at Brooklyn Criminal Court flashed before my eyes. Sitting eyeball to eyeball with Rojean, her head twitching, her voice guttural, her pupils needle points in her thin face. "Gotta get me out," she mumbled, her hands working in her lap. "Gotta get me out to feed my babies."

I'd looked down at the complaint just to be sure I'd read it right the first time. ". . . did cause the deaths of Tonetta, Todd, and Trudine Glover by means of . . ."

When we stood before the judge on the question of bail, she made her own plea directly to him: "Gotta get home, y'Honor. My babies alone, they need me."

"And besides," Marla went on, jarring me back to the smoke-filled present, "if this works out, there could be more. I place a lot of babies out of this group home on Staten Island, and as long as Feinberg's on the bench, the girls will need separate counsel. But I'd like to know I'm dealing with someone I can trust. I'd rather have you than some brother-in-law who questions everything and knows nothing. The last lawyer I had to deal with—God!''

"Hey," I said, "just keep in mind the only thing I know about Family Court is where they keep the juvenile delinquents.''

"That's the beauty part, sweetie. I'll teach you everything you need to know. For starters," she added, dropping her butt to the floor and crushing it with a black and silver pump, "we're not in Family Court. That's a poor people's court, and adoptive parents are used to better. So in the City we do adoptions in Surrogate's Court. Much nicer atmosphere. You'll see.''

If memory served, Marla had taught me everything I needed to know about wills in one long all-nighter just before the exam. I got a D in the course.

Marla'd said a D was no big deal.

CHAPTER TWO

I felt as if I'd been listening to Marla talk for a month. I'd begged her not to smoke in the car, so she lit up and held the glowing cigarette out the window, in the fond belief that the smoke would waft into the damp March breeze instead of back inside the vehicle.

"... hope nothing's really wrong with her," Marla said. She'd heard that the doctor who was scheduled to deliver Amber's baby was making a house call. "I mean, the last thing we need is a defective baby, right?"

"What happens if—"

"Depends," Marla replied, her eyes fixed on the road. We were on Victory Boulevard, a main highway on Staten Island, an uncharted wilderness to an Ohio girl transplanted first to Greenwich Village and then to brownstone Brooklyn. From the window of Marla's cream-colored Beemer, it looked a lot like Cleveland, even down to the depressing St. Patrick's Day rain.

"When people adopt through an agency," Marla explained, "they fill out a form listing what defects are acceptable and which are deal-breakers. Like they could handle a kid with a missing finger, but not a Down's syndrome baby. I thought it was a good idea, so I lifted a copy of the form when I left the agency, modified it a little, and now I get all my adoptive parents to sign it."

I pondered this in silence, tired of punctuating everything Marla said with incredulous exclamations. *You mean people actually choose between cerebral palsy and cystic fibrosis? If the kid's got a defect, they send it back to the manufacturer? What is this, adoption or buying stereo equipment, for God's sake?*

And I'd thought criminal practice was cold.

Marla took a left off Victory Boulevard, and we sped past the infamous Willowbrook State Hospital, euphemistically renamed the Staten Island Developmental Center— where Junior Greenspan might end up if he was lacking in the brain department. We then passed a giant enclosed mall, the first I'd ever seen inside the five boroughs.

"Looks a little like Cleveland," I remarked.

"God, yes," Marla agreed. "Depressing, no?"

Actually it made me feel slightly—very slightly—homesick for a place I hadn't lived in twenty years. And I cheered up a little, thinking that at least Amber, the birth mother, wasn't living in some hole waiting for her baby, but had a nice suburban home.

"Tell me again why Amber's in this group home," I asked. "I mean, it's a private adoption, right? The agency has nothing to do with it, so why—?"

Marla shook an exasperated head. "God, Cass, if you'd just *listen*. I told you, Doc Scanlon thought she might have a little trouble with her pregnancy; she was behind on her rent and couldn't work, so he agreed to let her stay at the home until she gave birth. The agency's charging her for the room, but it's a lot cheaper than an apartment. It's all perfectly legal; every penny the adoptive parents spend on her support has to be documented in an affidavit before the court, so there's no hanky-panky. Just a logical solution to a simple problem.''

The car—a four-year-old BMW; the adoption business must pay pretty well—took a wide left onto a road marked Platinum Avenue and traveled behind the mall into a complex of low-rise garden apartments, each a depressing replica of its next-door neighbor.

The development showed a positively stunning lack of taste, but it was clean and suburban-nice; bare trees poked spindly branches into the wan March sky. Lawns were still winter-pale, with outcroppings of black-edged snow; near the houses an occasional snowdrop poked a white, bell-shaped head above ground.

Marla turned a few times and pulled up before a huge false-brick two-family house. A regular American house, like the one the Brady Bunch used to live in. There was no sign at all that this place was occupied, not by one big happy family, but by the flotsam and jetsam of not-so-happy families.

The door opened and a very pregnant girl stepped out. She looked about fifteen, with lanky, mouse-colored hair and a pale moon face. She wore a pink smock over leggings; her swollen feet were jammed into pink slippers. She waddled over to the car.

My first impulse was to tell Amber to get the hell back into bed. But before the words escaped my mouth, Marla greeted the child with a ''Hi, Lisa'' in a voice so patently artificial you could have put it in coffee and not gained a pound.

Lisa looked at Marla with bovine sullenness. ''Hi, Ms. Hennessey,'' she said unenthusiastically. ''Mrs. Bonaventura sent me to tell you Doc Scanlon's with Amber. You can come inside, but you'll have to wait till he's finished.''

''Is something wrong?'' Marla and I both asked approximately the same question at exactly the same time.

"I don't know," Lisa replied. "But Doc looked serious when he came in, and you know how he is. Always smiling. Like Santa Claus," she added, a smile creeping over her plump face.

"Jesus" was all Marla said, but she slammed the car door hard and walked quickly, the heels of her shoes making little holes in the grass as she took the straightest path to the door, disregarding the curved flagstone path. I followed, wrapping my jacket around me and wondering how Lisa could stand being outside without a coat.

Inside, the place was homey, but institutional. Everything had been done to make it seem as though a family lived here—afghans over the rocking chairs, souvenir plates mounted on the wall, a colorful rag rug—but with a touch of impersonality. Like a Shelter Island summer house, with transient group renters season after season.

A middle-aged woman I took to be Mrs. Bonaventura came out of the kitchen, wiping her hands on a towel. She extended a still-damp palm and motioned for me to sit. I chose a rocking chair; she sat on the edge of an uncomfortable-looking sofa. She didn't bother urging Marla to sit; anyone with half an eye could see my colleague was bent on pacing and smoking until she'd seen the doctor.

"This is a nice place," I said lamely.

Mrs. Bonaventura smiled as though I'd called the home a palace. "We do what we can," she said. She was about five feet tall, with dark hair pulled back into a bun. Her accent could have been Spanish, Italian, Greek—Persian, for that matter—indefinably not American.

This was a deeply meaningful conversation, but it wasn't getting me closer to my client. But then I wasn't sure I was ready for another girl with a high school face and a mother's belly, especially one being seen by a doctor who might pronounce the product unfit for sale.

Jesus, stop thinking like that. I spoke to myself pretty sharply. I did not want to start talking like Marla, wearing armor clothes, peroxiding my hair. Smoking.

My colleague stubbed her cigarette into a cut-glass ashtray, the kind you see at stoop sales for fifty cents because nobody smokes anymore. Two hard twists of the wrist and the butt stopped smoking, ground into the glass by Marla's efficient hand. She reached into her Coach bag and pulled out a badly folded legal paper. She handed it to me with a casual air that was supposed to mean she'd almost forgotten this little detail. But I'd known Marla a long time, and something about the move seemed calculated. I went on the alert.

"What's that?" I said brightly.

"Oh, nothing much. I like to get a consent to adoption before the birth, then firm it up once the baby's delivered. Mrs. B. here is a notary, so—"

"How convenient." I fixed Marla with a stare I hoped conveyed amused tolerance for her naive attempt at manipulation. "I *can* read, you know," I pointed out. "I may have started this case not knowing much about adoptions, but there's this really handy reference book. Maybe you know it—it's called the Domestic Relations Law, and it contains everything you ever wanted to know about New York adoptions. Including," I finished, letting my voice carry a touch of steel, "the fact that prebirth consents aren't worth the paper they're written on. Marla, dear," I went on, matching her poisonous sweetness, "why are you asking me to have my client sign an unenforceable consent?"

She leveled a stare that should have had my hair falling out. "*I* know it's unenforceable," she said, spacing out the words. "*You* know it's unenforceable. But the little dears who give up their babies don't know it's unenforceable. It's just my way of making sure they know what they're doing is for keeps. If they really want to change their minds, they'll find out soon enough the consent doesn't matter until after birth—and by that time, they'll have signed another, valid consent."

I'd started shaking my head in the middle of her speech,

but it didn't stop her making her case. Now I said it flat out: "No, Marla. I will not take that form to Amber. I will not pretend she's signing a valid consent to adoption now when I know the consent is worthless. You brought me into this case as her lawyer, and that's who I am. Amber's lawyer. Not your patsy."

She shoved the paper back into her bag, then gave me an unexpected grin. "Hey, it was worth a try."

Mrs. Bonaventura asked us if we wanted anything to drink. I shook my head, and Marla muttered something about a neat vodka, cold, with a twist. She didn't get it.

Next thing I knew, Santa Claus was in the room with us. A young Santa, about fifty-five, with rosy cheeks and a tiny bud mouth hidden inside a neatly trimmed salt-and-pepper beard, laughing blue eyes, and a smile that could have melted the North Pole. A well-dressed Santa in a charcoal suit cut to fit his bulk, and handmade shoes on his oddly small feet.

"I'm Dr. Scanlon," he said, holding out a plump hand. I shook it; he squeezed a second or two longer than politeness dictated or allowed, then turned to Marla.

"She's okay," he said. "Fetal heartbeat strong. No sign of premature labor. Just a little spotting, some high blood pressure." He frowned and turned his attention toward the diminutive housemother. "She really should rest," he pronounced. "I've told her to cut down on her trips to the mall until the baby's born. It would be better if she stayed off her feet altogether, but—" He raised his hands, which were tiny compared to his swollen stomach, in a gesture of futility.

Mrs. Bonaventura shook her head regretfully. "You'll never get that Amber to stay in bed for two hours, let alone a week," she said in a dark-chocolate voice. Her prediction rang as portentously as anything said on the streets of Troy by the original Cassandra.

The mall we'd passed on the way to the group home was a huge complex of stores, anchored by Macy's, Sears, and Penney's. I had visions of a very pregnant teenager wandering through its covered, fountained vastness, clutching her distended belly and moaning in pain as she cruised the boutiques.

"Can't you order her to stay in bed?" I asked, my voice rising slightly. "After all, you're the doctor."

As soon as the words flew out of my mouth, I blushed for my stupidity. If I'd had a dollar for everyone who thought I could do something because I was the lawyer, I wouldn't have been standing in a group home on Staten Island making a fool of myself. I gave the bulky man a rueful smile by way of apology.

"I can strongly advise bed rest," he explained, locking eyes with me as though we were the only people in the room. His were blue and slightly bulging, pulling me into the seriousness of his words. "She's young and basically healthy," he said. "I'd admit her to the hospital right now if I thought she was in real danger. It would be better if she stayed as immobile as possible, but I can't prevent her from going for walks."

"I can," Marla interrupted. "I can and I will. If anything happens to that baby because she's tramping around that mall—"

"Amber always gets to go to the mall," dumpy little Lisa complained. "Whatever Amber wants, she gets. It's not fair."

"Lisa, not now," Mrs. Bonaventura said in a firm voice. She moved toward the sullen teenager, about to shepherd her out of the room, but the litany of grievances had just begun. ". . . her own room, her own phone line," the girl recited as the housemother all but pushed her into the next room.

"So can we see her or what?" Marla cut in.

Dr. Scanlon raised bushy, graying eyebrows. "Of course. Just don't upset her. Anything that can wait, should wait until after she gives birth."

I trudged up maple-banistered stairs after Marla, feeling like a sailboat caught in the wake of a liner. We passed room after room furnished with identical twin beds, matching pine dressers, and blue shag carpets. There were wall posters with huge blowups of the stars of "Beverly Hills 90210," rap groups whose names I didn't recognize, graduation photos of pimply boys—the proud fathers.

At the far end of the hall there was a big television room with fake leather couches crammed with teenaged girls in varying stages of pregnancy. All were white.

Amber had a room all to herself. She had a double bed instead of twins, fancier furniture with carved accents instead of plain pine, a Navajo-style throw rug over a beige carpet nicer than the blue shag the other girls had, and a white phone on the bedside table, the first phone I'd seen on this floor. It was a special room, a princess room. Lisa had a point; Amber had possessions and privileges the other girls didn't share. I wondered why, then filed the question for future reference.

The room was empty—well, not exactly empty; there were enough stuffed animals to fill a window at FAO Schwarz—but there was no one in the big bed or the straight chair next to it. I took the opportunity to look around while Marla went back down the hall to look for my client.

The room was a jumble of Care Bears, Hallmark cards taped to the walls, and posters with rainbows promising better tomorrows. Yet amid the rainbow-bellied bears was a white coyote, head raised to the ceiling in mid-howl, wearing a turquoise neckcloth. On the wall adjoining a "Just for Today" poster was a blowup of the Albuquerque balloon festival. The room seemed to have been decorated by two people with totally opposite tastes. I wondered which, if either, sensibility belonged to Amber.

Next to the window hung an unusual wind chime; I walked over to inspect it more closely. In addition to the usual tubes of tuned metal, there were silver-wrapped nuggets of semiprecious stones. I recognized a lavender amethyst, a rose quartz, an aquamarine. I was fingering a lemon-yellow stone when a voice behind me said, "Ms. Jameson?"

I turned. My client stood in the doorway, holding herself upright with one hand balanced on the door frame.

First surprise: Amber was no teenager. Twenty-three at least, she sat with a composed look on her perky face, manicured hands folded over her enormous stomach. She wasn't pretty, though her long, wavy hair had the kind of shine and bounce that sells conditioners. Her skin was fresh and rosy, her eyes clear blue. She looked like fun, like a ride on a roller coaster, like fresh-spun cotton candy, like a softball game on a breezy spring day.

Second surprise: Instead of a maternity top, Amber wore an oversized T-shirt that bore a replica of the *New York Post*'s most infamous headline: "HEADLESS CORPSE IN TOPLESS BAR." The latest in designer fashion for the mother-to-be. I couldn't help smiling; this kid had a sense of humor.

"Amber?"

She lifted a hand with French-polished fingernails and held it out. "Ms. Jameson," she said, her voice was low and sexy. She could have been the lawyer, so self-possessed was she, so firm and confident was her handshake.

"This is really interesting," I said, gesturing at the wind chime. I let my fingers play with the dangling gems, and a bell-like sound emerged, deeper in tone than I would have expected from the miniature metal tubes.

Amber beamed. "Ellie made it for me," she explained. "Ellie Greenspan," she added unnecessarily. "She's been just wonderful to me."

Amber touched a pendant at her throat with a manicured finger. "She made this, too."

I bent closer. It was a round, polished piece of amber, clear and pure, turning sunlight to gold as Amber held it toward the warm rays. It was cocooned in silver, caressed by a sterling hand—which, on closer examination, turned out to be the slim, naked body of a woman draped over the shining stone. She lay on the smooth surface as if she were embracing a lover, trying to bury herself in his naked flesh.

"Ellie says amber brings light into the body." The accompanying smile was both warm and secretive. "She says it's a good name for me because I'm bringing light into their lives with this baby."

There wasn't a whole lot to say to that, so I didn't say it. Amber motioned me to a straight chair next to the bed. I sat. Marla, back from her search in the hallway, stood behind me, ready to take charge, when Amber dropped her third surprise.

"Get out," she said, giving Marla one sharp glance. She turned toward me as though we were already alone. Marla opened her mouth to reply, then thought better of it and made an exit.

"I'll be downstairs when you're finished," she said. Her unspoken message: *and then you'll tell me everything that went on in here.*

I gave no sign that I'd understood that message. Whatever the reason, Marla had brought me in as Amber's counsel; my client was sitting in this bed, hands folded over an enormous stomach, not waiting downstairs, pacing and smoking.

Where to start? *What's a nice girl like you doing—*
No.
Why didn't you go for an abortion, like everybody else?
No.
How in the hell did you get mixed up with Marla if you hate her so much?

Actually, I liked that one. It had the advantage of blunt honesty, which I thought Amber would appreciate, given her quick dispatch of my colleague. But I never got the words out of my mouth; before I could speak, Amber asked, "So what did you think of Saint Christopher?"

"Who?"

"Doc Scanlon." She grinned. "Saint Christopher of the Golden Cradle. Patron saint of the unwed, the unloved, the unborn."

The penny dropped. "That was *Chris* Scanlon? The right-to-life guy?" I made a point of avoiding television discussions of the subject, so I'd read his name without ever seeing one of his numerous television appearances.

She nodded, a conspiratorial smile on her lips. "He's a real bullshit artist. But," she went on, "he's the one who got me this nice room and the private phone line. He told Mrs. B. I needed my privacy, since there were complications to my pregnancy."

Now I was ready for Question Two. "If you feel that way," I said, going back to the bullshit artist remark, "why didn't you have an abortion?"

Direct blue eyes raked me up and down, as though she could see just from looking at me that I'd marched for the right to choose.

And maybe those assessing—accusing?—eyes could see a newly graduated lawyer sitting in a waiting room at Planned Parenthood, sick to her stomach with worry, hoping against hope that what every cell in her body was telling her wasn't true after all. Maybe Amber could see that lawyer sobbing into her pillow after the procedure, thanking God it was legal. Going home, slipping into bed with a heating pad, calling in sick to work without telling anyone the nature of her illness. Telling herself it was a simple medical choice, not the end to a life-in-being.

If I'd had the child, she'd be fourteen. Old enough to sit in the television room of this house, belly swelled out to—

"You ever have a kid?" The question startled me back to the present; maybe Amber really could read minds.

I shook my head.

"I did. Four years ago. She died." Flat words, flat voice. Flat eyes that turned toward the window, but didn't see the rainy day beyond the glass. "She was only alive for a couple of days; I never even took her home from the hospital, but I knew I could never—" She choked on the words.

"I understand," I whispered. I didn't. I wasn't sure I wanted to, wasn't sure I wanted to remember every year the date that could have been celebrated with another candle on a cake but was instead memorialized by unexplained pain in my lower abdomen.

"No, you don't," Amber challenged. "And neither does that bitch Marla. She looks at me like I'm a prize cow about to give birth to a champion bull." The words accused me of complicity with Marla; they also had me wondering where Amber came from that she referred so readily to breeding stock.

"I just want him to have a good home, that's all." She folded her shapely hands protectively over her belly as a secret smile crossed her face. One hand left her stomach and reached for the delicate pendant, enclosing the golden stone in her slender fingers.

"Him? Did you have an amnio?" Enough of my friends had been through post–thirty-five births that I could speak Basic Pregnancy.

Amber nodded. She reached out a hand and touched the tiny wind chime that hung on a cup hook off the window frame next to the bed. The tinkling sound filled the air and mingled with her laughter. "Sure. Amnio. Ultrasound. The works. Nothing but the best for this cow."

"Okay, you told me why you couldn't abort, but why not keep the baby?" I was playing devil's advocate here; her reasons were clearly spelled out in the social work study Marla had given me. But I didn't want to rely on Marla for the facts; I wanted to hear the story from Amber's own lips. Especially since Amber had made it clear how little she liked Marla.

Amber took a big breath and let it out through puffed cheeks. As though she were practicing her Lamaze breathing. Her hand caressed the smooth, gleaming surface of her amber pendant as she talked.

"I liked the guy. I really did. I was pleased when he asked me out. And then—" She looked down at the piece of pet-rified sap. Her blue eyes stared up at me, and she started over.

"They call it date rape. Like you made a date just so

you could get raped. Like it wasn't really rape because he bought you dinner first. At an Indian restaurant.'' A harsh little laugh. "I swear I'll never eat curry again.''

Her fist closed around the amber talisman. "It's like he was two different people. The guy who asked me out, who kidded around over dinner, who was funny and smart and let me have all the mango chutney.''

She closed her eyes. Her fingers slowly moved around the amber in a sexy, swirling motion at odds with the hard words.

"He came all over my legs. He had me pinned down on my couch, held my arms back so hard I had bruises. I was crying but I remember being grateful, thinking that at least the sperm didn't really get inside, because I was moving too much, trying to keep away from him. But it only takes one of the little fuckers, and I guess one of them made it inside me.''

The psychological double-talk of the social work report was one thing; this raw account was something else.

"I can't believe you didn't abort,'' I blurted out. The minute the words left my mouth, I wanted them back. Marla had somehow alienated this girl; did she need another lawyer who sat in judgment, who refused to understand?

A single tear ran down her cheek. "If it was him inside me,'' she said, "if it was a dirty fucking rapist in here, I'd flush him out so fast—'' She shook her head. The tear glided away, but it left a track like a snail, visible when the light struck her face at a certain angle.

"But it's not,'' she went on, voice gaining firmness. "It's a baby. An innocent baby who never hurt anybody. So why should he die because of what his father did? If there's a family out there who can give him love, let them have him. I can't. I can't keep him, because every day he was alive, I'd think about that hot dirty scum running down my legs and maybe I'd take that out on the kid even if I knew better. I can't risk that. So when I saw their ad in the paper, I decided to give my baby a good home."

"By they you mean the Greenspans." Marla's clients. The childless couple who were pinning all their hopes on the woman in this bed.

Amber's face lit up. "I just love Ellie," she said. "I know she'll be a good mother to my Jimmy."

Jimmy?

A heavy-duty alarm bell went off in my head. Marla exuded confidence that Amber wouldn't change her mind, but naming a fetus didn't seem like a good sign.

She returned my quizzical look with a shy smile. "That's what I call him. Just between me and him." She gave her bulging tummy a proprietary pat. "I know Josh and Ellie will give him a different name, but to me he'll always be Jimmy."

"Look, Amber," I began, in my best lawyer-laying-down-the-law tone, "if there's any chance you might—"

"There isn't." She said it crisply. "Don't worry about me. I know what I want, and what I want is my life back. I want to go back to school, get my degree, get a job, travel. Meet a nice guy and get married. I don't want to be tied down with a baby I can't handle. Besides," she added, her voice softening, "I've spent a lot of time with Josh and Ellie, and I just know they're the perfect parents for my baby. I want you," she added, "to go and see them for me."

Fourth surprise: I hadn't counted on meeting the Greenspans until we had to appear in court. I knew the couple had spent time with Amber; she didn't need me to tell her they were okay.

Her face and voice turned suddenly shy; she looked more like a teenager than a woman of the world as she reached toward the night table, opened the drawer, and pulled out a card-sized yellow envelope. "For Josh" was written on the outside, in a fine-pointed calligraphic style.

"It's for Josh," she said unnecessarily. A faint blush tinged her cheeks. "His birthday is tomorrow," she added.

"It's a birthday card?" More alarm bells; something in

her hesitation said she might have a crush on the father-to-be. Another complication I didn't need.

"I sent Ellie one on her birthday," Amber replied, her blue eyes shining. "I really want Josh to have it, and even if I mail it today, it won't get there in time. And Marla told me you live in Brooklyn, so it won't be out of your way. Please take it to him. Please?"

I was about to say no when Mrs. Bonaventura, out of breath, burst through the door.

"He's here again," she panted. "That man's here."

"Who is he, Amber?" Marla demanded. Both women stood next to the bed, identical expressions of disapproval on their faces.

"What man?" I asked, not sure whom I was addressing.

It was Marla who answered. Her face was red, and she looked at Amber with a loathing she didn't bother to conceal. "It's your boyfriend, isn't it, Amber? The one who says he'll take care of everything, support the baby, if you change your mind about adoption."

She didn't wait for an answer. "Honey, please. I've been down this road before, and I guarantee you he'll walk out in a year, no forwarding address. Listen to me . . ."

I stood up from the chair and walked toward the window. At first I saw no one, then realized I was looking at a Staten Island street with Brooklyn eyes. Looking for a pedestrian when I should have been scoping out the cars.

He was in the silver-gray job down the block. I had no idea what make it was, but it was midsized, inconspicuous. He sat at the wheel with a newspaper open in front of him, as though that would allay suspicion. He could have been a boyfriend, nice-looking, around Amber's age. He glanced at the group home more than once, lifting his eyes from the paper and then hastily pretending interest in the news. He was a lousy stalker.

"Amber, do you know him?"

"Of course she—"

"Marla, I'm talking to Amber."

My client shook her head. "Never saw him before in my life," she said, her tone bored.

"And that doesn't worry you," I said, not bothering to conceal my disbelief, "being followed around by some guy you don't know?"

"He never did anything to me. Never even talked to me. Maybe," Amber speculated, "he isn't interested in me at all. Maybe it's one of the other girls here he's after."

Mrs. Bonaventura weighed in. "Then why did Heather say she saw you talking with him at the mall?"

"Because Heather's a stupid little twit," Amber replied. "She didn't see a damn thing; she just wants to get attention."

Marla stepped in front of the housemother and shook an angry finger in Amber's face. "If you have *any* intention of changing your mind about this adoption," she said, "you'd better tell me now, understand? No birth mother has ever backed out on one of my adoptions, and you'd better not be the first. Got that?"

Amber nodded, but the flash of defiance in her blue eyes worried me. If this adoption was really the piece of cake Marla had predicted, it was beginning to crumble.

It wasn't until we were halfway back to Brooklyn, on the sweeping expanse of the Verrazano Narrows Bridge—after I'd cursed Marla out for threatening my client, after I'd read Amber my own riot act about changing her mind, after I'd agreed with Mrs. B. that the police should be called—that I realized I still clutched in my clenched hand the birthday card Amber had given me for Josh.

I got the address from Marla, who was understandably reluctant to give it. Not as reluctant as I was to meet the Greenspans. Why, I wondered, was I always agreeing to do things I didn't want to do for people I didn't particularly want to do them for?

CHAPTER THREE

The Greenspans lived in a carriage house in an alley off Hicks Street. That meant bucks. It cost a lot to live in Brooklyn Heights, even more if you wanted to set up housekeeping in a place formerly occupied by horses. A brass plaque outside informed me that the building had been erected in 1843. Another, newer brass plate told me this was the office of Joshua Greenspan, Architect.

I rang the bell. As I waited, I admired the little row, a London mews unaccountably lost in Brooklyn, the tiny buildings like playhouses. The very first hints of spring were breaking through winter's icy shell; the snow was melting into tiny rivers at the edge of the street, and the warmth of the sun could be felt through winter coats.

The door was answered by a honey-colored woman in a burnt orange caftan. Her hair, skin, eyes, even lips all had the same golden honey glow, set off by the orange fabric and the gleaming gold around her neck. This had to be the wife; no maid could have afforded that eighteen-karat collar.

"You must be Ms. Jameson," she said, motioning me inside with a wave of her manicured hand. Her nail polish looked like melted pearls with just a glint of gold. I glanced down at my own ragged nails, way overdue for a filing, and stuffed them into the pockets of my peasant skirt.

"Mrs. Greenspan?" I let my voice rise slightly; the polite way to ask whether I could use her first name.

"Call me Ellie," she replied with a small smile. She led me into a living room that took me to another climate, another world. I knew Southwestern decor was up-and-coming here in the East, but this looked like the real thing. A Navajo rug on the floor showed elongated dancing figures in rich rusts and browns. On the sand-colored walls were basket displays, Indian pots on shelves, and another weaving, with deep turquoise lines that contrasted against the earth tones. Outside, the bushes bore rust-red knobs not quite ready to unfold stickily into new-green leaves; inside it was autumn in Santa Fe.

I could see where the miniature Navajo rug and stuffed coyote in Amber's room had come from. But could the sensibility that favored these mementos of the Southwest have thought Care Bears were cute? Or did babies reduce even the most sophisticated to outpourings of tastelessness?

Ellie led me toward the sofa, a butter-soft palomino leather item that made me wonder whether one of the house's former occupants had been transformed into furniture. "Would you like a drink?" she asked. "Or perhaps coffee?"

What I wanted and what I asked for were two different things. This was, after all, business, even if it was Sunday, so in a few minutes I sat on the dead-horse sofa sipping pretty good coffee and trying to think of something lawyerly to say.

My eyes kept roaming the room, caught by each exotic

artifact. "You must really love the Southwest," I said. "You have so many beautiful things from there."

The maple-syrup eyes lit up. "Oh, yes. You see, my dad was in the Army and we were stationed in Alamagordo for five years. I just loved it. I'd give anything if we could live in New Mexico, but of course Josh has his work . . ." Her voice trailed off and she looked away.

I followed her eyes to a huge terrarium in the corner. A miniature desert, it contained a small barrel cactus, a strange-looking plant spreading red-tipped arms out toward the couch, and several succulents I couldn't begin to identify.

I had heard there were architects in Santa Fe, but I didn't say so. Whatever compromises this woman had made for her marriage were none of my business.

"About this baby," I began. Not my most professional opening, but then I'd never transferred title to a child before.

"It's like a miracle," Ellie said. Her voice was soft and breathy, like Marilyn Monroe's, yet unlike Monroe she didn't use it sexually. Her sexuality was in that honey skin, in the planes of her face, the thick mane of hair tumbling over her shoulders, the utter femininity of her draped clothing, the manicured fingernails and waxed legs of a woman whose main job was to look attractive for her husband.

Women like Ellie Greenspan usually made my hackles rise. The working sheepdog's contempt for the shaved, beribboned poodle. This time, I reserved decision. Maybe it was the vulnerability of her little-girl voice, or the so-apparent sacrifices she'd made for Josh, but something forlorn in her touched me.

"I've wanted a baby ever since I can remember," she said, and I pictured a golden child rocking a doll with loving lullabies. "But first Josh had to finish school, and then he had his practice to establish, so we waited until the time seemed just right." Her face twisted into a wry grimace.

"And then I found out that those heavy, painful periods

I always seemed to get weren't just my imagination. I had endometriosis. I could conceive a child, but my womb wouldn't let me carry it to term.'' She looked away, and I wondered just who'd told her her pain was all in her head. Dear Josh, whose education came first, whose profession came first?

''We tried infertility specialists for years,'' she went on. ''It cost us a fortune, and all it did was make me feel more and more defective. It was so demeaning,'' she said, letting her voice trail off into a private world of humiliation.

''We even thought about a surrogate,'' she added with a faint blush, ''someone who could carry our own baby. But the legal complications . . .''

''Yeah. Baby M. and all that,'' I said. What I didn't tell her was that the case everyone in the country knew about was the sum total of my expert legal knowledge on the subject of surrogacy.

''Josh would have liked it better if we could have done it that way. Had our own, I mean.'' Ellie's tone was wistful. ''I was ready to adopt two years into the infertility program, but Josh was so set on having our own baby—our own genetic baby.''

Interesting. Still, I supposed couples arrived at decisions in different time frames.

''What changed his mind?''

Ellie's burnt-sugar eyes lit up. ''This,'' she said simply. She reached toward the coffee table and lifted a child's school binder notebook covered in plastic and decorated with a crescent moon.

''This is our Baby Notebook,'' she explained, opening the clasp. Inside were two folders, one with a sun and one with a star on the cover. She pulled open the rings and took out the sun folder.

''I sent for this without telling Josh,'' she said, handing me a desktop-edited newsletter with the logo of a sleeping baby and the word *Dreamchild* on top. Under the masthead were articles on how to make contact with birth mothers, how to arrange private adoptions, reviews of books on adoption no prospective parent should be without. Happy stories of adoptive parents who "finally, after years of avoiding other people's baby showers, had our own for little Melissa Marie."

I opened the newsletter. On the next-to-last page were the ads. "COUPLE WHO HAS EVERYTHING—EXCEPT A BABY TO LOVE. WE LIVE IN SUBURBAN SAINT LOUIS, IN A BIG WHITE HOUSE THAT FEELS EMPTY WITHOUT THE LAUGHTER OF A CHILD. MARRIED TEN YEARS, STILL DEEPLY IN LOVE, WE PRAY FOR A BIRTH MOTHER TO TRUST US WITH HER BABY. WE PROMISE YOU WON'T BE SORRY. WHITE ONLY. BOX 89743."

I read on. The only constant was the "white only" refrain. "Is this necessary?" I asked Ellie, pointing to the words in the first ad. I recalled the television room of Amber's group home, full of white teenagers bursting with soon-to-be-born white infants for the carriage trade.

"Well, yes," she answered, her eyes begging me to understand the pain behind the perky presentations. "We went to an agency first, and because Josh is over fifty and I'm over forty, they told us we couldn't have a white infant. But they said they could get us an older child or a baby with a medical problem, or a nonwhite baby. Josh had a fit. Not that he's a racist, because he's not, but when you're adopting a baby, you want one that looks like you. That could be your own."

"So that's why you chose a private placement adoption?" I asked, hoping she couldn't tell that I'd never heard the term before last week.

"Yes. I read about it in the *Dreamchild* newsletter. And I read about Marla. So I contacted her without Josh knowing, and she put me on a waiting list while I worked on Josh. At first, he wouldn't hear about adoption. The agency thing really soured him. He wanted me to call a Park Avenue infertility specialist he'd heard about from one of his clients. But," she paused for a delicate shudder, "I just couldn't go through that one more time. You have no idea how humiliating it is, how degrading, to be some doctor's experimental animal."

"So what changed your husband's mind?" She gave me a startled look, and I added, "About adoption, I mean."

"Oh, he started reading the newsletter and saw Amber's ad. I remember, we were sitting up in bed, watching Charlie Rose, and he pointed to the ad and said, 'This is the one.' Just like that," she said, shaking her head and smiling at the vagaries of the male sex. " 'This is the one for us.' And it was Amber's."

"Then birth mothers advertise, too?" I was surprised. "I thought it was kind of a seller's market." The look that crossed Ellie Greenspan's face made me blush. Without thinking, I had brought Marla's hard-boiled way of looking at adoption into the room.

"Sorry," I muttered. "Didn't mean it to come out like that."

She smiled an apology, but the wariness in her eyes didn't go away. It would be a while before she trusted me with another true feeling.

She reached for the notebook and opened the purple folder with the blue star on the front. Inside was another copy of *Dreamchild*, open to the ads page, with one ad highlighted in yellow. I remembered highlighters from my law school days; it was a surprise to see one used out of context.

The ad read: "WANTED: A TRULY LOVING COUPLE FOR A TRULY SPECIAL BABY. AGE UNIMPORTANT. WHAT IS IMPORTANT IS THAT YOU WANT TO GIVE A HOME TO A CHILD IN NEED. MY BABY NEEDS WHAT I CANNOT GIVE—A STABLE HOME WITH TWO LOVING PARENTS. NEW YORK AREA A +. PLEASE HEAR MY VOICE: I NEED YOU AS MUCH AS YOU NEED ME. AMBER, BOX 49350."

"What was so special?" I asked. "Not that this isn't a

nice ad,'' I amended, hoping I hadn't hurt her feelings again. "And now that I've met Amber, I think she is special. But from this ad—''

"I know what you mean," Ellie said. "When he first read it to me, I thought it was just like all the others. Except that this girl didn't mind about age and actually wanted somebody from New York. A lot of the birth mothers are from other parts of the country, and they think New York is a terrible place to raise a child. That was one strike against us. And then there's our ages, and the fact that Josh is Jewish. Most of the birth mothers want their children raised as Christians, and we're committed to giving our child the benefit of both his heritages. So just from the words 'New York a plus' Josh thought this girl might be more open to us. And,'' she finished with a triumphant smile, "he was right. Amber loved Josh's being Jewish, and she said her own parents were older when she was born, so she realized we could give her child a mature kind of love.''

"Sounds like a match made in heaven," I remarked. Not much else to say in the face of that radiant smile.

"Oh, by the way," I added, "where is Josh? I have something for him.'' I reached in my bag to get the birthday card Amber had pressed on me.

Josh Greenspan set my teeth on edge the minute he came out of his office. He wasn't tall, but his barrel chest and thick arms weighed down the room. He resembled the huge cactus squatting in his wife's terrarium, soaking up all the moisture and covering a soft interior with scary-looking spikes. At least, I hoped it was a soft interior, for the sake of the child his wife wanted so badly.

"Can't you order your client to obey Dr. Scanlon's orders?'' he began, not bothering with pleasantries. "Marla says Amber's out at the mall right now, in spite of what the doctor told her. Don't you have any control over her?'' He thrust out his chin, not his hand. The challenge hung in the air.

"Josh, please," Ellie's little-girl voice broke in. "I know how you feel, but—"

"But nothing," the bearded architect interrupted with a shake of his head. "Look, we're paying the bills, baby, we ought to have something to say about—"

"Josh!" Dusky patches appeared on Ellie Greenspan's cheeks. Her eyes sought mine, offering the kind of wordless apology women give one another when their men embarrass them. I tried to accept it in the same manner, shrugging ever so slightly.

The big man grinned, holding up a large paw in conciliation. "I'm sorry. It's just that we're getting so close to Amber's delivery date. If anything were to go wrong now—" He shrugged an apology.

"I understand," I said, meeting his grin with a cool smile. "If I could make Amber listen to Doc Scanlon, I would. But the real reason I'm here is that Amber asked me to bring you something, and since I live in the neighborhood . . ." I let my voice trail off; technically I was not a Heights resident, since my home-office was on the wrong side of Atlantic Avenue, but there was no point in advertising that minor fact.

Greenspan's eyes narrowed. "Bringing something? That's a new one." His laugh was a harsh sound and held no hint of humor. "Seems to me our Amber is usually asking for something, taking something. It's not like her to give back."

"Josh," came Ellie's admonitory voice. She sounded like she was getting into practice for speaking to a recalcitrant child. "I thought we agreed that Amber needed those things we gave her."

"What things?" Part of my mind said it was none of my business, but the other part remembered the words of the Domestic Relations Law governing permissible expenses to be paid by adoptive parents to birth mothers. I wasn't about to be Marla's patsy in covering up illegal payments.

"Oh, little things," Ellie said hastily. It was clear she

grasped the meaning of my question. "Like paying her phone bill so she can call her family back home in Kansas, her sister in Baltimore. Nothing out of the ordinary or unreasonable." The look she gave her husband was meant to insure his agreement.

It worked. He shrugged, then said, "Yeah, I guess sometimes I make more out of it than I should. I just hate to see you pouring money—and affection, too, don't forget that—down a bottomless pit like Amber. She'd suck you dry if she could, Ellie, you know she would."

Ellie shook her head. She moved as if to get up from the couch, then changed her mind and leaned back. "She's not much more than a child herself, Josh," she said. "She needs to know we care about her as a person, not just as someone carrying our child."

"I still think you romanticize her, baby," Josh said, his voice heavy with disapproval.

Then a slow smile spread across his face, a smile that took years off his age. He walked toward the palomino couch and parked himself next to his wife. He leaned toward her and grazed her golden cheek with his full lips.

"But that's why I love you, El. You have so much to give, so much love. I can't wait to see you holding our baby."

It was to throw up.

I handed over the card, watching the yellow envelope all but disappear into Josh's heavy, hairy hand. He opened it with a single rip, Ellie following his every move with hungry eyes.

He pulled out the card. It had a teddy bear on it, drawn in primary crayon colors, as if by a small child. "Happy Birthday, Daddy," it read. Either Amber had decided Josh was her surrogate daddy or she was sending him a birthday card on behalf of his unborn child. Either way, the card was weird as hell.

But Ellie, predictably, didn't see it that way. Tears welled in her eyes as she gazed on the sappy message inside, a message that hailed Josh as a wonderful daddy. "Oh, it's so beautiful," she breathed. "I'm putting it in the Baby Notebook, next to the one she gave me for my birthday." I was willing to bet Ellie's card had a similarly childlike motif and was addressed to Mommy.

Josh held the card with thick fingers that shook ever so slightly. I glanced at his face; his jaw was clenched and his mouth was set in anger. His face held all the thunder of a spring storm in the desert.

A white paper fell into Josh's lap. Ellie reached for it with her slender, elegant fingers. "A gift certificate from Baby Gap," she said delightedly.

"Nice," I commented. "A thoughtful gesture."

"Yeah," Josh chimed agreement, but his tone was wry. "A thoughtful gesture with our money. You don't really suppose she spent her own cash on this, do you, babe?"

"Josh, why do you have to be so cynical? Why can't you take something at face value, for a change?"

"Because with Amber, nothing is face value, that's why. She uses us, she takes and takes. I can't wait," he finished, emphasizing his words with the slap of his huge palm on the bleached coffee table, "till this baby's ours and that woman is out of our lives forever."

I hadn't known much about adoptions when I took this case, but I'd read a book or two since meeting Marla in the motion part, and one thing I'd learned about open adoptions was that the birth mother and the adoptive parents were supposed to be able to keep up contact after the baby was born. It didn't sound as if Josh was entering into the open adoption spirit at all. *Out of our lives forever* wasn't particularly realistic, since Amber knew the name and address of the people who were going to raise her child.

I left the carriage house with a feeling of trepidation that swept through me like the icy wind off the river.

"It just bothers me, that's all," Mickey Dechter said. We were not quite partners, since a lawyer is forbidden to go into practice with a non-lawyer, but she had an office next to mine and she gave social work services to many of the same clients I represented in court. I had without quite realizing it taken Amber's case in the secure belief that she'd help me with it, that she'd lend her considerable knowledge of human behavior to the enterprise. Now she was flatly refusing to have anything to do with an adoption.

"Oh, and it doesn't bother me?" I countered, trying to keep a lid on my rising anger, without much success. "Because I'm just an insensitive lawyer, right? I'm too crass, too—"

"I didn't say that," she retorted. Her voice held an edge of exasperated resentment. "If you'd just let me explain."

I sat back against my high-backed leather chair and said, "Explain already." I folded my arms across my chest to convey my earnest desire to listen with an open mind.

"I don't like adoptions," she said flatly. "I don't like the way they're conducted in this country, and I—"

Mickey and I had degenerated to conversation by interruption. It was my turn to break into her train of thought.

"What do you mean, the way adoptions are conducted in this country?" I stood up and walked toward the coffeepot for a refill, prepared to warm up Mickey's cup as well. Even a knock-down, drag-out argument was no excuse for depriving someone of coffee.

She waved her hand over her mug to signal that she'd had enough. This after I'd brewed total decaf in deference to her. I filled my own cup, took the pot back to the stove, and sat down to mix in the desired amounts of milk and sweetener.

"Do you realize," she began, fixing me with her earnest eyes, "that adoption agencies in the U.S. discriminate in ways the local McDonald's would get sued for? That in an adoption it's not only permissible but required to classify people on the basis of race, age, religion?"

I nodded. "Ellie told me she and Josh had trouble with

the agencies because of their ages and their mixed marriage.''

"That's what I mean," Mickey said. "If he was being fired from his job because he was Jewish or because of his age, he'd have a discrimination case, right?"

"Right."

"But it's okay for an adoption agency to deny him a child because he's too old or because his wife isn't Jewish. And don't get me started on race," she went on. I didn't; I didn't say a word, but she was off and running anyway.

"It used to be that white couples could adopt nonwhite babies, but now there's a big emphasis put on same-race adoptions. Which leaves a huge number of nonwhite children without homes while white babies are at a premium."

She leaned forward and lowered her voice, as if afraid of microphones in the coffee mugs. "They even try to match skin color among nonwhite families," she said. "As if a dark family shouldn't raise a light child."

"But doesn't it make sense for the adoption agency to give a baby to people who look as much like him as possible?" I asked. "Skin color is part of that; I suppose they look at other factors as well before they match—"

"Who says that's the only basis to make a family?" Mickey shot back. "Who says blond parents can't love a dark-haired child or that only light-skinned parents should raise a light-skinned child? Where is it written that an adoptive family is a second-best copy of a 'real' family?"

I opened my mouth to reply, then pulled myself back to the real issue at hand. "What does all this have to do with Amber?" I asked. "Her case has nothing to do with agencies."

"Oh, yes, it does," Mickey countered. She leaned forward on the couch—no easy feat at eight and one-half months pregnant—and tossed the words at me with a passionate intensity that would have gone down well on "The MacNeil/Lehrer Newshour."

"It has everything to do with society's bias toward bi-

ology. Look at the way we pay for babies. I'll bet every
visit your Ellie Greenspan made to a fertility specialist was
covered by insurance. But no one pays the costs of adoption. Which is society's way of saying that if you choose
to reproduce yourself, in spite of all the children already
born who need homes, we'll subsidize you. And if you
can't have your own, we'll help you find a white infant *if*
you're the right age, the right religion, live in the right
place, and have lots of money. If not—'' she shrugged and
held her out hands in a gesture that said, *You know the rest.*

"If not, what?" I demanded, deliberately obtuse.

"If not," she continued, letting her hands come to rest
on her swollen belly in a protective manner I was seeing
more and more as the delivery date loomed, "then you go
into the marketplace and make the best deal you can with
some poor kid who doesn't know which end is up, who's
going through her own crisis, who needs counseling before
she makes a decision that will affect her and her baby for
life—and all she gets is a desperate older couple waving
money in her face. She gets whipsawed between society's
supposed belief in adoption and its vilification of a mother
who gives up her baby."

I shook my head, recalling the "HEADLESS CORPSE"
T-shirt. "You haven't met Amber," I said. "A poor help-
less kid she's not. Besides, if you think she needs counseling, give it to her. That's why I need you, Mickey."

"Don't you get it, Cass?" Mickey fixed me with eyes
that had already decided, eyes that couldn't be reached. "I
refuse to take part in the adoption system. I refuse to par-
ticipate in something that came about because of society's
basic lack of respect for children. It's a direct result of the
narcissistic search for a perfect little replica—which can
only be satisfied by a white baby. And in a capitalist society, we therefore justify the creation by science of white
babies and the sale of white babies by birth mothers."

"Oh, now I'm a baby-seller?" I flung myself back on

the couch and shot a look of pure hatred at my friend and colleague.

"Nobody is selling a baby here," I went on, aware of the sullen edge to my voice. "Amber's expenses are going to be documented in affidavits filed in court. No payments are being made over and above what the law allows."

This remark was greeted by a superior smirk designed to let me know that only a naif with a law degree would believe such a fairy tale.

"I understand, Cass," Mickey said in a tone that reeked of empathy. "You think the fact that I won't help you with this case is directed at you personally."

"That when you say people are selling babies, you mean *I'm* selling babies," I cut in, my voice ragged. "Yeah, I'm *hearing* that," I said, parodying the self-help jargon I associated with social workers. "I guess I'm *feeling* attacked here."

"Cass, I'm not accusing you of selling babies," Mickey said in a tone so reasonable I wanted to rip her face off. "I *am* accusing you of choosing to become part of a system that treats white infants like commodities."

She paused, took a deep breath, and fixed me with eyes that pleaded for understanding.

"I have my own baby growing in here," she said, touching her belly with reverent fingers. "I know you have conflicted feelings about my pregnancy. But one of the things it's doing for me is making me sensitive—maybe too sensitive—"

I nodded fervently, but it didn't stop the flow of words.

"—to the whole issue of birth and babies. I can't help but think of the other ones," she went on, and so help me, her eyes filled with tears. I tried to dismiss them as the too-ready tears of the very pregnant, but it wasn't easy.

"I can't help but think of all the babies I used to see when I worked for BCW," she went on, naming her first employer, the Bureau of Child Welfare, the agency responsible for all the unwanted and abused babies born to people unable to care for them. "How can we continue to let those babies rot in foster homes while at the same time we reward white parents for making babies by the most artificial means?"

"Are you saying you'd help me if Josh and Ellie Greenspan were adopting a crack baby?" I demanded. "Mickey, this doesn't make sense."

"It does to me," she said with quiet stubbornness. Again her hands caressed the bulge around her middle. Again her eyes dropped to caress the unborn child with a look seen on Madonnas in Italian paintings. Again I was shut out— the barren woman who could never understand the feminine mysteries.

The worse-than-barren woman: the woman who could have given birth but chose not to.

I rose, picked up the coffee mugs, and slammed them down on my kitchen counter with a force that broke the handle off one of them.

CHAPTER FOUR

It's just like a closing, I repeated to myself, leaning back against the headrest on the passenger's side of Marla's sleek air-conditioned automobile. *You represent the seller; Marla's got the buyer. No big deal.*

It wasn't helping. This wasn't a closing, and the word *seller* reminded me all-too-forcibly of my argument with Mickey. And even though I was along for the legal ride and was not supposed to play social worker, I had a dark suspicion this was going to be a landmark awful day in my professional life.

We swung into the parking lot of—believe it or not—Our Lady of Pity Hospital, Marla making straight for the handicapped spaces right in front of the entrance. I wondered if she had a permit, then shook my head at my own naïveté. If Marla wanted a handicapped permit, she'd find a way to get one. Sure enough, she whipped a large plastic-coated card out of the glove compartment and tossed it onto the dashboard. She then swept out of the car in a cloud of expensive perfume. I followed, racing to keep up even though the heels on my shoes were half the height of the bronze pumps Marla wore. Did the woman ever *walk*?

As I grabbed the door Marla let close into my face, a blue-uniformed security guard nearly knocked me down. He shoved me out of the way unceremoniously and ran into the parking lot. I turned to look after him; was some poor woman giving birth out there, unable to make it into the emergency room?

Even from a distance I recognized Doc Scanlon's Santa Claus figure. He stood in a section of the parking lot marked "DOCTORS ONLY." His car was blocked by the same silver car I'd seen outside the group home the day I met Amber. The young man with the curly dark hair stood yelling at the doctor, his arms flailing. I strained to hear the words, but couldn't. The young man took a swing just as the security guard rushed up and grabbed him from behind.

I made my way into the lobby, catching up with Marla at the information desk. I started to tell her what I'd seen, but she waved me silent with an impatient hand.

The young woman behind the desk gave Marla a fish-eyed stare as she repeated, "We have no patient by that name."

"Yes, you do," Marla contradicted. "You've probably got her listed as a DNP."

I was about to show my ignorance and ask what that meant when a second security guard rushed up to the desk, a walkie-talkie at his chin. He started making a report to someone about the assault in the parking lot.

I turned to Marla. "The guy he's talking about," I said under my breath, "is the same guy who was hanging around the group home the day we visited Amber."

"He was *here*?" Marla's face and voice registered shock and alarm; her body stiffened as if for physical combat. She turned to the receptionist. "If you let him see her, you stupid—"

"Marla!" I said sharply.

"Lady, I told you," the woman behind the desk repeated, "we have no patient by that—"

I turned to the guard. "Did you get the license plate of the car he was driving?"

" '89 Ford Taurus, license plate P-I-Z-Z-A two-one," he spelled out, his mouth widening in a lizard grin.

"Pizza?" I repeated. "The man's tailing after Amber in a car with a license plate that says 'PIZZA'?"

"PIZZA Twenty-one," the guard corrected.

"That means twenty other citizens of the State of New York actually paid good money for a license plate advertising their favorite food. I can't believe it. Paying a fee for a—"

"Cass, who the hell cares?" Marla cut in. "I don't. He didn't get in, and that's all that counts. Let's get Amber's room number and get this thing over with."

"Don't you care that this guy just assaulted Doc Scanlon?"

Marla shook her head. "As long as my clients walk out of here with a baby, Amber can have a hundred boyfriends looking for her, and they can all hit Doc Scanlon for all I care," she replied.

The girl behind the information desk was losing patience. "Nobody here by that name," she repeated.

"Yes there is," Marla said in her slow-burn voice. "She's under a Do Not Publicize code because we're here to transfer her baby to the adoptive parents. We're the lawyers."

The magic L-word had the girl riffling through index cards, and two minutes later Marla and I were in an oversized elevator riding up to the maternity floor in the company of blue-suited medical personnel and one wheelchair-bound senior citizen with a bright, vague smile on her face.

Amber had a private room, courtesy of the Greenspans, so she wouldn't have to lie in bed next to a new mother cooing over her baby. It was a standard hospital room, cramped and functional, with a framed New York City Ballet poster on one wall and a window with a view of the parking lot on the other. Amber sat up in bed, pillows propped behind her, looking a bit frail. There were circles under her eyes, a pallid cast to her face, and her hair was lank and unwashed. In the late-March sunlight, she looked older, harder.

Marla took a worn leather cigarette case out of her purse and lit up. "There's no smoking in the hospital," Amber said with a pleased smile.

"Who gives a rat's ass?" Marla muttered.

"In that case," Amber countered with a bad-girl grin, "give me one. I stopped because of the baby, but now—"

The two of them puffed hastily, their nicotine high fueled by the knowledge that a nurse could walk in at any moment. They exchanged glances that spoke of covert pleasures, of hiding in the girls' bathroom and taking a few puffs before Chemistry class, of lighting up before outraged parents—or if their parents weren't outraged enough, grandparents—as a way of proclaiming adulthood. All the stuff I'd done before I quit.

A tiny—a very, very tiny—part of me wanted to bum a cigarette and prove I could be a bad girl, too.

About halfway through, Marla abruptly walked into the tiny private bathroom and tossed her lit cigarette into the toilet. She strode over to the bed and took Amber's butt away from her, then marched resolutely toward the john. A moment later she flushed away the physical evidence of their crime, though the smoke smell lingered in the air.

Marla reached into her capacious bag and pulled out a bluebacked legal document, folded in thirds like a racing form. She held it in the air and tapped it against her fingers.

"Is that the consent?" Amber asked.

Marla nodded. She was about to say more, but I decided it was my place to explain things to my client. "It's a consent to give temporary custody to the Greenspans," I said. "It permits them to take the baby home today, but it won't become permanent until you sign the consent to adoption before the Surrogate next month. The law gives you thirty days to change your mind. Forty-five in some circumstances," I amended, hoping she wouldn't ask what those circumstances were, even though I knew the answer; hoping that changing her mind wasn't something she wanted more information about.

Marla shot me a look; it was clear she didn't want Amber thinking along those lines any more than I did. But Amber's legal right to revoke consent wasn't going to go away just because we didn't talk about it.

I wheeled the bed table over in front of Amber. Marla opened the blueback and laid the legal form on the table, then opened her thick black pen and set it down on top of the neatly typed foolscap. "Read it first," she ordered.

Amber lifted the pen off the paper and let her eyes scan its contents; she raised the first sheet and read the second page with impressive speed. It wasn't until she reached page three that I realized I was holding my breath.

She raised her blue eyes to mine. "Looks okay," she said with a shrug meant to convey supreme indifference. But there was a slight tremor in the lower lip; Amber clamped her lips shut and picked up the pen. She signed on the space provided, with a savage quickness that made the signature a graffiti scrawl. Then she lifted her head in a proud gesture and stared straight ahead.

"There," she said. "It's done." She fell back against the pillows, letting her stiff shoulders go limp against their soft support. She pulled the thin blanket closer, as though feeling a sudden chill in the overheated air of the hospital room.

If signing the papers was this bad, what would it be like when Amber handed her baby to Ellie Greenspan?

She didn't have to hand the baby over physically. Many birth mothers, according to Marla, didn't want to see their babies after labor. They were afraid that holding the baby would break down their resolve to give it up for adoption. But in open adoptions such as this one, birth mothers often said good-bye to the infants, hoping the ritual of physically transferring the baby to its new parents would ease the pain of loss.

"Where's Ellie?" The male voice behind me made me jump. I turned; Josh Greenspan filled the door with his impatient presence.

"Not here yet," Marla replied. She narrowed her eyes. "I thought she'd be coming with you."

He shook his head. "I had to visit a construction site," he explained, "so I drove here in the four-wheel. She's bringing the Merc."

Where I came from, in the auto-conscious upper Midwest, a Merc was a Mercury. A good family car, if a tad flashier than the GMs we made just down the road at the Fisher Body plant. But here in the affluent East, a Merc was a Mercedes—and of course Joshua Greenspan, Architect, drove a Mercedes.

What was there about this man that brought out the snide in me? Was it the not-so-subtle air of entitlement that seemed to cling to him, the unspoken assertion that he owned a Mercedes because he deserved to own it?

I didn't give a damn how he felt about cars, but his sense of entitlement extended to the child; he deserved a son and heir, and if his wife was too defective to produce one, he'd buy the best.

I walked with quick, angry steps toward the window, deliberately fixing my eyes on a clump of deep-purple crocuses at the side of the hospital. This was my first and positively last adoption. I didn't like Josh, I didn't like Marla, and most of all, I didn't like myself. Who the hell was I to sit in judgment on a man I'd met once, a man who was moving heaven and earth to make his wife's motherhood dream come true?

Yes, it took money to adopt a child the way Josh Greenspan was adopting this one. Would I feel happier if Baby Adam were heading into a life of poverty instead of privilege? Would he suffer so much, having to choose between St. Ann's and Packer—only two of the best private schools in the city, conveniently located in Brooklyn Heights?

While I pondered this, Ellie rushed breathlessly into the room, beginning a disjointed explanation about traffic and directions. She sounded very young and very nervous. By the time I turned around, Josh had her in a bear hug, his huge paw soothing her back. It came to me that their relationship was as stylized as a ballet, with Josh as the strong, protective male, positively reeking masculinity from every hairy pore, while Ellie played the sensitive, feminine clinging vine.

Marla took over. She'd been here before, and she organized things like a cross between a sergeant-major and a cruise director. She rang the nurse and ordered Baby Adam to be brought from the nursery. She opened a second set of legal documents and handed them and her thick European pen first to Josh, then to Ellie for signature. Josh wrote with a heavy hand, while Ellie's elegant strokes resembled calligraphy. Neither looked at Amber before, during, or after the signing. It was as though they wanted to ignore her out of existence, to cut out the middleman so they could walk out of the hospital with their baby, pretending Ellie and not Amber had sweated through sixteen hours of labor.

Had nearly died. That was the part I couldn't put out of my mind. Unlike everyone else in the room, including Marla, I looked at Amber, looked closely at the pale skin and drawn face, the dark circles under the tired blue eyes. She'd had dangerously high blood pressure, Marla told me, and Doc Scanlon had performed a near miracle to keep her alive during the birth. And now no one spoke of it, no one acknowledged what she'd gone through to bring this child into the world.

I walked softly toward the bed, stopping just short of the wheeled table that still sat across Amber's chest. "Are you feeling all right?" I asked in a near whisper.

She nodded, but her lips tightened. "I might want to sue the bastard," she said.

It took me a moment; given the reason I was there in the first place, the word *bastard* threw me. Then I realized she meant Doc Scanlon. "He said you might have trouble," I pointed out. "He told you to stay off your feet," I added. "Which you didn't do. Instead, you went to the mall."

"He did something to me," Amber insisted. "I know he did. I was fine until I got in here, and then I nearly died. I could have died." Her voice shook, and she gripped the thin blanket with clawlike fingers.

"Not that anybody here would have cared one way or the other," she went on, bitterness choking her. "As long as the baby was all right, these assholes don't care whether I live or die. And I didn't have complications until the baby was almost out. That proves Doc Scanlon did it—he waited until it wouldn't hurt the baby, and then he gave me something to raise my pressure."

"Amber, this is—" It was verging on the paranoid, but I was trying to find a less confrontational way of saying that. Was this typical postbirth thinking by a woman trying to say good-bye to the living creature she'd carried for nine long months?

Maybe Mickey could have told me. If she'd been speaking to me.

"Here he is," the nurse crowed in a bright voice that sounded as incongruous as the early spring sun outside; Amber's mood required snow and ice, harsh winter winds, somber rain. And a voice of mourning, not celebration. Everything the Greenspans were gaining, she was losing.

The nurse placed the baby in Ellie's eager arms. Ellie smiled with a radiance that lit her from within, yet tears rolled down her cheeks like melting icicles. She pressed the blue-blanketed bundle close to her heart, then leaned her head down and laid her ear against the tiny chest, listening for his heartbeat. She closed her eyes and drank in the smell and sound of baby.

I did something I hadn't done in a long time: I translated the scene into a black-and-white photograph, the kind I always dreamed of seeing on exhibit at the International Center for Photography with my name neatly typed underneath.

Ellie's pale gold silk shirt would come out gray; her hair falling across her broad forehead would show blond only because of the way the light struck it from above. There would be interesting shadows on her face and in the folds of the blanket, but the focus would be Ellie's ecstatic expression as she listened to her child's life beating within his breast, and the baby's wide-eyed wonder as he met the woman he would know as mother.

I decided to reshoot in color, mentally bathing the scene in golden light. Amber light: the highlights of Ellie's straight, fine hair, the sheen of her blouse, the glints off the amber pendant she wore around her neck—the same pendant she'd given the mother of her golden child.

Josh walked over to them, and I took another mental photograph. This one was of a large, male hand with thick fingers adorned by a chunky gold band, reaching toward a tiny replica of a hand, touching the translucent baby fingers, lit from behind by the bed lamp next to Amber.

Even I knew enough psychology to realize that mentally taking artistic photographs of the scene was a damned good way to insulate myself from the emotion that threatened to swamp the room.

I turned my attention back to my client. She sat bolt upright in the bed, avidly taking in the expressions on Josh and Ellie's faces. There was something atavistic in the scene; I was reminded of old wives' tales about cats sucking the breath out of babies. Amber looked like a cat, staring without blinking, expressionless, predatory. Sly.

Was that a real insight or just another arty photograph?

She wore her pendant over a faded T-shirt that read in

huge block letters "JUST DO IT."

Then Amber caught me looking at her and gave a rueful shrug. Her smile threatened to turn into a flood of tears; she choked up and turned away.

I turned to Marla and whispered, "Could they take the baby outside? I think this is upsetting Amber."

Before Marla could take action, Amber shook her head and said, "No, please. I need—" She broke off, ducking her head. Her thick gold-brown hair shielded her eyes.

She gathered herself with a visible effort and said in a calm tone, "I need to say good-bye."

There was a tiny gasp of relief from Ellie. She clutched the baby tighter for a moment, then walked over to the bed and placed the blue-wrapped bundle in Amber's arms.

"Could . . . could everybody leave?" Amber asked. Her eyes locked onto mine, begging me to make sure she had a private moment before the final parting.

"No," Marla shot back. She was in full battle mode and looked ready to get a court order. Her clothes were bronze-hued; she resembled a statue of an armored woman warrior come to life.

"I'll stay," I volunteered. I looked past Marla and fixed my gaze on Ellie. "You have the rest of your lives with Adam," I said. "Please let Amber have a few minutes."

Ellie looked at me, then at Amber. Even though both Marla and Josh were trying to get her attention, to force her to acknowledge them, it was Amber she cared about. At last, she nodded and made for the door. Josh and Marla followed, but not before each sent dark, threatening looks in my direction.

I didn't want to do this. I didn't want to be here in this place of extreme joy and gloom, I didn't want to watch this farewell or witness the birth of a dream of motherhood.

I walked to the window and looked out into the burgeoning spring day; I was standing guard, but I didn't have to eavesdrop.

Outside, the trees were just beginning to waken; crocuses

poked purple and yellow heads above the newly thawed earth. Birds were making nests in the still-bare branches, getting ready for eggs that would hatch into nestlings.

New life. That was what spring was about. New life in bud and flower and bird and—

And babies. A sharp pain stabbed through my belly, the same pain I felt every year around the time I could have given birth. I could not imagine sitting in a bed with my baby, saying farewell forever. But if I had, if I'd had the courage to do what Amber was doing now, would my belly still hurt?

CHAPTER FIVE

Y ou can't do spring without e.e. cummings. I all but skipped along Clinton Street on my way from court, his rhythms bouncing in my head.

> when faces called flowers float out of the ground
> .   .   .
> —it's april(yes,april;my darling)it's spring!

And faces did float out of townhouse-sized gardens, cat-faced pansies and yellow trumpet daffodils, and suddenly the brownstone fronts were graced with bright yellow forsythia and creamy white apple blossoms. Life burst from every branch and the air had a soft, warm tang.

Even the animals were getting into the act. At the Arab market, where I bought hummus and *babaganoush* to dip Afghan bread into, a cat had given birth and tiny pussy-willow kittens tumbled on the floor.

I drank in a long breath of spring air, ready to believe at last that winter was over. Then I turned my steps toward my office and the client who waited there.

Spring was a relief after a long brutal winter, and today's meeting with Amber would bring relief as well. She was to sign the final consent, which Marla would finalize before the Surrogate next week. It was three weeks since she'd handed her baby over to Ellie Greenspan, three weeks during which I mentally held my breath.

I was late; I quickened my steps, but I was puffing when I passed the Japanese restaurant and turned to climb the steps of the four-story brownstone that housed my office, my apartment, the Morning Glory Luncheonette at ground level, and gave me one apartment to rent out for added income. I stopped on the way up to catch my breath, hoping Amber would be late, giving me a chance to read over the unfamiliar legal papers one more time.

She wasn't. Amber sat in a mission chair I'd received as a fee from an antiques dealer on Atlantic Avenue. She thumbed through an old issue of *New York* magazine, her glossy fingernails reflecting the sunlight that came through my picture window. The amber talisman around her neck gleamed gold, glinting in a teasing wink as she moved in and out of the sunbeams. She smiled and stood up as I entered, then followed demurely as I motioned her into my office. I set the briefcase on the chair next to my desk, waved Amber into one of the red leather client chairs, and took my place behind the desk.

Marvella Jackman, the best cheap legal secretary in Brooklyn, had placed Amber's file in the center of the desk along with the Domestic Relations Law, open to the section on private placement adoptions, and put away the other motions I'd been working on—part of a harmless fiction that let each client think hers was the only case that mattered.

I opened the file and took out the final consent form. ''This is—''

"I've changed my mind," Amber said. Her fingers caressed the amber pendant. The amber pendant Ellie Greenspan hand-made for her.

I've changed my mind. Four words that shook the world. They were shaking my world; what the hell would they do to Josh and Ellie? And to Adam: that was what really mattered. What would they mean to Adam?

My response was brilliant. "What?"

"I've changed my mind," she repeated. "I can't go through with it. I can't give up my baby."

"Amber, what's wrong?"

"Nothing's wrong. Everything's right. Everything's finally right," she replied. She sounded breathless, elated. High.

I almost asked her if she was on anything, if she'd taken drugs. I was so used to dealing with criminal clients, and so unused to regular people who could feel exhilaration by natural means.

"You want the baby back." I said it flatly, trying for a neutrality I didn't feel. Amber was my client, but it was Ellie Greenspan's face I saw in my mind's eye. The image of her pressing her face into Adam's tiny chest and merging her breath with his stayed with me, almost as if I'd really taken the photographs I'd pretended to shoot.

How in hell was I going to tell her her dreamchild had to go back to the shop?

Actually, I wasn't going to tell her. I was going to tell Marla, who would tell Ellie and Josh.

Marla. Jesus. Marla would kill me.

"What changed your mind?" Even as I asked the question, I remembered the silver car outside the group home, the dark-haired guy who'd assaulted Doc Scanlon at the hospital. The man Marla had identified as a lurking boyfriend, promising marriage. That was it. That had to be it. Marla, dear cynical Marla, had been right after all.

Amber looked into the sun, her bright blue eyes gleaming sapphire. "I lost one baby," she said, her voice a near whisper. "I can't let myself lose this one, too."

"But you knew—"

"No, I didn't," she replied, leaning forward in her chair. "I *thought* I knew. I thought I wanted to leave it all behind and go on with my life. But I can't stop thinking about him. I keep picturing him in his crib, crying for his mother. Crying for me. I keep wondering if he looks like me. Oh, I know Ellie will be a good mother," she explained, "but it hurts so much to think of her walking him to his first day of school instead of me. I can't let her keep him. I can't." Her voice broke, and she dropped her head into her hands.

For a moment there was nothing but the sound of sobs.

Thanks to the propensity of my Atlantic Avenue clients to pay me in furniture and collectibles, I had a nice collection of vintage posters on my office wall. I felt a sense of sisterly solidarity when ever I looked over at Rosie the Riveter flexing her muscles, hair bound up in a polka-dot scarf to keep it out of the machinery, her forties face determined. "We Can Do It!" the poster proclaimed.

I looked at Rosie now. We can do it.

But should we?

Amber raised her head; tears streaked her face. Her pink blusher had melted onto her hands; she brushed them on her black jeans with an air of apology. She gave me a watery smile, then said, "I can't stop thinking about Laura."

Laura? Another birth mother, I figured, someone who'd given up a baby and spent the rest of her life regretting the decision, searching for the child she'd—

"My first baby," Amber explained. "I was so young, but I had such high hopes. Jerry and I were married as soon as I told him I was pregnant. He was a good guy, Jerry. I knew he'd take care of me and love the baby as much as I did. But then, when Doc Scanlon told me she was sick, that she—"

"Doc Scanlon?" I was still reeling from the news of her

changed intentions; I was following this story about as easily as I would a discussion of nuclear physics.

"He delivered her. At first, he told Jerry and me she was fine. No problems. But then a couple days later, he said they'd found a heart defect. I never even took her home; she died a week later. It was nobody's fault, but—"

"Amber, this is not new," I said, gently, I hoped, but firmly. "No matter how bad you feel about losing Laura, that has nothing to do with this baby."

"Doesn't it? I thought I could let him go, but now that he's real, alive, I can't do it."

I looked down at the massive file on my desk. All that paperwork for nothing. All the hopes and dreams the Greenspans had put into Adam, and now—

Now what? Now Amber wanted her baby back. But under the laws of the State of New York, it wasn't at all certain she would get what she wanted.

"Once upon a time," I began, going into law professor mode, "there was a little girl named—"

"Baby Jessica," Amber cut in. She said the name with reverence, invoking the child taken from her adoptive parents in Wisconsin and returned, at two-and-a-half, to Iowa birth parents she had never known.

I shook my head. "Baby Lenore," I corrected.

Blank stare. I was telling her a story she hadn't heard before. Which was no more than I'd expected.

"This happened here in New York," I went on, "in"— I consulted the practice commentary to Section 115-b of the Domestic Relations Law—"1971." I was a first-year law student at NYU when the case hit the headlines, and its legal twists and turns had both fascinated and appalled me.

"Baby Lenore was adopted under the old law of New York State," I explained. "That law gave a lot of rights to the birth parents, so that when the birth mother petitioned to get the baby back, the adoptive parents weren't even allowed in the courtroom."

I transferred my gaze to the window at my right. Ornamental street trees waved in the stiff breeze, shaking pompoms of white and pink blossoms. Cotton candy clouds floated in the bright blue sky.

"When the judge ordered them to return the kid," I went on, wrenching my attention back to my client, "which happened after they'd had custody for at least three years, they scooped her up and went to Florida. It was a major heartbreaker of a case, and as a result, the Legislature amended the Domestic Relations Law."

I looked into Amber's guileless blue eyes. She seemed to be listening attentively, but would she really understand?

The innocence of spring seemed very far away.

"So the law in New York now," I finished, going for the bottom line before my client's eyes glazed over entirely, "is that you and the Greenspans are on equal footing in the eyes of the law. If they refuse to give up the baby, there'll be a hearing. You make your case for why the baby should be with you, and they get to make their case. The judge decides based on the best interests of the child. This isn't Iowa," I went on. "There the law favored the birth parents, just as New York did before Baby Lenore. That's why the Iowa couple got Baby Jessica back. If the Greenspans contest your revocation of consent—"

"There is something else," Amber interrupted. Her face was pale, but her tone determined. "I'm married."

"When?" All the other questions I could have asked were pushed aside as I went straight to the legal heart of the matter. "If it was after the baby's birth, it has no legal effect."

She allowed herself a tiny smile of triumph. "It was before," she said. "About a week before. I was big as a house, so the guy at Borough Hall looked at me like I was a whore, but I didn't care."

It flashed upon me that Amber knew the full legal implication of what she'd done, that she'd deliberately chosen to marry before the baby's birth so that her legal position would be stronger when she changed her mind. Then I discarded the thought; a woman who'd never heard of Baby Lenore was unlikely to know that a husband is legally presumed to be the father of a child born in wedlock.

On the other hand, one week before birth was perfect. Marla would have checked state records before she let the Greenspans start preliminary negotiations. But once papers were signed, once investigations were complete, who would monitor the county clerks' offices on the remote chance a birth mother would choose to marry a week before delivery?

I recalled sitting in the straight chair in Amber's room at the group home, listening to her sad tale of date rape. Anger ran through me like a hot flash; how dare this girl play on my emotions with a story like that, when all the time she'd known her intended husband could throw a monkey wrench into all the careful legal planning?

Was the rape story even true, or had she—

"What about the rape?" I'd abandoned all pretense of neutrality; I felt used and betrayed. I went into full cross-examination mode.

"What about that lovely image of the sperm running down your leg? Was that just a sob story, something you cooked up so the court wouldn't have to get the father's consent to adopt?" I stopped for breath. Amber sat still, her face a mask of endurance.

I raised my voice, letting my words assault her perfect calm. "Was this whole thing a scheme, Amber, a way to get Josh and Ellie to pay your expenses, buy you gifts, when all the time you knew you'd change your mind, that you had no intention of letting them have the baby?"

She shook her head. "No," she replied. "It wasn't like that. I really was raped. But," she went on, her voice shaking, "I was seeing Scott at the same time. I wasn't sure who the father was. But I thought I couldn't stand it if the baby turned out to look like him. If every time I played with my kid I remembered what that bastard did to me. But now—''

I waited for the inevitable. I wasn't going to help her, but I was beginning to feel something like sympathy. The young lawyer who'd agonized about her own unplanned pregnancy couldn't help but feel the pain of this young woman who'd made hard choices about her unexpected child.

"I don't care who the father is anymore," Amber concluded. Her eyes locked with mine, and again I felt her reading my thoughts. "I know I'm his mother, and I know I can give him a good home. And so can Scott. He says—"

"Scott." The wild card. The new husband. The guy in the silver car, waiting outside the group home. The guy who'd tried to assault Doc Scanlon at the hospital. The guy who rode around in a car with a license plate that read PIZZA 21.

My lawyer's mind went into gear, pushing aside thoughts of unwanted babies. "I'll have to talk to him. The court won't give the baby to you without first certifying him as a fit parent." I looked at my desk calendar. "When can I see him?"

"Now," Amber replied. The cool self-possession I'd seen at our first meeting was back. "He's downstairs in the car."

Nice. Maybe Amber had never heard of Baby Lenore, but she knew enough law to bring Scott along on this visit, somehow anticipating I'd need an affidavit from him as part of the altered legal proceeding. I agreed to her suggestion that she bring him up.

I twirled a yellow pencil in my hand as I waited. I recalled Marla's anger when she'd heard there was a man hovering outside the group home, following Amber. I'd protected Amber from her wrath, and now it turned out my cynical old friend had been right all along.

But when Amber came back, the man she ushered

through my door was not the man in the silver car. That boy had been stocky, dark, Italian-looking. This one was dishwater blond, with a baby face. He wore his hair long, slicked straight back, but its baby-fine strands fell over his forehead. A single earring dangled from one ear. And I mean dangled; this was no tasteful hoop; on closer inspection, it revealed itself as a full-length skeleton with moving parts.

He wore a Harley-Davidson T-shirt and jeans with holes in the knees. A leather belt held two knife sheaths; work boots completed his outfit.

"Ms. Jameson, this is Scott Wylie," Amber said, unmistakable pride warming her voice.

Scott mumbled something that might have been "Pleased to meet you," and folded himself into the red leather chair next to Amber's.

I got down to business. Poising my pen to take notes, I asked, "What do you do for a living, Scott?"

He shrugged, a quintessential Generation X gesture that seemed to put the question in some quaint museum of things people over thirty got hung up about.

"Done some construction," he said. "When there's work. In between, I work at the mall. That's where I met Amber," he explained, giving her a proprietary smile.

"I was a salesgirl at Victoria's Secret," Amber went on, "you know, that place with the lingerie."

I nodded. I jotted a note on a legal pad.

"Scott was working at Sears," Amber continued.

"We both used to take our dinner breaks at Friendly's," Scott said with a reminiscent smile.

"And one night I was there with my girlfriend, and Scott was with another guy from Sears, and there weren't enough booths, so the waitress asked if we minded sharing, and we said we didn't, so we shared the booth, and then Scott asked me out." Amber rattled on, her hands moving in her lap, her color rising. The cool young woman had turned simpering teenager.

"You were already pregnant?"

Color flooded her cheeks. "I wasn't sure," she said in a small voice. "I've never been that regular. Missing a period or two wasn't that unusual for me."

"You must have been showing a little," I persisted.

"My weight goes up and down. I just thought I needed to cut down on the Friendly's ice cream."

So far, so plausible. Young love at the mall, followed by an unplanned surprise, followed by marriage and a desire to start a family in spite of the odds. Maybe a little touch of soap opera, but nothing sinister. Until Amber decided the Greenspans should pay her medical bills.

"Are you still working at Sears?"

Scott shook his head. "Got a construction job for a while," he said. "When that shut down for the winter, I went to work at Macy's, in the stockroom."

I pressed him for the name of his boss, the duration of the job, his salary, the address where he and Amber were living—everything I thought the court would want to know.

Then I turned my attention to the harder question.

"You really think you could be a father to a kid who isn't yours?"

Scott lifted his shoulders again in the loose shrug that characterized his generation. This time the shrug said, What the hell, nothing matters anyway, so why not quit your job, get another one, raise a kid? It's all the same.

"I take it that's an affirmative." This conversation was making me feel like a teacher. Any minute now I'd be calling him "Mr. Wylie" in that snide tone I'd hated when I was in high school.

It was more than a little disconcerting for a card-carrying member of the generation that hadn't trusted anyone over thirty to be on the other side of the generation gap.

"I like kids," he said, an unexpected grin lighting his face. His teeth were perfect, a triumph of orthodontia. Scott, I realized, had been raised upper-middle class. So what was he doing working construction, meeting his future wife at the mall?

"Where did you grow up, Scott?" I asked.

"On Staten Island," he replied.

"Where on Staten Island?"

"Near La Tourette Park."

Amber leaned forward, an eager light in her eyes. It struck me she hadn't known the answer herself, that she'd married a man she knew little about.

"Near where Amber was living at the group home?" I pressed. "In New Springville or Westerleigh?" I named two working-class neighborhoods.

His mouth turned down into a sulk, and for a moment I wondered if he'd take the Fifth. He gave another shrug. "No, the other side of the golf course," he admitted. And it was an admission, the way he said it. As if he were confessing to coming from the wrong side of the tracks. Only Scott had come from the side of the park with the wide green lawns and big houses. The side where people went to Ivy League schools and earned advanced degrees. The side where you didn't sport work boots and box-cutting tools as a fashion statement.

They walked out of the office with their arms around each other's waist. Amber locked her fingers into Scott's belt loop with an air of ownership and seemed to lean her hips into his as if trying to melt into a single unit.

After they left, I sat amid the now-useless paperwork and cursed softly to myself. Which was a restrained response under the circumstances; I would have felt better if I'd swept the papers off the desk in a grand gesture of renunciation.

On some level I hadn't begun to think about consciously, I'd let Marla talk me into handling Amber's adoption in order to make up for Rojean Glover's dead children. I'd wanted more than anything to help save a child, help create a happy family.

I had to tell myself there was no reason Adam—correction: Jimmy—couldn't be happy on Staten Island with Amber and Scott.

Telling myself was one thing. Telling Marla was another. I called her office; her secretary said she was in Brooklyn Supreme, Part 52. I considered leaving a message but discarded the idea as too cowardly. Marla deserved to hear this in person, and soon.

I put on my linen blazer and headed out the door, prepared to intercept Marla in court.

This time no faces floated out of the ground.

"Let me get this straight," Marla said in a tone loud enough for the first two rows of the courtroom to hear. "I take you to meet your client on Saturday, she throws me out of the room, and on Monday she goes and gets herself married?"

I cast uneasy eyes around the courtroom. The judge was on break, but civil lawyers in the first row were finding our conversation too interesting for my taste. "Can we discuss this in the hall?" I asked, my voice an octave lower than Marla's.

The question was a mistake. Given the mood she was in, if I'd begged to stay in the courtroom, she'd have hauled me bodily into the corridor. She stood in the aisle between the first row of seats and the railing, feet planted apart, her arms crossed over her ample breasts—mad as hell and not giving a damn who knew it.

"That little bitch," Marla said, in an almost conversational tone, a tone that worried me even more than yelling. Marla quiet was far more deadly than Marla in full voice.

"I thought we could go see the clerk of the Surrogate's Court together," I said. "I'm not quite sure what happens next, what papers I have to file when."

"Oh, is that what you thought?" Marla countered, raising an eyebrow in exquisite disdain. The briefcases in the front row liked that one; I heard a snicker or two but didn't bother taking names. "You thought I'd help you take that baby away from my clients. You thought I'd let you get away with this piece of treachery, this—"

"Let me get away with what?" My voice rose in spite of myself. I didn't want to have this conversation in public, but I did want to understand what Marla was driving at. "What is it I'm supposed to have done here, Marla?"

"She gets married two days before she drops the kid," Marla said, her words etched in acid, "which is also two days after she meets you for the first time, and you've got the nerve to stand there and tell me you didn't give her a crash course in matrimonial law?" Her green eyes raked me up and down. "Save it, Cass. Save it for someone who might believe it."

She shook her head deliberately; her platinum hair moved in a well-sprayed unit. "I can't believe I let you do this to me. All the years I've handled adoptions, and I've never been outmaneuvered like this."

"If it makes you feel any better," I said, "I didn't know what she was going to do. She didn't ask me anything about marriage; she didn't tell me she was getting married. There was nothing said in that room you couldn't have heard."

She shot me a penetrating glance that held no softness. "Then why wasn't I there to hear it?" she asked sweetly.

I shook my head. I had no idea why Amber had insisted Marla leave the room, but I could tell it didn't matter. She was determined to believe I'd instructed Amber on the effects of a prebirth marriage on the presumption of paternity, and that was that.

"I should have known," Marla went on. "The minute that creep in the silver car came around, I should have known. In fact, I did know. But I let that little bitch tell me she didn't know him. Not that I believed her for a minute."

"Marla," I began, "I know how you feel. I'm not happy about this either." Understatement of the year; I'd rather face ten juries bringing back verdicts in murder cases than look at another adoption. "But this can't be the first time this has ever happened to you. Birth mothers have thirty days to change their minds, and that's what Amber did.''

''Did she?'' Marla radiated a steady, simmering rage that boiled to the surface like a geyser. ''Did she really change her mind, or was she planning this all along? Isn't that why she got married when she did—to strengthen her legal case? It seems to me her plan from the beginning was to string my clients along, get as much money out of them as possible, and then grab the baby. After they paid all her expenses and gave her presents and God knows what else.''

''Can't you sue for the money?'' I asked. Not a particularly strategic question, since I represented the potential defendant, but I was curious.

''Yeah, like the little bitch still has any of the money,'' she replied. Her foot, shod in a black flat with little jewels on the toe, tapped impatiently on the courthouse floor. ''Or if she does, she's socked it away someplace. The prospects of getting any of it back are not large. And my clients would rather put whatever they have left into another baby, not into legal fees for a case that won't get them anything.''

Another baby. I could hardly bear to imagine Ellie Greenspan saying good-bye to Adam, just as Amber herself had done three weeks earlier, then combing the ads in the *Dreamchild* newsletter for another birth mother to subsidize. The cruelty of Amber's decision came home to me yet again.

Marla locked her green eyes with mine. ''I swear, Cass,'' she promised, her voice as cold as a Disney stepmother's, ''I'll make you wish you'd never taken this case.''

Too late for that, I wanted to say but didn't.

Marla FedExed me her papers two days later. The top document was a court order, signed not by Sylvia Feinberg, the Surrogate we were scheduled to appear before, but by Judge Julius Hargrove of the Family Court.

Family Court. Marla had called it a poor people's court, had dismissed it as a place no self-respecting adoption lawyer would be caught dead in. And now she was serving me with an order from that very same court.

Why?

I skimmed the front page, my eyes eliding the legalese, trying to get to the heart of the matter. Finally, buried on the third page of the affidavit in support, I had it:

"I, Joshua Elliott Greenspan, am the biological father of the child known as Adam Greenspan, born Baby Boy Lundquist."

I recalled the slight tremor in Josh's hand as he held the birthday card Amber had sent him, the one supposedly from his yet-unborn son.

Happy Birthday, Daddy.

CHAPTER SIX

"I need your car," I said without preamble. I'd timed my visit to Mickey's office for the ten-minute window between clients, so I made it short and to the point.

She raised an inquiring eyebrow, but she opened her purse without comment.

"It's about Amber," I confessed, deciding my colleague deserved to know why her car was about to cross the Verrazano Bridge into Staten Island. "Something's come up and I need to talk to her right away."

Mickey handed over her car keys and said, "It's parked on Bergen, on the other side of Court. Near the taco place."

I nodded. Under other circumstances I'd have said something clever about the way Mickey's car gravitated toward parking places in front of spicy food emporia, but now I just wanted to get out of her office.

She didn't say I told you so, but the muscles around her

mouth were strained from the effort of not saying it.

I had directions from my interview with Scott. I'd told them I wanted to make a home visit, to be able to report to the judge what kind of home they could make for their baby. It hadn't occurred to me I'd be racing out to Staten Island to confront my liar of a client about the true paternity of the child she'd handed to Josh and Ellie that cold March day.

I could have called her on the phone, but I had to see her face when I told her what Josh was claiming.

I drove along Victory Boulevard to Richmond Avenue. Right on Travis, a narrow street that was overgrown with tall reeds on one side and developed into two-family houses that all wore the same drab green paint job on the other. I scanned the cross streets and pulled into a parking place just after the one I wanted. I was somewhere near the group home Amber had lived in before her marriage, but it was on the other side of the mall. I walked along the street, noting the well-kept lawns, the magnolias in full bloom, the basketball hoops on the sides of the houses.

The house Amber lived in looked like all the others. I walked up to the front door, which was guarded by an aluminum screen door with a curlicue C on the front, and rang the bell closest to me. A woman about my age opened the door and stood behind the screen. She had blond hair worn in short curls and held a fluorescent green substance in her hand.

"Yes?" she asked.

"I'm looking for Amber Lundquist," I said. "Or Amber Wylie," I amended. "I'm not sure which name she's using."

"She lives upstairs," the woman explained, punctuating her remark with a toss of her head. "The other bell."

"Oh. Sorry," I replied, and pushed the second buzzer.

A child came up behind her. Five, maybe, with red shoulder-length hair and a freckled face. "Aunt Betsy, Matthew hit Jason with—"

"I'll be right there, Erin," the woman said, leaning down. She handed the green blob to the little girl. "Here, take this Play-Doh back to the table, honey."

"Okay," she said and skipped away.

"They must be quite a handful," I remarked. I could hear the sounds of children at play—*at war* sounded more like it.

"Oh, they're not mine," the blonde replied with a laugh. "I baby-sit, and my niece comes over some afternoons to play with the other children."

Better you than me, I thought but didn't say. Amber appeared in the doorway just as the blonde disappeared into the grayness behind the screen door.

"Thanks, Mrs. Scanlon," she called after her retreating back.

"Who did you say she was?" I asked Amber as I followed her up the steps to the second level of the house.

"That's Betsy Scanlon," Amber replied. "Doc Scanlon's ex. She's renting the top floor to Scott and me."

"So the ex-wife of the doctor who delivered your baby is now your landlady," I remarked, not bothering to mute my sarcasm. "How many other little surprises have you got in store for me, Amber?"

My client shrugged. She wore an oversized man's dress shirt over flowered leggings; her feet were bare. "Why not? When I told Doc I needed a place for me and Scott to live with the baby, he said his ex-wife was looking for a tenant. Scott and I came right over. It's okay," Amber said with another shrug. "We'll need more space when the baby gets bigger, but it's okay for now."

It was a typical cheap construction-box apartment, with no frills and dead white walls, bare floors made of stained pine, and white venetian blinds on windows without drapes or curtains. There were no cardboard cartons, though; Scott and Amber must have unpacked their few belongings in record time.

The living room was a little bare of furniture, and what

was here looked hastily assembled from family castoffs, yard sales, and the Goodwill, but that was to be expected for newlyweds just starting out. I noted Ellie Greenspan's Santa Fe rug on the floor in the living room, and saw her crystal wind chime in the window.

"Are you still wearing that pendant?" I asked. No, demanded. Demanded to know how Amber could bear to use the things Ellie gave her while hurting her so deeply.

Amber's fingers went to her throat and she touched the amber talisman with a secretive smile on her face. "Why not?" she countered. "It's pretty. She gave it to me."

"She gave it to you when she thought you were bringing light into her life," I shot back. "And now you're taking it away."

This was not what I came to talk about. I was here to confront my client with Marla's bombshell, to ask her once and for all who was the father of the child she'd borne, to get enough truth out of her so I could walk into court and represent her without being afraid of what I'd learn. But those insolent young blue eyes infuriated me, made me realize how naive I'd been. How right Mickey had been to warn me against putting my faith in yet another aspect of the legal system.

I hate it when other people are right, and I'm stuck with the mess I made because I didn't listen to them.

Amber raked me up and down with eyes as sharp as fake fingernails. "I thought you were my lawyer," she said, cold contempt flattening her voice. "Why not let Marla take care of Ellie?"

"I don't like being used." I tried for the same calm, flat tone my client was using to such effect, but my rage got in the way.

Another twentysomething shrug of indifference. "I thought a lawyer was supposed to be used. To do whatever the client wants."

"You thought wrong. If I walk away from here convinced that you shouldn't have that baby, that's what I'll tell the court. You can find another lawyer.''

It was a bluff and her eyes knew it. They shone with triumph as she played her trump card. ''Doesn't the judge have to approve your withdrawal from a case?'' Amber's use of the correct legal terms told me she'd done her home-work, that she had me and she knew it. Sylvia Feinberg was not going to want to bring in a new lawyer at this stage. And unless she let me go, I was stuck representing Amber even if I knew her to be a liar who had deliberately used the Greenspans.

We were still standing in the bare living room. I decided to sit, to let Amber know I was prepared to stay here until I had what I'd come for. I walked over to the couch, which was covered in faded cabbage roses against a dark blue-green, and sat down, falling into its sagging upholstery as if into a swamp.

She folded her arms and remained standing.

''Who's the father, Amber?'' I asked conversationally.

She stiffened. ''I'm not sure,'' she said. ''I think Scott.''

''Marla served papers in which she claimed Josh was the father.''

''He could be.''

''He could be,'' I repeated. I didn't have to exaggerate my tone of disbelief. How the hell had I come to be sitting on this fourth-hand sofa listening to my client tell me she'd had sex with the man who was adopting her child?

''No wonder Josh picked your ad out of the *Dreamchild* newsletter,'' I remarked, remembering Ellie's glow of sur-prised pleasure when she told me how Josh had selected Amber out of all the birth mothers in the listings. ''He must have written the damned thing in the first place.''

She didn't bother confirming something so obvious, just walked back and forth along the cold wooden floor, her long toes reaching for the boards like prehensile append-ages.

She was thinking, searching for words to explain the unexplainable, to justify the unjustifiable.

Then she found them. "It was like I told you," she began. The insolent stare was gone; her eyes refused to meet mine. "We went out on a date. We had dinner, and the next thing I knew, he was ripping my clothes off. I told him I didn't want to, but he forced me. Then when I told him I was pregnant, he said he'd adopt the baby but his wife couldn't know it was really his. So he set up the whole thing with Doc Scanlon and Marla, made me pretend I'd never seen him before."

I was having a hard time accepting Josh Greenspan as a rapist, but even if Amber had consented to sex, it made sense that Josh would try to protect Ellie from knowledge of his affair with another woman. Especially another woman with working ovaries.

I decided to proceed as if I believed Amber's story—at least for the moment.

"So you decided to get revenge," I said. "Set him up to believe you'd give him the baby, then change your mind at the last minute. Pay him back for raping you. Good plan, Amber," I complimented my client, "except of course that you're hurting Ellie even more than Josh and she certainly didn't rape you."

Amber turned her face toward the window, where the April sun struck the crystal wind chime, making long rainbow streaks of color against the white wall.

"He hurt me," she said in a low growl. "He pinned me down with his big hairy arms and pushed himself into me. Then when I told him I was pregnant he grabbed me and—" Amber ran long fingers against her arm, rubbing herself as if to soothe the pain of that long-ago assault.

"He said he had to have the baby. He said he'd pay anything, anything I asked for. His eyes were crazy." She turned her own blue eyes on me, begging for understanding. "And after what he did to me, I didn't want his baby, so I said yes. And then I met Ellie, and I—"

She dropped her eyes, let her hands fall to her sides. "I wanted so much to make her happy."

She stood in silence for a moment, seeming to go deep inside herself. I'd never seen Amber so naked, so vulnerable.

"It's not revenge," she said at last. She turned the full force of her intense blue eyes on me. "It's the baby. He doesn't look like Josh, he looks like Scott."

"So your wanting him back depends on the outcome of a DNA test?" I asked. "Marla's petitioned the Family Court to order one, so we'll know soon enough who the father really is."

She shook her head. "That's what I thought at first," she replied, her voice a near whisper. "But the more I think about Jimmy, the more I know I can't live without him no matter who the father is. I want my baby, Ms. Jameson. I want him more than anything in the world."

Jimmy. It came back to that, to the silly name she'd called her unborn child when he nestled in her womb. If she hadn't named him, or if she'd called him Adam as a reminder that he was destined to become a Greenspan, maybe this wouldn't have happened.

"Could I see the baby's room?" I asked. It was an abrupt change of subject, but I wanted an antidote to the image of Josh forcing his heavy body onto Amber's.

"I want to be able to tell the judge that you and Scott are ready to give the baby a good home," I explained, trying to soften the investigative aspect of the situation.

Amber ushered me into the back bedroom with a triumphant smile. All the stuffed animals from Amber's room at the group home were lined up on a white shelf unit. A white crib with a Sesame Street mobile hanging over it sat in one corner of the room, while a matching changing table and chest of drawers flanked the opposite wall. A baby quilt with the letters of the alphabet appliquéed in pastels hung over the crib.

"Nice," I said.

There were cardboard cartons with a Kansas return address sitting open in one corner of the room. "Looks like you're getting baby presents already," I remarked.

"From my folks in Kansas City," Amber said. "And my sister in Baltimore."

"Scott's parents live here on Staten Island, don't they?" I asked. "I imagine they're pretty excited about their new grandchild."

Was I cross-examining my client or just making polite conversation? Amber looked at me as if she wasn't sure, and I couldn't have sworn which I was doing myself.

"Not really," she said in a small voice. "I wish they were. I'd love the baby to have grandparents close by, but they don't get along with Scott. They think his marrying me was a mistake."

"Amber, are you sure about this?" I blurted out. I looked at the nest she'd made for her offspring and realized it was a monumentally stupid question. Sure or not, Amber wanted this child and had made ready for it. What else did the law require? What else could I require?

She gave a long sigh. "Yes," she said, her tone firm. "I know I can raise Jimmy with Scott's help. I'm sorry about Josh and Ellie, I really am, but I can't let them keep him or I'll regret it for the rest of my life."

"Look, it's better this way," I said for the fifth time. "The last thing that kid needs is to become the Baby Jessica of Brooklyn."

"Baby who? Oh, that case in the Midwest. God, that was awful," Dorinda said, her eyes widening. "Can you imagine raising a child for two-and-a-half years and then—"

"My point exactly," I cut in. My finger hit the counter as punctuation for my words. "If those adoptive parents had given back the baby as soon as the birth mother changed her mind, they could have done their grieving and started over with a baby they could keep. And that poor kid wouldn't have been carried off crying for Mommy and getting used to a new name."

"You make it sound so simple," my old friend objected.

She was wiping glasses on a vintage fifties dishtowel with a red-and-blue rooster print. Her long, wheat-colored hair hung in a thick single braid behind her head. She could have auditioned for a revival of *I Remember Mama* and gotten the part hands down.

"I didn't say it was simple," I muttered. "Look, just pour me another iced coffee, will you?"

"You drink too much coffee," Dorinda pronounced. "I made some cold red zinger. You could—"

"I said iced coffee and I meant iced coffee," I replied. "This court appearance is the worst thing I've faced since Rojean's arraignment. I'm going to need caffeine and plenty of it, so zing me no zingers."

"O-kay," the proprietor of the Morning Glory Luncheonette sang as she strode to the oversized jar filled with the healing brew. She scooped ice into an old-fashioned soda glass and let the dark brown liquid flow into it. My mouth watered just looking at it; Dorinda, for all her pretenses to running a health food restaurant, had invested in a nice blend of Colombian, Javanese, and French Roast that stood up to ice very well. Of course, she had me as her consultant on what she loftily referred to as "stimulants."

"Sure, the Greenspans will feel terrible for right now," I went on, "but they'll get over it. They'll find another baby, and maybe the next Adam won't come with a cloud on the title."

The flippancy in my tone reminded me forcibly of Marla; I took a long swallow of the cold coffee to cover my sudden embarrassment.

Dorinda's gray eyes narrowed. "Oh, so you're doing the Greenspans a favor?"

I addressed my next remarks to the Formica counter. "The law's the law. All I'm doing is my job."

Why did I feel like a used car dealer?

"Cass, I can't believe you." Dorinda's normally soft voice was raised, and she shook her head. "It's not that easy. Here's a woman who wants a child so badly it hurts.

She finally holds this baby in her arms, feeds it, smells it—
and you think she can just give him up because the law
says she should?''

''Hey, adoption is about taking chances,'' I countered.
''Everybody who adopts has to face the possibility of the
birth parents changing their minds. Thirty days isn't a long
time in the law. Once that's over—''

My old friend came back with a one-liner I couldn't argue with, couldn't explain away, couldn't top.

''Thirty days is a long time if you're only a month old.''

> in Just-
> spring   when the world is mud-
> luscious

    I said the words to myself as I stepped back from the
curb to let a passing car splash the area where I'd been
walking a second earlier. The rain had stopped, but there
was water everywhere, dirty, muddy, ugly New York snow-
melt on top of April showers.

Mud-luscious, my——! The man was a fool, I decided,
as I surveyed the huge puddle separating sidewalk from
street in the crosswalk at Court and Atlantic. How was I
going to get around this without damaging my Italian
leather shoes?

Puddle-wonderful. What was so wonderful about puddles?

Of course the man who wrote those words wasn't trying
to propel himself over great brown puddles of probably
toxic mud without dirtying his new pumps. The man was
talking about childhood, when mud really was fun and puddles were wonderful and you ran out to play in new red
galoshes and floated paper boats on the high-flooded streets
of your small town.

He wasn't talking about making your way to court to
take a baby away from parents who'd already had a *bris*
for their son, who'd held him and rocked him and sung to

him and taken thousands upon thousands of pictures.

I walked into the courthouse at 360 Adams Street the back way, through the County Clerk's office and into the corridor leading to the single courtroom used by the Surrogate. Marla was already there, her possessions strewn on the front bench as though she'd spread out a picnic lunch. Her lavender briefcase was open; her butter-soft teal-colored leather bag sat next to her, its open top a gaping mouth, inviting pickpockets; papers sat in piles on the empty bench around her.

She looked up as I entered, staring at me with her game face. Hard, closed, prepared for battle.

I had expected as much. Whatever friendship we had shared was over now; we each had a client to represent, a job to do. And Marla couldn't be blamed for resenting my role in Amber's change of heart. Just as I couldn't blame her for Josh's claiming paternity.

Unless, of course, Marla had known all along that Josh—

Which would explain Marla's jumpiness, her desire to get an unenforceable consent out of Amber, her wariness about my meeting alone with my client.

"Let's talk outside," she said. Her hammered silver bracelets clanked as she rose; she wore the same silver outfit she'd had on the day we first agreed to work together.

She walked me to the end of the corridor, away from our courtroom. Oblivious to the No Smoking sign, she lit up, took a long drag, and let her words float out on a carpet of smoke.

"How much does she want?"

My response was less than brilliant. "What?"

"How much, Cass?" Marla persisted. "I know that's what this is about. The little bitch thinks she can hold Josh up for more money. I hate to admit it, but she's right. Josh and Ellie will pay another three thousand, but that's it. You tell her that, Cass. That's it. Three thousand and not a penny more."

CHAPTER SEVEN

I stood there stunned, silent, stupid while a hundred thoughts whizzed around my head like mosquitoes.

A nice simple adoption. A piece of cake.

Money. Amber wants money. That's what all this is about.

Marla could be disbarred for saying this.

I could be disbarred for listening to it.

"Amber doesn't want money," I said, my voice rising. Hoping against hope that my indignant denials were the truth. "She wants the baby back. She and Scott—"

"Spare me, Cass," Marla interrupted. "Let's cut through the bullshit and get down to business. The only reason Amber married that bozo was to get herself a husband at exactly the right time. It was a brilliant move; I take my hat off to both of you, and I'm willing to pay for my mistake in letting it happen. Just give me the bottom line."

It took a moment for the full import of my old friend's words to sink in, and when they did, the color rose to my face. "What do you mean you take your hat off to both of us? You *really* think I advised Amber to get married when she did, don't you?"

"I don't think she did it on her own," Marla answered with a grim smile. "She's a clever little bitch, but that took real legal genius."

"Gee, thanks," I said with all the sarcasm I could muster. "That means a lot coming from you."

"Just tell your client she can take the three thousand or face the fight of her life," Marla pronounced. She dropped her cigarette to the floor and crushed it with her silver pump.

"If you think I'm going to convey a completely illegal offer to buy this baby, you're—"

"Oh, you'll convey it, all right," Marla said with rock-hard certainty. "It's what your client's been waiting for and you know it."

"I wonder how Judge Feinberg would react to this little conversation," I said to Marla's retreating back. "I can't see her approving of lawyers selling babies outside her courtroom."

Marla's eyes held a malicious glint as she shot back, "What conversation, Cass? It's your word against mine." Her heels clicked on the pavement, and she swung the courthouse door open with a wide flourish.

And the hell of it was that I didn't really know how Amber would react. I couldn't convey the offer the same way I'd tell a criminal client about a plea bargain proposed by a district attorney, or the way I'd discuss a settlement in a civil case. What Marla had proposed was illegal, pure and simple.

But I wanted to hear Amber turn it down. I wanted to wave the money under her nose and watch her lip curl in disdain. I wanted to know she hadn't set this whole thing up just to squeeze a few more bucks out of Josh Greenspan.

So I went to the courtroom where she and Scott sat in the second row and motioned them into the hall.

Amber was dressed in schoolgirl mode, circa 1954: white blouse, plaid skirt, flat shoes. Her lush, thick hair was pulled back and tied with a big plaid bow. She looked about seventeen, and she carried a diaper bag with a big plaid Scotty dog appliquéd on the front. Scott, too, was dressed for court, wearing a suit and tie—a conservative tie—and black comfort-soled shoes that could pass at a distance for business wing tips. I noted with approval that the skeleton earring was gone from his right ear.

"I want to be very clear about this," I said, letting my voice drop to a register I hoped conveyed extreme seriousness. "Marla just made me an offer I ought to take straight to the District Attorney. And the only reason I'm not is the slim chance that you two would really consider taking it. Because if you would, then I'm off this case. And I need to know exactly what kind of people I'm representing here."

I laid out the offer. Three thousand dollars in return for Amber and Scott walking into the courtroom and withdrawing the revocation of consent. Three thousand dollars for letting Jimmy remain Adam Greenspan.

Before I'd finished talking, Scott was bouncing like a rapper, punctuating his movements with grunts of "No way. No fuckin' way. Sick fuck thinks he can buy our baby?"

Amber shook her head, a pitying smile playing around her lips. "That sounds like Josh," she said. "Money solves everything, according to him. But the answer is no, Ms. Jameson. Absolutely not. I won't take money for my baby."

"That's all I wanted to hear," I said, relief weakening my knees. As I walked back to the courtroom, I reflected that I had an ethical obligation to report the conversation I'd had with Marla to somebody. To Judge Feinberg, to the Kings County District Attorney. To somebody.

The door opened behind me; I turned. Ellie came in first, Josh holding the door behind her. Her face was devoid of makeup; she looked like a woman recovering from chemotherapy. At the court's insistence, she had brought the baby.

He was tinier than I remembered, and he was almost a month older than he'd been when I'd seen him last. He lay in her arms, sleeping. The still center of a storm that would sweep him forever into one family, cut him off from another.

The temperature around my body dropped twenty degrees; the sweat that had formed on my skin froze into a cold shroud.

Everybody knows the Bible story of Solomon and the baby claimed by two mothers. Everyone thinks they know how the mothers felt, how Solomon felt. Does anybody wonder what the lawyer for the mother felt?

I knew.

"All rise," the bailiff said. We rose. I gave a hasty, guilty glance back at the Greenspans. Ellie looked nearly transparent; Josh was the enigma. All the energy seemed to have been drained from him. He held Ellie's thin hand in his big paw and stared straight ahead, refusing to acknowledge Amber's existence. He lumbered out of his chair when Judge Feinberg took the bench, then fell back like a rag doll. The masculine force of his personality seemed to have seeped out of him.

It was my motion, which meant I argued first. The advantage: I could set the stage, characterize the facts, define the issues. Disadvantage: I laid out my cards for Marla to trump when it was her turn.

I needed something to grab the court's attention.

"Joshua Greenspan lied to this Court," I began. "He also lied to his wife. He pretended to be the disinterested adoptive father of this child when the fact was that he raped Amber Lundquist while married to Ellie Greenspan."

I sensed a stir at the opposing counsel table, but didn't

bother to look over at Marla. The judge's eyes opened a little wider, which was all I cared about.

I continued my indictment, letting some of my indignation at Josh's clumsy attempt to buy Amber off fuel my argument. "He used Amber as an unpaid surrogate mother to produce a biological child he intended to manipulate this Court into letting him adopt. He filed perjurious affidavits, he concealed vital information from the social workers preparing the pre-adoption investigation. And, yet, for all this—"

I let my voice go up and paused dramatically. Now for the zinger. "For all this," I went on, "he is *not* the biological father of this child."

I had a moment's pure satisfaction as I heard the gasps and murmurs from the rows behind me. Judge Feinberg banged a gavel and the noise subsided.

I had her complete attention. Sylvia Feinberg was a slight woman, thin as a dancer, with jet-black hair—no gray, courtesy of Grecian Formula—pulled back into a bun. Her cheeks were streaked with badly applied blusher, and her eyes had a raccoon ring of eyeliner. The wine-dark lipstick she favored was continually rubbing off onto her large front teeth. She was easy to caricature, easy to imitate with her no-nonsense bluntness. But she had a mind few judges could equal; she'd been number one in her class at Columbia and was mentioned more than once for the New York Court of Appeals.

"My client tells me," I explained, "that she had a menstrual period between Mr. Greenspan's assault and the pregnancy. She cannot be absolutely certain as to the paternity of the child, which is why I am more than willing to submit to the DNA test already ordered by the Family Court, but—"

"Counselor," Judge Feinberg interrupted, "what bearing, if any, does paternity have on the issues before this Court?"

If any. That was the clincher. Those were the words that

told me Judge Sylvia was way ahead of me, that she knew exactly how I was going to answer that question, that she knew better than I what the legal ramifications of this case were. I felt like a golfer taking a swing she knew would carry the ball straight down the fairway.

"A child born in wedlock is presumed by the State of New York to be the child of the marriage," I replied, stating what we both knew. "And this child was born at a time when Amber Lundquist was married to Scott Wylie. I offer the marriage certificate in evidence, Your Honor." I handed the document to a court officer, who ferried it to the clerk for marking.

As I relinquished it, I tried not to picture an extremely pregnant Amber slipping out of Mrs. Bonaventura's benevolent clutches and sneaking away to Staten Island's Borough Hall for a brief marriage ceremony, while the indignant housemother thought she was at the mall. That picture smacked too much of the kind of calculation Marla had accused me of masterminding.

I pressed my advantage.

"It should be noted for the record that Mr. Wylie, whether or not he is the biological father of this child, is presumed to be its father. And his consent to this adoption was never obtained. The adoption is therefore voidable at his will."

I took a breath. "We are here today, Your Honor," I went on, "solely on the issue of temporary custody. We ask that this Court return the child to its birth mother pending a full hearing. As this Court knows, New York law provides that the best interests of the child take precedence over any claims, however legitimate, on the part of the adult litigants." A nod from Feinberg; I was speaking her language.

"The question, of course, is what constitutes the best interests of the child. I am certain that my opponent will make a case that the best interests of this baby would be served by leaving custody with her clients until the larger issues are resolved. I could counter this argument by reciting the virtues of my client as the baby's birth mother or by relying solely on the law of paternity in wedlock.''

I looked up from my papers and locked eyes with the judge. For a brief moment I put myself in her place. Solomon. Cutting the baby in half.

Doing my job was hard enough; I couldn't imagine doing hers.

I pulled out my big gun: Nanette Dembitz. New York's most famous Family Court judge, she had written a controversial book entitled *Beyond the Best Interests of the Child* in which she argued passionately that what children needed more than anything else was stability: one family, one home.

The way Feinberg lit up at the mention of Dembitz's name, I knew I had her. I zeroed in for the kill with Baby Jessica, giving the good judge the same argument I'd used on Dorinda: better now than later. Amber would win eventually—why make the baby wait to bond with the woman who would be his lifelong mother? I tossed in a couple of barbs at Josh—he shouldn't benefit from his lies; he'd used Amber and the Court—but the heart of my argument was the trauma to the baby if he was passed from hand to hand, his world shaken up by the vagaries of the adults in his life.

By the time I'd finished, I believed it myself.

''Mr. Greenspan is not a rapist, Your Honor,'' Marla began. A good opening. ''In fact, he is the one who was used. Yes, he had consensual sex with Amber Lundquist.''

I gave a tiny nod of approval; it was the best tack Marla could take. Sex yes, rape no.

''And afterwards Amber came to Josh, told him she was pregnant, and asked him for money which she said was for an abortion.''

More than a slight emphasis on the *said*. She punched home her meaning by adding, ''The amount Amber asked for was seven thousand dollars, Your Honor.''

I turned toward the second row. Scott's face reddened with anger, but Amber, cool and calm, contented herself with a decisive shake of the head. I turned back to the judge.

"It's a common scenario, Your Honor," Marla continued, her tone contemptuous. "It's how a young woman blackmails a married man into paying her to keep the affair from his wife. She pretends pregnancy and asks for abortion money, which is really hush money."

I had a quick flash of Amber's princess room in the group home, of the way she manipulated Doc Scanlon. Amber had a way of exacting favors from men. Was Marla's sordid little story completely out of the realm of possibility?

But she turned down the three thousand Josh offered through Marla. And she did it flat out; she didn't counter with a higher figure. No, I decided; this was Josh's best hope of deflecting Amber's accusation of rape. Nothing more.

"Imagine her surprise," Marla continued, sarcasm filling her voice, "when Josh Greenspan refused her the money and said he wanted to adopt the child instead."

Marla dropped her hands, heavy with silver rings, onto the counsel table and gazed up at the bench. "Your Honor, Josh Greenspan did what any husband would do—he protected his wife from knowledge of his affair, knowledge he knew would hurt her. He paid Amber's expenses and arranged for her to advertise in the *Dreamchild* newsletter, which his wife subscribed to. It was his sincere hope that he could adopt the child he'd fathered without his wife ever knowing the baby's true paternity."

It was good stuff. Plausible, told with just the right amount of I'm-sorry-and-I'll-never-do-it-again humility.

"Nevertheless, Counselor," interrupted Judge Feinberg, "it appears Ms. Lundquist married less than a week prior to the birth of the child. Given the law of New York State regarding the presumption of paternity, does it really matter which sperm ultimately connected with her ovum?" I looked at Sylvia Feinberg with new respect; I wasn't sure I'd ever heard the word *ovum* in a sentence before.

"It did to Mr. Greenspan," Marla replied. "He resisted the concept of adoption for a long time in hopes of producing a child from his own gene pool. And this woman," Marla swept her hand toward my side of the table, "deliberately misled Mr. Greenspan into believing the child she was carrying was his. She had no intention of giving up this child, Your Honor. She defrauded the Greenspans, promising them the baby in return for their paying her medical expenses, knowing she was going to change her mind at the last moment. She lied to everyone, including this Court, in order to get revenge."

"Revenge for a rape that never happened?" I said the words loudly enough to be heard, not loudly enough to put me on the record.

"Counselor," Judge Feinberg admonished, holding up her hand. But I'd made my point.

"The only issue that matters here is what disposition will best serve the interests of this infant child," the judge went on. My heart leapt; she was repeating the words I'd used; a good sign.

Marla's stainless-steel voice showed the strain. Strident at the best of times, it now had an edge that sounded unpleasantly like chalk on a blackboard.

"My clients love this child," she said. "No matter who the biological father is. To take him away now and give him to a woman who lied and cheated and blackmailed, who used him as a weapon against the man who refused to pay her blackmail—how can that be in the baby's best interests, Your Honor?"

She stopped, gripping the counsel table with white knuckles. "Ellie Greenspan is the only mother this child has ever known, Your Honor." She stopped and hung her head, the platinum hair falling over her face like a shield. If I hadn't known her better, I'd have sworn she was hiding tears.

I expected Feinberg to adjourn while she thought about her decision, but she straightened her glasses and began to talk.

"I have nothing but sympathy for Mrs. Greenspan," she began.

My heart jumped, we'd won. "No matter who the father of this child may be, she has opened her heart to him. She has acted honorably throughout this proceeding. Her husband has not, and it would appear that Ms. Lundquist has likewise kept crucial facts to herself instead of telling the full truth to this Court. But, as Ms. Jameson rightly argues, the issue here is the best interests of the child. I find that those interests will be served by placing the child in the custody of the people most likely to prevail on the law, namely, Mr. and Mrs. Scott Wylie."

The sound that came from behind me could have been made by a wounded animal mother fighting for her child's life against a bloody-toothed predator. It was primitive, agonized, horrible.

It was Ellie Greenspan.

"I see no reason to delay the process of bonding," the judge continued, in a flat voice that refused to acknowledge the existence of anything as sloppy and unjudicial as emotion. "So the child will be delivered to Mrs. Wylie within the hour. So ordered," she finished, banging the gavel with a sharp rap that sounded like a gunshot.

We had won, but I felt no elation. I was as numb as if I'd succeeded in winning an acquittal for a serial killer. Behind me, Ellie sobbed, repeating, "No, no," over and over in a rhythmic chant of denial.

"Your Honor," Marla called out over the noise. "I've prepared the papers for a stay. I ask that you consider—"

"No, Counselor," Sylvia Feinberg intoned, her thin lips drawn into a rictus of embarrassed sympathy. "I will not issue a stay. You'll have to appeal to the Second Department."

Marla was ready. "Then let the record show that I'm

serving opposing counsel with notice of appeal and motion for a stay. I intend to proceed to the Second Department at once, Your Honor.''

She handed a blueback to the clerk and offered me an identical copy. No surprise; it was what I'd have done in her place.

''That is your right, Counselor,'' Judge Feinberg said. She rose and left the bench, swirling her black robe around her as if to envelop herself in the symbol of her position.

I turned away from the front of the courtroom, ready to stand by my client as she accepted the fruits of her victory.

Ellie Greenspan sobbed into the baby's blanket, her head shaking from side to side as if she were a survivor at an airplane crash site, totally unbelieving of the tragedy that had befallen her.

Josh sat next to her, his arm wrapped protectively around her shoulder, but his face was blank, his body devoid of energy. It was as though the life had been sucked out of him, leaving an empty shell.

Marla looked sick, her round face pale and sticky. She locked eyes with me in a mute appeal. I motioned Amber and Scott into the hall, leaving Marla to deal with the Greenspans.

''Let's give them a few minutes,'' I said. I walked Amber and Scott to the rear entrance of the courthouse; we stepped out into the glorious April morning. Scott lit up a cigarette and offered a drag to Amber, who sucked in a lungful of smoke and passed it back to him.

I took the opportunity to explain the ramifications of the appeal Marla would undoubtedly file, and the upcoming Family Court appearance. The baby's blood had already been taken and typed at birth; it was no problem to use a sample for DNA testing. From the smug look on Scott's face, I had no doubt of his confidence in his own paternity.

After about ten minutes, I reluctantly followed an eager Amber back inside. She walked straight to the courthouse and flung open the door. Ellie sat in the front row, her arms around little Adam as though shielding him from a tornado. Josh sat, white-faced, next to her. Court officers hovered discreetly. Marla was nowhere in sight.

"Where's your lawyer?" I asked, addressing whichever Greenspan cared to answer.

Josh came to life; a bitter smile edged his lips and a glint of malice lit his eye as he replied, "At the Appellate Division. She went to get a stay."

CHAPTER EIGHT

Blood rushed to my face. I'd been careless; I'd been compassionate, giving Ellie a few minutes alone in which to say good-bye. But she didn't want to say good-bye. Instead, she held her baby while Marla slipped out of the courthouse and made a dash for the appellate court she hoped would countermand Judge Feinberg and order the baby to stay with her clients pending appeal.

I looked into Amber's accusing face. She knew instinctively that we'd been had.

"I'd better get over there right away," I muttered, making for the courtroom door. Hoping it wasn't too late, and knowing I'd given Marla plenty of time to get an order signed.

Before I reached the door, it swung open and Marla marched in. But there was no look of triumph on her face. She shook her head. My client was going to walk out of the courthouse with her baby after all, no thanks to me.

Ellie gave a long, drawn-out wail. Marla walked toward her; she shrunk away as if from a rapist. And all the while Josh sat like a statue, unmoving, unseeing.

Finally, it was over. Finally the tiny red-faced creature, who had woken up and begun to cry, was pried from Ellie's iron grip and placed in Amber's welcoming arms. Finally I walked out of the courthouse with my client and said good-bye at the curb. And walked all the way home before I remembered I meant to tell someone about the terrible offer Marla had made to buy Amber's baby.

When the going gets tough, the tough go to the movies. And drink a little too much, and sit in their offices until after ten at night drafting motions in cases they know for a fact are going to plead out at the next appearance.

Anything except remember. Anything except hear again that awful animal cry of a mother deprived of her baby.

I sat at my desk, two days after my appearance in Feinberg's courtroom, wiping sleep from my eyes, trying to concentrate on a set of subpoenas in a case that wasn't on the calendar for another month.

The doorbell rang. I jumped in my chair; even criminal clients didn't come ringing the bell at 11 P.M. I might get a phone call from the station house, or a message from night court that one of my clients was about to see the judge, but personal visits were something I discouraged.

I walked to the door and looked through the peephole.

It was Scott. The streetlight outside my window glinted off his lank blond hair. He pounded on the door, then stood back in indignation when no one appeared.

What the hell—

Only one way to find out. I opened the office door and stepped into the foyer, then unhooked the safety lock and opened the outer door. Scott all but burst into the hallway.

"Where is she?" he demanded, his head swiveling in an attempt to see around me into my office.

"Amber? Not here, Scott. Why would you—"

"Don't lie to me, bitch," Scott said. He shoved an angry hand into my chest and pushed me out of the way.

He strode through the double doors into the waiting room of my office. "Amber," he called. "Amber. Get out here, you cunt."

"What is this about?" I yelled after him. Pretending Scott was acting like a distraught husband out of his mind with worry for his wife, not a small-time hood eager to break kneecaps. Pretending I had some control over the situation.

Scott reached my desk in the other room. He lifted his hand, then brought it down in a sweeping motion that cleared the objects off the top and sent them crashing onto the hardwood floor.

"Shit!" he screamed. "Double fucking shit!"

I almost smiled. I'd tagged Scott as a spoiled brat from the right side of the tracks, and here he was throwing a tantrum in front of my very eyes, regressing in seconds from twentysomething cool to two-year-old fury.

I *almost* smiled. But two-year-olds with knife sheaths on their belts are not that funny, especially when you're the target of their unbounded rage.

"Amber is not here," I repeated, sounding firmer than I felt. Hoping a touch of maternal calm, teacherlike authority, would defuse the situation. Hoping Scott wouldn't realize I had no clue what the situation really was. Pushing to the back burner the questions I couldn't answer but which were beginning to crowd out all other thoughts, including those about my own safety: if Amber wasn't here, where was she? And where was the baby?

"I told you to stop fucking with me," Scott replied. He marched back to where I stood in the doorway between the waiting room and the office proper. He stuck his finger in my face and fixed me with eyes that looked capable of anything.

"Nobody double-crosses me and gets away with it, so you damn well better tell me where that little—"

"Scott, what the hell are you talking about?" I shouted, pushing the finger aside with shaking hands. His rage terrified me, but so did the thought of letting him see my fear.

"What's the point of these games, huh?" He gave my chest another pointed push. It hurt. There were going to be bruises.

"We had it all set up. The meeting, the payoff, then we split. I had the car all ready."

Meeting, payoff—what was going on here? But in some corner of my mind I suspected I knew. I was afraid I knew. A cold draft wound around my ankles like a cat; my knees weakened and I leaned against the doorjamb to keep them from buckling.

The baby. Where was the baby?

"I had that fucking car checked over by a top mechanic," Scott continued. Spittle formed at the corners of his wide mouth as he talked; it seemed vital that he convince me how well he maintained his car. "So why wouldn't it start when I went to the parking lot to get it, huh?"

"Parking lot?" I jumped on the one thing that might pin down some information. "What parking lot, where?"

He snorted. "Like you don't know, Ms. Smart-ass Lawyer Bitch. At the mall, where else? At the mall where you met Amber while I was at the fucking gas station trying to get some meatball to come look at my engine. The only question here is, where did you take her from there? She's not here, I can see that, but where—"

"The mall. The Staten Island Mall? That's where Amber is?" Relief surged up through my legs and settled in my upper thighs; I tottered to a chair before I slid down the wall onto the floor.

Amber was safe. The baby was safe. They were at the mall, waiting for this blockhead to pick them up in a car that had—

Scott followed me to the chair in a single bound, snaked

his arm around my neck, and held me in a choke grip that had me gasping for breath.

"You made a side deal with her, didn't you?" When I didn't answer, he screamed, "Didn't you?" in a banshee screech that should have brought six black-and-whites to the front door.

My response was to gag and claw at his arm with fingers that had all the tensile strength of overcooked spaghetti. He looked at me with speculation in his gray eyes, then let up ever so slightly on the choke hold. Blessed air surged through my lungs, and my body sagged with a relief my mind knew was all too premature.

"Okay, don't tell me where she is," he continued in a deceptively reasonable tone. "Just give me your share of the money and I'm out of here."

Money. Whatever lingering wisps of hope I'd had that Amber and the baby were waiting forlornly at the mall to be picked up like any normal mother and child evaporated. Money. What money?

Money for selling the baby. Apparently Amber and Scott were more than willing to listen to the Greenspans' desperate offer—so long as the amount was readjusted upward.

"You were the one who told us Greenspan would pay," Scott went on. "Only Amber was smart enough to know he'd pay more than three thousand. And then you two went behind my back—"

I wore a shroud of cold sweat. "No, I didn't, Scott," I said in a very tired voice. But how to convince him?

It came to me suddenly that he wasn't as tough as he pretended to be, that he was playing a role. Sean Penn in any number of cheap street-boy movies. So I delved into my own bag of cinema clichés and said, "In my right pocket. Just pull it out and you'll see where I was all evening."

The quick puzzled frown between his eyebrows was followed by a nod of understanding. He knew where I was going with this; we'd seen the same movies. Communication by cinema. Welcome to the Global Village.

His bony hand plunged into the right pocket of my silk baseball jacket and pulled out a rectangle of cardboard.

"Read it," I ordered. Playing Kathleen Turner in the ill-fated movie about V.I. Warshawski.

"Angelika Film Center," he read, sounding out each syllable. "So what? Anybody could say they were at a—"

"It's a computer receipt, Scott. Read the date and time."

"April 20," he said obediently, "Friday. Seven-o-five P.M. showing of . . ."

"It's a Chinese movie," I explained. "I was in the movie until almost nine, then took the train back to Brooklyn. Unless you think Amber's developed a sudden taste for post-Communist Chinese cinema, you can be sure I haven't seen her tonight."

A long sigh accompanied Scott's release of his arm around my neck. "Ah, fuck," he said. He struck his own thigh with an outstretched palm, like an old codger slapping his knee, but there was no humor in the gesture.

"She's gone," he whispered. "She and the baby and the money."

"Gone where, Scott?" I pressed. "If you tell me everything you know about tonight, maybe we can—"

"Maybe you can put me in jail?" The challenge came out halfhearted; Scott had lost a lot of his edge since realizing at last that I knew considerably less than he did about Amber's activities.

"That's not important now," I countered. "What is important is that we find the baby."

"It may not be important to you," he objected. "But it's number one on my hit parade." A nice Sean Penn line. I tried to come up with something Kathleen Turner would have been proud to say. But before the words formed themselves in my mind, Scott was on his way to the door.

"Scott! Get back here!" The irony wasn't lost on me; for the past five minutes I'd hoped against hope that Scott would walk out and leave me alone, and now it seemed like the worst thing that could happen. I needed him to lead me to Amber, to the baby, before it was too late.

The outer door slammed. I jumped from the chair and ran after him, flinging the door open to the cool April night. Scott ran with awkward haste down Court Street, then jumped onto a big shiny motorcycle I hadn't known he possessed and took off with a roar.

I made a fist and hit the doorjamb so hard the pain reverberated to my elbow.

My fingers still tingled as I picked up the phone to call the police. Detective Button at the 84, I decided. He'd know which precinct to notify on Staten Island.

I had a moment's pause: should I call? Was it ethical for me to turn in my own client? My mind reviewed hastily the obligations of a lawyer regarding future crimes. Then I stopped myself. This was no time for an ethics opinion. There was a baby's life at stake. Just dial the phone and worry about ethics later.

As I punched the numbers into the phone with shaking hands, it was not Amber's pink-white baby whose image haunted me. Instead, it was Rojean's children: Tonetta, hiding behind her mommy's skirt, fingers in her mouth, looking at me with huge puppy eyes; Todd, white baby shoes scuffed and worn, oversized shorts falling around his skinned brown knees; baby Trudine, with her two-tooth grin and full head of fine black hair.

I won my case, and the Glover children died. It made me a kind of accessory before the fact.

I'd won Amber's case, and she and her baby were missing. I wasn't going to be an accessory a second time.

The man whose heavy bulk filled my doorway could only have been a cop. He had thinning black hair, a basset hound face, and an air of perpetual disappointment.

"Ms. Jameson," he said rather than inquired, "I'm Detective Aronson, Staten Island Detective Unit. May I come in?"

Staten Island? I'd called Brooklyn—why was I getting

Staten Island? And why so quickly—he couldn't possibly have crossed the Verrazano Bridge in the three minutes since I'd put down the phone.

"Of course," I said, opening the door and admitting Aronson. He stepped in and surveyed my client waiting room as if taking inventory. Then he walked uninvited into my office and sat, not on one of my red leather client chairs, but in the larger chair behind the desk. The seat of authority. My chair.

I declined the gambit, remaining standing behind one of the client chairs instead of sitting down. "Do you want me to tell you what happened, or—"

"You represent a woman named Amber Lundquist," he began, in a weary, heavy voice, "also know as Amber Wylie."

"That's her married name," I replied tartly. "It's not an alias."

"I didn't say it was," he said without inflection. "Ms. Jameson, where were you between eight and ten this evening?"

"What does that have to do with Scott coming here and threatening me?" I countered, astonished that a person who called the cops to make a complaint was being asked to provide an alibi.

"Just answer the question, ma'am."

"Am I being charged with something?" My voice rose in disbelief. As a defense attorney, I was not always a fan of New York's Finest, but this was—

"No, ma'am," the detective said, but the lines around his mouth tightened, as if he hated to admit that he didn't have grounds for an arrest.

"Then what is this about?" I said. I stepped away from the chair and paced the floor. Adrenaline surged through me; first Scott invaded my life, and now the cops were acting as if I'd committed the crime of the century.

"Where were you, Ms. Jameson?" Aronson persisted,

his voice hard. "Were you at the Staten Island Mall, by any chance?"

"Staten Island—" I broke off, astonished. How could he know about the mall? I hadn't had a chance to tell him what Scott had said about meetings, about deals.

"No, I—" I stopped in mid-sentence and walked to the waiting room, where my jacket hung on the rack. I went to the pocket and pulled out my Angelika ticket, with its computerized statement: date, time, movie. What a night—providing the same alibi twice.

I handed it to him. He took it and stared for a moment, then turned it over in his big hand, as if hoping for a message in code.

"Just because you have a receipt doesn't mean you saw the movie," he intoned. "You could have paid for this and then headed straight for the mall, trying to give yourself an alibi."

"I was with a friend," I said. Anger warred with fear as I realized this man was serious; I was a suspect in something, but I didn't know what.

Or did I? Somehow the detective knew about the mall; did he know about Scott and Amber's attempts to sell their baby? And did he think that I, as Amber's lawyer, was part of the plan? I gave him my friend's phone number without protest, hoping he'd call right away and let me off the hook.

He didn't. He pocketed the piece of paper I'd written Sandy's name on and leaned back in my chair. "Tell me about this Amber," he invited.

"She's my client," I said, disbelief edging my voice. Surely he knew about lawyer-client privilege.

"Look," I went on, "I called you. I called because Scott Wylie came into my house and—"

"What do you mean, you called us?" Aronson shot back. He sat up in the chair, leaned forward in an attitude of intimidation. "Lady, I'm here because Joshua Greenspan was assaulted in the Staten Island Mall."

"Assaulted?" I grabbed the back of the client chair and

gave serious thought to sitting down in it before my knees gave way.

"By Scott," I murmured.

"Now, how would you know that, Ms. Jameson?"

"Because he was here. Which is what I've been trying to tell you since you walked in that door. Scott came here looking for Amber. He was convinced I—"

I broke off, unable to say the words. *He thought I'd helped Amber sell her kid and then split the money with her.*

It was time to sit down. I slid onto the red leather chair, no longer caring who sat in the seat of power and who didn't.

"Look, we know she had an accomplice," Aronson said. "She was seen leaving the mall and getting into a car. Someone drove her away from there, with the baby."

"What kind of car was it?" I asked. "Did you get a description of the driver? Which direction did it—"

"I'm here to ask the questions, not answer them, Counselor."

Typical cop. So I sat as quietly as I could with adrenaline surging through my veins like cheap booze and answered all his questions.

When we came to the events outside the courtroom Wednesday, my voice faltered and I found myself looking at the floor.

". . . three thousand dollars," I mumbled.

"You say Ms. Hennessey approached you?" Aronson repeated, not bothering to hide his skepticism. "But you didn't report it to the judge or the District Attorney or—"

"No," I admitted. "Things happened so fast, and then— I didn't want to add to Ellie's troubles."

"You'd better think up a more plausible excuse, Counselor," Detective Aronson advised, "since Mr. And Mrs. Greenspan say that you approached their lawyer with an offer of money in return for relinquishing rights to the child."

I sat in numb silence after that, refusing to answer any more questions on the grounds that the answers might tend to incriminate me. As a defense attorney, I'd always been a fan of the Fifth Amendment, but I'd never actually used it before.

Until now.

I fell into bed around three A.M., but sleep was fitful and unsatisfying. The next day was Saturday, which meant the good citizens of Staten Island were off work and ready to search the swamp for the missing baby they'd heard about on the morning news. I put on my old clothes, borrowed Mickey's car, and drove across the Verrazano Bridge to join the search party.

It was almost sunset when we found Amber, but the search continued till after dark, in the hope—or fear—that Baby Adam would turn up as well. It continued, but without me. I had seen enough of death for one day.

"These things happen," Matt Riordan said. I'd fled to the comfort of his co-op apartment on Fifth Avenue after watching the emergency services cops pull Amber's swollen body out of the swamp. I'd stood under a hot shower, washing away the cold and damp and smell of death for a long time. Now I sat wrapped in a royal blue velour man's robe, big white men's socks on my feet, sipping Scotch that should have been in a museum.

My sometime lover lifted a glass of his miracle Scotch to his lips. "If I fell apart every time I lost a client, I'd—"

I held up a warning hand. "Look, the clients you take, you expect them to get fished out of swamps on Staten Island. This was supposed to be a simple adoption, not the Gotti trial."

His answering smile was composed of equal parts amusement and condescension. "I have been known to represent innocent people," he said.

"Yeah, right. The last time you represented someone who didn't deserve twenty to life was when you were with the Manhattan D.A.'s office. But the important point here is that this isn't about you and your practice—it's about me.'' I took a deep swallow of my own Scotch and let its smoky warmth burn my throat. Thank God for alcohol, I thought. It always comes through.

"First Rojean, now Amber,'' I said. There was a ragged edge to my voice I didn't like. So I medicated it with another swallow of single-malt.

"Cass,'' Riordan said, an edge of exasperation in his rich, jury-seducing voice, "you can't go through life blaming yourself every time one of your clients dies or screws up.''

"Screws up,'' I mimicked. "Yeah, I'd say selling your baby constitutes screwing up, all right. How can you . . . ?''

"How can you?'' he countered. He marshaled arguments, fixing me with the same intense stare I'd seen him use on Juror Number Six in his last Godfather trial. "You've been a criminal lawyer for almost twenty years, Cass. You need a thick skin for this kind of practice, and up to now, you've had it. You didn't put those poor kids into the bathtub and you didn't help Amber sell her baby. So why not cut this self-indulgent guilt trip and get down to finding out what happened to Amber?''

"Finding out.'' I stared into the amber liquid in my glass. Amber, clear and bright and golden, reflecting sunlight. The amber pendant. Amber's maple-syrup hair. Ellie telling Amber she fit her name because she was bringing light into their lives with her baby. Amber, pulled from the swamp, dripping weeds, her face a puffy blur.

"I identified the body,'' I murmured. I picked up the heavy cut glass and drained the rest of the Scotch in a long fiery swallow. Under ordinary circumstances Riordan would have called it a sacrilege to treat his Scotch like fraternity chug booze, but this time he just sat and watched as I worked things out my own way.

"It wasn't the sea," I went on. "So there wasn't as much damage from fish, and she wasn't in there all that long. But she was puffy and pale and—" I broke off before I got to the part about the foam bubbling out of her nose and mouth. I took another swallow of the burning-sweet liquid.

"She was gruesome," I said.

I looked up into my companion's deep blue eyes. They held a compassion I seldom saw. "Could I have another drink?"

He poured. I was over my limit and we both knew it, but he didn't say a word, just filled my glass with more of the amber nectar. I took a sip and let the Scotch burn my tongue with its smoky, biting taste.

"After what she did, I'm not sure I care who killed her." I let that thought lie on the couch between us. "I'm not saying she deserved to die. Exactly. But why should I worry about who killed her? Hell," I went on, throwing back a shot of booze like a gun moll in a forties movie, "whoever killed Amber was a better human being than she was. It's hard to imagine someone worse than a woman who'd sell her own baby."

The courtroom voice was soft and seductive as Riordan asked the only question that mattered: "What about the baby?"

"What about the baby?" I let all the frustration I felt fill my voice as I faced the adversary on the other end of the couch. "You think I know where the baby is? You think I helped Amber line up buyers, that I told her to get married so she'd have an airtight legal claim to the baby? You think I—"

"You know I don't think any of that," Riordan replied, his tone as soothing as the Scotch he poured. "But I do think you could help locate the baby if you asked the right questions."

"The cops are covering Staten Island like a heavy fog," I countered. "What can I do that they can't?"

He shrugged. "I don't know. Maybe nothing. But I do know you are going to be impossible to live with—even more impossible than usual, that is—unless you get off your ass and try."

There was nothing in those words that would have caused a normal person to break down in tears. So why did I lean into Riordan's broad chest and sob like a child, letting him hold me close until the tears dried up?

CHAPTER NINE

I walked toward the Greenspan house, almost but not quite able to ignore the Sunday morning pageant of early spring, the hyacinths tall and dignified, the tulips green nodules not yet in bloom but poised on the brink of glorious color, the forsythia reaching golden-yellow arms into the blue sky. I wanted to enjoy it, to revel in spring poetry.

> Spring rides no horses down the hill
> But comes on foot, a goose-girl still.

But spring had lost its magic; all I could see was the tiny little life who had been passed from mother to mother—and now was God knew where. One mother was dead; I was on my way to see the other.

If Ellie didn't shoot me on sight, it would be a miracle. I hadn't counted on the press. Stupid of me. I'd somehow

108 • CAROLYN WHEAT

assumed I could just walk up to the door of the former stable and ring the bell. Instead I confronted a gauntlet of eager reporters, print and television, trying to get quotes.

"Are you a friend of the Greenspans?" a petite blonde asked, shoving a microphone to within an inch of my mouth. "Have you known them a long time?"

"How is Mrs. Greenspan reacting to the loss of her baby?" an Asian woman asked, photogenic concern etched on her smooth young face.

But the dangerous one was a disheveled print reporter who'd studied in the School of Jimmy Breslin. He sidled up to me while the media types signaled their cameramen and said out of the side of his mouth, "Ms. Jameson, can we talk when you leave here?"

"I don't think so," I muttered back.

He raised an eyebrow and regarded me with amusement. "Oh, I do think so, Counselor. Because if you don't agree to talk to me, I tell these bozos who you are. And then—" He waved an arm at the phalanx of mannequin telejournalists and their camera people. The gesture took in the news vans parked at the entrance to the mews, and even embraced the two cops guarding the cul-de-sac, cigarettes cupped under their hands, as well as the little knot of rubberneckers who stood gossiping and drinking coffee from paper cups.

"I see what you mean," I replied. Half of being a lawyer is knowing what to concede and when. "Do you know the neighborhood?"

The reporter lifted a shoulder in what might have been an assenting shrug. "Hey, I'm a Brooklyn boy," he bragged.

"Yeah, by way of Buffalo," I shot back. Enough people mistaked my Ohio accent for Buffalo that it was worth a try just to wipe the smug smirk off the guy's face.

"Howdja know?"

My turn to shrug. "We could sit on the Promenade when I get out of here," I offered. "You buy me a coffee and

I'll tell you whatever you want to know.''

And you'll tell me a few things in return, I thought but didn't say aloud. The other half of being a good lawyer is cross-examining people without letting them know you're doing it.

I rang the bell. I couldn't believe my own nerve in standing here expecting either Josh or Ellie to give me the time of day, but I had to try convincing them I hadn't known what Amber was going to do with their baby. And, apropos of surreptitious cross-examinations, I had to find out more about Josh's Friday night meeting with Amber at the mall.

The door was opened by a woman who looked to be in her mid-seventies. She stooped; she raised her head awkwardly to meet my eyes. "Yes?" she asked in a voice like a raven's.

"Uh . . . I'm—That is, Ellie knows me," I said, trying to find the right words. "I wonder if I might come in, Mrs. Greenspan." I'd been lucky with the reporter from Buffalo; maybe my guess that this was Josh's mother would hit the mark as well.

It didn't. "It's *Miss,*" she corrected. "I'm Joshua's aunt. Norma Ruditz," she continued, holding out a lank hand dotted with liver spots. I took it and shook my way into the foyer.

"Come in and sit," Miss Ruditz invited. Her voice held the memory of thousands of cigarettes smoked over the years. She walked stiffly toward the palomino couch, her out-thrust head preceding her at an awkward angle. I reminded myself to pick up some calcium tablets at the health food store before heading home.

As the aunt settled herself, I decided on my approach. I hadn't said I was a friend, but the elderly lady seemed to assume as much. Could I find out a little more about Josh's movements from her before Ellie showed up and had me thrown out?

"It must be awful for Josh and Ellie," I began. Short on originality, but perhaps enough to open a floodgate or two.

Norma Ruditz shook her head slowly from side to side. "I warned them," she said. "I warned them about adopting a baby from some shiksa they never met before." Her bird-of-prey eyes raked me up and down.

"You're not Jewish," she pronounced.

I shook my head.

"Then you should pardon the expression. It's nothing personal, you understand. Just that people should be with their own, deal with their own, marry their own. Have their own babies and if they can't, at least adopt from their own." She spoke with a singsong cadence that wasn't exactly a Yiddish accent but was instead the natural result of having grown up in a home where Yiddish was the primary language.

If every Jewish birth mother took the same view, she'd refuse to give a baby to a man married to Ellie. It came to me slowly that this was Aunt Norma's point—that the tragedy began for her the day Josh married out of his faith, and that in her mind the rest followed inevitably.

It was also clear that she had no idea Josh was claiming paternity.

What a comfort she must be to Ellie in her hour of need. Maybe I wouldn't get thrown out, after all. A fellow shiksa might be a welcome relief to a woman shut up with Norma's parochial views on mixed marriage.

"I told him to go to the Jewish Family Services. My friend Mitzi's oldest went there eighteen years ago, they gave her the sweetest little girl. Such a talent, she graduates this June third in her class at—"

"What are you doing here?" a shrill voice interrupted. I turned. Ellie Greenspan stood in the doorway to the bedroom, her hands on her hips, her face a mask of accusation.

"How dare you come here after what you did?" She took a stride forward, bursting into the living room with all the force and fury of a tornado. She strode up to where I sat on the couch and stood over me in an attitude of menace. I wondered for a moment if her slender-fingered hand would reach out and slap me across the face.

For a strange, long moment I waited for it, almost wanted it.

I looked up into Ellie's sunken eyes, challenging her. "What did I do, Mrs. Greenspan?" I said with deliberate calm.

It was a calculated risk. I figured enough people, from Josh to the media to Marla, were busy commiserating with her, urging her to explore and express her pain, that a dose of cool reason might penetrate her shield of anger.

"You stole my baby and gave him to that woman to sell." Her voice cracked on the last word. She turned and walked away with a swiftness that startled me.

That was what I'd thought at two o'clock in the morning, but it wasn't true. I summoned the strength to say so to Ellie's face.

"No, I didn't. I presented legal arguments to a judge who made a ruling. Neither I nor Judge Feinberg had reason to believe Amber intended to do anything except give the baby a good home."

"That's not what Marla says," Ellie countered. She sat in the armchair with the turquoise sand-painting print and folded her legs under her like a child.

"Marla," I echoed. I asked the question I should have put to one of the Greenspans on Wednesday in court. "Did you or Josh authorize Marla to offer three thousand dollars to—"

"We did not," Ellie cut in, her voice a laser cutting through glass. "That's exactly what Marla said you'd say. She warned us about you, said you'd try to put everything on her. Well, it was your client who sold my baby, who met Josh at the mall Friday night, who—"

"Did he give her money?" I jumped in with both feet; this was what I'd come for: to hear every horrible detail of how my client spent her last hours on earth.

"We told the police everything," Ellie replied. Her voice had a dead sound. Indignation was giving way to exhaustion. I suspected she was talking to me only because throwing me out would be too much trouble. And maybe having someone on hand to blame took some of the pain away, if only for a little while.

I pressed my luck. ''Then it won't matter if you tell me, too.''

She sighed. ''I suppose not. Yes, Josh went there Friday night. She called him Thursday, the day after we were in court, and said she'd changed her mind again. That we could have Adam back if we paid her ten thousand dollars.''

''And you agreed.''

''We had to,'' Ellie replied in her breathy voice. ''She said we'd never see him again, that she'd take him across state lines to a— Let me remember her exact words.'' Ellie closed her eyes and leaned her head back on the chair. Her hair hadn't been washed; it hung limp and lank. Her face was without makeup; she looked old and worn. ''She said if we didn't pay, she'd give our son to a family who really cared about him. Cared enough to pay, she meant.''

She sighed, opened her eyes, and sat up again. ''Josh met Amber at the mall at eight-thirty. She was with Scott, but she did all the talking, according to Josh. Scott said to meet him at the entrance to Macy's, so Josh walked all the way through the mall. Then when he got there,'' she went on, her tone as bitter as unsweetened chocolate, ''there was no Amber and no baby. Scott jumped out and hit him, then demanded the money. But Josh had already paid Amber, so he had no money. Scott hit him some more, then ran away.''

''Scott worked at Macy's,'' I commented. ''Maybe he knew some kind of back way through the store.''

''It was near the loading dock,'' Ellie confirmed, but her voice had lost interest.

I continued my train of thought. ''So the last time Josh saw Amber, she was alive.''

''Josh didn't kill Amber,'' Ellie said. It was a flat statement of fact, not an indignant protest. "If he had," she began, then stopped herself with a hard clamp of her jaw.

I finished the thought for her. "If he had, he'd have taken the baby with him. He would never have killed her while there was a chance of getting Adam back."

She flashed me a wintry smile. "I'm glad you understand everything, Ms. Jameson," she said.

Ellie's eyes glazed, and she stared at a spot on the wall about ten inches to the left of my face. "After the court ruling," she began, "I was devastated. I'd lost the baby and found out my husband had an affair with that little slut, all in one day. Even though Marla filed an appeal, things didn't look promising. I kept trying to tell myself we could start again, find another baby, but it was no good."

She turned her head and gazed directly into my eyes, pulling me into her pain. "One minute he was there, next to my heart, and the next minute he was gone. Can you understand that? Gone—as if he'd died in my arms. As if he'd fallen into the river and drowned. As if he'd been kidnapped. Gone. I couldn't think about another baby—all I could do was think about Adam."

She stared unblinking at my face. "Even now, I keep hoping— Do you know what I hope, more than anything?"

I shook my head. I wasn't sure I could stand finding out.

"I hope with all my heart that Amber sold my baby. I hope somebody paid good money for him, and took him home, and that he's warm and dry and fed. Can you believe it?" She shook her head.

"Three days ago I hoped he'd go to college. Now my best hope is that he was bought and paid for and isn't lying in the swamp waiting for hikers to stumble on."

I opened my mouth to say something, but what the hell was there to say?

When I left the Greenspan house, the gaggle of reporters crowded the door, pushing microphones into my face and shouting the same stupid questions I'd already refused to answer.

"How is Mrs. Greenspan holding up?"

"Did Ellie know Amber was going to sell the baby?"

"Can you comment on the rumor that Josh Greenspan offered money to the birth mother to—"

My print reporter friend leaned against the brick wall, a wry smile on his young face. He held his head at a cocky angle that demanded a tilted fedora for the full effect. I was willing to bet he'd seen *The Paper* at least ten times. He lolled by the wall as though nothing on earth could move him from the spot, but as soon as I cleared the gauntlet, he'd find a way to follow me, to make sure I walked along Remsen to the Promenade and didn't cut along home through the narrow brownstoned streets of the Heights.

I had already decided I could get more from him than he could from me, so I strolled along the tree-lined block past the Brooklyn Bar Association building, past the stately town houses with the seven-foot windows lined with old lace curtains, past huge oak doors with leaded glass and chandeliers winking through the tall windows. I pictured carriages pulling up in front of these grand houses, men in frock coats opening the doors for ladies in long skirts and tiny slippers. I pictured the men scraping mud off their boots on the wrought-iron scrapers that were part of every home's stoop railing. I pictured a gaslit world of charm and manners, an Edith Wharton world, an age of innocence without baby-sellers or—

Who was I kidding? Babies were born into abject poverty, sold into brothels, farmed out to foster mothers who starved them in that gilded age that knew evil as plainly as we know it today. If the Greenspans had lived then, the same tabloid journalists would have surrounded their house, working for Hearst or Pulitzer.

On that note, I turned around and faced the man whose footsteps had dogged mine for the past half block.

"What's your name, anyway?"

"Artie Bloom," he replied, pushing an aggressive hand in the direction of my midriff. I allowed mine to be given a jerky shake as he named as his employer the least obnoxious of New York's three tabloid papers. We walked in silence toward the river. Already I could see the tip of Manhattan's skyline from the middle of Remsen Street; it grew larger as we approached the Promenade.

The Promenade—or, more accurately, the Esplanade, a name few know and fewer actually use—that straddles the edge of Brooklyn Heights runs along the top of the Brooklyn-Queens Expressway. As a result, there's always a hum of traffic underfoot. But this doesn't stop the place from being a haven for mothers with strollers, dog walkers, elderly people sunning themselves on benches, young lovers embracing at the railing.

I motioned Artie to a bench near the circle that ended the Promenade. He sat and looked at me expectantly. "Well, did you get anything out of her?"

"Nice subtle approach, Bloom," I commented.

He shrugged. "You don't ask, you don't get."

I had to laugh. "Yeah, you're right. And, no, I don't think I got much out of her. Just what the cops already knew, that her husband went to meet Amber that night to make a deal for the baby."

Artie Bloom leaned forward eagerly. He had an open face with freckles and sandy-red hair that frizzed like Art Garfunkel's—an all-American boy, the cereal-commercial kid all grown up.

"Did you know she was going to sell the baby?"

"Bloom, I thought you were smarter than the blow-drys back there or I wouldn't have agreed to talk to you. Think about it: would I risk my license to do a thing like that? And if I had, would I tell you about it?"

He pulled back a moment and gave me an assessing stare. "No to the second," he agreed. "I don't know you well enough to answer the first."

"I see. And how many other reporters have given that question a little thought?"

"Gotta admit, I'm not big on sharing with my fellow

journalists," the boy reporter replied with a rueful shake of his head. "Never did work and play well with others."

"But nobody's printed anything accusing me of assisting Amber in the deals."

"Hey, nobody wants to get sued," he shot back. "Every lead has to be confirmed by at least two sources before we can print what we—"

"So all you have so far is Marla Hennessey's word that I helped Amber set things up."

Now the look on the young face was one of amused admiration. "Good guess, Counselor."

"It's no guess," I answered. "I've known Marla since law school. She doesn't like losing, and she's not above hinting that the game was rigged when she does lose."

"If you didn't know what your client was going to do, you must feel guilty as hell."

"You don't know the half of it, Bloom. But one part of our little deal is that I am not going to tell you how guilty I feel. I am not going to see my name in print any more than it has to be. I'm going to tell you things on deep background. Very deep background. No attribution."

"Jeez," he said, letting out his breath in a disgusted whoosh. "Has everybody your age seen *All the President's Men*?"

I laughed. "Damn right. Now, what do you know that I don't?"

He flipped open his steno pad and made a show of consulting his shorthand scribbles. "For one thing, Josh wasn't the only mark," he said. "There was a meeting three days earlier with a Staten Island couple who wanted a baby, and she was dealing long-distance with a couple in Kansas City and another in—"

"Amber's parents live in Kansas City," I cut in, my voice quickening with excitement. "Maybe she was going to—"

He laughed. It was somewhere between a laugh of derision and a boyish crow of triumph. "Parents! Your client was an orphan, Counselor. A Mount Loretto girl.''

"Mount Loretto," I echoed. I was stunned but not surprised. It was just one more lie in what was becoming an intricate web of deception. "Isn't that on Staten Island?"

"Yeah," the boy reporter replied. "It's on Prince's Bay, near Tottenville. A big old Victorian orphanage, straight out of Dickens."

"So the presents from Kansas City were from other adoptive parents," I mused aloud. The clashing tastes represented by Amber's room at the group home began to make sense. The Santa Fe decor came from Ellie Greenspan, the Care Bears from the Midwest.

"They told the cops they expected Amber to deliver the baby to them this weekend," Artie said. "They sent her money for the trip. But then so did another couple in Baltimore."

Baltimore. Where Amber's mythical married sister lived.

"So she was going to rip off Josh and then take the baby to one of them," I speculated.

"Maybe," Artie replied. "There was also this local couple." He consulted his steno pad. "Kyle and Donna Cheney. They have one adopted kid and wanted another. They live in Westerleigh, which is about two miles north of the Davis Wildlife Refuge."

"What difference does that—" I began, then broke off. "Oh. That's where Amber's body was found."

My companion nodded. "They claim they dropped out of the bidding, but who knows?"

"This makes me sick," I muttered. I turned away from the panorama of skyline and silver water, looking back at the stately brownstones that lined the Promenade. The trees were beginning to bud; pink and white blossoms festooned the branches like tissue paper decorations. It was a gorgeous day, the kind you want to bottle for use on a bleak winter morning, and here I was talking about a baby on sale at the mall.

118 • Carolyn Wheat

"Yeah, me, too," Artie said. He stood up from the bench.

"You owe me a cup of coffee," I called.

He stopped and looked around, as if hoping to find a coffee shop in between the benches. "Okay," he said grudgingly. "But I gotta make it quick. Where do you want to go?"

"How about the Staten Island Mall?"

CHAPTER TEN

"What are all those birds doing over—" I began, breaking off as the import of Artie's smirk hit me. Clouds of gulls swirled around a large, flat mound of earth, treeless and vast, sitting on the opposite side of Richmond Road from the mall.

"That's the landfill," I guessed aloud. The appearance of a squat brick building with New York City Department of Sanitation on it in silver block letters confirmed my brilliant deduction.

"The biggest sanitary landfill in the whole entire universe," Artie cheerfully volunteered. "One of the perks of being the Staten Island reporter for my paper is that I got a full guided tour. It measures—"

"Do I look like I care, Bloom?" I shot back. We had just passed the turnoff to the marsh where Amber's body had been pulled from its watery grave; I was in no mood for a sightseeing trip through garbage.

Across the road—a six-lane highway, to be exact—stretched a huge parking lot surrounding the giant mall anchored by three major department stores.

It was a perfect metaphor for late–twentieth-century urban life: a highway to nowhere with a mountain of garbage on one side and a shopping mall on the other. We pulled into the parking lot and found a space near the main entrance. As I closed the door on the passenger side of the car, I looked back across the road at the cloud of gulls hovering over the landfill. A few strays had made it to this side of the road; carrion birds circled Macy's, their harsh cries ringing in my ears as we stepped into the Emerald City of shopping: the Staten Island Mall.

"Where are we going?" I asked Artie. He was moving at a rate of speed that had me hustling to keep up.

"Having some ice cream," he tossed back over his shoulder.

I was about to remark that I hadn't really accompanied him to the mall for food, when I remembered that Amber had met Josh Greenspan at Friendly's.

We stepped out of Macy's into the mall proper, a cavernous space broken up by fountains and escalators and cute little carts with cute little *tchatchkes* sold by cute little women with perky smiles.

There was an information desk; I picked up a folding map of the mall printed in three colors and raced after Artie, who was moving at a speed hard to keep up with even for a hardened New York pedestrian.

We walked the length of the lower level, passing athletic shoe stores, clothing stores for teenagers, The Body Shop, Victoria's Secret—

"That's where Amber worked," I said abruptly. I had a sudden vision of her and Scott in my office the day she told me she wanted her baby back. I'd thought that was the worst news I could hear regarding this adoption. Now I looked back upon that moment with fond nostalgia.

Artie stopped, causing a woman walking behind him to

swerve her stroller and hit the wall. She glared at him and kept moving.

"Maybe someone in there knew her," he said, lighting up like a kid expecting to see Santa. He took a step toward the store, and I knew he had to go in and try his luck.

I waited outside; his quest for a sidebar held no interest for me. One thing I was sure of; Amber hadn't confided her plans to a fellow salesgirl. She was a keeper of secrets.

Artie came back out, disappointment written on his freckled face. "They're all new," he said. "No one remembers Amber."

We came to the center atrium, which boasted a fountain and two escalators on either side, rising to the mall's second level. We stepped on and were wafted upwards, as sun poured through a skylight onto the tinkling water below. Friendly's was right there; it had a corner location that beckoned shoppers to take a break and try the Wattamelon, an imitation watermelon slice made of raspberry sherbet with a lime sherbet rind and chocolate-chip seeds.

It was an off-time, somewhere between late lunches and early snacks, so the place was pretty empty. A boothful of teenaged girls sat in the front, giggling over large sundaes topped with mountains of whipped cream. A young mother spooned orange sherbet into the eager mouth of a toddler in a stroller, while an older child sat next to her and licked chocolate from his spoon with single-minded concentration.

At the cash register a middle-aged man the color of iced tea perched on a stool and counted receipts. His hair was cropped short, with gray tufts at the ears. His face was pockmarked, like pancakes ready to turn. He wore a brush mustache with more than a hint of gray.

"Are you the manager?" I asked. I hoped Artie would have the sense to stay in the background; I had the feeling this was not a man who wanted to see himself in the media.

"Who's asking?" he replied, not looking up from the receipts. His name tag read "Herman Tolliver."

I sized him up and decided on the truth. Something about

him said he'd resent being jerked around. "I'm a lawyer," I explained. "I represented the woman they found in the swamp."

He raised his eyes from the receipts and lifted a single eyebrow. "Go on," he said.

"Well, I guess I feel—" I looked down at the counter, at the receipts in neat piles.

"—responsible," came out in a tiny voice I wasn't sure was audible.

I looked up; Herman nodded understandingly. So understandingly I had to blink and grab my lower lip with my teeth.

"Had a nephew," Herman Tolliver said. "Nice kid. Gave him a job in here, had him cooking in the back. Hoped I could change his ways, get him away from the street trash he was running with. Damned if they didn't find him dead of an overdose, from shit he copped right here in the mall, from some fool down at the Chess King." His head moved from side to side, sorrow and regret etched in the lines of his moon-pocked face. "Thought I was giving the kid a break; I was only bringing him closer to his death."

My turn to nod. The fellowship of the responsible. This meeting of the "I was only trying to help" society is now called to order.

"Did you see my client in here Friday night?" I asked.

"Yeah," Herman said. "She and her husband and the baby came in about eight-thirty, stayed till almost nine. I sure hope they find that baby," he added.

I wasn't going to touch that one. I could only do this if I didn't think about the baby. "Did you see anyone else with them?"

"Sure. Like I told the cops, first they were alone. Then a man came in and joined them. They all left together."

"Where was the baby all this time?"

"In a carrier thing. Like a car seat. I remember when I first saw them, I was worried about the baby. People can't relax and enjoy their food if there's a screaming baby in the place. I figured he was bound to wake up and start bawling any minute, but he never did.''

"Did you see them leave?''

"Sure. I took their money, said something nice about the kid. People like it if you talk nice about their babies.''

"Do you still have their receipts? Did the other people order anything?'' I was getting eager, sure I was on to something.

"Gave them to the cops.''

Artie decided he'd been quiet long enough. "Do you know who waited on them?''

Tolliver pursed his thin lips and I thought he'd refuse to answer. But finally he said, "Her name is Sonia. She only works nights on account of her mother. Alzheimer's,'' he explained. "She lives right near the mall, over in Heartland Village.''

Tolliver gave Artie the address. "She's home all day, comes in here at six, three nights a week. Not tonight, though, so you'll have to catch her at home.''

We thanked him and turned back to the mall, back to the bustling shoppers and the carts full of useless little objects: crystals hanging from black silk cords; neckties with the Three Stooges on the front; rubber stamps and colored ink-pads.

One cart stood twenty feet or so from the entrance to Friendly's. A bored-looking Asian woman of about twenty perched on a stool next to it. Rainbow crystals in different shapes and colors winked at me.

Artie walked straight to the cart and started fingering the hanging pendants.

"You like?'' the salesgirl asked in a high, birdlike voice.

"Nice,'' Artie replied. Then he dropped his pretense of interest and asked, "Were you here Friday night?''

"When lady with baby here?'' she chirped. "Cops all over place, ask everybody.'' She deepened her voice and put a frown on her doll-like face to act the part of the police officers. " 'What you see? You see baby?' "

Then she gave an enormous grin and said, "Just like on TV. *NYPD Blue.* Favorite show."

"So did you see the baby?" Artie persisted. He had his steno pad out; she eyed it with avid interest.

She nodded. "First see woman with baby come out of Friendly's," she said, gesturing toward the entrance. "One man she with go this way," she added, pointing in the direction of Sears.

But Josh Greenspan had gone to the entrance at Macy's, so the man who went in the opposite direction had to have been Scott.

"Younger man?" I asked, falling into her habit of omitting articles. Artie gave me a glare, but the cart owner didn't notice the change of interrogators.

"Yeah," the girl replied, nodding vigorously. "Lady stay with other guy, while blond guy go down escalator."

I pressed my luck. "Did you see the older man give the woman anything?"

"Someone come to buy," the crystal seller said with a regretful nod. "I sell bracelet with pink heart. When I look back, man going that way." She pointed toward Macy's.

It made sense; Josh, following instructions, headed for the Macy's entrance, where he was supposed to take possession of Baby Adam. Scott, planning an ambush at the loading dock, sprinted down the rear escalator to get there first, while Amber, who had already taken Josh's money, went—

"Where did the lady go?" burst out of me. "The one with the baby? Did you see her?"

"Go toward kid place," the Asian girl said, pointing toward a mall exit to the right of where we stood. It was an entrance that wasn't connected to a large department store, but led straight to the parking lot.

"Kid place?" Artie echoed. He lifted eager eyes from his steno pad; he looked as if he were writing his lead paragraph in his head.

"I show. Mary, you watch cart?" she called out. The plump gray-haired woman at the necktie cart gave a nod. The girl bounced off the high stool and headed toward the exit. There were food places lining the way, and the last storefront was occupied by miniature amusement park rides for children.

The kid place.

"She go out here, sit on bench," the crystal seller explained. She pointed to a cement plaza with royal blue metal benches. "I go out, too; time for cigarette. So I there when she get into car; tell cops all about it."

Car? Artie and I looked at each other in wild surmise.

"What car?" I demanded.

Artie cut in. "Can you describe it?"

The girl rolled her eyes toward heaven, as though seeking divine guidance, but the beatific smile on her face said she was only too glad to be the center of an admiring audience.

"Japanese car," she said. "Not brand-new but pretty good shape. Silver-color car."

I drew in a sharp breath.

The girl kept on. "License plate was—"

"PIZZA twenty-one," I interrupted, unable to contain myself. "It has to be."

She shook her head, her smile fading. "Was going to say, couldn't see plate. Covered in mud."

Artie took down the girl's name and thanked her; she went back into the mall with obvious reluctance, relinquishing her role as star witness with difficulty. Then the boy reporter turned to me and said, "What's all this about pizza?"

I told Artie about the silver car outside the group home, about the curly haired man who'd argued with Doc Scanlon at the hospital, about the vanity plate as reported by the security guard.

"If we can get to this guy before the cops," he said,

bouncing on the bench like a kid anticipating a ride on the roller coaster, "we can—"

"We can get ourselves busted for obstructing governmental administration," I finished brightly, as if the prospect delighted me.

"Counselor," he intoned, adding decades to his age with a drop of his voice, "this is what is known in my business as a scoop. I am therefore going to run this plate, find out who this guy is and where I can find him, and I am going to confront him with the fact that he was seen picking up a woman who is now dead. You can either join me or stay here with your thumb up your—"

"If you don't call Aronson," I interrupted, not waiting to find out where my hypothetical thumb was going to be, "I will. We can't just—"

"Counselor, we don't know this guy was anywhere near the mall. For all we know, he was having dinner at Gracie Mansion with the mayor and the cardinal. All I'm suggesting," Artie went on in a tone of exaggerated patience, "is that I find out who he is before we do anything."

That I couldn't argue with. I started to look for the nearest pay phone, but he reached into his jacket and pulled out a tiny cellular job. It made funny little noises as he unfolded it and punched in a number from memory.

Welcome to the twenty-first century. In less than three minutes, Artie folded the plastic toy and said, "His name is Jerry Califana and he owns a pizza parlor in Tottenville. Which I guess is why he has PIZZA twenty-one on his car."

"And you want to go out there and talk to him before the cops figure out who he is," I said.

"Hey, I just got this sudden taste for pizza," he replied with a shrug and a boyish grin. "You coming?"

"I'm coming," I said, following him like a puppy. "But if he was anywhere near the mall when Amber was killed, I'm calling Aronson."

"After I get my scoop," the boy reporter insisted.

By the time we reached Artie's battered Chevy, I'd convinced myself I wasn't concealing evidence because it wasn't evidence yet. As soon as it became evidence, I'd turn it over to the cops like a good citizen.

This was the kind of reasoning that would have earned me an A in law school, but I had the uneasy feeling Detective Aronson wouldn't be giving me any prizes for it.

"Marla was right," I said as Artie slid into the right lane, following the expressway sign marked Tottenville.

"About what?" Artie replied absently.

"She said this guy hanging around Amber was bad news. She was afraid he was going to convince her to change her mind about the adoption."

"But she married Scott," Artie objected.

"Yeah, but what if she didn't want to go along with Scott's little scam?" I turned in my seat, trying to engage Artie's attention without distracting him from the all-important task of not driving us into a ditch.

"What if she called this pizza guy and asked him to meet her so she could slip away from Scott and save her baby? She knows Scott's going to ambush Josh at the entrance to Macy's, so she meets Mr. Pizza—"

"His name is Jerry," my companion amended.

"Jerry," I substituted. "She meets Jerry at the kid place, gets into the car with the baby, and—"

"And good old helpful Jerry drives her to the swamp, bops her on the head, drowns her in a foot of water, takes the money and the baby, and goes home to Tottenville to make pizza."

"You make it sound stupid," I said.

"It is stupid."

"Thanks. Why don't you come up with a scenario that explains it, then?"

"Your client is not out to save her baby from Big Bad Scott, for starters," Artie began. "Look how she conned Scott into running away while she pocketed the cash Greenspan gave her. She's got buyers lined up out of town, and she intends to sell the kid to one of them. Only she doesn't want Scott in on the deal. So she sets him up with Josh, disables his car—don't forget Scott couldn't get his car started in the parking lot.'' Artie lifted a hand from the steering wheel to shake a pudgy finger at me.

"Both hands on the wheel, please, Bloom," I pleaded.

He complied. "She jumps in the car with Jerry, expecting him to take her to Kansas City," he went on. "Only Jerry gets greedy, decides he can make money on the baby without cutting Amber in. He drives to the swamp, kills her, and takes the cash and the kid."

"Which means he's probably in Wyoming right now, and we're making a trip to an empty pizza parlor," I pointed out. "I knew we should have called Aronson."

I slumped in the passenger seat, silent as Artie made his way through the narrow streets of the sleepy little neighborhood known as Tottenville. It was at the end of Staten Island, where Prince's Bay met Arthur Kill, the inlet separating the island from the New Jersey mainland.

He took a turn on a side street, and a brick pizza restaurant appeared in mid-block.

The pizza parlor was called 'At's Amore, and it had a big neon pizza in the window on which was a caricature of a man it took me a full minute to realize was supposed to be Dean Martin.

I laughed aloud; Artie Bloom, pulling his car into a space behind a teal-green station wagon, asked why. "When I was a kid," I explained, "I thought it was the pizza pie that hit your eye."

"What are you talking about?"

"It's a song. From the fifties. 'When the moon hits your eye like a big pizza pie, 'at's amore.' So I used to think it was the pizza that— Oh, forget about it."

The restaurant itself was a slice of the fifties here in the hard-edged dystopian nineties. Although, come to think of it, all of Tottenville seemed stuck in a time warp: one-family houses complete with fences and trees and dogs tethered to clotheslines; a little business district with mom-and-pop stores; nobody with skin darker than a Sicilian's, and well-tended front yards decorated with Virgin statues and plastic birds—Our Lady of the Flamingos.

I went inside, followed by Artie, and was enveloped by warm air smelling of tomato sauce and garlic. No fancy Northern Italian cream sauces here, no penne in vodka with yellow peppers, or squid ink pasta with morels. In fact, I suspected . . .

I opened the menu. I was right. The word *pasta* appeared nowhere; you could get spaghetti with meatballs or marinara sauce or plain butter-and-garlic. And the waiter would not spend three minutes discussing precisely how *al dente* it was going to be or detailing which region of Italy the grated cheese came from. We were talking plain Southern Italian here, no more—and no less. The sauce would roll on the tongue thick and oily, would stick to the spaghetti and linger on the palate, would flavor the pizza and coat the chicken cacciatore, would satisfy like no upscale yuppie Italian food managed to do.

I was hungry all of a sudden. Hungry for a slice of pizza with a thin but strong crust, melted cheese, zippy sausage. The place smelled like heaven, like the old Elbow Room Pizza Parlor on Euclid Avenue in Cleveland, where we hung out after school, having driven across town for no other reason than that we had drivers' licenses and the keys to the family car.

"Are you Jerry Califana?" Artie asked, after we'd ordered and paid for two slices.

The man's eyes narrowed. "Who wants to know?"

So he wasn't in Wyoming after all.

"I was Amber Lundquist's lawyer," I began. "I saw you—"

"Lawyer?" He backed away slightly, putting distance between us. It was the equivalent of placing a wreath of garlic around his neck.

"But I'm not," Artie cut in smoothly. He reached his pudgy, freckled hand toward Jerry. "I'm a reporter."

Jerry looked from me to Artie and back again, as if weighing his options. He gave a quick, decisive nod and said, "I want people to know the truth about Amber." His big hands clenched into fists at his side; in his pizza apron he looked like a butcher; for a moment the splotches of tomato sauce could have been blood.

"That's what I'm here for," Artie said. "To listen."

In two minutes we were sitting at a front table, hot pizza slices in front of us, Jerry straddling a chair and leaning forward as if he couldn't wait to pour his deepest secrets into the boy reporter's tabloid ear.

"How did you know Amber?" Artie began. He lifted a slice to his lips and took a big bite, licking the strands of hot mozzarella that dripped from the pizza. I wondered how he was going to take notes while balancing pizza on his fingers.

Jerry sighed, a long sigh that spoke of a good deal of history between him and my dead client. "I was married to her."

CHAPTER ELEVEN

Artie and I both stared at the man in the white apron. My farfetched theory that Amber had decided to save her baby from Scott's plans didn't seem so crazy now that there was an ex-husband on the scene.

"We got married when Amber was eighteen and I was twenty," he went on, glancing at Artie to make sure the reporter was taking it all in. "She was pregnant, so naturally, I did the right thing." He blinked his altar boy eyes, dark chocolate eyes that brimmed with remembered pain.

"At least it seemed like the right thing then," he went on, looking down at the tabletop. "My mother tried to tell me about her, said she was no good. Even said she didn't think the baby was mine, that Amber was a slut and made it with a lot of guys besides me. I thought she was just, you know, being a mom."

"You two meet when she was at Mount Loretto?" Artie asked, in an elaborately offhand way.

Jerry stared; a look composed of equal parts awe and street challenge: how come you know my business?

I gave my companion a silent nod of approval; Totten-ville was about five miles from the orphanage. It was a good guess, and judging from Jerry's stunned face, it had hit the mark.

"Yeah," Amber's ex-husband admitted. "I used to hang out over at the end of Sharrott's Road, by Prince's Bay," he explained, as though that said it all. Apparently it did to Artie; he nodded and made a note in his steno pad. "She used to walk by the bay, and we kind of ran into each other."

The stocky Italian looked down at the floor, and a dull flush crept into his cheeks. "It's where we used to make out," he explained. "I can still hear the sound of the little waves on the sand."

"Amber told me she'd had a baby before," I prompted, since he'd stopped talking to look inward. "She said the baby died. That must have been very sad." The words were inadequate and I knew it, but I wasn't expecting Jerry to tell me how inadequate.

"Sad. Shit." He lifted a ham fist and brought it down hard on the little round table. So hard it shook. "You ever look at a white coffin the size of a fucking shoe box and know it's got your own baby inside?" His voice was ragged; his eyes bored into mine with intense passion.

"It was hell," he went on, with the air of a man who knew the full import of the word. "One minute I had a brand-new kid, I was passin' out cigars like a big man. Next minute I'm standin' in the hospital with Doc Scanlon tellin' me it was a fluke of nature or some fucking bullshit."

"Doc Scanlon?" I said, surprised to hear a familiar name. "What did he have to do with—?" I caught Artie's glare of disapproval, but I persisted. "Oh, he delivered Amber's first baby, too, didn't he?"

"What do you mean, 'too'?" Jerry's voice rose, as did

his color. "You mean that bastard delivered the new kid, the one that's missing?"

I nodded; it was public knowledge. No reason he shouldn't know what the *Post* hadn't bothered printing.

"I knew it!" Jerry burst out. He stood up from the little wire-backed chair as though remaining seated was a physical impossibility. He walked toward the back wall of the parlor, where travel posters of Italian cities hung in cheap frames.

"Knew what, Jerry?" Artie Bloom prodded. "You said you wanted people to know the truth. So what is the truth? What did you know?"

"I knew she sold this kid to Scanlon just like she sold mine."

A moment of silence, bewildered on my part, greeted this announcement.

"I thought your baby died," I said, genuinely confused. "And now you're accusing Doc Scanlon of selling it. Was there a second child?"

Jerry shook his head in urgent denial. He stepped closer to our table with every word, advancing on us as though to convince us of the truth of his words by physical force if necessary.

"No, no, no," he repeated. "You don't get it. Those bastards stole my baby and faked the death. The baby wasn't really dead; they sold it to some rich couple and split the money."

Wow. We were talking major paranoid fantasy here, and the wide, intense brown eyes told me he believed every crazy word he was saying. I glanced at Artie; his face was avid with the deep desire to believe Jerry—the scoop potential was enormous—but his blue eyes held a healthy skepticism.

"Doc Scanlon?" he said, letting his tone convey his disbelief. "Dr. Christopher Scanlon, who's on the board of at least six charities, who appears on television on behalf of unwanted children, who makes at least two hundred thousand bucks a year legitimate? That Doc Scanlon?''

''Yeah, that Doc Scanlon,'' Jerry shot back. ''That hypocrite. He and Amber faked a death certificate and pretended my Laura was dead when the truth was that bitch never wanted the baby and was only too happy to take the money and run. She hit me with divorce papers a month after Laura supposedly died.''

Laura. My first meeting with Amber came back to me: sitting on a hard chair next to her bed at the group home, watching her face go slack as she talked about the baby she'd lost.

When she told me she'd changed her mind, she said she couldn't lose another child after burying Laura.

And now the father of that child said Amber faked the death and sold the baby.

''Lots of people get divorced after a baby dies,'' Artie pointed out with a shrug. ''Doesn't mean they—''

''That's not all,'' Jerry cut in, his words coming more quickly. Little flecks of spittle leaked out the sides of his mouth; he seemed determined to convince us by sheer speed if nothing else.

He lowered himself onto the wire-backed chair and leaned forward in the eager stance of conspirators everywhere. He lowered his voice so the secret would be heard by as few people as possible.

''I got the records,'' he said. He was so close I could smell the garlic on his breath. ''I got a copy of the death certificate and compared it with the hospital records. That baby was healthy as a horse the day she was born. The record says so.''

I was transported back in time to my earliest years as a lawyer with the Legal Aid Society. How many clients had wandered into my office with shopping bags full of papers that were going to transform their lives, prove to everyone how they'd been swindled or done wrong? Jerry Califana had the same air of obsession.

''Then, two days later,'' he went on, tapping his large

finger on the table, "there's a note says she has a heart defect all of a sudden. Out of the blue. And we don't even get her home from the hospital before she dies. I never even held her." The voice broke and he turned away.

Babies die. People die. And it's not always someone's fault. Even a lawyer, trained to fix blame, could see that.

I wondered if Artie Bloom did. Or would he use this man, parade his appalling delusion across the pages of his paper, feed his paranoia and then drop him when the story had run its course?

Then another thought struck me. Did this grieving man, weeping for a child dead how many years, hate Amber enough to kill her?

Damned right he did.

I could believe, with a suddenness that took me aback, that Amber could have been greedy enough, ruthless enough, to sell her own baby and fake its death. Elaborate, even for her, but I'd seen enough of the pain she'd inflicted on Ellie and Josh Greenspan to suspect that creating grief had been a hobby.

But Doc Scanlon. A man with a secure place in the community, a man who made at least two hundred thousand dollars a year without breaking the law, a man with everything to lose and very little to gain—why would he have aided and abetted Amber by faking official records?

As I gazed at Artie's impassive face, I realized it didn't matter what I believed. What mattered was that Jerry Califana had a bedrock conviction that Amber had sold his baby and put him through hell. And for this he had decided she would pay with her life.

"What did the baby die of?" Artie asked, then amended his question to reflect Jerry's delusion. "What did Doc Scanlon tell you she died of?"

"She had a hole in her heart is what the doc said," Jerry replied in a morose, darkly suspicious tone. "He said it just like that," the burly young man went on, "like I was some kind of dummy who couldn't understand big words. I may make pizza for a living,'' he said, the corners of his mouth turning downward, ''but I went to CSI for two years. I can tell the difference between a valve and a ventricle.''

I was still figuring out that CSI stood for College of Staten Island when Artie asked, ''So which was it, valve or ventricle?''

Jerry Califana looked around nervously, as though worried that there might be a microphone hidden in the garlic powder. Then he wet his lips and said, ''I could show you.'' He spoke to Artie, but his eyes gave me an appraising stare. I wondered why, then realized it was one thing to talk to a reporter, another to slander a doctor in the presence of a lawyer. But Artie was his best hope of having his story told, and I was with Artie.

''Be right back,'' Jerry said, then disappeared through the kitchen door.

I leaned toward Artie. ''You can't be serious about running this story,'' I whispered. ''Doc Scanlon will sue your—''

''I know,'' Artie replied, his voice a hoarse whisper. ''But I've gotta see this stuff. Can you see the headline? 'RIGHT-TO-LIFE DOC SELLS BABY, S.I. FATHER CHARGES.' '' His blue eyes glittered with excitement; I wondered whether his fevered imagination was drafting the opening paragraph of the story or composing his modest acceptance speech for the Pulitzer Prize.

Jerry Califana returned with a black metal lockbox. He opened it with ease, his big fingers manipulating the lock as though he'd opened it many times before. I had a sudden picture of him sitting in a chair, late at night, taking each piece of paper out and looking at it, hoping to see something new, something that would clinch his case against the doctor.

The first item on top was a four-by-five-inch baby picture. Jerry lifted it reverently and laid it on the table, carefully brushing away imaginary crumbs before letting it touch the surface.

"She's a beautiful baby," Artie said. I noted the use of the present tense; the boy reporter seemed more than willing to support Califana's delusion that his daughter was still alive.

There followed a birth certificate, a death certificate, and several postnatal medical records from Our Lady of Pity Hospital.

"See, here's where the doc checks 'none' under 'heart defects,' " Jerry explained. "Then the very next day, there's a note about decreased vascular activity."

"So where were you Friday night?" Artie asked, his tone innocently conversational.

The pizzamaker's jaw dropped. He gave Artie the kind of look he'd have given a giant cockroach and replied, "What's that got to do with my Laura?"

"Nothing," Artie responded breezily. "Nothing at all. That's the night your ex-wife bought the farm, that's all. Or should I say the swamp."

The boy reporter had a sound grasp of cross-examination. I looked at him with new respect.

"I don't have to tell you anything," Jerry said, the sullen tone of his voice reverting him to the teenager he'd been when he met and married Amber.

"No, you don't," Artie agreed. "And I don't have to print anything about how Amber sold your baby."

"You mean you won't write anything about Doc unless I tell you where I was on Friday night?"

"That's right," Artie confirmed. "See, my interest in all this is Amber. That's what my editor sent me to Staten Island for. Now, don't get me wrong," he added, spreading his pudgy, freckled hands in a placating gesture, "I'd like nothing more than to break a big story about Doc Scanlon selling your baby, but first I've got to come up with something on Amber's murder. So, what's it going to be, Jerry? You going to answer my question, or am I going to walk out of here and forget all about your baby?"

Jerry gave it serious thought. He looked at the documents

spread out on the pizza table like cards in a poker game, then up at Artie's face, which gave him no quarter. Then he muttered, "She asked me to meet her."

I couldn't believe it. Aronson was going to kill me. Artie and I had managed to locate the man in the silver car, the man who'd picked Amber up at the mall and driven her to her death. And here he was, sitting at a table in his own restaurant, admitting everything to a reporter and a lawyer.

"At the mall?" Artie prompted.

"Hell, no," Jerry replied, shaking his head. "At this place called the Native Plant Center."

"The what?" I asked.

"It's part of the Greenbelt," Artie said absently, as if that was supposed to tell me something. "It belongs to the New York City Park system," he added.

"Where is it?"

"Across from the mall," Jerry explained, his voice dropping as he realized the full implications of what he was saying. "Right next to the Davis Wildlife Refuge."

"Let me get this straight," I began. "You—"

"Why not let him start at the beginning," Artie said.

I clamped my mouth shut and waited for Jerry to collect his thoughts.

"She promised to give me all the documents," Jerry said at last. "She practically admitted Laura was still alive and that she knew who adopted her. She promised to give me everything, including the name of the couple who had Laura."

"In return for what?" asked Artie.

"Twenty thousand dollars," Jerry answered. He wiped a big hand across his face and went on. "She told me to be at the Native Plant Center parking lot at nine o'clock, to wait for her to come. So I did. I got there at eight-thirty and sat in my car until nearly ten. I had the money; I took a second mortgage on this place, but she never showed."

I looked over at Artie. Was he buying this? Here was a man with every reason to kill Amber, a man whose car fit the description of the one she'd been seen getting into at the mall, and we were supposed to believe he was sitting idly in a parking lot doing nothing while his ex-wife drowned less than a mile away?

One thing was certain: no force on earth was going to move Arthur H. Bloom from that wire-backed chair until he had his story.

No force on earth except one. The door opened and a big man walked up to the counter. A big man with the face of a basset hound and the disgusted expression of a cop who sees civilians meddling in police business.

Detective Milt Aronson walked over to the table and said, "What are you two doing here?"

I hoped to hell Artie wasn't going to say, "Having pizza."

Instead he gazed up at the big detective with the eagerness of a kid greeting a favorite uncle. "Are you going to arrest Mr. Califana?" he asked.

Jerry jumped up from his chair and looked around wildly for a place to hide.

"You want a press release, call DCPI," Aronson retorted, naming by initials the police information office. "Just get the hell out of here."

Artie looked at me, as though expecting me to weigh in with a speech about the rights of the press under the First Amendment, but I was happy to accept the reprieve. I took a few bills out of my wallet, threw them on the table, and hustled Artie out the door, glad Aronson wasn't going to grill us about how we happened to be there.

On the way to his car, Artie turned and looked back toward 'At's Amore. "Let's wait a few minutes," he said. "See if Aronson takes Califana out in handcuffs."

"If he killed Amber, where's the baby?" I said, heartlessly throwing rain on his parade. "He's the one person in the country who doesn't want Adam; if for some reason he decided after all these years to kill Amber on the exact same night she's selling her new baby, which is a pretty farfetched coincidence, then what did he do with Adam?''

Artie opened the door to his car and got in, then leaned over to unlock the passenger door for me. I jumped in beside him; within minutes the Artie Bloom Express was on its way back toward the mall.

"You buy his story?" I asked as we sped along the expressway.

"Makes a certain amount of sense," Artie replied. "Amber's ditching Scott and taking her baby out of state. She decides to get herself a nice going-away present from her ex. So she agrees to meet him at the Native Plant Center, only she never gets there because she's busy getting killed."

"By someone who picks her up at the mall in a silver car very much like the one Jerry happens to own," I finished, not bothering to hide my sarcasm. "His story won't last five minutes once Aronson starts questioning him."

"I don't know," Artie said, shaking his head. "It's not like I can't see Jerry killing her, because I can. But would he kill her before he found out what she knew about his kid?"

"You're assuming there's something to find out," I countered. "What if Amber was just playing on his obsession, lying to him about the baby being alive? If he found out that she was jerking him around, he'd kill her so fast—"

Artie took his eyes off the road and locked them with mine. "Did he strike you as that good an actor, Counselor?"

I remembered the look on Jerry's face as he opened the lockbox that held the sacred talismans of his lost child. No, I decided, Artie was right. Jerry Califana believed with every cell of his being that his Laura was still alive. So if he killed Amber, it wasn't because he'd come to see that she was lying about his child's death. And he wouldn't have killed her if there was the slightest chance she had information that would lead him to Laura.

"You know, Scott may not be off the hook here," I

mused as we raced along the expressway.

"How do you figure that?" Artie replied, giving me a sideways glance.

"He jumps Josh only to find out that Amber already has the money," I said. "So he runs for his car, hoping to find Amber and the baby waiting for him. Instead, he finds a car that won't start and no Amber. And, more important, no money."

Artie nodded; I pressed my luck. "So he hops on the motorcycle and takes off. He knows Amber double-crossed him. She ditched him at the mall and disabled the car. So he tracks down Amber, kills her, and then races to my house pretending he's looking for her when he knows damn well she's already dead because he—"

"Where's the baby all this time?" Artie countered. "And what about the silver car? Does Jerry—or whoever Amber's accomplice is—just stand there and let her get killed? And isn't coming to your house to establish an alibi pretty sophisticated for a lump like Scott?"

"Hell, Bloom, we know where the baby is," I answered, my voice dropping. I didn't want to say the words—didn't want to think them—but the reality I'd been pushing away ever since Amber was found had to be faced.

"In the swamp," I said, lowering my eyes and trying not to form the picture in my mind's eye. "Scott killed Amber and the baby, then tried to make it look like Amber successfully ditched him and left the state with Adam."

"Why would he destroy an asset worth at least ten thousand dollars?" Artie retorted. It was as cynical a reply as anyone could have made, and it cheered me no end.

CHAPTER TWELVE

"He never should have let her come here," Mrs. Bonaventura said mournfully. She struck me as a woman who said most things mournfully; the entire world seemed not to live up to her expectations.

Artie Bloom and I sat on identical chintz-covered chairs, placed with geometric precision across the room from the sofa. The group home seemed smaller and quieter this time; of course Marla wasn't with me, filling the air with smoke and pacing up and down.

"Why did he?" I asked. I sipped at my weak iced tea. My hand came away wet after I placed the sweating glass on a straw coaster.

"I don't know," the older woman replied. "It just happened. One day he showed up at the door and she was with him. I wondered because she was older than the other girls, and he treated her different from the beginning."

"How do you mean different?" I'd seen it myself; seen

the private room, decorated with a lavish hand, seen the private telephone line, seen that Amber was the princess of this little castle. What I didn't know was why.

Artie's steno pad was nowhere in sight. We'd agreed that since I'd met Mrs. Bonaventura, I should conduct the questioning. I had the feeling that if Mrs. B. realized the press was sitting in, we'd be out on our respective ears in short order.

"That room used to hold three girls," the housemother confided, "but Doctor made me move them out and put Amber in there alone." Her voice was laden with grievance. I had a sudden picture of her gleefully ridding the master bedroom of Amber's furniture and moving three spartan single beds into the space.

"Then he said she needed a private telephone line." Again the disapproving tone invited me into a game of Ain't It Awful. "He said the adoptive parents who wanted her child were paying for it, but I saw the bills. That line was in her name, but he paid for it with his own money."

Interesting. Ellie Greenspan had led me to believe that she and Josh financed Amber's link to the outside world; was Amber collecting expense money from them for extras Doc was already paying for? And what of the Kansas and Maryland couples? I was willing to bet they both kicked in.

I shook my head and tried for a tsking sound that said I couldn't agree more. "And look how she paid him back," I ventured. Hell of a thing to say about my own client— but then look how she'd paid me back.

I was answered by a malicious gleam in Mrs. Bonaventura's black eyes. I had a moment's vision of her wearing a fringed shawl, Tarot cards spread before her, candles flickering behind her head. She was a natural gypsy, and I leaned forward expectantly as she opened her mouth, certain she would tell me she'd seen Amber's treachery in the stars.

I wasn't disappointed. "I told him," she said with lip-smacking satisfaction. "I warned him not to trust that little snip."

I hadn't heard that word since my Grandma Winchell went to live at the Home. If Amber was only a snip, I wondered what it took to make a bitch in Mrs. B's lexicon.

"She was in and out of here whenever she pleased," the housemother complained. "All the other girls had rules, curfews. In by ten on weeknights, eleven on weekends. And even during the day, we kept an eye on them. They'd spend all day at the mall eating hamburgers and drinking milk-shakes if we let them. Gaining weight, smoking—all the things that would be bad for the babies."

"The babies are the most important thing," I said gravely, unsuccessfully trying to push away Amber's image of her-self as a prize brood cow. I didn't dare meet Artie's eyes. Laughter lay just below the surface of my diaphragm, ready to leap into my throat and destroy my rapport with Mrs. B.

"Of course," the housemother agreed. Her head bobbed up and down in an awkward nod; the bun wobbled as she moved. "That's what our adoptive parents pay for, healthy babies. And while there are no guarantees," she went on, as though instructing a prospective adopter in the vagaries of genetics, "we try our best to give our little mothers healthy food and a quiet lifestyle."

"Except for Amber," I said, gently working the house-mother back to my agenda.

"She went out whenever she felt like it," Mrs. B. com-plained. "She'd go to the mall, see the girls she used to work with. I told Doctor he ought to make her stay home," she confided. She looked directly at me, deliberately ex-cluding Artie from the conversation, as though his mascu-linity prevented him from understanding.

"I wasn't surprised when I found out she slipped out and got married," she continued. She sat back and clamped her thin lips shut. "It's just the kind of thing I warned Doctor about."

"And what did he say?" I lifted my glass to my lips,

hoping to hide the eagerness I felt. We were finally getting to the heart of my interest—Doc Scanlon. I felt sure Mrs. B. would rather cut out her tongue than criticize her boss, but if I could couch my questions in serious Amber-bashing, I had a chance of opening her sealed lips.

"Oh, he's like all men," she responded with a curdled smile. Again I fought down the urge to laugh. How was Artie going to get usable quotes from this interview? "A girl like Amber can twist them around her little finger."

"I wonder what else he paid for besides the private line," I said, infusing my voice with a sisterly bitterness I hoped would match my companion's mood.

"It wasn't just him," Mrs. B. said defensively. "Those poor people who wanted her baby just couldn't give her enough. She had her own portable television, a CD player." She shook her head. "Of course, I didn't realize there was more than one couple giving her things. I thought the presents from Kansas City were from her own family."

This was old news. I needed a lever into something I didn't know. I gave the matter some thought, but before I could come up with something, the boy reporter jumped into the conversation.

"I understand there was a burglary at Doc's office," he began, his tone conversational. I tried not to look as astonished as I felt; he'd been holding out on me.

"Not just the office downtown," Mrs. Bonaventura confirmed, her tone thick with relish, "but right here in this house."

"Two burglaries?" Artie exclaimed. "I knew there'd been one at the office on Victory Boulevard," he went on, "but I didn't know there was one here, too."

"Oh, yes," the older woman said with a grim nod of her head. In some corner of her mind, she seemed obscurely to blame Amber for this as well—and maybe she wasn't wrong. If Amber got her special treatment because she had something on Doc Scanlon, she might well have obtained her knowledge through burglary.

But then there was Jerry Califana—were the records he'd brought out for Artie Bloom's perusal taken from Doc Scanlon's office?

"When did these burglaries happen?" Artie inquired, a look of solicitous interest on his freckled face.

"Oh, the one here was six months ago," Mrs. B. replied. "It was cold outside, but no snow. November, perhaps."

Six months ago Amber had been four months pregnant. At four months, you could probably commit burglary. Breaking into this house didn't require the skills of a cat burglar by any means, and Doc's office was on the first floor.

"Do you remember what was stolen?" I asked.

"Nothing," the housemother said with a shrug of her black-clad shoulder. "That's why Doctor didn't bother to report it. He said there was no harm done. But me," she went on, "I would have called the police anyway. Even if all they did was mess up some old records nobody cared about."

"Old records?" I tried to keep my voice innocently curious, but Mrs. B. wasn't that gullible.

"Nothing important," she said with a snap of her jaw. Closing the barn door before any more horses managed to escape.

"Adoption records?" I persisted, but to no avail. My hostess rose from her chair and made for the door.

"It was nice of you to come," she said with wooden politeness. "I must be getting back to work now."

Artie rose more slowly; I was afraid he was going to push our luck with a parting question, but he bowed to the inevitable.

We stepped out into a fine April afternoon. The sun was high in the sky; there were soft green leaves on the trees and dandelions winked at us from the square, mowed lawns.

"Old adoption records," I said. "I wonder how old."

"And you thought Jerry Califana was just your average paranoid," Artie teased. "Maybe he's right—and it looks like he's got the records to prove it."

"Where to now?" I asked as we crossed the street, making for Artie's antique Chevy.

"I want to see where Amber lived," the boy reporter said, "maybe talk to her landlady. And I want to talk to that waitress from Friendly's. She lives right around here, as I recall."

He opened his steno pad and checked the address Herman Tolliver had given him. Then he drove around the block and pulled up in front of a tract house that looked like all the other houses on the street, moss-green and boxy, with spindly white-blossomed trees in the front yard. Three minutes later we were sitting in a living room, courtesy of Sonia Rogoff.

"It's kinda like having a baby again," the waitress said, glancing at the senile mother who sat in an oversized orange chair. "Only she weighs a hundred and twenty pounds and has a mouth on her somethin' awful," she added, giving her mother a conspiratorial grin. The old woman smiled and, as if in response to her daughter's prompt, said, "Fuck you, bitch."

Sonia's grin widened. "See what I mean?" she said, inviting us into the conspiracy. "She always was a pistol, my ma."

"Always was a pistol," the gnomelike creature repeated with a satisfied nod.

"Yeah, Ma, a real pistol," the waitress said. She turned her attention to Artie and me, but every so often she let her eyes slide to where the old woman sat in a chair too big for her.

"See, that's why I work nights," Sonia explained. "I gotta stay with her all day, and then when the kids come home, I can go out. Not that I go anywhere except work," she added. "Four nights a week I'm schleppin' ice cream, and seven days I'm changin' diapers and takin' Ma for walks."

I would have asked why. I would have asked how—how can you give her your life? How can you keep on day after day after day? How can you bear to look into the petlike, vacant eyes of a woman who must have been strong and tough and funny once upon a time?

Who knew malls had saints working the night shift?

"So you remember the couple with the baby?" Artie asked, not bothering to keep the eagerness out of his voice. With every witness we talked to, he saw his story getting bigger and bigger. If nobody bombed a major capital, he had hopes of the front page.

"Yeah," she replied, but a frown crept between her eyebrows. "What TV station did you say you were with? Where's the cameras?"

"I'm not a television reporter," Artie replied, his smile dimming only slightly. "I write for a newspaper."

"Oh, a newspaper," Sonia repeated. "I thought maybe it was *A Current Affair*. Me and Ma, we watch that all the time."

"All the time," the old lady agreed, nodding like a car toy.

"About Amber Lundquist," Artie prompted. "You saw her the night she—"

"Not just that night," Sonia interrupted. She wore a tank top and cutoff jeans; her long, ropy legs ended in worn moccasins. She sat with one leg tucked under her like a teenager, but her pert face was lined with wrinkles brought on by too many days in the sun.

"You saw her there before?" Artie flipped open his steno pad and sat poised for an answer that would take him to the front page.

"Lots of times," Sonia said with a conspiratorial nod. "She used to come in when she was still pregnant. And I seen her with this other couple, too."

"What couple? Can you describe them?"

She lifted her bare shoulders in a shrug. "Dunno. They were pretty ordinary. She might have been Spanish, but he was just a guy. Light brown hair, kind of a thin face."

"Kyle and Donna Cheney," Artie guessed, his eyes lighting up. "She's Cuban; her name was Donna Pacheco before she married."

"They're the ones who claim they dropped out of the bidding for Adam?" I asked.

Artie nodded. Sonia glanced from the boy reporter back to me with an avid face, drinking in the scandal that was juicy enough for *A Current Affair* even if Artie had no cameras with him.

"How do you remember them so well?" I cut in, suddenly suspicious. This woman served a lot of ice cream to a lot of people; she could hardly have known Amber was going to turn up dead in a swamp. So how come she had total recall of Amber's visits to Friendly's?

Artie didn't like the question, but Sonia Rogoff didn't seem to mind. "I don't know," she said, "it's like when I'm at work I'm so happy to be out in the world with regular people, I like to watch them. And watching her was like following a story on television. First she's pregnant, then she has the baby, she's with this guy, then with that guy."

It made sense. "So this one night," she continued, taking in both Artie and me with her inviting glance, "she and her husband come in together, only they weren't exactly together. She and the baby sat in one booth and the husband was alone in the booth behind—at first."

I broke in for clarification. "By the husband, you mean Scott? A blond guy?"

She nodded. "We got a policy of three or more in a big booth, and I hadda tell both of them they couldn't sit there if they was alone. So she says she's waitin' for someone, so I let her stay, but I hadda make him move up to the front where the smaller booths are."

"Did he give you a hard time?" I asked.

"At first, he started to, but then she give him a look could freeze a pancake on a griddle, and he gets up and moves. I remember thinkin' if they was together, why not sit in the same booth, y'know?"

She shifted her gum from one side of her mouth to the other, revealing the chipped tooth that gave her a rakish, motorcycle mama look. "But he went quiet, I'll say that for him," she went on. "Then this other couple come in and sat with her. They didn't wanna order nothin' at first, but I told them they couldn't stay without they bought something."

"When was this?" Artie asked.

"Two, three nights before she was killed," Sonia said. "Let me think. I worked Monday, but not— No, it was Wednesday, Wednesday about seven-thirty."

Amber died on Friday night. That Wednesday she was in Surrogate's Court indignantly rejecting the notion that she wanted money in return for her baby. Yet that night she'd sat in a booth at Friendly's discussing an offer from yet another set of would-be parents.

"Did they seem—" I began, then broke off as I searched for words. Did they seem what? Like a couple desperate enough for a baby to buy it in the mall?

She shrugged. "I didn't notice much," she said apologetically. "It was a busy night and I had a boothful of teenagers hasslin' me for more water, more napkins. Makin' assholes outa themselves, y'know."

"Assholes," Ma repeated with her vacant grin.

"You're a pistol, Ma," Sonia said without turning her head. Then she frowned in thought and added, "When I brought their sundaes, the girl pointed at the guy in the booth and said something about him being the father. Which made me even more curious, y'know, like why he wasn't sitting with her if he was the father of her baby. But then I started thinkin' maybe he was the father but he wouldn't admit it, wouldn't pay support or nothin'. I know a little something about that," she went on, "since the father of my twins done the same thing sixteen years ago."

"Asshole," Ma pronounced.

"You got that right, Ma," Sonia agreed without turning her head. "Course I don't say that to the twins," she said in a lowered voice. "Don't wanna make them feel bad about their dad, even if he is what Ma says he is.''

"Did the guy in the booth ever talk to the couple?" I asked. "Did he come back to where they were sitting?''

She shook her head. "Not then," she said. "After the couple left, the guy gets up and goes back to where she's sitting and slides into that booth.''

"Back to the last time you saw Amber," Artie prompted. "Did the same thing happen, with the two different booths?''

"No," the waitress replied. "The woman come in with her husband and the baby and they all sat together. Then a middle-aged guy comes in and sits with them.''

"Josh Greenspan," I said, thinking aloud.

Sonia nodded. "Yeah," she agreed. "I seen him on channel five news. Course,'' she went on, leaning toward us as though to shield her mother from the sordid side of life, "if I'd a known what that little bitch was up to with that baby, I'd a taken and shoved an ice cream scoop up her you-know-what.''

I wasn't at all sure what good that would have done, but I applauded the sentiment with an empathetic nod. "He was real intense, the guy," she explained. "He didn't want to order nothin' either, but I knew Tolliver would give me a hard time if I let people sit in the booth without payin'. He was different from the other couple, though—he couldn't take his eyes off that baby. I started thinkin' maybe he was the grandpa, y'know, like maybe he was the girl's father and he was there to make the guy pay support.''

Sonia shook her head; her hair, which had been badly streaked, was growing out dark roots. She turned to Artie and asked, her tone plaintive, "You sure you don't know nobody at *A Current Affair*?''

"*A Current Affair*," Ma Rogoff repeated with a sage nod.

CHAPTER THIRTEEN

W_e walked back to the Chevy in silence; before Artie turned the key in the ignition, he pulled out his pocket phone and talked to someone at the paper. Then he turned to me.

"Kyle and Donna Cheney live in Prohibition Park," Artie said, putting the car into gear.

"Where?" I had a Staten Island map open on my lap, but that name appeared nowhere.

"It's called Westerleigh now," my companion explained with a smug little smile. "But when it was built in the twenties, the streets were named after dry states and anti-booze politicians. Hence Prohibition Park."

"You are just a fund of Staten Island trivia."

"Hey, when my editor assigned me to this beat, she told me to learn everything I could about this borough, and by God—"

He broke off as we reached the corner of an unmarked

street. "Where the hell are we?"

I consulted the map. "Take a right, then a left," I ordered, a smug smile of my own playing around my lips.

Kyle and Donna Cheney lived on a wide street with large, lush yards, attached garages, and houses that looked lived in. As we drove toward the split-level stone-and-white house, Artie said, "This one's mine, Counselor. I doubt these people would be thrilled to spill their guts to a lawyer."

"Whereas they'll be happy to see themselves quoted in your paper as would-be baby-buyers," I countered. But as we walked toward the house, I stayed back, letting Artie make the moves. He walked toward the door and rang the bell.

The door was answered by a short woman with dark hair and a pale face. She gave Artie a wary once-over and asked in a gruff tone what he wanted.

"Mrs. Cheney?" he began. "I'm sorry to disturb you like this. I'm a reporter for the—"

"Go away. I don't want to talk to you people." Her voice rose.

I stepped forward and spoke into the screen door. "I'm not with the press," I called, holding up a conciliatory hand.

"I don't care who you are or what you want," she shot back. "I don't want to talk to anyone about what happened to that girl. It's nothing to do with me or my family, an I don't want anyone coming around here and botherin us."

"Mrs. Cheney, all I want is to—" I wasn't quite sure what I wanted, but it seemed important to find out what she had to say about my client. And maybe she and her husband hadn't decided against dealing with Amber; maybe they'd been at the mall the night she was killed.

"I don't care what you want," she shouted, her voice rising into a screech. A man next door called through his screened window, "You need some help there, Donna?

Want I should call the cops?''

She shook her head. "Thanks, Bernie," she called back, "but they were just leaving." She said the words with a pointed little smile of triumph, knowing we had no choice but to obey.

A white van with a rosebush painted on the side pulled into the driveway; the motto on the side was "Cheney Nursery and Landscaping. Our Business Is Growing."

A tall, thin man with sandy hair and a nervous face stepped out of the van and strode toward Artie and me.

"What's going on here?" he demanded.

"Are you Kyle Cheney?" I said before Artie could speak.

He nodded. His wife called out, "They're from the newspapers. Don't talk to them."

"I'm not a reporter," I clarified. "I'm a lawyer. I represented Amber Lundquist."

"Oh, my God," Kyle said. "We didn't— That is, I—" He clamped his thin lips and started again.

"My wife and I have nothing to say. We never paid Amber any money, and the last time we saw her was Wednesday night. So please leave us alone."

I turned toward Artie's car, but the boy reporter was made of sterner stuff. "You already have one adopted child, named Aaron, right?" He didn't wait for an answer, but plowed ahead. "And you wanted another one, so you met Amber at the—"

Kyle Cheney's face, which was ruddy and marked with severe acne scars, paled. He took a step forward, clenched his sinewy hands into fists, and said, "Get the hell away from me and my family."

Artie took one last shot. "If you won't talk to me," he said, "I'll have to get my facts from other people. Don't you want the chance to tell your side of the story?"

"No," Kyle said. He turned and strode toward his house, where his wife waited inside, barricaded behind a screen door.

Artie shrugged, then opened his car door and motioned for me to get in beside him.

"Looks like not everybody wants to get on *A Current Affair*," I remarked, recalling Sonia Rogoff's wistful ambition.

"Can't win 'em all," Artie replied in a cheerful tone. "Besides, I can always say they refused to talk to me, make that sound like they must have something to hide."

I opened my mouth to protest that this was a pretty low trick, then recalled that I'd done the same to people taking the witness stand at a trial. When it came to treating people decently, there wasn't much to choose between Artie's job and mine.

We drove toward Richmond Road. There were blue-and-white police cars on the side of the road where Travis Avenue began. It was the turnoff that led to the Davis Wildlife Refuge, where Amber's body had been recovered. I studied the cars while Artie negotiated the intersection. No ambulance, no morgue wagon, no Crime Scene Unit.

No body. No baby. Thank God.

Artie took a right off Richmond Road and pulled into the undeveloped parking area. Aronson stood in a little knot of men and women. Something was up—but what?

"Find something, Detective?" Artie shouted. He was only halfway out of the car, but the questions poured from his mouth. He slammed the door behind him and raced toward the blue-and-white cars parked in the mud-rutted lot.

"What is this place?" I asked no one in particular. It wasn't the Davis Wildlife Refuge. It was too close to the main road for that, and it had no official Parks Department insignia.

A green-uniformed Parkie replied, "It's the Staten Island Native Plant Center. Part of the Greenbelt."

The place Jerry Califana claimed Amber had told him to wait for her.

I walked across the muddy ruts, which were not as dry

as they looked at first glance, trying not to think about the effect on my shoes.

Aronson came straight to the point. "You knew she had a car?"

"A car?" I echoed.

"Yeah, a car. Did you know she had one?"

"You mean Scott's car?"

"No, I mean a car in her own name," the detective replied, holding onto his patience with visible difficulty. "Did she ever come to see you in a car, or give any other evidence of car ownership?"

"No," I said, beginning to see where this line of questioning could be leading. "You mean you found her car? The one she was planning to take off in?"

"What do you know about that?" Aronson's thick eyebrows knotted, and he glared at me, suspicion in every line of his face.

I glanced at the other cops with Aronson, as if hoping to enlist their support. "Detective, she wasn't going to walk to Kansas City or Baltimore. If she ditched Scott on purpose, which it looks like she did, then she either went with an accomplice or she had her own car ready somewhere. It stands to reason."

Aronson stood back and pointed to a white hatchback flecked with mud. "Can you identify this vehicle?"

I stifled a smile at his police-report style. "No," I said. "I've never seen it before."

He shook his head back and forth. He drew in a breath and expelled it through pursed lips, a silent whistle. He looked at me as though trying to decide whether to let me in on a secret. Then he said, "I'm going to inventory this car, Counselor. I want you to stand by in case you can identify whatever we find inside."

The words hung in the air; I wondered what he expected me to say. Did he think I'd make Constitutional objections to his search? If Amber had been alive, I'd have raised holy hell and he knew it, but dead clients have little interest in the Fourth Amendment. And with a missing baby, any objections I might have made to the search would be quickly overruled in the name of what the courts call exigent circumstances.

Besides, he didn't want to know what was in that car any more urgently than I did.

The trunk held nothing I couldn't have predicted: Baby stuff and more baby stuff: a diaper bag, a duffel with little cotton outfits and what looked like dozens of doll-sized white socks, a giant box of Pampers, one Sportsac tote with clothes Amber herself might have worn, an extra pair of sneakers—

Sneakers. Amber's feet had been bare; a sandal had been found nearby. Surely if she'd expected to go hiking into the swamp, she'd have changed her shoes. Which didn't mean much; obviously she hadn't walked voluntarily to her death.

There was nothing visible to the naked eye in the front or backseats—typical of a New York car, even on Staten Island. You didn't leave even a faded T-shirt on the floor in case a thief decided it might cover something of value and break your car window. Even if nothing was stolen, the cost of window replacement was high enough to cause New Yorkers to put "No Radio" signs in their windows. Urban legend had it that one pissed-off burglar broke the window anyway and left his own sign reading "Then get one, sucker."

Aronson stood back while another cop pried open the glove compartment. Wearing surgical gloves to protect whatever prints could be found, he pulled out a sheaf of documents.

The top one was a death certificate for Laura Marie Califana.

Artie's story in Monday's paper was entitled "Heartbreak Kid." It wasn't on the front page, but it was the first thing that hit your eye on page three, with a big picture of the cops dragging the body out of the swamp.

Dorinda gave me a quizzical look as she brought over my French cruller; the only time I read newspapers is when one of my clients makes the headlines. Which, fortunately, doesn't happen often.

I read the first paragraph, holding the paper closer to my face than I liked to admit I needed to.

"She even sent me an early Mother's Day card," mourned Carla Stebbins, would-be adoptive mother of the unborn child carried by Amber Lundquist, 25, whose drowned body was found in a Staten Island swamp Tuesday night. Stebbins and her husband Timothy live in the Mission Hills district of Kansas City; they say they paid Amber over $5,000 in the expectation that she would choose them as the adoptive parents of her baby.

Little did they know that Amber made the same promise to Josh and Ellie Greenspan of Brooklyn Heights and to Rita and Mark Tripp of Baltimore.

"I always hated Mother's Day before," Carla said, wiping a tear from her eye. "It was a day I'd spend in a deep depression, thinking about the baby I couldn't have. Until this year, until Amber called our 800 number and told us about her baby."

800 number? Call 1-800-INFANTS. Had there been an 800 number in the Greenspans' ad in the *Dreamchild* newsletter?— Or had Josh decided to skip it since he knew the only birth mother he wanted was the one carrying his child?

Artie didn't say. I read through more heartbreak, with quotes from the Baltimore couple, echoing the sense of loss and betrayal. I was beginning to feel annoyed; where was the hard news? Where was something I didn't know?

Then I came to the last paragraphs:

. . . legal fees, and other expenses related to interstate adoptions. "My lawyer can help us," Amber is quoted as telling the Stebbins family, "but she doesn't come cheap."

Ms. Lundquist was represented by Cassandra Jameson, of Brooklyn. Ms. Jameson denies that she had knowledge of her client's activities.

I was shaking when I lowered the paper into my lap.

Damn Artie Bloom! I'd spent the day tromping around Staten Island with him, playing Lois Lane to his Clark Kent, only to have him screw me in print.

I could sue his ass off. I would sue his ass off. I'd drag him into court so fast his head would—

And what would that get me? More publicity, more exposure. More people thinking that where the smoke got this thick, there had to be fire.

The words were true; I was Amber's lawyer. But putting that fact directly after Amber's alleged boast that her lawyer—conveniently identified as female—didn't come cheap was tantamount to accusing me of brokering babies.

But was it libelous? Even though the last time I'd heard the word *libel* was in my first-year Torts class, I knew that what Artie had done was perfectly within his paper's legal rights.

Still, I ate the cruller in three huge bites, washed it down with the last of my iced coffee, and raced upstairs to get a second legal opinion. Fool for a client, and all that.

Matt Riordan answered on the second ring. He was on his way to federal court to handle one of his more notorious clients—I could have read all about it on page five of Artie's paper—but he confirmed my suspicion that bringing suit would be the worst option I could exercise.

"But the article does raise an interesting point," he went on, in his mellow courtroom voice. "Could this expensive lawyer be your friend Marla?"

That thought would have crossed my mind eventually, I told myself.

"But then why would she bring me in as Amber's lawyer?"

"Why did she say she brought you in?"

"Nice cross-examination technique," I said approvingly. "She said it was because the judge insisted that Amber have her own lawyer."

"Assuming that's true," Riordan said, "it might mean the judge had reason to suspect Marla was doing something that wasn't kosher."

"Good point. But she never said anything to me about it. She meaning Judge Feinberg, not Marla," I explained. Seeing my name in the paper had unhinged me; I was usually more articulate than this, even in the morning.

"The judge wouldn't necessarily put it on the record," Matt pointed out. Then he added, "Look what having you in the case has done for her."

"Done for who?" I said ungrammatically. "Marla? What do you— Oh."

I stopped. "I get it. I think."

"Think about it, Cass," he urged, warming to his theory. "Suppose Marla was in this scam with Amber from the beginning. Suppose Marla taught your client how to play the legal system so that she'd get the baby back. Then when everything hits the fan, who's the attorney of record?"

I gave him the answer he wanted. "Me," I said. "Marla set me up to hold the bag. While she scoops in the cash and kills Amber?" I didn't wait for a reply, so caught up was I in this new, horrifying, and perversely satisfying scenario.

"Which means the lawyer Amber mentioned to the Kansas City couple isn't me but Marla." I thought about that for a minute. "She just tells the couple there's a new lawyer in the case in order to squeeze more cash out of them."

"It's only a theory," Matt Riordan said, the clotted-cream complacency in his tone undercutting the pose of humility.

The phone gave an all-too-familiar click; one of us was being summoned by Call Waiting. We said hasty good-byes and I switched to the other call. It took a minute to switch gears, to realize I was hearing from a prospective client.

"... saw your name in the newspaper," the diffident male voice said. He talked so low I could hardly hear him, as though he were sneaking a call to his mistress with his wife in the other room.

"My wife and I—" he began, then choked and started again. "That is, we both wanted—we tried everything, and now the agency says it's a three-year wait at least. We just—we can't wait three years, Ms. Jameson." He was near tears, and I could hear a snuffling sound in the background.

"Now, honey," he murmured; it took a moment for me to realize I wasn't honey, that his wife was sobbing next to him.

It took another moment for me to realize what this call was about.

They think I can buy them a baby.

It hit me like a wet snowball, sending a cold trickle down my neck in spite of the balmy spring weather.

I was so shocked I just stood there, holding the phone away from my ear. Then I slammed it down; only later did I realize how rude and insensitive I'd been.

But how do you find words to tell people you're not what they think you are, when what they think is that you're a monster and a savior rolled into one?

CHAPTER FOURTEEN

I got back to my office around six o'clock, having spent a long day in court trying to pretend interest in my other cases. Marvella Jackman was just covering her word processor with a plastic shroud. "There's a girl wants to see you, Ms. Jameson," she said in her West Indian lilt. "Said she was from that group home where the other one come from." The other one was Amber, so this must be—

"Her name is Lisa, and she's waiting downstairs at the Morning Glory."

Lisa. I had a quick vision of a dumpy, lumpy teenager in a pink smock top, her swollen feet jammed into flip-flops, her doglike eyes riveted on Doc Scanlon. Unformed, without personality or flavor or individuality, she seemed to represent a mental construct called "teen mother."

What was she like when she wasn't pregnant?

Tattooed. She was tattooed. And pierced. Five rings in

each ear, a golden knob on one side of her nose, and a tasteful little hoop decorating one plucked eyebrow. A black leather vest with nothing underneath and a little black skirt that emphasized rather than hid the baby fat chubbiness of her thighs. Her legs ended in black combat boots with little white socks peeking over the high tops.

"Lisa?" The simple greeting turned from statement of fact into question as I tried to connect this punk queen with the pink blob I remembered from the group home.

"Ms. Jameson," she replied, her voice still the high childlike near-whine I recalled. She plopped into one of my red leather client chairs; I tried not to think what it would feel like on bare skin after about five minutes.

"I'm really glad you're here," I began. "I have some questions I'd like to ask you."

"Sure," the girl said, moving her gum from one side of her mouth to the other. It was black gum, which went with the polish on her bitten nails. She looked like Vampira's teenage sister.

"But first," she continued, "I want to ask you to be my lawyer. After what you did for Amber—"

"What I did for Amber?" I cut in. "Amber's dead, Lisa. I don't know what you mean."

"I mean you got her baby back. Before she died. I been thinking." Lisa shifted the gum one more time and put her hand on the corner of my desk. "I want to give my baby a good home. I want to raise her myself. I want to change my mind."

I raised my eyes to heaven. First phone calls from desperate parents who thought I could buy them a baby, now this.

"Lisa, I—" I paused and looked into the girl's eyes. They were a watery blue and had a childlike innocence underneath the heavy eyeliner and mascara. "How old are you?"

She stiffened, took the defensive stance of somebody

who's been asked a question she doesn't want to answer. "Seventeen," she replied.

I shook my head. "Not how old you're going to be someday. Now."

"Fifteen." Lowered eyes, something that might have been a blush under brown-tinged makeup. "But that doesn't mean I can't be a good mom," she challenged.

I looked across the desk at the three-colored dragon winding along her arm, from elbow to bare shoulder, at the rose tattoo on her wrist, at the baroque design that circled the other arm like a bracelet. "How did you hide those at the home?" I asked.

She tossed off a shrug. "Oh, most of these are temporary," she replied. "I just want to see how they look before I get them done for good. Besides," she added wistfully, "I can't afford anything this fancy right now. I'm saving up for the dragon."

"And the piercings?"

Another shrug. "I just took out all the rings." She picked up a strand of mouse-colored hair and twirled it around a finger. "That Mrs. B. made me take them out," she added. "The bitch."

"You didn't like her?"

"She was mean," Lisa replied. "She made all kinda remarks about the way I looked and made me wear this dorky polyester shit from the mall. So I'd look 'respectable' when the adoptive parents came to visit."

"Gotta admit," I said, "you fooled me."

Lisa grinned. Her teeth were spaced widely apart. "I guess I fooled them, too," she agreed. "Like they really didn't know I came from Mount Loretto."

"Mount Loretto?" I echoed.

She nodded. "Sure. Me and most of the other girls at Mrs. B.'s came from there. Doc Scanlon used to come around Mount Loretto once a week to give us checkups, and if someone was knocked up, he'd talk about adoption and set them up with a couple who'd pay their expenses. I

knew a bunch of girls who gave up their babies, so when
Eddie and me got into trouble, I told Doc right away. I
knew he'd take care of me.''

"Eddie's the father of your child?''

"Uh-huh. And at first I agreed with Doc that giving the
baby up made sense on account of Eddie's got another year
on his sentence, but now—''

"Sentence?'' I asked it like a question, but somewhere
down deep I was less than surprised.

"Yeah. He's doing a split bit for burglary. Two to six.
He'll be out next year if he don't stab a guard or something.''

"I take it he wasn't in jail when you—''

"Course not. He was out on bail. But then his Legal Aid
made him plead guilty. So I decided Doc was right and I
should give up the baby on account of I couldn't raise her
by myself. But now I been thinking it over and—''

She wanted to talk about now, but I had questions about
then.

"How did the adoptive parents react when you told them
the father of your baby was in jail?'' Again I knew what
the answer had to be, but I wanted this artless child to say
it in her own words.

"Oh, Doc took care of that. He said I should tell them
I didn't know who the father was, that it could have been
five or six guys. So I put down these guys from school,
and I stuck Eddie's name in the middle and Doc had Ms.
Hennessey send them all papers to sign giving up their right
to the baby just in case they were the fathers. I don't think
she told the couple Eddie was in jail.''

I was willing to bet she hadn't. Even my limited experience in the world of adoption had taught me that adoptive
parents cherish a fond hope that the father of their unborn
child is a nuclear physicist with a yen for teenagers. If they
can't have a graduate-student mom who had a brief but
passionate fling with a professor, they can at least dream
of a birth father who isn't serving time. And burying the

true father in a list of innocuous possibles was a good way of letting the adopters conjure up a fantasy of teen love between basically good kids who made a mistake.

"So most of the girls at Mrs. B's came from Mount Loretto? What about the others?"

"Some of them had boyfriends at Arthur Kill," Lisa said. I nodded; if Doc found some of his brood cows at Mount Loretto, it made sense that the studs would be at Arthur Kill Correctional Facility.

"Doc used to work over there, too. He'd get talking with the guys, find out if they had pregnant girlfriends—white girlfriends—and then offer to set them up with a nice deal. That's how some of the older girls came to the house."

"I suppose the adoptive parents didn't know about those fathers either," I said.

"I dunno," Lisa replied. "Listen," she said, leaning forward, "I really want you to help me get my baby back. I talked to a welfare caseworker, and she says I can get money for an apartment and everything just as soon as I get custody."

I ran a hasty mental check: had I asked all the questions I could reasonably expect an answer to, or was there something else I should dig for before I told Lisa I couldn't help her recover her baby?

Her response was typical teenager. She hurled herself out of the red leather chair and shouted, "You fucking bitch. You tellin' me I can't be a good mother?" She lunged at me, her heavily ringed fingers nearing my face.

For a moment I thought she was going to hit me. For a moment I almost wanted her to. I wanted to feel a fist in my face, to let someone punish me for the suffering I'd caused, however inadvertently. But then she stopped herself and gave me a contemptuous look that stripped me naked. "I bet if I wanted to sell my baby, you'd get her back for me, wouldn't you, bitch? Wouldn't you?"

Before I could answer, she flung herself out the door. I

fell into the chair behind my desk and breathed heavily for a minute or two.

It was one of those Village apartments that started out as a student share—two bedrooms, four female law students. I remembered study sessions with huge vats of spaghetti cooked by Angela Romanelli, the femme fatale of our class. We'd scarf down pasta and shoot legal questions at one another until we felt ready to face Professor Lerner's Torts class in the morning. Even though NYU had a large number of women students for its time, we felt the need to band together, to support one another in our assault on the citadel of the male-dominated profession we were determined to conquer.

Now the apartment was Marla's alone. The bare-plank bookshelves supported on cinder blocks had been replaced by walnut-and-black wall units, but the oversized law texts were still there: the blue Crim Law book, the brown Torts book—huge, heavy volumes filled with outdated law. The giant pillows stacked in the corner had gone the way of the bookshelves; there was now a Laura Ashley love seat covered in a Chinese red fabric with tiny flowers. Matching Chinese red mini-blinds adorned the casement windows. A tasteful Matisse print hung over the sofa; once the walls had boasted the finest collection of feminist posters on the Eastern seaboard. There were fewer candles.

"Jeez, Marla," I said, reverting to my student self as I looked around at a place where I'd been young, "how long's it been?"

She shrugged. "Dunno," she replied. "Were you here for the party I gave when Angela made partner at—"

"Did she?" I asked delightedly. "Make partner?"

"I guess you weren't," Marla said. "I thought I invited you, but maybe you were out of town or something."

"I can't believe I didn't know she made partner, though," I mused. "But then we haven't seen much of each other. Wall Street and Legal Aid don't socialize after law school."

"No, you Legal Aid types are too snobbish," she retorted. "Too busy saving the world to have time for those of us who just want to make a living."

Typical Marla, she swept out of the living room into the kitchen on this note, cutting off my chance to rebut. I plopped onto the love seat and noted that it concealed a hidden bed; it was hard as a rock.

"Want something to drink?" she called.

"Sure," I called back. "Can I use your bathroom first?"

"You remember where it is." Statement, not requiring a reply.

I walked down the cramped corridor that connected the living room with the two bedrooms. The one Angela and Becky used to share was now a study, with the usual paper-strewn desk and battered file cabinets. I smiled, noting that the feminist posters had found a museum in here; they were curling at the edges and sported torn spots where they'd been taped several times too often, but at least they hadn't been junked.

It was the second bedroom that stopped me cold. I remembered it with two single mattresses on the floor, one for Marla and one for Susan Whatever-Her-Name-Was from New Hampshire—Indian print throws on the beds, more bookshelves made out of salvaged building materials, Lava Lamps, psychedelic rock posters, woven baskets the size of baby carriages, a bong and cigarette papers next to a cigar box full of badly rolled joints.

Now it was a preteen girl's fantasy bedroom. White eyelet swathed the bed from dust ruffle to sham pillows piled in a heap at the head. The bed itself was a brass curlicued affair, and the curtains at the window repeated the white eyelet motif. On the walls were framed posters similar to the ones at Marla's office. A primary-color Winnie the Pooh poster showed the famous bear floating in the air, holding a balloon. On the other wall Ratty and Mole and Mr. Toad walked arm in arm along a country lane. Baby pictures and framed valentines completed the decor.

I hadn't known Marla had a daughter.

I said as much when I returned to the living room, ready to take in more liquid after using the bathroom.

"Daughter?" she said blankly. "What do you mean?"

"The bedroom," I said, beginning to think I'd made a huge mistake. "I couldn't help noticing—"

"That's my bedroom," Marla replied, her eyes narrowing. "I don't know what makes you think—"

"I'm sorry," I said, blushing furiously. "I didn't mean—"

I stumbled around, trying to salvage the situation and knowing it was impossible. No matter what I said, the damage was done.

Even as I backtracked and explained, the feeling stayed with me that this was not the bedroom of a forty-something woman. It was presexual, virginal, untouched.

I could not imagine making love to a man in such a room.

Did Marla?

I wasn't going to make the mistake of asking that question. But there were others I was determined to get answers to, others I could no longer afford to refrain from putting to my old friend.

"Why did you really want me in this case?" I perched on the edge of the sofa and reached for the Scotch-rocks Marla handed me in a heavy, hand-blown glass.

"I didn't," Marla said. I knew her well enough to give a tiny nod of approval for the overly blunt answer. It was supposed to shock and wound me, to knock me off-balance so I'd be less able to follow up.

"So who did?" Before Marla could open her mouth, I added, "And don't tell me it was Feinberg. That horse expired some time back."

"Amber," she said. Her gray eyes bored into mine. "The little bitch started hassling me about having her own lawyer. She wouldn't tell me why, just made it clear that it was a deal-breaker. And Josh was so hot for this baby and no other—I swear, Cass, I had no idea why at the time.''

The gray eyes took on a guileless note of sheer, misunderstood innocence that took me aback. It was so unlike Marla, who must have forsworn feminine wiles at the age of six.

''I should have suspected,'' she went on, her mouth twisting as though the lemon peel in her martini had soured her mouth. ''I should have realized only a man who thought his magic sperm had done the deed would be that crazy. Hell,'' she went on, picking up the cigarette in a ceramic ashtray and taking a long drag, ''I knew the whole story about how he fought adoption, insisted that Ellie go through every quack procedure in the book. I should have known the conversion was too quick, too complete, to be for real.''

I sat back on the sofa and regarded my old friend. She was wearing Indian silk pajamas; Persian slippers with upturned toes adorned her wide, small feet. Sitting on the overstuffed ottoman, smoking, she resembled the caterpillar in *Alice in Wonderland.*

''Protesting too much?'' I lifted the glass to my lips and let the Scotch hit my tongue. Cutty Sark, good but not great. But then, Marla was a gin woman and couldn't be expected to understand the mysteries of Scotch.

Marla's lipsticked mouth widened into a smile. She gave a small congratulatory nod and said, ''Josh told me from the beginning. Swore me to secrecy, said Ellie must never know.'' She shook her head. ''Pure soap opera. I told him it was a dangerous situation, that all the cards were in Amber's hands. But he had such a thing about the baby being his.''

She took in a deep drag and let the smoke out in a long, gray stream, then twisted the butt into the ashtray. ''God, men,'' she said.

''What about Doc Scanlon?'' I said, trying to sound casual as I moved the conversation to the topic I really came to discuss. ''How many times have you worked with him?''

She shrugged. ''I don't know. Quite a few, I guess. He

has that group home, he meets a lot of girls through his work at Mount Loretto and—''

''Mount Loretto?'' I cut in. ''Did you know Amber was a Mount Loretto girl?''

She grimaced and reached for another cigarette from the inlaid wooden box on the coffee table. ''I do now,'' she said grimly. ''She not only lied, she produced a fake birth certificate. She was some piece of work, your client.''

''She was my client thanks to you,'' I shot back, then waved away the indignant reply that seemed to be on the way.

''You heard about this Jerry Califana?'' I asked. ''Amber's ex-husband?''

''The guy who says Amber sold his baby? God, what a pathetic delusion.''

''Is it a delusion? If Amber faked her birth certificate, maybe she and Doc Scanlon faked her baby's death certificate five years ago. Why couldn't—''

Marla rose from the ottoman; cigarette in hand, she began to pace. The Persian slippers made little scuffing sounds on the parquet floor.

''He wouldn't,'' she said flatly. ''Doc wouldn't do a thing like that.''

''Why not?'' I shot back. ''Because he's a saint, or because there wouldn't be enough money in it for him?''

Another thought struck me. ''Were you working with him back then? Could you have done the adoption for whoever ended up with Amber's baby?''

''Nobody ended up with Amber's baby,'' she retorted. ''The poor kid's dead and buried.''

She took in another long drag and looked toward the window. Little buds were starting on the tree in back; baby leaves poked out from near-bare branches. In the yard next over, a weeping cherry tree drooped pink-dotted branches like a woman sobbing.

''I shouldn't tell you this,'' Marla mumbled. ''Attorney-client privilege. But I'll say this much: Doc came to me when Amber's baby died. He was afraid she and that husband were going to sue for malpractice. Now does that sound like a man who faked a death?''

I shook my head. "What about the Mount Loretto connection?" I persisted. "Did Doc meet Amber there before her marriage?''

"What if he did?''

"I'll take that as a yes," I said. I finished the last of the Scotch, letting it burn my tongue and then swirling an ice cube in my mouth to cool myself.

"How many other prospective birth mothers did Doc find at the orphanage?''

"What do you mean by—''

"I talked to Lisa," I cut in. "You remember Lisa, from the group home. She says Doc trolls for babies at Mount Loretto, at Arthur Kill, at—''

Marla gave a contemptuous shrug. "What if he does? The girls are old enough to sign a consent form.''

Something in the belligerent stance told me Marla was hiding something.

"Are they?" I persisted. "Are all of them old enough, or are some of your little brood cows still in foster care? Don't you need Family Court approval before a foster child can give her baby up for adoption?''

"Don't try teaching me the law, Cassie," Marla countered. "I've been doing this work for fifteen years now, and I—''

"Why?" I cut in, suddenly realizing that was the question I wanted answered above all others. "Why did you specialize in adoption law?''

She stiffened. She stood there in her sky-blue-trimmed-with-silver pajamas, her absurd slippers on her feet, and gazed at me with the look of a deer about to be struck by a moving van. Her gray eyes went blank; her face sagged.

She lowered herself onto the ottoman and faced me. Her voice went from strident to husky-soft as she said, "I was adopted.''

CHAPTER FIFTEEN

It fell into place. I'd met her parents at our law school graduation; they seemed tiny, birdlike people next to her broad-shouldered bulk, but I put that down to the vagaries of genetics. This revelation explained her deep commitment to the adoption process, her choice of adoption as a specialty.

"My parents were good to me," she said fiercely, as though I'd accused them. "They never made me feel different or unloved. I liked being adopted, I liked being chosen instead of coming into a family by accident."

"I could see that," I said. I was trying to tread cautiously, aware I was about to hear more than I'd bargained for.

"It started when I was eight," she went on. Perched on the ottoman, one leg underneath her and the other swinging at her side, she now looked like a little girl dressed up for Halloween.

"At first, it was just this woman who'd sit in her car and watch me at the playground. I asked my parents about her, and they told me to report to the teacher if I saw her again. The next time, she came out of her car, walked up to me— I was sitting on a swing—and told me she was my real mother and she'd come to take me home."

"Jesus," was all I could say.

"I screamed and cried and said I already had a real mother and a real home. But she didn't care; she said I'd learn to love her because we had the same blood in our veins." Her last words reeked of sarcasm.

"She got my name and address from one of the social workers," Marla went on, her tone deliberately flat. "She wasn't supposed to know where I was, things were very secret in those days, but the social worker was new and she believed in things being more open, so she gave in and told my birth mother where to find me."

"That must have been a horrible experience," I said.

"It was only the beginning," Marla replied. She reached for a cigarette; her hand shook as she struck the match to light it. "My parents went to court, got a restraining order against her, but she still didn't stop. She stalked me at school, followed me to church, brought a petition for return of custody—she made my life hell. At one point, a Family Court judge actually made me visit with her even though I cried in court and said I didn't want to. I visited every other Sunday for a year before the judge finally realized she was crazy as a bedbug; she'd been telling me over and over again how if she couldn't take me home, I'd be better off dead."

"My God. No wonder—" I cut that thought off in a hurry; I'd been about to say, *No wonder your bedroom is a little girl's safe haven.* No wonder you wear armor clothes and keep people at arm's length. No wonder you hate Amber with such a passion.

"Yeah," she echoed, her voice street-tough. "No wonder I'm a bitch on wheels. No wonder I'll do anything to make sure my adoptions stick. I don't want any other child going through what I went through. Children deserve stable homes with parents who want them; they don't deserve to be little prizes for people who couldn't get their lives together when it counted.''

"Marla, I—" I began, then stopped as I realized I didn't really have the words.

She shot me a glance that was pure Marla—aggressive, cynical, taking no prisoners. "If you're about to tell me you feel my pain, you can—"

I laughed. "Hell, no," I replied, knowing now that sympathy was the last thing she wanted. "What I feel is pissed off. How could you think I'd sell a baby, for God's sake? In the first place, I knew absolutely nothing about adoptions until you got me into this."

"When people see the kind of money they can make by selling babies, they tend to learn fast," she replied. Her direct gaze held no apology. "Then when I learned about the marriage to Scott, I figured I knew why she wanted her own lawyer."

"Thanks to Artie Bloom," I said, "everyone in the five boroughs thinks the same thing."

I looked down at my empty glass and considered asking for another Scotch. The first one had been pure heaven; the second would slide down my throat so easily, and then—

And then I'd be too drunk to care who killed Amber or what was happening to my reputation as a lawyer. Not good.

"What about the others?" I said, only half-interested. "Lisa said you told her to name a bunch of guys who could have fathered her child, so the adoptive parents wouldn't know the kid's father was doing time. How often do you—"

"Out," Marla said. She rose from her ottoman like a queen stepping off her throne. She pointed to the door.

"Time to go, Cass," she said, her voice unyielding. "No more questions, no more accusations. Just get out of here."

I went. I walked out the door and down the curved staircase to the bottom of the Village brownstone building I'd occupied in my student days. It was like leaving a piece of my past. A piece that would never be the same; I could never again look at Marla Hennessey without seeing that little Halloween girl and her pure white bedroom.

Where to now? I wanted more on Doc Scanlon. The man Amber called Saint Christopher of the Golden Cradle.

What I hadn't realized at the time was that ''Golden Cradle'' was the nickname adoption people gave to the high-cost agencies that guaranteed perfect white babies for exorbitant fees. Was Doc Scanlon a one-man Golden Cradle? And were his fees more than the law allowed?

I had an idea the former Mrs. Scanlon might have the answers, so I walked to the subway and headed for South Ferry. The boat ride was bracing; the view of the Manhattan skyline spectacular. When I hit the Staten Island side of the bay, I realized I hadn't a clue how to get to Betsy Scanlon's house, but I did know it was near the mall. That meant bus number 44 according to the signs posted over the long corridors leading to the bus terminals.

It was a long, meandering ride that gave me plenty of time to think. Too much time; the entire enterprise seemed crazy now that I was wending my way along totally foreign streets. I asked the driver to let me know when we came to Travis Avenue; he did and I dismounted just short of the mall and the landfill.

I walked along Travis, looking for the side street where Amber and Scott had lived. On one side were neat rows of mustard-colored tract houses; on the other, undeveloped swampland. I passed a small driveway with a chain suspended between two poles. A sign with a Parks Department maple leaf proclaimed the William T. Davis Wildlife Refuge.

Amber's last refuge. The place where her body had been found. And it was mere steps away from the cross street where she'd lived. Why hadn't I realized before how close the refuge parking area was to Betsy Scanlon's house?

Because I'd been in a car before. Because I didn't know the area. Because when I'd come to Betsy's the first time to see Amber, I had no idea she'd be pulled dripping wet from the swamp.

I turned my gaze away from the refuge and walked toward the house occupied by Aunt Betsy's Playroom. Which house was it? They all looked alike; was there anything distinguishing—

The letter C. The screen door had a C on it. Which was odd, now that I knew the house was owned by Betsy Scanlon. Or was it? Was she renting, the C referring to her landlord? Or had she bought the house from people named C, and kept the screen door?

Who cared? The important thing was that once I recalled the C, I found the house. There was, thank God, a light in the window. She was home; I hadn't made this ridiculous trek for nothing.

I rang the bell and waited. The door was opened just a crack by a chunky woman with short blond curls and a face that had once been cute but now showed lines around the mouth and puffs under the eyes. I could picture Betsy Scanlon as a cheerleader, the kind of girl who in my day would have worn pink angora sweaters and put little bows in her teased hair.

"Mrs. Scanlon?" I said, making it a question for purposes of courtesy. I reminded her who I was.

"Oh, yeah, Amber's lawyer," she said without enthusiasm. She opened the door and, instead of inviting me inside, stepped out onto the concrete porch. She closed the door behind her and lowered herself onto the top step. She pulled a pack of cigarettes out of her pants pocket and offered me one.

"I don't smoke in the house," she said, lighting up and enveloping both of us in a cloud of menthol, "on account of I've got kids in there all day."

I nodded. I'd had the entire bus ride to come up with an opening question, and I still didn't have one. "It was terrible about Amber," I began.

"Yeah," she said.

"Were you home that night? Did you see her go out?"

Betsy shook her head and expelled smoke. "No, I was at my brother's, baby-sitting my niece. When I got home, everything was quiet, but then the cops came and started asking questions."

This was getting me nowhere; it was time to throw out a fast one and see what came over the plate. "You and Doc never had children?"

Her blue eyes widened. The lines around her eyes disappeared, but only for a moment. Then she squinted, adding ten years to her face. "No," she said. She turned her face away, looking toward the other houses on the street.

Did I dare ask why? I was pondering how far to push her when she said, "He couldn't. And before you ask, I would have adopted but he wouldn't hear of it."

"Interesting," I said, trying for a noncommittal tone and failing. "He may be the best-known pro-adoption doctor in New York City, and he wouldn't adopt a kid himself."

I looked straight into Betsy's sky-blue eyes, eyes that couldn't possibly be as innocent as they looked, and said, "I wonder if it was because he knew too much. That he couldn't play the denial games other adoptive parents get into."

Her wry answering smile contradicted her baby-doll eyes. "Yeah, I know what you mean. They all want to think their baby's a genius, when the truth is most birth parents are losers who didn't know how to work a condom."

She drew in a long breath and let it out in a heavy sigh. "But I don't think that was it, not really," she said at last.

The baby blues locked onto mine and she said, slowly and deliberately, "He didn't want a child because he wanted to be the child in our marriage. He didn't want my energy, my time, my love given to anyone but him. He's easily the most selfish man I've ever known."

I sat in stunned silence, amazed that she would say these things to a stranger. Or perhaps it was because I was a stranger, and we were sitting in the dark, that the words flowed so freely.

"He seems so charming," I said at last. "Almost boyish."

"The trouble with boyish charm," Betsy replied, her words floating on a stream of menthol, "is that it usually comes attached to a boy.

"Hell," she went on, dropping the cigarette onto the walk and stepping on it with a sneakered foot. "It took me seven years to figure out that just because he made me feel special it didn't mean he thought I really was special. He makes everyone feel that way. His nurse thinks he walks on water, and as for that Mrs. B.—anyone with half an eye can see she'd cut off her right tit if he asked her to."

That was an image I wanted out of my mind at the earliest opportunity. "Would she lie for him?" I asked.

"Like a rug," Betsy said. "Not that I know what she'd have to lie about," she added. "As far as I know, Chris's business is on the up and up."

"There's a guy out in Tottenville who thinks your husband stole his baby," I said, matching her tough-girl tone. "He says Doc faked the baby's death, then put it up for adoption, with the cooperation of the man's wife."

"That's bullshit," Betsy shot back. "Hell, there are enough girls who want to give up their babies. He doesn't have to take one away from someone who wants to keep it."

"Would it make a difference if the wife was Amber?"

"You mean—wait a minute, you mean this baby you think Doc stole was hers?"

I nodded; the blue eyes narrowed. "That changes everything," she said in a low voice.

"You think he might have done it for Amber?" I didn't

want my eagerness to scare her off, but I couldn't suppress it entirely.

"She was a real bitch," Betsy said, as though that said it all. And it did, but not in a way that would be admissible in a court of law. She reached into her pocket for another cigarette, cupped her hand around it to shield it from the spring breeze, and lit it. We sat in silence; I waited for her to stand up, go into the house, and shut the door in my face.

"He was scared," she said at last. Her cigarette had gone out, but her lips still caressed its tubular bulk. "He made a mistake about the diagnosis. He kept talking about how Amber and her husband could sue and wipe him out."

She opened her eyes with a suddenness that resembled a doll being raised from its sleep mode to wakefulness. "In the old days, you had a baby that wasn't quite right, you went to church and lit a candle. Today, you sue the doctor, even if it wasn't his fault. It's like everybody thinks they're entitled to a perfect baby."

"Amber's baby wasn't perfect?"

"I don't know exactly," she said. She turned the full force of her blue eyes on my face, willing me to understand. "Once he said it would be better if the baby died; that the real money came when a child would be disabled for life. I'm not sure what he meant, but—"

"I am," I said grimly. "He was right. A wrongful death action for a baby doesn't bring much in the way of damages, because the court looks at how much the child might have contributed to its parents' support in the future, but a suit for damages when a baby needs lifetime care could run into the millions."

"And the next thing I know, he tells me the baby's dead," Betsy said. "He tried not to sound too relieved, but I could tell it was a big weight off his mind."

"Had Amber talked about suing him?" I asked. "From what I knew about her, if she thought a living baby would bring more money through a lawsuit, she wouldn't have agreed to the phony death scam.''

She screwed up her face in thought; the wrinkles around her mouth and eyes deepened. ''I don't know all the facts,'' she said at last. ''In fact, I don't know any of them. I just know he worried a lot less after Amber's baby died. And he was placing a lot of babies for adoption at the same time, so I suppose he could have given Amber's baby to one of those couples. But it sounds pretty far out,'' she continued, shaking her head.

''This whole thing is pretty far out,'' I replied. ''But the bottom line is, Amber's dead and the baby's missing.''

She turned her head away. ''Yeah,'' she said softly, a touch of regret crossing her face like a cloud streaking across the sun.

''If you remembered Amber from before,'' I asked, ''why did you let her rent your upstairs apartment?''

'' 'Cause Doc asked me to,'' she said. ''God, you don't know what I do because that man asks me to. Sometimes he stops on his way to his office up on Victory and asks me if he can use my washer and dryer. Which means I do his laundry for him while he sees patients. He stops by and borrows my car whenever he feels like it. Sometimes he doesn't even ask: every time I try to get the keys back, he forgets them in his other pants.''

She looked down at her cigarette, suddenly aware there was no smoke coming from it. She relit the tip and took a long, deep drag.

''He talked me into taking Amber as a tenant—of course, he didn't tell me it was her, but I recognized her the minute I saw her. I couldn't believe he took her as a patient after he was so afraid she'd sue him last time she had a baby.''

''You think she blackmailed him?'' I asked bluntly.

She shrugged. ''Could be,'' she replied. ''I wouldn't put it past her. And he's not a guy who'd stand up to that. He's a soft man; he'd give her what she wanted—even if it was something of mine, like the apartment.''

It was getting chilly on the little cement porch; I would

have liked an invitation to step inside. But Betsy needed
her smoke the way I needed oxygen, so I resigned myself
to staying a little longer on the cold hard steps.

"You know when he served me with our divorce papers?" Betsy asked. "I mean, we both wanted the divorce,
I knew it was coming, but—but he walked up to me on
my birthday and handed me the summons. On my birthday!
Can you believe it?"

I shook my head. Boyish Chris Scanlon didn't seem the
type.

"When I burst into tears," Betsy went on, "he gave me
this puzzled look. Like 'what did I do?' He could never
just say something nasty to my face and be done with it;
he had to pretend he was the good guy and just happened
to hurt my feelings."

It was a fascinating sidelight, but it wasn't getting me
anywhere. I turned toward the tall reeds on the other side
of Travis Avenue and said, "I didn't realize you lived so
close to the wildlife refuge."

"Used to be we called it a swamp, couldn't wait till it
was drained and the land put to good use," Betsy said.
"Now the Sierra Club types call it a goddamn wetland and
the damned thing never will be drained." Spending the day
with toddlers seemed to engender in Betsy Scanlon a need
to smoke and swear, to let her bad-girl adult take over after
a day of wiping little noses.

"So you never went over there, never walked around the
nature preserve," I persisted.

"Nature preserve, my butt," Betsy replied with a snort
of derision. "It's a swamp. What's to see? Weeds as high
as a second-story window, squishy grass under your feet, a
few mangy old birds. Hell, no, I never went in there, and
neither did anyone else in the neighborhood. Just a bunch
of fairies from Manhattan, wearing hiking shorts, that's the
only people ever went in there."

It took me a moment to dislodge my mind from an image

of Tinker Bell wearing LL Bean shorts and little tiny hiking boots, but I managed it.

"What about when you were a kid?" I prompted. "A place like that would have been a kid's paradise where I came from."

But Betsy, I decided, hadn't been a kid the same way I had. Her happiest days would have been spent, not exploring the undeveloped land near her house, but playing dress-up or serving tea to her dolls. She had, in short, been a girly kind of girl, and the tall weeds held no fascination for her then or now.

I was halfway to the ferry terminal on the bus before I remembered the most vital piece of information: the color of Betsy Scanlon's car, the one her ex-husband was given to borrowing. It was silver.

CHAPTER SIXTEEN

The more I thought about it, the more I liked it. Amber was killing her golden geese, raking in as much cash as possible before taking off with her baby. She had Jerry meeting her in the parking lot where she'd stashed her getaway car, so why not ask Doc to pick her up at the mall and squeeze a final blackmail payment out of him on the way?

But Doc doesn't want to pay, doesn't want Amber holding her information over his head for the rest of her life, so instead of taking her to the Native Plant Center, where she'd stashed her secret car, he keeps going on Travis Avenue and forces her into the swamp. He uses Betsy's car partly to disguise himself, partly because it's handy, only a block away from the wildlife refuge.

A soft crime for a soft man. A man who might have faked a baby's death, not really for money, but to get himself out of a possible malpractice suit for misdiagnosing a nonexistent heart ailment. A man who might have let Amber's blood pressure climb a little too high during the birth, hoping she'd die of natural causes, but who wouldn't risk his license to make sure she didn't come out of the anesthetic. At the time, Amber's accusation had seemed postnatal paranoia; now it made sense.

The clincher: of all the possible suspects, Doc Scanlon was the only one who could get rid of Baby Adam quickly and quietly. All he had to do was put the kid into the pipeline, take full advantage of his nationwide network of desperate would-be parents, send him out of state for adoption by some couple in Arizona or Oregon.

Did Doc have an alibi for Friday night? How could I find out?

I snapped on my television set the minute I walked into my living room. It was sheer habit; there was nothing I wanted to watch, but I needed to hear a human voice.

I was halfway to the bathroom when the import of the news announcer's words penetrated my consciousness.

"The body of Scott Wylie, missing since Friday, has been found in an undeveloped area near the Fresh Kills landfill on Staten Island," the portentous male voice intoned. "Wylie, aged 24, was wanted for questioning in the drowning death of his wife, Amber, and the disappearance of the child known as Baby Adam."

It was déjà vu all over again as I watched the cops haul yet another body out of the swamp. The only difference was that I didn't have soaked feet. The announcer went on. ". . . exact time of death has not been determined, but Wylie has been in the water for at least two days. Police theorize he was riding his motorcycle along an isolated stretch of Victory Boulevard when he was struck from behind by an unidentified hit-and-run driver. There is as yet no sign of the missing infant."

There was a picture of Scott, a young, hopeful kid with a solemn look and slicked-down short hair. High school

186 • CAROLYN WHEAT

graduation, I assumed. It was a far cry from the earringed punk I'd known.

I sat down hard on the mission rocker.

Scott was dead. And had been for several days.

It was another brick in the case I was building against Doc. I had my eye on Scott for one of the burglaries of Doc's office, with Jerry penciled in for the other one, which meant that Scott knew Amber was blackmailing the good doctor. So in order to get free, Doc had to kill both Amber and Scott.

"Could I speak to Artie Bloom, please?" I asked, trying to sound like a lawyer instead of an outraged citizen who wanted the boy reporter's head on a plate.

"Who may I say is—"

"My name is Cassandra Jameson," I cut in, "and I need to talk to Mr. Bloom about a breaking story."

She took my number and promised to beep Artie. Less than two minutes later, the phone rang.

"I take it you saw the news last night," he began. "All the time we were wondering if Scott grabbed the kid and took off, he was decomposing. I hear the body was a real bloated mess, looked like a zeppelin."

"Charming word picture, Bloom," I said. "But that's not why I called." I explained my theory about Doc, gratified to hear a sharp intake of breath on the other end of the line. The boy reporter was impressed, no doubt about it.

"Counselor, I can't run any of this," he said at last. "My paper isn't going to let me libel a guy like Doc Scanlon without a hell of a lot more than speculation. And that's all you've got here, spec—"

"What time did Scott die?" I cut in. "What did the cops say about the car that hit him? Did they examine the motorcycle yet? What's the cause of—"

A long, heartfelt sigh greeted my questions. "Aronson said the cycle was struck from behind by a vehicle with a high bumper, probably a four-wheel drive. One of those yuppie Jeeps.''

I digested this; so much for Betsy's silver car as the murder weapon.

"Does Doc own a four-wheel?''

Another snort. "A minute ago you had him in the silver car picking up Amber. Now you want him in the four-wheel ramming Scott. You can't have it both ways.''

"Why not? The cops don't have an exact time of death for either Amber or Scott. Why couldn't Doc borrow his ex-wife's car, pick up Amber, take her to the swamp and kill her, then use his own car to run Scott off the road?''

"Why? Why change cars? And how does he know where to find Scott? What does he do, look in his crystal ball and sees Scott zooming along Victory on his cycle?''

"Maybe Scott went home to look for Amber,'' I improvised. "He races around the house, but she's not there. So he leaves, but by now Doc's killed Amber. Doc's in the wildlife refuge parking lot, which fronts Travis Avenue, remember, when he sees the motorcycle racing by; he jumps in his car—''

"Aha,'' Artie said, as he gloated. "Which car? The silver one or the four-wheel?''

"Aha yourself,'' I shot back, inspiration fueling me, "he's got both cars there. He brought his own four-wheel to the parking lot, borrowed Betsy's car in case anyone saw him pick Amber up, and now he jumps into his own car, leaving hers in the lot. After he kills Scott, he comes back, moves his wife's car back to the street near her house, and drives home in his own four-wheel, which you haven't admitted he owns yet, but he must or you wouldn't have let me—''

Artie sighed. "It's a Trooper,'' he admitted. "But why does Amber get into the car with him in the first place?''

"That one's easy, Bloom. Amber's cashing in all her chips. She's ready to ditch Scott and take Baby Adam on the road, but before she goes, she wants every penny she

188 • Carolyn Wheat

can get. So she sets up a meeting with Jerry to sell him information about his dead kid, and she decides to take one last whack at Doc Scanlon. Only she never makes the meeting with Jerry because Doc's more desperate than she realizes."

"The scary thing is this makes sense," Artie said, his tone glum. "I only wish I could print it."

He hung up. I stared at the phone for a minute, realizing too late that I hadn't raked Artie over the coals for the way he'd treated me in print.

The irony of it shot a quick jolt of anger through me. He could hint that I was a baby-seller without a qualm, but he didn't dare make an allegation like that against Saint Christopher of the Golden Cradle without proof.

It was up to me to supply that proof.

He smiled that disarming smile, the one that would have had me making a quick mirror check of my makeup if I'd met him in a bar. He gave a shrug and made a deprecating movement with his mouth.

"You got me," he said. His blue eyes twinkled at me from under slightly lowered lids. Bedroom eyes. Eyes that seduced and promised, eyes that wanted my understanding.

Eyes I didn't trust for a minute.

"You ask me if I deliberately went into Mount Loretto looking for pregnant girls," he repeated. "You wonder if I asked my patients at Arthur Kill Correctional Facility about pregnant girlfriends. The answer is—absolutely." He nodded firmly. He opened his mouth to continue, then stopped as if working on the most effective way to phrase his next words.

"I believe in life," he said simply. "Call me a right-to-lifer, I don't mind. I have never stopped a woman from getting an abortion if that's what she wants," he explained, locking his blue eyes onto my face. "But if I can offer her an alternative, if I can help her find a home for her baby,

I will. I plead guilty, Ms. Jameson. I go where the babies are."

I had come prepared for bluster. I had come expecting to hear a long defense of Doc Scanlon's pro bono work and a heated denial that he used it to round up pregnant teenagers. Instead, he'd copped a plea right off the bat. It left me with at least thirty questions I didn't have to ask.

I hastily shuffled through my mental index cards and decided to up the ante. He was a charmer; how would he deal with outright rudeness?

"You go where the white babies are."

He raised an eyebrow. "I've never denied my services to any woman on account of race," he began. "I have programs for—"

"I'm sure you do," I said, waving away his disclaimer, "but all the girls at the group home were white. Whatever services you give the others, it's the white babies who get placed in the best homes."

He sighed and looked over at the wall where his diplomas hung, framed in shiny dark wood. The other three walls were covered with collages of babies and smiling mothers. There was no way to tell whether the mothers holding infants were birth mothers or adoptive parents. Which might have been the point.

"I can't change the world, Ms. Jameson," he said at last. "I wish, I truly wish, that every child regardless of race or age or physical condition could find a loving home. But should I deny a couple a child because they prefer to adopt within their own race? Should I refuse to help a birth mother make the most difficult decision of her life because she's white?"

This was getting me nowhere. I'd come to Doc's Victory Boulevard office in hopes of confronting him with enough evidence that he'd break down and admit something, anything I could take to the police. So far, the advantage was all on his side; he now knew I was suspicious, but he also knew I didn't have any concrete proof.

"You told Lisa to lie about the father of her child," I said. "You helped her bury the real father in a bunch of names so the adoptive parents wouldn't realize Lisa's boyfriend was doing time. Do you do that kind of thing often?"

His smile was full of Irish charm and his blue eyes twinkled as he replied, "Counselor, I don't draft court papers. The lawyers do."

I gave him a steady look, but a sour taste formed in my mouth as I realized where he was going with this. "Which means that if any of this comes to light, you'll blame it all on Marla Hennessey," I translated.

Good cross-examination requires keeping the witness off-balance. "What about Amber's first child? The one who may or may not have died?"

Doc Scanlon's jolly Saint Nick face assumed a mask of solemnity. "A tragic loss," he said. "The child's father has never accepted his baby's death. At first, he blamed me, threatened to sue for malpractice."

"I know," I said, nodding agreement. "But now he's convinced the baby never died, that you and Amber put it up for adoption."

"Bereaved parents can convince themselves of many things," Doc said. The tiny smile that played around his rosebud mouth, half-hidden by his beard, told me I was getting nowhere fast. He could play this game all afternoon.

"Where were you the night Amber died?"

He opened his mouth to reply, but I cut him off. "And don't tell me you were home watching television. You were seen at the mall." I stared straight into the guileless blue eyes, hoping he wouldn't see the bluff.

"I doubt that, Ms. Jameson," he replied genially. "Since I wasn't there. And neither was my Trooper," he added, his eyes glinting with pleasure at the shock on my face.

"You'll be interested to know that once I heard how Amber's husband died, I insisted the police examine my car. They found no trace of Jamage, no evidence whatsoever that it was involved in an accident. So it couldn't have been the vehicle that struck the young man's motorcycle and forced him off the road.''

Later that night, I wondered if Scott could have gone off the road into the reeds by accident. Sheer coincidence. Nothing whatever to do with the fact that his wife lay underwater not two miles away, in another part of the same wetland preserve. Just another careless motorcyclist riding without a helmet.

''Christ, it was hit-and-run at least, Counselor,'' Artie Bloom said in a tone of disgust. I'd reached Artie at his home number; his paper went to bed at eight-thirty, so he'd already filed whatever story he'd written on the case. ''Aronson said there was a hell of a dent on the back fender of that cycle. Somebody in a four-wheel or a pickup truck clipped him pretty—''

''Pickup? You didn't say pickup before,'' I said accusingly. ''You said four-wheel drive.''

''Something with a high bumper,'' Artie clarified. ''Could have been a Jeep or a van or a light pickup truck. And, in case you were wondering, Josh Greenspan agreed to let the cops examine his Bronco. No chipped paint, no damage.''

''Does Califana's pizza parlor deliver?'' I mused aloud. ''What kind of—''

''Yeah, like he's gonna deliver pizzas in a big red pickup truck. This is Staten Island, not fucking Texas.''

''Which means?''

''Which means he's got a bicycle with a thermal pizza box on the handlebars. I can't see that running Scott Wylie off the ass end of Victory Boulevard, can you?''

I could not. I hung up the phone and looked at the clock. Eleven P.M. Not too late to call an old law school friend, I decided.

I took a leaf from Marla's book of bluntness and began, ''Doc Scanlon says he's not responsible for what lawyers put in affidavits. Which means if push comes to shove, he'll roll over on you so fast—''

"I suppose this colorful language is part of being a criminal lawyer?" Marla interrupted, her tone a meld of sweetness and suspicion. "One problem with being a criminal lawyer is that you tend to see crime everywhere. There's nothing in my affidavits for me to worry about."

"Isn't there?" I countered. "How many of your birth fathers are in jail? How many birth mothers are wards of the State? How many—"

"Cass, you're blowing smoke," Marla cut in. By the way she exhaled, I figured, so was she. I could almost see a blue stream coming out of her disdainful mouth.

The hell of it was, she was right. I was trying to get her to roll over on Doc, to tell me something that would incriminate him, would put him square in the middle of something really illegal, not just borderline sleazy. I was certain there was a lot more iceberg below the tip I'd uncovered.

I switched tactics, pulling out a weapon I probably should have used earlier.

"They're your clients, Marla," I reminded her. "How can you let him get away with it?"

"What are you talking about?"

"Josh and Ellie. If Doc killed Amber, then he knows where Adam is."

Silence on the other end of the line. A pregnant silence, punctuated by the long, drawn-in breath of a smoker pulling the last puff out of a cigarette.

"Go on."

"He's got the connections to place Adam anywhere in the country," I said. "While the cops were grid-searching the swamp, he probably had Baby Adam on a plane to Tennessee, in the arms of a grateful—"

"Cass," Marla interrupted, "I know for a fact Doc hasn't made any placements since Amber's death. None. No local, no interstate. Nada, zip, none. So if that's your big insight into Amber's death, you can forget it."

She clicked the receiver down on her end of the line, leaving me holding a dead telephone.

It was spring; the night was cool and fresh and laden with tomorrow's rain. As I went to bed, a line from e.e. cummings floated into my half-asleep brain:

> all ignorance toboggans into know
> and trudges up to ignorance again:

I hoped to hell my ignorance started tobogganing into know sometime soon.

CHAPTER SEVENTEEN

"That lunch special will kill you dead," Dorinda remarked. She refilled my iced coffee glass and gave my boneless spareribs over pork fried rice a disapproving stare. Normally she didn't allow customers to bring in food from other restaurants, but since I held the mortgage on the brownstone that housed the Morning Glory, she made the occasional exception.

"Look," I said, wiping grease from my lips with a blue napkin, "every once in a while a girl needs cholesterol. It's a fact of biology."

"If you're trying to blame this on menopause," she said with a toss of her head, "I have some wonderful herbal remedies you ought to look into. Black cohosh is—"

"Spare me," I said, raising greasy fingers to the sky. "I'm not a fan of political correctness at the best of times, and when it comes to food—"

She'd plaited her hair into a complicated knot of braids

the color of new rope; the sun poured in through the window and bathed her in a golden halo. Dorinda, goddess of health, turned and poured an iced orange zinger for a weedy-looking man with a toothbrush mustache at the other end of the counter.

She was, of course, right. The spareribs, which had tasted like a little bit of Chinese heaven when I lifted the first one to my lips, were congealing into an inedible mess at the bottom of the aluminum tray. The ones I'd already eaten lay like concrete in my belly. I pushed the dish away and resolved to put more distance between me and the Good Taste Chinese Takeout on Court Street.

"If Doc Scanlon didn't send Adam out of state," I mused aloud, "then where is he?"

I resolutely pushed aside the thought that he was in the swamp. Artie Bloom's confident assertion that Baby Adam was worth too much on the open market to be killed echoed in my head. Whoever murdered Amber and then Scott knew the full retail price of a white baby.

Dorinda cruised past, a pitcher of water in her hand, refilling glasses. "Where would you hide a baby?" I asked.

"Where would you hide a needle?" she countered, her blue eyes widening as she contemplated the question.

"In a haystack?" My voice rose in disbelief. "You're not taking this seriously. I'm trying to—"

"No, not a haystack," my old friend said, "a sewing basket."

"Dorinda, it's 1994. Who the hell has a sewing basket, for God's—"

"I do."

Of course she did. How else would she get appliqués on her vintage aprons; how else would she put oversized decorative buttons on men's tuxedo shirts; how else would she mend the antique blouses she picked up for a song? And where else would she hide a needle?

It was like something out of Edgar Allan Poe. You hide a needle in a sewing basket, among other needles that look just like it. You hide a letter on top of a desk filled with other letters. You hide a baby—

I had it!

I set the iced coffee glass down with a bang and tossed a couple of bills on the counter to cover it, then called out a quick thank-you to a puzzled-looking but pleased Dorinda, and took the steps up to the office two at a time.

I was hoping to catch Mickey and borrow the keys to her car before she took off for the afternoon. She'd been working half days for the past three months; we hadn't seen much of each other since our last conversation about adoption and motherhood.

Marvella Jackman raised an inquisitive eyebrow as I came through the door. It was after two P.M.; I should have been in Part 25 on a drug case.

"Glad you're here, Ms. Jameson," my secretary sang out. There was an odd look of anticipation on her face. "Ms. Dechter call about an hour ago; she's on her way to the hospital. Pains coming three minutes apart now, so—"

"Oh, my God. Mickey's having the baby!"

So obsessed had I become with the missing Adam that my first thought was *She's probably using her car.*

Which left Marvella's. It took a hefty bribe to get her to part with the keys to her ten-year-old Lincoln Town Car, which she polished religiously every weekend right after church, but she finally handed me the bunch.

"I'll be careful," I promised.

"You'd better be, Ms. Jameson," she warned. "Anything happens to that car, I can't be responsible for what my Covington will do." Covington Jackman, a carpenter by trade, had muscles Arnold Schwarzenegger would have envied. I doubted he'd actually harm me physically, but I pocketed the keys with some trepidation.

"Call Judge McGarvey and adjourn my two o'clock," I called as I ran out the door. "Tell him I've got food poisoning."

Which, judging by the way the spareribs were acting in

my stomach, wasn't going to be a complete lie.

I drove Marvella's car along Victory Boulevard, passing Doc Scanlon's office and giving an involuntary backward glance. As if the doctor would somehow sense I was driving past, on my way to discovering where he'd hidden Baby Adam until it was safe to place him with a new adoptive family.

Unless Marla had lied to me about Doc's not placing a child since Amber's death. But after what she'd revealed about herself, I doubted she'd cover for Doc if he'd ripped Baby Adam out of Ellie Greenspan's arms for profit.

Of course he could have shipped the baby out of state last night, or used another lawyer besides Marla to handle the adoption. If he'd done either of those things, I could be on a fool's errand, which was why I hadn't called Detective Aronson before setting out from Brooklyn. I had to have more than a brilliant insight brought on by Dorinda's sewing basket and Edgar Allan Poe. I couldn't see Detective Aronson accepting my purloined baby theory without a struggle.

I eased the huge car into the right lane, turned onto Richmond Avenue, and cut another right just across from Willowbrook Park, heading into the development known as New Springville.

I started the great parking space hunt, not as tricky a proposition on Staten Island as on Manhattan, but still something that took a sharp eye and quick reflexes. I slipped in behind a station wagon and killed the engine, then sat a moment and considered my strategy.

It was at this point that I realized I didn't have a strategy. I had a bedrock-solid belief, a conviction that rang as true as Edgar Allan Poe's bells. And I had the advantage of surprise. Betsy Scanlon was not expecting me to walk up to her door and ask if Baby Adam lay in one of the Sears cribs in the sun room.

That was how you hide a baby: put it in with other babies, in a place where people see children come and go, where one more infant can pass unnoticed. Aunt Betsy's

Playroom was the perfect hiding place for Adam Green-span—and I was all but certain he was taking his afternoon nap with the other little boarders.

My theory was that Betsy was just a caretaker, without a stake in the baby-selling scam. She was hiding Adam for Doc, one more little favor for her ex-husband, like doing his laundry or letting him drive her car to the mall. I doubted she was making a profit.

Why did I believe Betsy wasn't working the scam along with her ex-husband? I didn't know; I just felt somehow that she wasn't a woman who could be a party to selling a baby.

But how to reconcile that with the obvious fact that if she had custody of Amber's baby, she was an accessory to Doc's crime?

The completely half-baked nature of this venture slowly came home to me as I sat in the car, slumped behind the steering wheel, thinking about how to accuse a woman I hardly knew of keeping a child from the parents who loved him. For whatever reason, she'd chosen to abet her former husband instead of telling the police she had the baby. She'd chosen to let Ellie and Josh Greenspan live in terror instead of letting them know their baby was alive. She was not likely to invite me into her house and confess that Baby Adam was the third kid from the left in the crib room.

I mentally drafted an affidavit in support of a search warrant; if Detective Aronson had my suspicions, he'd have to get a warrant to search the premises. Did he have enough evidence to get one?

No. That was the problem. Everything I had was built on a hunch supported by a feeling, not something a judge would consider reliable evidence to justify violating Betsy Scanlon's Fourth Amendment rights.

Of course, if I told the cops what I suspected, they could work toward getting the kind of evidence that would stand up in court. But how much time would that take? And how long did Doc intend to leave the baby at Betsy's? For all I knew, he had a couple flying in from Atlanta, ready to exchange unmarked bills for a bundle of joy formerly named Adam. Any interest on the part of the police could lead to Adam's being hustled out of the jurisdiction before they could get a warrant.

No, surprise was not just my best advantage, it was my only hope. And it would be lost if the police began nosing around; Betsy would tell Doc, and the baby would quietly disappear into the gray-market pipeline.

I couldn't leave Staten Island without testing my hunch. But how to get inside Aunt Betsy's Playroom without letting the former Mrs. Scanlon know what was on my mind? And how would I know Baby Adam when I saw him? The truth was, all babies looked pretty much alike to me. Baby Adam would be younger than most infants farmed out to day care, but did I really know a seven-week-old from a four-month-old? Would I even know a boy from a girl if he wasn't swaddled in baby blue instead of pink?

And suppose I managed to identify him; how was I going to get him out of the house? Even if I was right and Betsy was a reluctant accomplice rather than an active conspirator, she really wasn't going to hand me a baby and wish me luck. She'd kept Adam a secret for several long, horrible days—why would she surrender him now?

All this wasn't helping. If I kept on sitting here and ruminating about my choices, or lack thereof, I'd accomplish nothing. At the least, I had to go to Betsy's and get her to invite me into the house—something she'd pointedly not done the last time I visited. We'd sat outside in the cold, ostensibly so she could smoke, but the truth was, she didn't dare ask me into her living room, in case Adam began to cry and I began to wonder what a baby was doing in day care after dark.

I hefted myself out of the creamy leather bucket seat and opened the door. I had to do something before I talked myself out of doing anything. I closed and locked the door to Marvella's car and walked quickly along Travis Avenue. On one side of the road lay the orderly development, houses arranged in neat rows like grade-school children out for a walk. On the other side of the road lay the swamp, where Amber and Scott had met their deaths.

I turned a corner and reached the street where Betsy lived, the street where I'd gone to confront Amber about the paternity of her child, back when I really thought she and Scott intended to make a home for their baby.

I stood for a moment and looked at the house. From the outside there was no way to tell that nearly twenty children played and slept and cried and laughed inside. But some neighbors must have seen the children come and go, and one more baby could easily have come and stayed without causing the kind of comment that would be expected if a newborn suddenly popped up in someone else's life. Even those neighbors who had slogged through the swamp with me in search of Amber and Adam, who devoured the news reports and were on the lookout for Baby Adam, could be forgiven for not thinking the baby might be with Betsy.

I started up the walk, trembling slightly as I considered how close I might be to finding the baby whose unfocused blue eyes had begun to haunt me. The baby I was accused of selling.

That thought allowed me to push the bell. I stood waiting, still without a clue as to what I was going to say when Betsy came to the door. I quickly ran through a mental file of possible reasons for my presence on her concrete steps: a question about Doc's office burglaries; another clue regarding Amber's first baby; a fictitious witness who saw Scott at Betsy's house after the mall incident. But before I could formulate a plan, I noticed a small red-haired girl playing in the yard at the side of the house. She was on the grass next to a driveway made of cement squares someone had painted in red, white, and green blocks.

I decided to strike up a conversation with her; if Betsy came out while I was talking to the kid, she wouldn't suspect that I was there to collect Adam Greenspan. I hoped.

I walked over to the child. "Hi," I said. My tone was a little too bright, the voice of a person who talked to children the way she talked to small dogs who nipped at ankles.

She looked up at me with wide blue eyes. She held one of those wooden paddles with a ball hung on a rubber band; she bounced the ball idly, without rhyme or rhythm, as she talked.

"When you were a little girl, did you bite your nails?" she asked. She didn't look at me, but her tone implied that this question was to be taken seriously. She wanted solid information.

"Didn't everybody?" I replied.

"Melissa doesn't," the kid announced. "And Fern doesn't and Randi doesn't. But I do and so does Tasha and Brian and—"

I had the feeling this could go on. I held out my self-manicured hand and said, "Well, I stopped, and look how long my nails are now."

"I'll stop when I'm six," the child said firmly. She nodded to show her determination, then hopped away, skipping along the painted squares of the driveway, hopscotching her way to the scraggly lawn. She turned and hopped back, carefully stepping on the green squares and avoiding the red.

"How old are you?" I asked; it was the kind of question a non-child person asked.

"Four years and eight months," she said, tossing off the answer without looking up.

"That's a good age," I remarked.

"No, it's not," retorted the kid. "I'd rather be sixteen. That's my favorite age."

"Because you could drive a car?" I ventured.

She nodded. "And because I'd be big like my cousin."

The child stopped suddenly and measured me with her eyes. "How tall are you?" she asked.

"Five feet five inches," I answered.

She considered my answer, then rejected it. "You're three greens and a half," she countered. Then she demanded, "Tell me how tall I am."

I gave the matter some thought. "I'd say you were about three feet."

"No," she replied with a decisive shake of her head. "I'm two red ones."

Red ones?

It took a minute. Then I glanced down at the painted squares of concrete and realized she was using them as her unit of measurement. And she was right; if you laid her little body down on two of the red squares, her head would be at one end and her sneakered feet at the other. As for me, I was about three and a half green squares, which were twice as large as the red.

Were all kids this clever at four years and eight months?

Betsy Scanlon rounded the corner and came toward us. She looked frazzled, out of breath. "I was running a load of laundry in the basement," she explained. "I didn't hear the bell, but Tyler said someone was at the door."

I ran through my list of ruses and was about to ask Betsy if she knew anything about Doc's burglaries when the child said, "Aunt Betsy, can I have a graham cracker sandwich with peanut butter for lunch?"

"I don't think so, Erin," Betsy replied. "I made tuna salad this morning. We'll have that."

"But I hate tuna," the kid said, screwing up her face into a getting-ready-to-cry pout.

And then the penny dropped.

Erin.

Not *Aaron.*

And I knew.

I knew why the screen door had a *C* instead of an *S.*

I knew why Betsy had kept Baby Adam a secret instead of letting the police know he was safe and sound.

I knew who had borrowed the silver car the night Amber was killed.

I had come to the right place, but for all the wrong reasons.

CHAPTER EIGHTEEN

Betsy had mentioned that her niece, the one she was baby-sitting the night Amber was killed, sometimes came to the day care center. She just hadn't mentioned that her niece was named Erin or that she was adopted almost five years ago, at the same time Amber's baby supposedly died. Or that the *C* in the screen door stood for Cheney, the name Betsy had borne before she married Chris Scanlon.

My thoughts whirled as I looked at the child whose copper hair and blue eyes suddenly reminded me of Amber. I'd come to this house convinced Doc Scanlon had persuaded his ex-wife to take one more chance for him. Convinced she was an unwitting or at least unwilling accomplice to his scheme.

This changed everything. Betsy wasn't unwitting or unwilling; she'd known exactly what she was doing and why she was doing it. It wasn't about money, it was about helping her brother Kyle keep the child he loved. The child Jerry Califana remembered as Laura.

The Cheneys hadn't met with Amber at Friendly's to buy Baby Adam, but to pay Amber enough money so that she'd let them keep Erin. Amber was killing all her golden geese that night; why not milk Kyle Cheney for one more payoff, one more lump sum that would insure him against the birth father who could turn his daughter into Staten Island's own Baby Jessica?

I turned and started a brisk walk away from the house; there was nothing to be gained by confronting Betsy. The best thing I could do was get into the car and drive straight to the One-Two-Two precinct and get Detective Aronson to come out and talk to Betsy. He could get his warrant based on—

A hand touched my shoulder. I jumped and whirled, half-expecting to see a gun. But Betsy's hand held nothing more threatening than a pirate ship made of Legos.

"I came to ask a couple of questions about the burglary of Doc's office," I began, hoping my face didn't betray my total lack of interest in said burglaries. Or my deep desire to get free of Betsy and make a getaway in Marvella's car.

"No, you didn't," Betsy contradicted, her tone flat. "I know what you came for." She looked from me to her niece, then back into my eyes. "But he's not here. Doc sent the package last night."

Sent the package? What was this, a rerun of "Mission: Impossible"? What kind of stupid underworld code was this supposed to be?

"Aunt Betsy, can I have a peanut butter sandwich on graham crackers?" Erin repeated. "I don't like tuna, and I want—"

Which is when I realized that Betsy wasn't talking like an imitation drug dealer, but like an adult disguising a mention of sex in front of a child. Except that it wasn't sex we were discussing, but the disposal of a baby boy.

"Erin, go into the kitchen and ask Ramona to make you

a peanut butter sandwich. On bread," Betsy added.

"But I want graham—" the child protested.

"Now."

Erin's face crumpled into a pout, but she went. She opened the door as though it weighed a hundred pounds, pulling it with her skinny arms and dragging her body through the doorway with obvious reluctance, as though going in to face punishment rather than Wonder bread.

Now that the kid was gone, we could speak freely.

"No, he didn't," I said with a confidence I suddenly realized was based on solid evidence. "Doc didn't sent any package last night, and he's not going to send one tonight or any other night. That's why Adam is still here, isn't it? Because Doc won't lift a finger to help you."

The look on Betsy's face encouraged me to continue. "You called him the most selfish man you ever knew, and you were right. He handed Amber's baby over to your brother because he was afraid Amber and Jerry might sue him for malpractice. It was the path of least resistance. But this—putting Adam into the gray-market pipeline—this doesn't benefit him, so he won't do it. Which is why Adam is still here, not halfway across the country."

"No, he's not, he—"

"Come on, Betsy," I cut in. "We both know what happened. We both know Kyle killed Amber so he could keep his own kid. And if he'd been smart instead of sentimental, he'd have killed Adam too. But he couldn't. He brought the baby back here, hoping you could convince Doc to sell him to some couple out of state. But Doc refused. So now you have a baby you don't know what to do with."

I looked at Betsy's face, which had a haggard quality in the bright afternoon light. Dark rings circled her deep-set eyes; the eyeliner had smudged and she looked like a blond raccoon.

"Come inside," she said at last, softly but seductively, as though inviting me to a tryst.

The invitation gave me pause. Why was she asking me to view the evidence?

Because she couldn't let me leave.

Or because the evidence was no longer there.

Was she taking me into a room full of babies, none of whom were Jimmy Lundquist-Wylie/Adam Greenspan, just to prove Amber's child had never lain in the crib room?

It made more sense to run for the car than to follow Betsy inside the house. I turned away, measuring with my eyes the distance from the side door to the end of the drive-way.

Or was she inviting me inside because she knew it was over? If Doc wouldn't help find a new home for Adam, then someone someday was going to make the same connection I had, and she might as well get it over with.

It made as much sense as any other explanation I could come up with. And besides, I needed to see Adam, to know that he was really alive and drawing breath, not lying in the swamp ballooning up with gases.

I followed Betsy down the hallway of the apartment, past the wooden pegs where a dozen little jackets and slickers hung. I nearly tripped on a car seat.

The babies were lined up in their cribs. Five in all, they lay in a row like sausages, bundled in terry-cloth suits with animals embroidered on the breast. A blue suit with an elephant—was that Adam Greenspan? Not the pink with the teddy bear; that must be a girl. But the yellow with a duck or the green with a giraffe—or was the green child too big? Did Adam have hair?

I looked from one baby to another, my eyes shifting with a panicky uncertainty. Now that I'd seen Erin, I knew I was in the right place; Adam had certainly been hidden here since Amber's death. And since Kyle Cheney had no desire to sell the baby, he was probably still here, if only I could pick him out.

"He didn't mean to do it," Betsy said. "Things just got out of hand."

That was one way to describe the deliberate murder of two human beings.

"Kyle and Donna love that child to death."

"Yeah," I replied. "I guess they did."

"You could take the baby and not tell the police about Kyle," Betsy offered. But there wasn't much assurance behind the words; she knew it was over.

Betsy stepped into my line of sight. "Adam's the one in the yellow suit," she said with a small, wry smile.

He was tiny. Tiny and squinched-up and red-faced and bald. Not a pretty picture—unless you were Ellie Greenspan.

I wanted to scoop him up and take him straight to Brooklyn Heights. Probably not the soundest way of proceeding legally, but I wasn't particularly concerned with legalities. I wanted this child returned to a home where he'd be loved, not just stashed. I was sure Betsy had taken good care of him, but he deserved to be with people who wanted him more than they wanted the sun.

"Kyle doesn't want to kill him," Betsy said, shaking her head.

I caught the present tense.

"But he will if Doc won't help?"

"He won't have a choice. It's better than having the police find him here."

"They'll know he was killed after Amber," I pointed out. "They'll know he had to be someplace between then and now."

"But they won't know where. They won't have any reason to connect the baby to me or to Kyle."

"You can't let him kill Adam." I said it as a statement, hoping against hope it was true.

She shook her head. "Not if there's another way."

"Is there another way?"

"You could pretend you found him. You could take him

to those people in Brooklyn, tell them they can have him back if they don't tell the police how he came to them.''

''Betsy, this doesn't make sense,'' I said, but my protest was halfhearted. However strange her reasoning, if there was a chance I could walk out of here with Adam, I was prepared to encourage her fantasy that this could somehow all be settled without reference to the New York City Police Department.

Not that I was particularly eager to involve the cops. If I took the baby to the precinct and dumped him in Detective Aronson's lap, I'd be listening to the Miranda warnings in nothing flat. Aronson was still convinced I was the mastermind behind Amber's scams; he would never believe I'd located the baby through sheer logic and a familiarity with the work of the late Edgar Allan Poe. And by the time he investigated Betsy and found evidence to support my contention, I'd be on the six o'clock news, hiding my face under my jacket as the cops paraded me past the minicams, and solemn anchorpersons would tell the world an arrest had finally been made in the Baby Adam case.

I could take him to Artie Bloom. I laughed aloud at the picture that would make; I could see myself dashing into the city room, the baby propped on my hip, shouting ''Stop the presses.'' Artie could play Jimmy Breslin to my Son of Sam.

I could call my lawyer. Riordan could arrange a meeting with Aronson, but then I'd be branding myself as the kind of person who needed a lawyer like Matt Riordan. A guilty person.

What I could not do was take Adam back to Josh and Ellie and pretend they'd boarded him with Aunt Betsy for three days. I was an officer of the court; if I wanted to keep practicing law—let alone walk around like a free citizen— I was going to have to tell someone in a uniform what I knew.

Betsy had to know that. So how could she just let me have Baby Adam?

Was she really so certain her brother would put an end
to the baby's short life? Was turning him over to the police
the only way she could avoid having the child's blood on
her hands?

I'd never worn a baby before.

I felt like an opossum, as seen on public television in
grotesque close-up. Adam was a weight, not unlike a back-
pack, only on the front. But he was alive, wriggling,
breathing; I couldn't take my eyes off him, couldn't just
treat him like a load.

He was a person, a little proto-person, and his life was
wholly in my hands. He was in a sling; as soon as Betsy
strapped it onto my chest, I could see how she'd snuck the
baby into her house. Wear a loose raincoat over this thing
and all people would think is that you'd put on a pound or
two; the baby could hide under a cloak, strapped to the
chest.

I hastened toward Travis Avenue, where I'd left Marvella's car parked on the side of the road next to the tall,
feather-topped reeds of the Davis Wildlife Refuge. The
irony of walking toward the place where Baby Adam's
mother had been fished out of the swamp like an old boot
wasn't lost on me, but I didn't care to dwell on it either.
The sooner I was away from this watery, treacherous landscape the better.

I took one last paranoid glance behind me as I crossed
the avenue.

He was there.

All I could see, all I knew, was that there was a man
and he was moving more swiftly than I. He was fast and
he was coming straight at me. I couldn't see him, but I
knew who he was, who he had to be, without looking back
for a confirming glance.

I fumbled in my jacket pocket for the keys, my fingers
slipping on the cool metal edges. I kept my eyes firmly on
the swaying pampas grass; to look back was to invite my

pursuer closer, to make him appear, big as life, in front of me. Not looking kept him at bay.

Or at least that was the theory. The reality was that I stood, knees wobbling, fingers clumsily pawing the keys which seemed to have taken on a life of their own inside my pocket; they kept wriggling out of reach. And as I fumbled, his steps came closer, pounding the blacktop as he ran across the road toward the car.

I grabbed the keys and thrust the first one into the lock. Why, I wondered frantically, had I been such a goddamn New Yorker, locking the car on a lonely Staten Island road to protect it from thieves who didn't exist instead of leaving it open so I could make a fast getaway?

Too late now. The key wobbled in my hand, refusing to enter the door lock.

Then the bunch slipped from my hand and clattered on the road. I looked; he was halfway across the road, racing toward me, arms pumping as he ran. A racer's run. An athlete's run.

I had to bend down, pick up the keys, get my fingers around the door key instead of the trunk or gas tank keys, put the key in the lock, turn the handle, open the door, get into the car, and drive away before Kyle Cheney reached me.

It couldn't be done.

Acting on some kind of instinct I didn't know I had, I cupped Adam's melon head in my left hand, retrieved the keys with my right and stood back up in one swift motion. Then I thrust the largest key into his face, aiming as much as possible for the eyes.

He howled and grabbed his face. I swung my shaking hand toward the car door, put the key into the lock, turned it, and opened the door. Ignoring Kyle's scream of rage and pain, I lowered myself to the carseat level of the car. Two more seconds and I'd be inside, safe.

Adam and I would be safe.

Strong, wiry hands grabbed my shoulder, spinning me

around. Blood dripped from his nose, but his sinewy hands had lost none of their strength. I struggled to get inside the car, to put the key into the ignition so I could leave Kyle in the road, take off for safety. I still had my left hand on Adam's soft head; he whimpered as I jerked my body down into the driver's seat.

Kyle had both hands on my arm now; he pulled with all his considerable strength. I looked wildly around; wasn't there someone walking by, someone in a car who would see us and stop?

Cars sped by, on their way to Victory Boulevard, but no one so much as slowed to look at us.

Then I realized anyone watching would think we were having a family squabble, and would avert their eyes, certain they shouldn't interfere.

I swung my left arm, elbow first, at Kyle's midsection; he saw the movement and jumped back with a grunt. Then he pulled with renewed vigor, and because I was off-balance, I nearly fell out of the car. The keys were still in my right hand. I moved back toward the car, trying to crawl in before Kyle had me out altogether. He grabbed at my right hand, but I kept it out of reach, blocking with my body.

The keys were everything. I couldn't drop the keys, no matter what. The keys had to go into the ignition, had to get us out of here.

"Give me those keys," he demanded. His hands were everywhere, huge bony things that gripped and grabbed and pulled at me. Strong fingers reached out and took possession of my hand; no amount of struggle could keep him from wrenching the keys out of my fingers.

"You'll break my—"

"Who cares? Give me the keys." And he chopped at my arm with the flat of his hand, then wrapped his fingers around the bunch of keys, scratching me as he pulled them away.

I lunged out of the car, my hand grabbing at the keys.

He raised his arm and flung the entire bunch into the tall reeds. They arced into the air like a silver ball, then fell somewhere in the forest of grass.

Gone. The keys were gone.

CHAPTER NINETEEN

I stood a half second in paralyzed wonder. My whole object had been to get in the car and drive away, to leave Kyle standing in the road, to whisk Baby Adam off to sanctuary. And now I had no keys, no way to move the car. Nowhere to go.

Kyle turned toward me, a smile of triumph on his face. He took a step closer; I turned and ran toward the neat rows of houses that flanked the wildlife refuge.

I'd learned the key trick in a woman's self-defense class. As I stumbled along the sidewalk next to the tall reeds, I tried to recall other words of wisdom.

One thing was that I wasn't supposed to be a hero. Disable your attacker and run for help, that was the basic idea. Which meant that instead of racing into an isolated swamp full of egrets, I should have been heading across the road toward the houses. I should have been ringing doorbells, begging people to call the cops, attracting as much attention as possible. Not doing the one thing that would give Kyle maximum advantage, namely letting myself be herded into a desolate area where he knew the terrain and I was hampered by ignorance, bad shoes, and a baby.

That was the theory.

But every time I tried to step off the sidewalk and into the road, every time I leaned toward the houses on the other side of the reed-festooned refuge, Kyle cut me off, harrying me like a big wiry sheepdog, forcing my steps back toward the swamp.

But maybe there were people in the refuge. Maybe there were park employees, naturalists. Birdwatchers. Hikers. Teenagers making out. Kids exploring.

Anyone.

I was having trouble catching my breath. No runner, I was used to an occasional brisk walk along city sidewalks to boost my cardiovascular system.

I hadn't boosted it enough. There was a sharp pain in my side and I gasped for air like a leaky balloon. Any second now, the vise-grip of Kyle's strong hand would grab my shoulder, bring me to the ground, smashing Adam's head on the—

No. That couldn't happen. I had to keep going, had to reach some kind of safety.

I lurched toward the driveway entrance to the wildlife preserve. My turn must have surprised Kyle; he took a moment to orient himself before following me into the copse of trees that sheltered the forest-green sign with the maple leaf on it, the sign that said this land belonged to the New York City Parks Department. There was a building dead ahead. A flat-topped, utilitarian structure of indeterminate use. I had no idea whether it was occupied. But I headed for it anyway, hoping there was at least a caretaker inside.

It beat trying to tell my story to egrets.

I was so intent on making it to the green building that I failed to realize there was no one behind me. Kyle was gone.

Which, in retrospect, should have told me something.

But all I could think of was getting through the barnlike double doors before a large hand reached out and pulled me down into the mud. All I could think of was safety, sanctuary. All I could think of was Adam.

He was wailing now, a birdlike cry that would have had me worried if I hadn't had other things to worry about. Were babies supposed to cry like that? Bouncing him around in the snuggly probably wasn't improving his mood any.

The door was heavy. It slid open sideways, like the door of a warehouse. I gasped for breath as I pulled at the handle with both hands, straining my limited upper body strength. Maybe it was time I joined a gym, made friends with the Nautilus machines.

Inside, it was dark, the kind of dark you expected in a tunnel. A rich, brown darkness that smelled of mulch and loam and fertilizer. As though I'd opened a door into a mole burrow.

Long wooden tables stood in the center of the open space, with seedlings on trays, growing under dim light. I grabbed for breath and looked around, but I couldn't see another person in the blue-tinged light from the overhead rods.

This, I realized, had to be part of the Native Plant Center, which supplied ferns to local parks and gardens. Which meant there had to be someone in a Parks Department uniform somewhere close by.

But where?

And where was Kyle?

I whirled around, half-expecting to see him in the doorway, blocking the only exit I knew. But there was no one in the crack of light I'd left when I pulled the door open.

Turning had been a mistake; the bright sunlight brought purple and red spots in front of my eyes, which had to adjust to the dark all over again.

I took a tentative step forward and called out, "Is anybody here?"

No reply.

I walked closer to the table upon which the seedlings stretched spindly green arms up to the stingy ceiling light. What grew here? Who grew it and why?

More to the point, where the hell were they?

"Just stay right there," a voice commanded.

I froze.

"Who's there?" I called out, my voice higher and more panicky than I would have liked it to be. "Kyle, is that—"

"Kyle's right here," the voice, which was not Kyle's, replied. "Just stay put, and everything will be all right."

It was the kind of voice you used when talking to a very crazy person. A very crazy person who might kill a newborn baby if you said the wrong thing.

"No, it won't," I shot back. I had to get control of this somehow—which wasn't easy, considering I couldn't even see the person I was talking to.

"I don't want to have to call the police," the man said, his voice tinged with exasperation.

"Why not?" I countered. "Sounds like a good idea to me. Call the cops—please."

"You don't want me to do that," the reasonable male voice replied in a tone that promised infinite patience. "Just let Kyle have the baby and everything will be all right."

"You know Kyle?"

"Sure do," the voice said. "He and Donna come in here all the time, pick up seedlings."

Of course. That was the piece I'd been trying to remember ever since I realized that Kyle killed Amber. The Cheneys had a landscaping business; that meant they knew the workers in the Native Plant Center. The man whose face I couldn't see had every reason to trust Kyle, and no reason at all to trust me.

"Listen to me," I begged. "I don't know what Kyle told you, but—"

The figure stepped closer. He wore the forest-green fatigues of the Parks Department, and his face already had the weathered brown of an outdoorsman in spite of the early spring weather. His forearms bulged, and his face wore a look of stubborn determination.

"Kyle told me about you," he said, his voice tinged with contempt. "He told me how you and that dead girl planned to sell the baby. I was there when they fished that girl out of the kill, and I—"

"So was I," I interrupted. "I was there, too, and I knew her when she was alive and I didn't kill her and I don't care what Kyle told you, I am not trying to sell this baby. I want to take him to the police. Kyle killed Amber, and—"

"Kyle?" The man threw back his head and laughed. "You're the lawyer they been talking about on TV. You tried to sell this here baby and you want me to believe Kyle killed that girl?" He shook his head and took another step closer.

"Where's Kyle?" I asked. It seemed vital that I know. Was he creeping around behind me? Had he gone for help? Would he appear in the doorway, ready to cut me off if I tried to make a run for it?

The Parkie shook his head again. "You just stay there," he ordered.

I turned and bolted for the door. His footsteps followed; I reached out and grabbed a rake, tossing it behind me as I ran. It clattered in back of me, and I heard a curse that told me my pursuer had run into it.

I reached the door and slid through, then gave a huge shove, trying to close the door enough so that he would find it harder to squeeze through. Then I dashed in the direction I hoped would take me to the road, where I could flag down a car and find a phone, call for help.

I hadn't the slightest idea where I was going. All the

trees and reeds looked alike. I ran down a large path that seemed well trodden, and I hoped it led to the road.

It didn't. I stumbled over a tree root and caught myself, grabbing for rough bark that scraped my palm. I shoved my foot back into the Italian loafers that had seemed like sensible shoes back in Brooklyn but hadn't been made for slogging through swampland or hopping over roots. There was a walkway made of flat planks ahead, allowing the birdwatcher to cross the watery inlet without getting his or her feet wet. It probably led deeper into the swamp, where birds' nests were hidden among the tall reeds. It was unlikely that it led to the road, to the mall, to civilization.

If I went forward, I headed into swamp, away from help. But I also headed away from Kyle, away from the Parkie he'd recruited to his cause.

Did Parkies carry guns? I hastily ran through my jumbled memory banks, searching for the New York statute defining the term peace officer, but to no avail. I took a quick glance backward. Was that reed swaying a sign that someone was hidden behind the green curtain? Was the sound I heard merely the breeze playing with the branches, rattling the tall grasses—or was someone moving through the swamp, hot on my trail?

I had no idea. All I knew for certain was that if I stood still, someone would come crashing out of the foliage eventually. Movement seemed like a good idea. Movement made me feel as though I had a semblance of control over the situation, over my own fate and that of Baby Adam.

When I reached the planked walkway, my shoes made hollow thudding sounds. I stopped dead, then moved forward more slowly, walking on the balls of my feet and trying to keep the heels from striking the wooden slats. It slowed my progress, but it felt worth it. Creeping along silently was better than advertising my presence with bouncy steps.

Mercifully, Adam had stopped crying. I looked down at his fuzzy head, blue-purple veins like rivulets on the bald scalp. Then I glanced at the water flowing under the plank bridge, at the tall reeds overhead, picturing a baby in a basket floating along the swamp water, picturing Moses among the bulrushes. God had looked out for baby Moses; I hoped He'd do the same for little Adam.

If I kept going in this direction, would I reach the other side of the wildlife preserve? Would I come out on Victory Boulevard? I could flag down a car there, maybe locate a telephone. Get help.

That thought cheered me. I picked up speed once I stepped off the planking and put my feet back on hard-packed dirt. The path narrowed; I brushed past reeds and bushes, shielding Adam's bobbing head with my left hand and using my right to push green stuff out of the way.

I jumped lightly over a puddle, then came to a stop as I realized there was no more path. Reeds grew up all around me; there was no clear way through them. I pushed aside a bunch and peered through the green curtain, but the growth was equally dense in every direction except back-ward.

There was no more path. Should I keep going, bush-whacking my way through the tall growth? Or should I turn back, hoping for another way out of the wildlife preserve?

Adam gave a tiny little cry. I looked down at him. Huge, unfocused blue eyes tried to fix themselves on my face and failed. His head bobbed and he cried out again. It seemed a cry of pleasure rather than pain, but it was impossible to know for sure. An incredibly tiny hand reached out from the snuggly and grabbed at the air. He opened and closed his fingers and squealed again.

"Shut up, kid," I murmured. "Let's not advertise, shall we?"

"Too late," a laconic voice said. I jumped a foot, then turned in dismay. Kyle Cheney stood five feet away from me, a silver gun glinting in his hand.

"You don't want to hurt the baby," I said quickly. Hop-ing it was true.

"No," he said. "I don't." But before I could breathe a sigh of relief, he added, his tone regretful, "I don't want to, but I will."

"You didn't before," I pointed out. I was shaking so hard I grabbed at a reed to lean on; a bad choice, since it bent over and nearly landed me in the swamp. A part of my mind was totally awed by the way I seemed able to carry on a normal conversation while trying very hard not to look at the gun pointed at my midsection; the other part of my mind knew I'd taken leave of my senses. That I was babbling in hopes that if I kept my mouth moving, I'd stay alive.

He gave the accusation some thought. "I didn't want to hurt anyone," he said at last. "But Amber wouldn't leave me alone. She kept saying all she had to do was go to court and she could take Erin away from us."

"So you gave her money," I finished the thought. "You must love your daughter very much."

Kyle's face wore a pinched look I suspected wasn't just the result of his recent troubles. He looked like a man on the verge of a nervous breakdown, a man who took far too many things far too seriously.

"I do," he said. "And so does Donna." He squinted into the bright overcast sun. "We lost so many babies," he went on, speaking as much to himself as to me. "So many dead babies."

"Miscarriages?" I asked. "Is that why you adopted?" I had to keep him talking, had to keep him from coming any closer. He could still shoot at five feet away, but the more distance I kept between us, the better my chances of survival were. And maybe, just maybe, if he focused on his love for his own child, he'd see that he couldn't insure her happiness by killing someone else's baby.

"Two stillborn, four miscarriages," he recited. "And one baby that lived for six days. Six days, twelve hours, and forty-one minutes." He swallowed; his oversized Adam's apple bobbed like a piece of food caught in his throat. "That one was Kyle, Junior," he added.

His eyes swerved away. "I really think Donna would have killed herself if we'd lost another one," he said. His voice was thin, strained, repressed, as if it had been years since he let his lungs fill to capacity. "She tried once, with pills. So when Betsy said Doc could get us a baby—" He broke off and swallowed again. "It was a miracle. She was a miracle."

I recalled the sun glinting off her copper hair, hair that was going to go brown and wind up the color of maple syrup, like her mother's. "She's a great kid," I agreed. "I can see where Amber's threat to take her away from you would make you crazy."

Poor choice of words.

"I wasn't crazy," he snapped. He raised his gun arm just a little, pointed the weapon a little straighter. "I was doing what I had to do to protect my family." He gave me a look that begged me to understand. "I gave her money," he said, his voice a plea. "I gave her whatever she asked for. And then she came back and said there was a father who could screw up the adoption, that I had to pay him off, too."

"It wouldn't have been that easy," I objected. "She'd have had to admit she helped Doc fake Erin's death. She'd have risked prosecution herself."

It seemed more than a little late to start giving Kyle Cheney legal advice.

He shook his head. "Look at Baby Jessica," he pointed out. "Those parents lost their daughter and there wasn't anything about fraud. As soon as I saw that birth father, I knew it was all over."

He saw the father? When? When could Kyle have seen Jerry Califana?

Then I remembered Sonia Rogoff's account of the night she saw the Cheneys with Amber.

"Oh, no," I breathed. I closed my eyes; the picture Sonia had so vividly painted came back to me. "Amber pointed to a booth in the front and said the man sitting there was the father, right?''

Sonia thought Amber meant the father of the baby who lay next to her in the car seat.

But that wasn't Amber's meaning. She was pointing to a man she identified as the father of the child Kyle and Donna had raised for four years and eight months. Erin Cheney, born Laura Marie Califana.

''She told you Scott was the father,'' I whispered, ''and that's why you killed him.''

''We couldn't let him take our daughter,'' Kyle replied. His Adam's apple jumped; a vein throbbed in his forehead. His nervousness permeated his entire being; he looked like a man who hadn't slept in weeks. Maybe years. I suspected Kyle had never been able to forget the gray-market nature of Erin's adoption, had never entirely relaxed since the day the baby was placed in his wife's hungry arms.

''He didn't care about her,'' Kyle continued, his voice ragged. ''He just wanted money, like Amber. But he could have screwed us, he could have walked into court and taken my child away, just like that Baby Jessica case.''

I looked directly into Kyle Cheney's pale blue eyes, eyes the color of acid-washed denim. ''Except for one little thing,'' I said, trying for a gentle, believable tone of voice. ''Scott wasn't Erin's father. Erin's father is named Jerry Califana and he owns a pizza parlor in Tottenville. He's still alive and he still wants his daughter back. You killed the wrong man.''

''That's bullshit,'' Kyle shot back, so quickly I knew he understood the enormity of the accusation. ''You're just trying to mess me up. You'd say anything to keep me from shooting you right here and—''

''Yes, I would,'' I agreed. I rested my hand on top of Adam's peach-fuzz head in a gesture that soothed me at least as much as it did him. He was a weight, a gentle, breathing weight on my chest; a real living creature connected to me in a way I'd never known before.

I had to keep him alive.

"I sat at a table in Jerry's pizza parlor," I went on, trying for a calm, conversational tone. "The first thing in his lock-box was a picture of his baby girl. He loved her as much as you love Erin. He's not out for money. He's a father, just like you."

"That's bull—"

"No, it isn't," I said firmly. He had a gun; the truth was my weapon, and I wasn't going to let go of it. "Jerry was waiting for Amber at the Native Plant Center parking lot at the same time you picked her up at the mall in your sister's car. You probably drove right past him on your way here."

Kyle drew himself up and visibly groped for control. "That doesn't matter if the guy never finds out Erin is his child," he said, trying to convince himself. "And he won't find out if you aren't there to tell him what you know."

"You aren't going to shoot me," I said with far more confidence than I felt.

"Actually, I had wondered about that," I went on, willing myself not to focus on the silver weapon. "I wondered why you didn't shoot Amber instead of drowning her. Then I remembered where we are. Half the cops in the NYPD live on Staten Island. Hell, you shoot off a gun here, you'll have twenty off-duty cops on your tail in a matter of minutes."

Kyle's eyes narrowed. "I have a silencer," he said softly.

"I didn't notice a—" I began.

He stepped forward too quickly for me to react; I tried to maneuver my way out of his path, but it was too late. He closed the distance between us, grabbed my shoulder with one sinewy arm, and jammed the gun deep into my abdomen. "If I fire into your stomach, it should muffle the noise."

CHAPTER TWENTY

Essentially, the advice my self-defense teacher gave regarding guns was to give the attacker whatever he wanted. Unless, of course, he wanted your life. Which was exactly what Kyle Cheney did want. He wanted me dead, and however reluctantly, he wanted Adam dead.

My teacher's advice in that situation was to take the advanced class.

I hadn't.

If I tried to push the gun away, Kyle could pull the trigger and put a hole through me the size of a basketball. If I karate-chopped his throat or jammed the heel of my hand under his chin, the gun could go off by reflex, even if I managed to throw him off-balance. The same was true for the instep-stomp or the knee to the groin. All good defense techniques, but not against someone armed.

But he hadn't shot Amber. He could have, but he didn't.

Instead, he'd marched her to the heart of the swamp and pushed her down, then held her underwater till she drowned.

"You're not really a killer," I repeated, hoping to hell the statement was still true. It seemed a remarkably naive thing to say to a man who'd killed twice and stood ready to dispatch two more innocent people.

"I threw up in the bushes after Amber died," he said, his voice so thin it sounded as though it hurt him to talk. "I— God, she took so long to die. It was so much harder than I thought it would be. I thought I hated her so much that I could hold her head underwater and be glad her life was ending. But I couldn't. It was horrible. It took forever, and she gurgled and kicked and clawed at my face. It was horrible," he added again.

He shuddered. I looked at his face and saw that there were healing scratch marks along the acne scars. Why hadn't someone noticed them before?

Because he was a landscaper. Because his face was constantly scratched by tree branches, thorns, whatever.

I swallowed. The gun was becoming a familiar presence now, its hardness bruising my sensitive stomach. "You must love Erin so much," I said again. "How will you ever explain to her what you did?"

He shook his head; his lank hair fell across his scarred forehead. "I never will; she'll never know," he said firmly.

A kick and a push. Kick straight into his shin, then jab my elbow into his arm, shoving the gun away. Or was it dug too deeply into my flesh for that? Could I swing away from him, drop to the ground, swerve out of the way of the barrel?

I doubted it. He'd pull the trigger before I got out of the way and the bullet would embed itself in my body, maybe not directly in my stomach, but somewhere painful and lasting. I'd crumple to the ground, clutching my oozing belly, screaming in agonizing pain, bleeding my life away in the muddy water.

I had been shot once—not in a vital organ, but my shoulder still ached when rain was on the way.

It was aching now. I glanced up; the clouds that had loomed all morning were more threatening, gathering with sinister purpose overhead. It was going to pour any second.

Would that help?

I didn't see how.

The only weapon I had was my mouth. I resolved to keep it moving as long as I could, to keep Kyle talking instead of shooting, to force him to relive the horribleness of Amber's death, hoping it would deter him from killing again.

It wasn't going to be enough. Not when weighed against his love for a little red-haired girl.

My hand still rested on Adam's peach-fuzz scalp. He was so small, so defenseless. He'd fallen asleep in the snuggly, his head drooping to one side like a sunflower.

Keep him talking, I told myself. Talking isn't shooting. Maybe there's a way out of this somehow. He can't keep killing forever.

"She had papers somewhere," I speculated. "Papers that would prove Erin was really her child. And I don't think you knew she had a car stashed at the Native Plant Center, or you'd have broken in and found the documents in the glove compartment." The ones Detective Aronson hadn't let me examine. The ones I was guessing had a connection to the adoption of Erin Cheney. I pushed that thought aside and kept talking.

"Which means you probably went to your sister's house and ransacked the apartment."

His pale blue eyes widened. His thin mouth tightened. He jammed the gun one more millimeter deeper into my gut. I'd struck a nerve. I kept speculating.

"So when Scott came home looking for Amber, you followed him and ran him off the road."

Kyle opened his mouth to protest, then squeezed it shut. "Yeah," he admitted, but his eyes didn't meet mine. His

Adam's apple bobbed up and down as he swallowed convulsively.

And the truth dawned on me. "You know, you're a terrible liar," I said, keeping my tone light.

His voice was a croak. "What are you talking about?" He shoved the gun in deeper. I grunted and tried to move back. He tightened his grip on my shoulder and pulled me closer to him.

"Tell me what you mean," he ordered.

"You were still in the swamp with Amber," I pointed out. "And then you took the baby to your house, where Betsy was. You drove Betsy home and she went inside with the baby. So you were nowhere near your house when Scott came home. It was your wife who searched the apartment and followed Scott, wasn't it?"

"No!" he said, the sharply emphatic tone of his voice enough to tell me I'd hit a nerve. "She had nothing to do with it! She doesn't know anything about all this. She—"

"She was driving your landscaping van," I cut in, raising my voice to override his protest. I recalled its white bulk in the driveway of the Cheney house, recalled the red lettering, the rosebush design.

"It had a logo on it, Kyle," I pointed out. "Someone somewhere is going to remember that a big white van that said "*Our Business Is Growing*" was driving along Victory Boulevard when Scott's motorcycle went off the road. And if the cops examine the bumper, they'll find traces of the cycle's paint job."

I stopped for breath. The skin around Kyle's eyes went white; the rest of his face went a deeper red.

"They won't find anything," he said, his voice ragged. "The van's being painted. I ordered a new bumper."

I shook my head. "Maybe," I said. "But even so, the van's distinctive. Somebody's going to remember seeing it at Betsy's the night Amber died; somebody's going to ask too many questions and get answers that don't add up. And when they do, it won't just be you who goes down. It will be Donna, too.''

I had my weapon. It might not be made of metal or capable of blowing a hole in his midsection, but it was going to work. It was going to work because Kyle Cheney's whole life was about being a good father to Erin and a good husband to Donna.

"Is that what you want?" I persisted. I had to keep my breathing shallow; the gun was lodged so deeply in my diaphragm that each breath hurt a little more. And with every word I said, I ran the risk of pushing him over the edge, of causing him to pull the trigger just to end the agony of listening to me.

"If you confess to both killings," I said, swallowing hard against the utter depravity of my suggestion, "maybe we can keep Donna out of it. Maybe Erin can keep one parent.''

"Why should I? Why not just kill you and get it over—''

"Kyle, if you were going to kill me, I'd be dead fifteen minutes already," I cut in, making my tone weary. Pretending there was no fear, only boredom. "You did it once, but you can't do it again. Not up close like this. And you can't live your whole life looking over your shoulder, wondering when someone's going to figure it all out. Betsy knows what you did; Doc at least knows you've got Adam, and he's probably got a damned good idea how you got him. Do you really think you can trust Doc to go to the wall for you and Donna?''

Kyle swallowed; the Adam's apple bounced in his skinny throat like an orange in an ostrich gullet. He was a funny-looking man, all angles and oversized parts: hair too sandy and thin; nose too sharp; knuckles huge knobs on his rough hands. But as he squinted into the white clouds, his face took on the look of a martyr about to die for his faith.

Being a good husband and father was the only thing Kyle lived for, the thing that made him a man. And I was playing on those feelings, using them to save my own skin.

And Adam's. I caressed the soft, vulnerable head and worked on that thought. I was saving Adam, not just myself.

Yeah. That made it all right. My stomach turned over as I realized I was working out a deal, plea-bargaining in a swamp to let a killer go free. And it wasn't just for Adam. I knew now that even if Kyle managed to pull the trigger and leave me for dead, he'd pick the baby up and find a way to keep him alive. So this deal wasn't for Adam, it was for me. And for Erin.

I swallowed hard and kept talking. "I can get you a good lawyer," I continued, hoping my voice sounded more confident than I felt. "The best. Matt Riordan." I had no right in the world to offer the services of Manhattan's highest-priced criminal attorney, but I decided it was about time Riordan did a little pro bono work. And if Kyle bought what I was saying, he'd be copping a plea to Amber and Scott's murders, not splashing the story on the front page with a trial, so Riordan wouldn't be spending too much of his expensive time on Kyle's defense.

And Donna would have to deal with Jerry Califana's inevitable lawsuit for custody of Erin, but at least the little girl would have one parent she could count on.

I'd taken this adoption because I had a need to save a child, to atone for Rojean's children.

For a long time, I thought the child I was destined to save was Adam Greenspan.

Now I knew it was Erin Cheney.

I stood for what seemed like a long time, waiting for Kyle's reply. Waiting to find out if I was going to be dispatched to a bloody, watery grave, or if I'd walk out of the swamp with a confessed murderer in tow.

At last, Kyle lowered the gun. He took a long look at it, then lifted his sinewy arm and threw it as hard as he could into the heart of the swamp. He turned to me, despair on his face.

"Do you think they'll let me see her one more time? Say good-bye?" His voice broke on the last word.

"We'll go back to Betsy's," I promised. "We can call Detective Aronson from there."

And we did. The good father walked next to me, his hand cradling my arm. He made no sound, but tears glinted on his face, making crystal tracks like snail residue on the acned cheeks.

Then the rain started and washed away the tracks.

CHAPTER
TWENTY-ONE

Her name was Miranda. *Oh, brave new world, that has such people in it!* And now the world had a new person, courtesy of Mickey Dechter.

I carried a copy of *Goodnight Moon* in one hand and a bouquet of lilacs in the other—peace offerings; tributes to lay at the feet of the newborn goddess.

But as I mounted the steps to the hospital doors, other children followed behind, their sorrowful eyes unblinking, unforgiving. Erin Cheney, her blue eyes accusing, looking so like Amber's in her rosy face, asked, "Where are you taking my daddy?" Tonetta Glover, deep brown eyes wide with terror, begged, "No bath, Mommy." They followed me up the stairs and into the elevator, on the way to greet Mickey's new miracle, Miranda.

I had no right to be here. That was the message the ghost children sent to me with their troubled eyes.

If I'd had a daughter, would I have done what Kyle Cheney did? Would I have killed for her?

I didn't know. I'd never taken the test.

My steps slowed as I approached the room number the woman at the reception desk had given me. Part of me wanted to turn and run home, to hide my face.

Sleeping Beauty. I thought about Sleeping Beauty, about how at the christening party all the good fairies brought her gifts. And then the Black Fairy swept in, all clouds and portents, and gave her the "gift" that would put her in a coma for one hundred years. I was afraid Mickey would look at me with the same horrified face Sleeping Beauty's mother must have shown the Black Fairy on that christening day.

I squared my shoulders and stepped into the double room. One bed was empty; the woman on the other bed looked up from her magazine and gave me a two-word message: "Sun room," she said, then went back to her article on "Breastfeeding Today."

I thanked her with a nod and hastened back into the corridor.

There was still time; I could leave before Mickey saw me. I could take my dark cloud away and not cast a shadow over mother and child in the sun room.

And not see Miranda? Not greet the child I'd felt kicking in my friend's swollen belly? Not make peace with the woman who'd been my friend and partner, the heart to my brain?

This wasn't about me; it was her day, her milestone. Hers and Miranda's.

I turned my feet in the direction of the sign that said, "Sun Room" and tried to compose my face in delight mode.

Once in the doorway, gazing at Madonna and child, backlit by strong afternoon sun, my expression became real, delight became real.

She was breastfeeding. One corner of her terry robe was pushed back discreetly; the baby sucked at a brown-pink tit, with lips that pushed in and out with the regularity of a metronome.

She didn't see me; her eyes gazed down at the tiny bundle of hunger and need. Her face wore the rapturous expression of Madonnas everywhere. I carefully set the flowers and book on the carpet and swung the camera around my neck up to shooting position.

The first shot gave me away; the click of the shutter, then the whir of the automatic film advance. Mickey turned and gave me a slow welcoming smile; I took a second picture, then a third. I moved in closer; I knelt and shot Miranda at eye-level, loving the way the sun caressed her damask cheek, marveling at the tiny eyelashes like feathers, at the button nose. Essence of baby: that was what my photographs would convey.

I took a close-up of the tiny hand, waving in the air, backlit by golden sun, the fingerprints outlined in relief. Miranda kicked her miniature foot; I focused on that, aware that what I'd probably get would be a peach-colored blur.

She closed her eyes and the lips stopped working. Mickey gently eased her breast out of the baby's mouth and closed her robe. She cuddled Miranda close to her, resting the wobbly little head on her shoulder and giving the fragile-looking back a hefty pat to bring up the burps.

The sound made us both laugh; it could have come from an overweight alderman with a cigar stuck in his face, it was so loud.

"God, she's amazing," I said, meaning it even as I realized it could be said of all babies, not just this one.

But Mickey didn't mind. "I can't believe she's really here," she said. "That she's really mine. That they're going to let me take her home and keep her forever."

I lifted the camera and took another shot. Mother and child: Mickey's face glowing with pride and joy, Miranda sleeping the deep trustful sleep of very new life.

"Oh," I said, recalling my duties as a visitor, "I brought you stuff." I walked back to the doorway and retrieved my flowers and book. "I hope you don't already have six copies of this," I said, handing her the bedtime classic.

"Thanks," Mickey said, taking it with her free hand. "It's hard to imagine Miranda being old enough to read to, but—"

"But it will happen before you know it," I finished. I felt awkward, as though clichés and banalities were the only proper conversation under these circumstances, as though the only way I could be sure I'd left my black cloud outside was to position my camera between me and my feelings.

I turned away, my face betraying me. I couldn't look at the radiant pair, illuminated like medieval saints by the golden light of the afternoon sun.

The Black Fairy had outstayed her welcome. I turned to go.

"Cass?" Mickey called softly.

"Yeah?" I replied without looking back.

"You did it," she said. "You found the missing baby, and you found out who killed your client."

I nodded. I didn't want to talk about it, especially with Mickey. She'd hated the adoption from the beginning, and now she'd been more than proved right.

"Who has the baby?"

"Josh and Ellie," I replied. "The adoptive parents."

"I'm glad."

"Me, too."

"What about the other child?" she persisted. "Amber's first baby, the one she pretended was dead."

"Erin," I said. It seemed important to give the little girl her name. Her adopted name; Jerry Califana still thought of her as Laura, but it was as Erin that I'd made her acquaintance.

"Erin's with her mother," I replied. "But she and Jerry, the birth father, are talking about a visitation schedule. Jerry could upset the whole adoption, but so far he's willing to go slow, to let Erin get used to the idea that she has another daddy."

SWINDOLL
LEADERSHIP
LIBRARY

Immanuel

JESUS CHRIST:
CORNERSTONE OF OUR FAITH

JOHN A. WITMER
CHARLES R. SWINDOLL, GENERAL EDITOR

WORD PUBLISHING
Nashville•London•Vancouver•Melbourne

IMMANUEL
Swindoll Leadership Library

Published in association with Dallas Theological Seminary (DTS):
General Editor: Dr. Charles R. Swindoll, President
Managing Editor: Dr. Roy B. Zuck

The theological opinions expressed by the author are not necessarily the
official position of Dallas Theological Seminary.

Library of Congress Cataloging in Publication Data:

Witmer, John Albert, 1920–
Immanuel : Jesus Christ, cornerstone of our faith /
John Albert Witmer : Charles R. Swindoll, general editor.
p. cm.— (Swindoll leadership library)
Includes bibliographical references and index.

ISBN 0-8499-1369-1 (hardcover : alk. paper)

1. Jesus Christ—Person and offices. I. Swindoll, Charles R.
II. Title.   III. Series.

BT202.W597   1998   98-15085
232–dc21   CIP

Printed in the United States of America
98 99 00 01 02 03 04 05 06 BVG 9 8 7 6 5 4 3 2 1

In memory of my parents,

Albert F. and Mary E. Witmer,

who dedicated me to the service of God before birth
and by personal example and precept guided me
as a child of twelve to saving faith
in the Lord Jesus Christ

Contents

Foreword

ONE OF THE MOST PROFOUND Bible studies ever held took place on a dusty road between Jerusalem and Emmaus. Two discouraged disciples on their way home encountered the resurrected Jesus, but they failed to recognize Him. Unsure, uncertain—certainly unnerved—by recent events in Jerusalem, they had developed a "crisis of faith" as they tried to reconcile what they had seen with what they believed.

Jesus understood their confusion . . . and He offered solid answers from the Word of God. "And beginning with Moses and all the Prophets, he explained to them what was said in all the Scriptures concerning himself" (Luke 24:27). The Bible had the answers to the disciples' questions, and the answers focused on the person and work of Jesus Christ.

Jesus Christ . . . Son of God . . . Messiah . . . Savior . . . the Word . . . Son of Man . . . King of kings and Lord of lords . . . the second person of the Godhead is clearly the central focus in God's drama of redemption. His first coming was so significant that it serves as the dividing line of history for most of the world. And yet, tragically, many Christians know only a small fraction of what the Bible teaches about our Savior and Lord.

John Witmer has done us all a great service by distilling what the Bible teaches about Jesus Christ. Much like a careful archaeologist, John has diligently dug through God's Word and brought to the surface the riches about Jesus Christ found within its pages. Like treasures held up to the light, he allows the various facets of the person and work of Christ to flash their brilliance.

Where was the Son of God before His birth in Bethlehem? What part did God's Son play in the Old Testament? What is He doing now? What will He do in the future? Witmer addresses these and numerous other questions by taking us back to the Word of God for authoritative answers. As Jesus did with the disciples on the road to Emmaus, Witmer has taken us aside in this volume to explain "what was said in all the Scriptures concerning [Jesus]."

Read through this book carefully . . . and prayerfully . . . if you hope to glean the maximum benefit from its pages. Look up the passages of Scripture and allow *all* God's Word to open its treasures to your gaze. As you do, you will respond as the disciples on the road to Emmaus, "Were not our hearts burning within us while he talked with us on the road and opened the Scriptures to us?" (Luke 24:32). You will come away from this study with a deeper love for our Lord and Savior Jesus Christ.

—CHARLES R. SWINDOLL
General Editor

Introduction

Our Lord Jesus Christ is the most important and significant person identified with humanity in this cosmic scene. This excludes, of course, God the Father and God the Holy Spirit, who together with the Lord Jesus—also called "Immanuel," which means, "God with us" (Matt. 1:23; Isa. 7:14)—constitute the eternal triune Godhead. This emphasis on the importance of the Lord Jesus is part of the eternal plan of the triune Godhead for this cosmos from its beginning—the angelic creation—to its consummation—the creation of new heavens and a new earth (Rev. 21:1). God's declared intent is "that in everything he [Jesus] might have the supremacy. For God was pleased to have all his fullness dwell in him, and through him to reconcile to himself all things, whether things on earth or things in heaven, by making peace through his blood, shed on the cross" (Col. 1:18–19; see 1 Cor. 15:27–28). God the Father also desires that the Lord Jesus Christ and His sacrificial death be the focus of faith and commitment for Christians as well.

It is fitting, therefore, that we should study closely what the Bible teaches about the person and work of our Lord Jesus Christ. This involves the totality of the Scriptures, the Old Testament as well as the New, because, as God's angelic messenger told the apostle John, "the testimony of Jesus is the spirit of prophecy" (Rev. 19:10). Many Scriptures make it clear that the existence and ministry of our Lord Jesus Christ did not begin with His birth in human form as the Virgin Mary's baby in Bethlehem (e.g., John 1:14–15, 30; 17:5; Gal. 4:4; Phil. 2:7). He existed eternally as the Word (John 1:1–2), the second person of the Godhead, and was active in preincarnate ministry and revelation in the Old Testament.

Our analysis of the biblical teaching concerning the person and work of Jesus Christ falls into four major divisions: The Preincarnate Word of God, the Incarnate Son of God, the Glorified Christ of God, and the Reigning King of God. In His preincarnate existence and ministry He is called the Word (John 1:1, 14; 1 John 1:1; Rev. 19:13). In His incarnate life and ministry He is frequently called the Son of God (e.g., Matt. 3:17; 14:33; 16:16; 17:5; Mark 1:1; 3:11; 5:7; Luke 1:32, 35; John 1:34, 49; 11:27; 17:1; Rom. 1:3–4; 8:3; 1 Cor. 1:9; 2 Cor. 1:19; Gal. 4:4; 1 Thess. 1:10; Heb. 1:2–3; 4:14; 10:29; 1 John 3:8, 23; 4:9–10, 14; 5:9–13, 20; 2 John 3; Rev. 2:18). In His present ministry He is at the right hand of God the Father in heaven as the glorified Christ (Ps. 110:1; Matt. 22:44; 26:64; Mark 12:36; 14:62; 16:19; Luke 20:42; 22:69; Acts 2:33–36; 5:31; 7:55–56; Rom. 8:34; Eph. 1:20; Col. 3:1; Heb. 1:3, 13; 8:1; 10:12; 12:2; 1 Pet. 3:22). In His future ministry He will reign on earth as "King of kings and Lord of lords" (Rev. 19:16) over the millennial kingdom of righteousness and peace, on the throne of his father David (Luke 1:32–33). These four divisions embrace the person and work of Christ from eternity past to eternity future and all of cosmic time between. That is a subject broad enough and wondrous enough to cause any mere human being to bow in humble adoration and worship before the Lord Jesus.

Colossians 1:15–20 stands as a marvelous capsule statement of Christology—the organized theological discussion of the person and work of Christ. Obviously not all four divisions of this subject are stated in these verses, but its broad scope is outlined, from His participation in cosmic creation as "the image of the invisible God" through the final reconciling to God of "all things, whether things on earth or things in heaven, by making peace through his blood, shed on the cross." This means that finally even Satan and his demonic hosts and all unrepentant human beings will be brought into submission and will be obliged to confess "that Jesus Christ is Lord, to the glory of God the Father" (Phil. 2:11). This includes the judgment of eternal torment in the lake of fire for Satan and his cohorts (Rev. 20:10; 19:20) and all unregenerate human beings (20:11–15).

Part 1

THE PREINCARNATE
WORD OF GOD

One

THE WORD OF GOD AS A MEMBER
OF THE TRIUNE GODHEAD

W E USE THE TITLE *Word* in speaking of the preincarnate Lord Jesus Christ because Scripture uses it in John 1:1–5. The identity of the Word with Jesus Christ is stated in verse 14: "The Word became flesh and lived for a while among us. We have seen his glory, the glory of the one and only Son, who came from the Father, full of grace and truth." In fact, John 1:1–5 can serve as that capsule Scripture passage for this first division of our study of Jesus' person and work. It covers His eternal existence, His identity and relationship with God, His participation in the triune Godhead's work of creation, and His involvement with humanity as its source of life ("and that life was the light of men," v. 4). Interestingly the apostle John is the only biblical author who used the title *Word* for Christ (John 1:1, 14; 1 John 1:1; Rev. 19:13).

Through the centuries biblical scholars have wondered why John used this title, especially since he presented it without any explanation, simply stating, "In the beginning was the Word." Many have suggested that it had a meaning well known to his readers. They surmise that John, being a Jew and familiar with the Old Testament, was aware of the gradual personification there of "the word of the LORD" (Ps. 33:4, 6; see Pss. 107:20; 119:89, 105; 147:15, 18) and the wisdom of God (Job 28:12–28; Prov. 1:2–33; 8:1–9:6). This biblical personification of the wisdom of God is carried

1

forward and accentuated by two of the Jewish apocryphal books, the *Wisdom of Jesus ben Sirach* and the *Wisdom of Solomon*.

Numerous scholars also relate John's use of this title to its occurrence in the religious philosophy of the flourishing Alexandrian Jewish colony represented primarily by Philo in A.D. 40–50, who combined his Jewish convictions with strong influences from Greek philosophy into a confusing doctrine of the *logos* (the Greek noun translated "word") that involves God and an intermediary between God and mankind. In effect, Philo personified the divine *logos* but refused to deify him, since to the Jews, God is one in the absolute sense. Bromiley concludes his discussion on Philo by writing, "the logos seems to be a convenient link between the Creator God and the world which he has made."[1]

The teaching concerning the *logos* that Philo borrowed and adapted goes back at least as far as Heraclitus (ca. 525–475 B.C.), who considered the law of change the only thing that does not change, which is the *logos*.[2] This cosmic principle of the *logos* was adapted by the Stoics (200–100 B.C.) who identified Zeus as the universal *Logos*—who is reason, who never changes his mind, and who permeates all things through sparks of divine fire called the *logoi* that control the development of each thing.[3] As with Alexandrian Jewish Hellenism as represented by Philo, the concept of the *logos* in Greek philosophy, despite use of the same Greek word and a few superficial similarities, does not correspond to the apostle John's revelation concerning Christ the eternal Word of God, His incarnation, and His ministry in the past, the present, and the future.

Actually the Greek word *logos*, which was in common usage, refers both to a concept, idea, or inward thought and to the verbal expression, spoken or written, that gives expression to that idea and communicates or reveals it to others. The inward thought remains invisible and unknowable until it is expressed audibly or visibly in a word (*logos*). This is exactly and beautifully the relationship between the first and second persons of the Godhead (John 14:8–11; Col. 1:15; Heb. 1:3a) and undoubtedly is the reason John was led to refer to Christ as "the Word."

Philip Schoff wrote, "John (and he alone) called Christ the 'Logos' of God, *i.e.*, the embodiment of God and the organ of all his revelations. As the human reason or thought is expressed in word, and as the word is the medium of making our thoughts known to others, so God is known to himself and to the world in and through Christ as the personal Word. . . . 'Logos' designates the metaphysical and intellectual relation . . . of Christ to God."[4]

THE WORD OF GOD ETERNAL WITH
GOD THE FATHER AND GOD THE HOLY SPIRIT

The first revelation the apostle John gave concerning the Word is a declaration of His eternality—"In the beginning was the Word" (John 1:1a). This statement obviously is designed to remind the reader or listener of the opening sentence of the Bible—"In the beginning God created the heavens and the earth" (Gen. 1:1). In part because of this similarity, Lewis Sperry Chafer spoke of the Gospel of John as the theological beginning of the New Testament. John undoubtedly viewed the word *beginning* in the two passages as referring to the same starting point.

Whether one agrees with John in this identity of the beginning, at whatever point a person places the beginning of John's statement, at that point "was the Word" (John 1:1). The Word did not come into being at that time; He did not come into being before that time; He simply *was* at that time, eternally existent as God Himself. In your mind's eye you can make a point to mark the beginning of time and of all things except God, and at that point the Word was; in other words, He was eternally existent. John used the imperfect tense of the Greek verb translated "to be," which signifies existence at the point mentioned, in this case eternally. To underscore this truth John later stated, "He was with God in the beginning" (1:2), affirming the Word's possession of the same eternality as God.

Although numerous Scriptures speak of Jesus' preexistence before His incarnation (e.g., John 1:14; 3:13, 17; 17:5; Gal. 4:4; Col. 1:15–17, 19; Heb. 1:6; 10:5; 1 John 1:2), they do not automatically teach His eternality. The Jehovah's Witnesses and some other cultists teach that Jesus existed before the Incarnation but deny His eternality, teaching that He was the first creation of God. Few Scriptures besides these in John 1 teach the eternality of the Word of God, and most of those do so only by inference. The clearest is Jesus' own statement, "I tell you the truth . . . before

Abraham was born, I am" (John 8:58). To claim mere preexistence Jesus would have said, "Before Abraham was born, I was." Instead he took God's covenantal name with Israel—"I AM" (Exod. 3:14)—and claimed eternal existence. In addition, Scriptures that equate Jesus' deity with that of God the Father (e.g., Phil. 2:6; Col. 1:15, 19; 2:9; Heb. 1:3) state His eternality by inference because of the eternality of God.

Our finite minds have comparatively little difficulty conceiving of eternity stretching without end into the future. Believers in the Lord Jesus Christ have received eternal life (John 3:16, 36). This signifies primarily spiritual life, a quality of life, the life possessed by God and bestowed by God (17:3); but eternal life also will continue forever—it will never end (6:50–51; 10:28; Rev. 22:5). Scripture also makes it clear that all unregenerate human beings also will exist forever, but in eternal torment, not eternal life; they will be separated from God in the lake of fire (Matt. 25:41, 46; Rev. 20:10–15). That is the horror of dying without trusting the Lord Jesus Christ and receiving the salvation and eternal life provided by God's grace. Awareness of that eternal torment that awaits the unregenerate should spur all Christians to greater personal evangelism and support of evangelistic and missionary agencies.

It is much more difficult, however, for human beings to conceive of eternity past, of existence stretching back into the past without beginning. But this is true of God (Deut. 33:27; Pss. 41:13; 90:2; Isa. 44:6; 48:12; 57:15; Rom. 1:20) and according to John is true of the Word as well. This fact of His self-existence is what the Lord Jesus, the incarnate Word, declared concerning Himself, as stated earlier, when He told the Jews who debated with him, "I tell you the truth, before Abraham was born, I am!" (John 8:58). By this statement Jesus was claiming for Himself exactly what God had claimed when He told Moses, "I AM WHO I AM. This is what you are to say to the Israelites, 'I AM has sent me to you'" (Exod. 3:14). The Jews understood Jesus' claim, because "at this, they picked up stones to stone him" (John 8:59), judging Him guilty of blasphemy.

Logic—some might even say common sense—demands that eternality and self-existence be true of someone or something. It is inconceivable that everything, including God, just suddenly sprang into being out of nothing. In the past, secular scientists have considered matter to be eternal. With the splitting of the atom and other discoveries concerning matter, secular scientists in more recent years have attributed eternality also to energy. However, the scientific law of entropy—the principle that the amount of available energy is always decreasing in a closed system such as our universe—argues against energy being eternal. Through the years Christian scientists have argued for the eternality of God in opposition to atheistic secularism, and in more recent years they have used the latest scientific discoveries to press their insistence that God must be the eternal One.

Logic also demands that the simpler and less complex always be produced by the more complex, not vice versa. That which possesses life and personality is more complex than that which is inanimate and impersonal; therefore, logically, life and personality cannot have been produced from matter or energy. The eternal, self-existent God of the Bible, therefore, is the only logical explanation of all things; He must be the eternal, self-existent One. The apostle John stated that this eternality and self-existence belongs to Jesus Christ, the Word.

EQUALITY OF THE WORD IN FELLOWSHIP
WITH GOD THE FATHER AND GOD THE SPIRIT

John's second statement about the Word in John 1:1 is, "the Word was with God." Most commentators agree that in His eternal existence the Word was in continuous association and fellowship with God. The verb "was" repeats the imperfect tense of the Greek verb translated "to be" in the first clause of this verse. In addition, a number of commentators note that the Greek preposition translated "with," when it occurs with the accusative case of the noun as here, describes the two persons involved as face to face in an equal and close relationship (see 1 John 1:2; 2:1). Vincent summarized the significance of John's statement as follows: "the divine Word not only abode with the Father from all eternity, but was in the living, active relation of communion with Him."[5]

The apostle John's third statement in John 1:1 further emphasizes the equality of the Word with God the Father and God the Holy Spirit: "and the Word was God." Because the Greek word translated "God" *(theos)* has no definite article in the Greek text, the Jehovah's Witnesses, who believe

Jesus is a divine being but not fully and truly God, translate the clause, "and the Word was a god." This is a form of the ancient heresy of Arianism and in effect is a repetition of Philo's error. It is rejected as grammatically unsupportable by such Greek scholars as Henry Alford and A. T. Robertson, who call attention to the parallel construction in Jesus' statement to the Samaritan woman by the well of Sychar: "God is spirit, and his worshipers must worship in spirit and in truth" (John 4:24). Another parallel construction is found in John 1:49, which reads, "you are the King of Israel," where the word translated "king" occurs without the definite article but is properly translated "the king." Concerning this construction E. C. Colwell stated (in what is called Colwell's Rule), "Definite predicate nouns which precede the verb usually lack the article . . . a predicate nominative which precedes the verb cannot be translated as an indefinite or 'qualitative' noun solely because of the absence of the article; if the context suggests that the predicate is definite, it should be translated as a definite noun."[6]

The word *logos*, which has the definite article in all three clauses in John 1:1, is clearly the subject of the first two clauses. It is obviously meant to be the subject of this third clause even though in the Greek word order it follows the word translated "God" *(theos)*. Robertson pointed out that in Greek the first position in the sentence or clause, as here, is often given to the predicate "simply because, as a rule, the predicate is the most important thing in the sentence."[7] Here the fact that the Word is God is the most important thing. First position in the clause or sentence is also given frequently for emphasis, which may also be involved here. John undoubtedly wanted his readers to know that the Word truly is God.

Had the article occurred with the word *theos* as well as with *logos* ("the God was the Word") it would have meant that the totality of what constituted God was expressed in the Word, thus denying the doctrine of the Trinity and supporting the ancient heresy of Sabellianism, a form of Modalistic Monarchianism (see page 84). It also would have denied the personal distinctiveness and the relationship between the *logos* and God the Father, stated in the second clause and in verse 2. The clause as stated by John means that the Word *(logos)* possesses the character of God *(theos)* and is God in substance and essence.

As Tenney wrote, "The three statements of v. 1 bring out three different aspects of the nature of the Word. The first speaks of his preexistence, the second of his distinctiveness, and third of his deity."[8] Then in verse 2, in the apostle John's characteristic mode of writing, he repeated two of the ideas from verse 1 for emphasis—the eternal existence of the Word and his eternal face-to-face relationship of fellowship and equality with God. Correctly translated and interpreted, these two verses contribute to the recognition, development, and formulation of the biblical and Christian doctrine of the Trinity. This is the doctrine that the one eternal God of the Bible subsists in a Trinity of Persons—Father, Son (or Word), and Holy Spirit.

The doctrine of the Trinity is a biblical doctrine, not in the sense that it is stated in any one verse of Scripture but in the sense that its recognition and formulation are demanded by a wealth of biblical evidence such as this passage. In this regard 1 John 5:7 as it occurs in the King James Version ("For there are three that bear record in heaven, the Father, the Word, and the Holy Ghost: and these three are one"), though an excellent statement of the doctrine of the Trinity, has no early Greek manuscript support and probably was not in the original letter written by John but inserted later.

On the one hand the Bible clearly teaches that there is one God (Deut. 6:4; 4:35, 39; Rom. 3:30; 1 Cor. 8:4, 6; Eph. 4:6; 1 Tim. 2:5). The Bible also clearly teaches that three persons—God the Father, God the Son, and God the Holy Spirit—possess and utilize the attributes of God, exercise the prerogatives of God such as accepting worship and forgiving sins, and clearly are identified as God. The Bible, therefore, presents God the Father, God the Son, and God the Holy Spirit each as equally and eternally God, constituting the one God, and yet each as a distinct person in fellowship and cooperative activity with each other. As Jesus expressed it to the Jews in Solomon's Colonnade of the temple, "I and the Father are one" (John 10:30). Jesus was not claiming simply unity of goal or interest but unity of nature, as the Jews clearly recognized (10:33). Jesus later expressed a personal interrelationship with God the Father, as seen in His doing the works of God (10:37–38).

Other Trinitarian passages of Scripture include the baptismal formula given by the resurrected Jesus Christ to His disciples at their commissioning before His ascension: "Therefore go and make disciples of all nations, baptizing them in the name [singular] of the Father and of the Son and of the Holy Spirit" (Matt. 28:19). The three persons of the triune Godhead were involved in the annunciation by the angel Gabriel to the Virgin Mary (Luke 1:35), the baptism of Jesus by John the Baptist (Matt. 3:16–17), and Jesus' Upper Room Discourse with His disciples the evening of His arrest (John 14–16). The three persons of the Godhead are joined together in the benediction of 2 Corinthians 13:14, the introduction of 1 Peter 1:2, and the discussions of 1 Corinthians 12:4–6 and Ephesians 4:4–6. Some Old Testament implications of the Trinity include the Aaronic benediction for the sons of Israel (Num. 6:15–16), Jacob's benediction on Joseph's sons (Gen. 48:15–16), and the threefold occurrence of "holy" in Isaiah 6:3. The latter could also be a Hebrew way of expressing emphasis on God's holiness. Much additional biblical evidence could be given in support of the doctrine of the Trinity.

Although the statement of the doctrine of the Trinity is simple—"We worship one God in trinity and trinity in unity without confounding the persons or dividing the substance" (Athanasian Creed)[9]—its explanation and comprehension are difficult, even impossible in the ultimate sense, because it is utterly unique and transcends human earthly experience. Many illustrations of the Trinity can be suggested, such as the human individual composed of body, soul, and spirit. (However, others believe the Bible teaches man consists of only two parts—material and immaterial.) Some like the illustration of an egg, which consists of shell, white, and yolk. This illustration logically breaks down, however, because each part of the egg is only that part of the egg, not the whole egg. Each person of the Trinity, on the other hand, is completely God and at the same time a distinct person from the other two persons. Perhaps the closest natural thing to an illustration of the Trinity is light, which consists of three different kinds of rays and yet forms one light. This is appropriate since the Bible states "God is light" (1 John 1:5), but in the end even this illustration logically breaks down.

In the final analysis all illustrations of the Trinity prove inadequate to fully explain this unique reality. Bernard of Clairvaux wrote, "How can plurality consist with unity, or unity with plurality? To examine the fact closely is rashness, to believe it is piety, to know it is life, and life eternal."[10]

The Puritan divine John Arrowsmith said, "The Trinity is a mystery which my faith embraces as revealed in the Word, but my reason cannot fathom."[11] Once again in this volume a thorough discussion is not appropriate; but I must confess that despite the numerous times I have taught the doctrine of the Trinity as clearly as I could, each time at the end of the course I had to confess to myself and to the class that, although I could explain the doctrine adequately and believe it wholeheartedly, I did not comprehend it in the sense of fathoming its depths of meaning. I take solace in the reputed wry remark attributed to Jonathan Edwards, another Puritan divine, concerning the Trinity: "He who would deny it will lose his soul, and he who would too much seek to understand it will lose his wits."

THE WORD WORKING WITH GOD THE FATHER AND GOD THE SPIRIT

In Creating All Things

The apostle John followed his revelations concerning the person of the Word and His eternal relationship and identity with God (John 1:1–2) with a revelation concerning the involvement of the Word in cosmic creation. He wrote, "Through him all things were made; without him nothing was made that has been made" (1:3). This supports the idea that the "beginning" in verses 1–2 is to be identified with the beginning in Genesis 1:1. Here the tense of the Greek verb translated "were made" (more literally "came into being") presents the creative process in all its complexity and progression. The words "through him" signify the agent of an action. The statement that follows—"without him nothing was made that has been made"—is more than Hebraic antithetical parallelism (the repetition of the same idea in a negative statement). It is a specific denial of the ancient Gnostic heresy of the eternity of matter and of the participation of angels or aeons in the creative process.

John's presentation of our Lord Jesus Christ's involvement as the Word in the creation of all things is supported by other Scriptures. Later in this chapter John wrote, "The world was made through him" (John 1:10). The apostle Paul declared, "For by him all things were created: things in heaven and on earth, visible and invisible, whether thrones or powers or rulers or authorities; all things were created by him and for him" (Col. 1:16). Similarly the writer of the Epistle to the Hebrews described the Son as God's Heir "through whom he made the universe" (Heb. 1:2).

Elsewhere in the Scriptures creation is attributed to God (Gen. 1:1–2:4; Exod. 20:11; Job 38:4; Ps. 90:2; Isa. 44:24; Acts 14:15; Rom. 1:20; Heb. 11:3; Rev. 10:6), understood in most cases to mean God the Father. In a few Scriptures God the Holy Spirit is mentioned as involved in creation (Gen. 1:2; Job 33:4; Ps. 104:30). Also in at least two verses God's Word is said to be His instrument of creation (Ps. 33:6; Heb. 11:3), and frequently creation is described as the result of His speaking (Gen. 1:3, 6, 9, 11, 14, 20, 24, 26; Pss. 33:9). In Proverbs 8:27–31 the wisdom of God is personified and described as involved in creation. Elsewhere wisdom is spoken of as God's instrument in creation (Ps. 136:5; Prov. 3:19; Jer. 10:12; 51:15). The point of this is that Scripture presents God the Father, the Word of God—the Lord Jesus Christ—and the Holy Spirit of God as involved in God's work of creation without specifically identifying the Word or the Holy Spirit as members of the triune Godhead; yet they must be, because creation is God's work. Perhaps the Old Testament verse that best clarifies the Trinity in the work of creation is the statement, "Let us make man in our image, in our likeness" (Gen. 1:26). The first point to notice here is that God is quoted as speaking to Himself, a suggestion of the Trinity's involvement in creation (see 3:22; 11:7; Isa. 6:8). Then there is the use of the plural pronouns "us" and "our." Most Old Testament scholars consider this an example of the "plural of majesty," but these pronouns may well imply God's subsistence in a Trinity of persons in light of other biblical evidence.

A New Testament verse that clearly states the relationship among the members of the Godhead in God's work of creation is 1 Corinthians 8:6. There the apostle Paul emphasized that, in contrast to the false gods represented by the idols worshiped by the pagans, the triune God of the Bible worshiped by Christians is the only true God. This God involves "the Father, from whom all things came and for whom we live; and there is but one Lord, Jesus Christ, through whom all things came and through whom we live." Thus God the Father is identified as the primary source, as well as the goal, of everything, and Jesus Christ, the Word, is identified as the agent of accomplishing everything. This verse is one of the clearest in setting forth the relationship between God the Father and God the Son in the work of creation. It presents what theologians call the "economic order" of the triune Godhead, the relationship among the three members of the Trinity in carrying out all the work of God. In summary, creation is from God the Father through the Lord Jesus Christ (the Word) by means of the Holy Spirit of God.

That Jesus Christ should be the secondary agent of God's creation is appropriate; as the Word He is the person of the Godhead who reveals God and makes Him manifest. Just as a word is an expression of a human person's thoughts, so the Word of God is the expression and manifestation of God. Since Scripture makes it clear that creation is a means of God's revelation of Himself (Ps. 19:1–6; Rom. 1:19–20), it is fitting that the Word of God be involved in it. Likewise, as discussed in chapters 4–7, it is appropriate that the Word is the member of the Godhead who became incarnate (John 1:14) as the Lord Jesus Christ.

In Sustaining All Things

Scripture also indicates that in relation to His creation God is not an absentee landlord. He did not create the universe to abandon it to the operation of inherent principles, the position generally associated with Deism, a view that rose to some prominence in England and in western Europe during the latter seventeenth and eighteenth centuries. It is also the position of secular science with its discovery of supposedly absolute, inviolate laws that control the operation of the universe. To the contrary, in his messages to Job God made it clear that He is in immediate control of His complete creation and all of its creatures (Job 38–41). To the same point the apostle Paul wrote that "in him [Christ] all things hold together" (Col. 1:17). Similarly, the writer of the epistle to the Hebrews stated that God's Son is "sustaining all things by his powerful Word" (Heb. 1:3). The apostle John undoubtedly had the work of sustaining creation in mind when he wrote concerning the Word of God, "In him was life, and that life was the light of men" (John 1:4). Robertson correctly concluded, "The permanence of the universe rests, then, on Christ far more than on gravity. It is a Christo-centric universe. . . . Christ is the controlling and unifying force in nature."[12]

SUMMARY

The biblical truth that Jesus Christ existed prior to His incarnation as the infant Jesus is stated in a number of Scriptures (John 1:14–15, 18, 30; 3:13; 6:62; Phil. 2:5–6). Jesus Himself asked God the Father to "glorify me in your presence with the glory I had with you before the world began" (John 17:5). Only the apostle John, however, identified the preincarnate Christ as the eternal Word who subsists eternally in intimate relationship with God and is identified as God. This introduced the doctrine of the one God of the Bible who subsists as a Trinity of persons. And this, in turn, as well as the apostle John's revelation of the eternal Word's participation in the creation of all things, led to a discussion of the relationship of the three persons of the triune Godhead—God the Father, God the Son (or Word), and God the Holy Spirit—in all the work of God, including the work of creation of all things and the subsequent sustaining of all things.

Two

THE PREINCARNATE MINISTRY
OF THE WORD OF GOD

———◦◉◦———

THE PREINCARNATE MINISTRY of the Lord Jesus Christ as the eternal Word of God began with His participation in the cosmic creative activity of the triune Godhead, discussed in the preceding chapter (Gen. 1:1–2:3; John 1:3; Col. 1:16). His ministry continues in His involvement in sustaining creation in its orderliness and predictability, which people can observe and describe (Col. 1:17). Until the moment of His incarnation as the baby in Bethlehem, however, was His preincarnate ministry limited to these two activities? His very designation as the Word implies otherwise because it suggests visible expression and manifestation and audible communication and revelation. His identity as the Word means that to become incarnate He had to be a member of the Godhead. It also means that He is the member of the Godhead manifested visibly and communicating audibly in the Old Testament. Some evidence supporting this conclusion is definite, while other evidence is more tenuous.

THE PREINCARNATE MINISTRY
OF THE WORD AS THE ANGEL OF THE LORD

One line of evidence for the preincarnate ministry of the Word of God is the ministry of the Angel of the Lord in the Old Testament. The Hebrew word translated "angel," as well as its Greek equivalent, means a person sent as a deputy or representative and a messenger. In fact, the English word *angel* is in effect a transliteration of the Greek word *angelos*. God used members of His angelic hosts as His representatives and messengers, for example, Gabriel (Dan. 8:15–26; 9:11–27; Luke 1:19–20, 26–37), other unnamed angels, such as the two at Jesus' tomb (24:4–7), and the two at Christ's ascension (Acts 1:10–11). The Angel of the Lord who ministered in the Old Testament, however, is a unique representative and messenger of God, as we will discuss. He is in a class by Himself.

This fact is demonstrated by an examination of the recorded appearances of the Angel of the Lord in the Old Testament. The first was to Hagar, the Egyptian servant of Sarai. Sarai gave her to Abram, Sarai's husband, as a concubine when Sarai was infertile (Gen. 16:1–3). When Hagar conceived, she despised her mistress, who dealt with her harshly. As a result Hagar fled from the household (16:4–6). As Moses recorded, "The angel of the Lord found Hagar near a spring in the desert" (16:7). The Angel instructed her to return to Sarai and submit to her. He explained that she would bear a son whom she should call Ishmael and from whom would come many descendants (16:9–12). Hagar gave this name to the One who appeared to her: "You are the God who sees me" (16:13). Some say her identifying this person as God was an error. But note that Moses, the author of Genesis, writing under inspiration of the Holy Spirit, wrote, "She gave this name to the Lord who spoke to her" (16:13).

This Hebrew word for "Lord" is translated in the King James Version and American Standard Version as *Jehovah*, an effort at transliterating the Hebrew word *YHWH*, a four-letter word called the tetragrammaton. A better transliteration is *Yahweh*. When the Jews came to the word *Yahweh* in reading the Old Testament, they refused to pronounce it. This was out of worshipful respect for God and to insure against their blaspheming "the name of the Lord" (Lev. 24:16), a sin punishable by death. Instead they would say either *ʾAdōnāy* ("Lord") or *ʾElōhîm* ("God"), whichever was appropriate in the context. As the Jewish scribes produced their scrolls, they added vowels to the consonants of the Hebrew word for Lord. These vowels are reflected in the English name Jehovah. The word *Yahweh* more accurately reflects the Hebrew consonants.

Further evidence of the careful use of the name Yahweh (LORD) is the statement by God recorded in Isaiah 42:8: "I am the LORD; that is my name! I will not give my glory to another or my praise to idols" (see 43:3, 15). In light of this, for Hagar to identify one of God's angelic hosts, a created spirit being, as Yahweh may seem at first glance to be a mistake. Yet this in fact indicates that the Angel of the Lord is the same as Yahweh.

The facts found in the incident of the Angel of the Lord's appearance to Hagar are repeated in many of His other appearances. It is verified, for example, by His appearance to Abraham (whose name was changed from Abram in Gen. 17:5) when he was about to sacrifice his only heir and son Isaac as a sacrifice to God, as God had commanded (22:1–10). As Abraham stood with the knife in his hand poised above Isaac on the altar, the Angel of the Lord called to Abraham to stay his hand (22:11–12) and provided a substitute sacrifice of a ram caught in a thicket (22:13). Abraham considered the Angel of the Lord who spoke to him to be the Lord Himself, for he "called that place, 'The LORD Will Provide'" (22:14). Also he wrote that the subsequent covenantal promise spoken by the Angel of the Lord was a declaration of the Lord Himself (22:15–18).

Moses knew that the Angel who spoke to Hagar was God Himself, as he wrote in Genesis 16:13, because of his own personal experience at the burning bush, recorded in Exodus 3. "There the angel of the LORD appeared to him in flames of fire from within a bush" (3:2). The account continues, however, "When the LORD [no longer the Angel of the LORD] saw that he had gone over to look, God called to him from within the bush" (3:4) and instructed Moses to remove his sandals because "the place where you are standing is holy ground" (3:5). God then identified Himself as "the God of your father, the God of Abraham, the God of Isaac and the God of Jacob" (3:6). Later God identified Himself as "I AM WHO I AM," and He instructed Moses to tell the Jews in Egypt, "I AM has sent me to you" (3:14). The name I AM is linguistically related to Yahweh.

During the theocracy, when God ruled His people Israel and delivered them from their enemies and oppressors through sovereignly chosen judges (Judg. 2:16–19), the Angel of the Lord appeared at least twice to judges in calling them to their ministries. One occasion was an appearance to Gideon while he was threshing wheat secretly "in a winepress to keep it from the Midianites" (6:11). After first calling this person "the angel of the LORD" (6:11–12), the author of Judges (who was Samuel, according to the Jewish Talmud) called him "the LORD" (6:14, 16–17, 23, 25), as did Gideon (6:15).

Evidently equating the Angel of the Lord with the Lord Himself, Gideon requested permission to bring an "offering and set it before you" (6:18). When Gideon returned with a young goat and unleavened bread, the Angel told him how to prepare it as an offering on a rock. Then the Angel touched the offering with a staff, and it was consumed with fire from the rock and the Angel disappeared (6:19–21). Realizing he had truly seen and talked with the Angel of the Lord, Gideon was afraid he would die (6:22). In response to the Lord's assurance of peace, Gideon "built an altar there to the LORD there and called it 'The LORD is Peace'" (6:24).

In preparation for the birth and ministry of Samson, the Angel of the Lord next appeared to the infertile wife of Manoah, announcing to her that she would conceive and give birth to a son who "is to be a Nazirite, set apart to God from birth" (13:5). When the woman told her husband, Manoah prayed for the Angel's return to give them further instructions, a request God granted (13:8–14). When Manoah prepared a burnt offering to the Lord in response to the Angel's suggestion, the Angel ascended into heaven in the flame of the sacrifice on the altar (13:19–21). "We are doomed to die!" Manoah told his wife; "We have seen God" (13:22). Being more theologically perceptive, Manoah's wife responded, "If the LORD had meant to kill us, he would not have accepted a burnt offering and grain offering from our hands, nor shown us all these things or now told us this" (13:23).

The significant thing about the appearances of the Angel of the Lord to both Gideon and Manoah and his wife, in addition to his identity as the Lord given by both Gideon and Samson's parents, is his acceptance of their worship in the form of sacrificial offering. The created angels of God explicitly refuse to accept worship, saying to those who would do so, "Do not do it! . . . Worship God!" (Rev. 19:10; 22:8). The acceptance of worship by the Angel of the Lord is further evidence that He is the Lord Himself, the preincarnate Word of God.

The Angel of the Lord is mentioned in a number of other incidents in the Old Testament. One is the appearance of the Angel of the Lord to Balaam's donkey (Num. 22:22–27) and then to Balaam himself (22:31–35). In this incident the only possible basis for such an identification is relating the Angel of the Lord's declaration to Balaam, "speak only what I tell you" (22:35), with Balaam's statement to Balak, "I must speak only what God puts in my mouth" (22:38). Further possible but unclear evidence can be found in Moses' declarations, "Then the LORD opened the donkey's mouth" (22:28) and "Then the LORD opened Balaam's eyes" (22:31).

Still other incidents are the Angel of the Lord's appearance and message "to all the Israelites" (Judg. 2:1–5), His appearance to Elijah when he fled into the wilderness from Jezebel (1 Kings 19:5–7), His directing Elijah to confront Ahaziah's messengers (2 Kings 1:3) and Ahaziah (1:15), His judgment on the camp of Assyrian soldiers in siege around Jerusalem (19:35) in answer to King Hezekiah's prayer (19:15–19), His appearance to King David (1 Chron. 21:16) and his message to the prophet Gad (21:18) when God judged Israel for David's numbering of the people.

The Angel of the Lord is mentioned frequently in the visions Zechariah recorded in his prophetic book. For example, the Angel of the Lord is the man "riding a red horse . . . standing among the myrtle trees in a ravine" (Zech. 1:8), as verses 11 and 12 make clear. In the vision of chapter 3, Joshua, the high priest of Israel, was seen "standing before the angel of the LORD, and Satan standing at his right side to accuse him" (3:1). Zechariah then identified the Angel of the Lord as "the LORD," whom he quoted as saying to Satan, "The LORD [referring to God the Father] rebuke you, Satan!" (3:2). Joshua's filthy clothes and turban were changed "while the angel of the LORD stood by" (3:5), and then "the angel of the LORD gave this charge to Joshua" (3:6).

This review of the preincarnate ministry of the Word of God as the Angel of the Lord brings several observations to mind. Of first importance is the fact that His ministry was primarily to leaders of God's chosen people Israel—Abraham, Moses, Gideon, the parents of Samson, David, Elijah, and Zechariah. These appearances also involved the support and protection of Israel, illustrated by His appearance to Balaam and his donkey and his judgment of death on the Assyrian army. Even His judgment of death on Israel for David's prideful numbering of the people ultimately benefited both the king and the nation.

At the same time it is interesting, perhaps even significant, that the ministry of the Angel of the Lord in his first two appearances was "on behalf of a friendless and comfortless person who is not even included in major features of the Abrahamic covenant,"[1] namely, Hagar. This certainly demonstrates God's concern for all downtrodden, needy, oppressed, and poor human beings regardless of race, and reveals His infinite grace, mercy, and comfort. These divine attributes also are displayed in the Angel of the Lord's provision of a substitute sacrifice for Isaac and His provision of food, encouragement, and guidance to distraught and fearful Elijah.

It is important to point out that the Angel of the Lord's defense of Joshua the high priest against the attack of Satan in Zechariah's vision prophetically illustrates the present ministry of the glorified Lord Jesus Christ as "the one who speaks to the Father in our defense" (1 John 2:1) whenever believers sin. Similarly, the Angel of the Lord's provision of a substitute sacrifice for Isaac prophetically illustrates the sacrifice of the incarnate Christ, God's "one and only Son" (John 3:16, 18) as our Substitute, "the righteous for the unrighteous" (1 Pet. 3:18; see Heb. 9:26, 28).

THE PREINCARNATE MINISTRY OF THE WORD AS THE ANGEL OF GOD

Related to the preincarnate ministry of the Word of God as the Angel of the Lord are a few incidents in which He is called the Angel of God. The first of these is another appearance and ministry of comfort, encouragement, and revelation to Hagar (Gen. 21:14–21). For the second time Sarah demanded that Abraham send Hagar away, this time because Ishmael mocked Sarah and Isaac (21:9–10). The bread and water Abraham gave Hagar were soon exhausted in the wilderness, and Hagar left her son under a bush to die while she went some distance away so she would not witness his death (21:14–16).

The Angel of God appeared to Hagar and told her God was aware of her plight (21:17–18). "Then God opened her eyes and she saw a well of water" (21:19), providing life-giving refreshment. Although the conclusion is not irrefutable, the Angel of God here seems to be equated with God. The account adds that "God was with the boy as he grew up" (21:20).

The identity of the Angel of God with God is clearer in the account of His appearance to Jacob while he was with Laban in Haran (31:11). The angel of God told Jacob, "I am the God of Bethel, where you anointed a pillar and where you made a vow to me" (31:13). In that previous dream on the way to Haran the Lord had spoken to Jacob and said, "I am the LORD, the God of your father Abraham and the God of Isaac" (28:13). When Jacob awoke from his dream, he said, "Surely the LORD is in this place" (28:16), and "This is none other than the house of God" (28:17). In the morning he set up a stone as a pillar and consecrated it with oil and called the place Bethel (21:19), which means "House of God."

The Angel of God is mentioned again in the account of the Israelites' departure from Egypt under Moses' human leadership. When the Israelites were pinned against the Red Sea with the Egyptian army in pursuit, "Then the angel of God, who had been traveling in front of Israel's army, withdrew and went behind them. The pillar of cloud also moved from in front and stood behind them" (Exod. 14:19). Here the pillar of cloud is identified with the Angel of God, but previously we read, "By day the LORD went ahead of them in a pillar of cloud to guide them on their way and by night in a pillar of fire to give them light" (13:21). Thus the Angel of God seems to be identified with the Lord.

THE PREINCARNATE MINISTRY OF THE WORD IN OTHER OLD TESTAMENT THEOPHANIES

These appearances of the preincarnate Word of God as the Angel of the Lord and the Angel of God are called theophanies ("appearances of God"), since such appearances are by a member of the triune Godhead. Other appearances of God also are recorded in the Old Testament, which are undoubtedly a part of the preincarnate ministry of the Word of God. In fact, since the eternal Word is the member of the Godhead who manifests and reveals God visibly and audibly, as we have seen, all appearances of God in the Old Testament are part of His preincarnate ministry. What is often difficult to settle is whether a particular appearance is that of God or of a member of His angelic host.

One such case is the record of Joshua's experience after crossing the Jordan River (Josh. 3) and the circumcision of all the males of Israel who had been born in the wilderness (5:2–9). As "Joshua was near Jericho, he looked up and saw a man standing in front of him with a drawn sword in his hand" (5:13). In response to Joshua's question, "Are you for us or for our enemies?" (5:13), the man replied, "Neither . . . but as commander of the army of the LORD I have now come" (5:14). Joshua apparently concluded that this was an appearance of the Lord, because he "fell facedown to the ground in reverence" (5:14). This act of homage was accepted by the man, which was something a mere angel would not be willing to do (Rev. 19:10; 22:8–9). In fact, after commanding Joshua, "Take off your sandals, for the place where you are standing is holy" (Josh. 5:15), the "commander of the LORD's army," now identified as the Lord, gave Joshua directions for the conquest of Jericho.

Another example is the coming of the three men to Abraham in Mamre (Gen. 18:2). Here Moses settled the issue, however, by introducing the incident with the statement, "The LORD appeared to Abraham" (18:1). Although the visitors are called men three times (18:2, 16, 22), one is also identified as "the LORD" (18:10, 13–14, 17, 20, 22, 26–33). After God revealed to Abraham his intentions for Sodom and Gomorrah (18:20–21), "the men turned away and went toward Sodom" (18:22). Apparently only two of the men departed, because "Abraham remained standing before the LORD" (18:22).

A third instance is Jacob's experience the night before he met his brother Esau and was reconciled with him. Jacob was alone, having sent his family and all his possessions across the river Jabbok, "and a man wrestled with him till daybreak" (32:24). The man wrenched Jacob's hip in an effort to overpower him, but Jacob refused to let him go "unless you bless me" (32:26). He renamed Jacob Israel, "because you have struggled with God and with men and have overcome" (32:28), and He "blessed him there" (32:29). "So Jacob called the place Peniel, saying, 'I saw God face to face, and yet my life was spared'" (32:30).

Concerning this incident the prophet Hosea wrote, "As a man he struggled with God. He struggled with the angel and overcame him; he wept and begged for his favor" (Hos. 12:3–4). Then Hosea wrote of Jacob's earlier encounter with God: "He found him at Bethel and talked with him there—the LORD God Almighty, the LORD is his name of renown!" (12:4–5). This inspired commentary confirms the fact that the man with whom Jacob wrestled was the preincarnate Word of God in a theophany.

Still other possible theophanies of the eternal Word of God in the Old Testament include the man who joined Shadrach, Meshach, and Abednego in Nebuchadnezzar's fiery furnace. Nebuchadnezzar said, "Look! I see four men walking around in the fire, unbound and unharmed, and the fourth looks like a son of the gods" (Dan. 3:25). Later he said, "Praise be to the God of Shadrach, Meshach, and Abednego, who has sent his angel and rescued his servants!" (3:28). Daniel had a similar experience when he was thrown into the lions' den (6:16–17). The next morning when King Darius saw Daniel unharmed (16:19–21), the prophet told Darius, "My God sent his angel, and shut the mouths of the lions" (6:22). The conclusion that these incidents are theophanies of the preincarnate Word of God as the Angel of the Lord is appropriate, but not absolutely certain.

Bible students are divided on whether the "man dressed in linen" (10:5) who appeared to Daniel by the Tigris River was a theophany of the preincarnate Word of God as the Angel of the Lord, or whether he was a member of God's angelic host. In support of His identity as the Angel of the Lord is His glorious description (10:6) and His extensive revelation to Daniel of Israel's history from that time forward to the completion of God's program for His chosen people (10:12–12:13). Such a description and such a revelation are appropriate as part of the ministry of the eternal Word of God. (Bible students who conclude this is a member of God's angelic host do so because he was delayed in responding to Daniel's prayers by "the prince of the Persian kingdom" until "Michael, one of the chief princes, came to help me" [10:12–13]. They say no prince could delay the Son of God, but the prince of Persia could delay an angel.)

Although the preincarnate ministry of Jesus Christ as the eternal Word of God began with creation (John 1:3), much of it was directed to God's chosen people Israel (1 Cor. 10:1–4). As already noted, the pillar of cloud and fire that led and protected the Israelites out of Egypt and through the wilderness to Canaan was a preincarnate theophany of the eternal Word of God. In the wilderness the Lord provided manna (Exod. 16:4–5, 35; Josh. 5:12) and quail (Num. 11:31–32) as food for Israel. The Lord also punished Israel when they turned away from Him, but He delivered them from their enemies when they repented and returned to Him (Pss. 105; 106). This seems to be confirmed by Isaiah in his review of God's care of Israel: "In all their distress he too was distressed, and the angel of his presence saved them" (Isa. 63:9). It is also likely that the visible manifestation of the glory of God to Moses, Aaron, Nadab and Abihu, and the seventy elders of Israel (Exod. 24:9–11) and to the people of Israel (24:16–17), to Moses by himself (33:21–23), and to the prophet Ezekiel (Ezek. 1:26–28) were theophanies of the Word of God. In fact, "it is safe to assume that every visible manifestation of God in bodily form in the Old Testament is to be identified with the Lord Jesus Christ"[2] in His preincarnate role as the eternal Word of God.

The emphasis in this chapter on the eternal Word of God ministering in the Old Testament as the Angel of the Lord, the Angel of God, and in other theophanies is not intended to minimize the importance and role of either God the Father or God the Holy Spirit. It simply presents the evidence that the eternal Word of God as a member of the triune Godhead had an active ministry in Old Testament times before His incarnation as the Lord Jesus Christ. In addition, it recognizes the truth of Scripture that God the Father is "invisible" (John 1:18; 6:46; 1 Tim. 1:17; Col. 1:15; 6:15–16; Heb. 11:27; 1 John 4:12) and that God the Holy Spirit also is invisible. The member of the Trinity called "the Word" is the One who manifests and reveals God in incarnate form as Jesus Christ and in preincarnate form as the Angel of the Lord and in other theophanies.

Three

THE OLD TESTAMENT ANTICIPATION OF THE
INCARNATION OF THE WORD OF GOD

FTER THE APOSTLE John introduced the eternal Word, who is associated with God as a member of the triune Godhead and was involved in God's work of creation (John 1:1–3), he revealed that "the Word became flesh and made his dwelling among us . . . the One and Only Son, who came from the Father" (1:14). This incarnation of the Word (the Son) as Jesus Christ, the One who has made known the invisible God (1:17–18), suggests that a divine master plan was being carried out. Recognition of such a plan is consistent with the biblical portrait of God as the all-wise Sovereign (Pss. 103:19; 104:24). The Incarnation was not a spur-of-the-moment decision on God's part.

Scripture elsewhere makes it clear that God has a master plan that stretches from eternity to eternity and embraces all created beings, all created things, and all events. Psalm 33:11 reads, "But the plans of the LORD stand firm forever, the purposes of his heart through all generations." Not only is this plan devised in God's infinite wisdom, but also it is carried out by His infinite, sovereign power. "The LORD does whatever pleases him, in the heavens and on the earth, in the seas and all their depths" (135:6). The prophet Isaiah asked, "For the LORD Almighty has purposed, and who can thwart him? His hand is stretched out, and who can turn it back?" (Isa. 14:27; see 46:8–11). King Nebuchadnezzar of

Babylon learned concerning "the Most High . . . who lives forever" that "His dominion is an eternal dominion; his kingdom endures from generation to generation. All the peoples of the earth are regarded as nothing. He does as he pleases with the powers of heaven and the peoples of the earth. No one can hold back his hand or say to him, 'What have you done?'" (Dan. 4:34–35). When Nebuchadnezzar acknowledged God's sovereign control of His universe, he said, "my sanity was restored" (4:34, 36).

The crux of this eternal master plan of God is the redemptive death of Jesus Christ, His incarnate Son (the Word) as a sacrifice for sin to provide salvation and eternal life to all who believe. As the apostle Peter explained to the Jews on the Day of Pentecost, "Jesus of Nazareth . . . was handed over to you by God's set purpose and foreknowledge; and you, with the help of wicked men, put him to death by nailing him to the cross" (Acts 2:22–23). To provide a perfect sacrifice for a redemptive death required the Incarnation, as Peter told his readers: "He was chosen before the creation of the world, but was revealed in these last times for your sake" (1 Pet. 1:20). Similarly, the author of the epistle to the Hebrews wrote, "Therefore, when Christ came into the world, he said . . . 'a body you prepared for me'. . . . Then I said, 'Here I am . . . I have come to do your will, O God'" (Heb. 10:5, 7). The author concluded that "we have been made holy through the sacrifice of the body of Jesus Christ once for all" (10:10).

One part of this master plan difficult to understand is how it can include the eternal choice by God of everyone who will believe in Jesus' sacrificial death while at the same time maintaining that their faith in Jesus' death is their free choice. This is true also of those who refuse to accept the offer of salvation. In fact, this conundrum between God's eternal plan and human will involves all events. Ultimately the answer rests in the mystery of God's omniscience and His sovereignty, but the Bible teaches both the certain execution of God's plan and free will in human choices. For example, the Roman soldiers who crucified Jesus freely chose to divide Jesus' clothing among them and cast lots for his seamless undergarment (John 19:23–24), but their actions had been prophesied in Psalm 22:18.

Contributing to the human choice of salvation is the convicting ministry of God the Holy Spirit (John 16:7–11) and His efficacious calling (Rom. 8:29–30). Such a choice is part of God's master plan. The apostle

Paul told the Ephesians that God "chose us in him before the creation of the world" and "he predestined us to be adopted as his sons through Jesus Christ, in accordance with his pleasure and will" (Eph. 1:4–5). He added, "In him we were also chosen, having been predestined according to the plan of him who works out everything in conformity with the purpose of his will" (1:11). Paul also told the Thessalonians that "from the beginning God chose you to be saved through the sanctifying work of the Spirit and through belief in the truth" (2 Thess. 2:13), and he told Timothy that God "has saved us and called us to a holy life—not because of anything we have done but because of his own purpose and grace" (2 Tim. 1:9).

The goal of this eternal master plan of God is fourfold. The first objective is the exaltation and glorification of Christ, the eternal Word, who willingly humbled himself to become incarnate and to suffer death as a sacrifice for sin in the plan of God (Phil. 2:5–11; see 1 Cor. 15:25–26; Rev. 19:16). A second objective is "that now, through the church, the manifold wisdom of God should be made known to the rulers and authorities in the heavenly realms, according to his eternal purpose which he accomplished in Christ Jesus our Lord" (Eph. 3:10–11). Ultimately this is to be "for the praise of his glory" (1:12, 14) and "to the praise of his glorious grace" (1:6) "so that God may be all in all" (1 Cor. 15:28). A third objective is to bring "many sons to glory" (Heb. 2:10–13)—believers who are "conformed to the likeness of his Son, that he might be the firstborn among many brothers" (Rom. 8:29). A fourth objective is the final defeat and judgment of Satan and all his followers, both angelic and human (Rev. 20:10–15; see Heb. 2:14) and the removal of physical death (1 Cor. 15:25–26).

In view of the fact that the preincarnate Word was ministering to God's chosen people Israel in theanthropic (i.e., deity in human form) appearances during Old Testament times, and since God's eternal plan for His incarnation and sacrificial death was already set, it is not surprising that revelation concerning the incarnation and sacrifice of the Word was presented in what is called prophecy—disclosure in advance of something that will happen. Such prophecy concerning the Incarnation and ministry of God's promised Messiah, our Lord Jesus Christ, is not the total content of Old Testament prophecy, but it is a significant part of it. Since in all its details it is part of God's eternal plan and since God has infinite ability to carry out His plan, why not reveal it in advance as encouragement or warning to God's people? As the Angel of the Lord in theanthropic appearance said to Abraham before the impending destruction of Sodom and Gomorrah, "Shall I hide from Abraham what I am about to do?" (Gen. 18:17).

OLD TESTAMENT ANTICIPATION IN PROPHECY

God's promise to His chosen people Israel of a Messiah permeates the Old Testament and includes prophecies of the Incarnation and ministry of a unique person, even one divine. Some of the prophecies are vague and veiled, but others are quite clear and specific in details. These prophecies are found throughout the Old Testament from the opening chapters of Genesis to the book of the prophet Malachi.

Genesis 3:15. The first Old Testament prophecy concerning the Incarnation and ministry of a Deliverer was part of God's sentence of judgment on the serpent for having led Adam and Eve into sin. God said, "I will put enmity between you and the woman, and between your offspring and hers; he will crush your head, and you will strike his heel." The vagueness of this prophecy is seen in the fact that many commentators suggest that Eve's exclamation at the birth of Cain—"With the help of the Lord I have brought forth a man" (4:1)—is an expression of her hope that he would be the promised offspring to bruise the serpent's head. Ironically, the first murderer, Cain, proved to be the offspring of the serpent instead! As the outworking of God's plan is recorded in Scripture, the offspring of the woman is Jesus Christ, whose heel was bruised in His arrest, trial, and crucifixion. In turn His bruising of the serpent's (i.e., Satan's, Rev. 12:9; 20:2) head began with His resurrection and ascension to heaven and will be consummated when Satan is bound and thrown "into the Abyss" for the millennium (20:2–3) and then thrown "into the lake of burning sulphur, where the beast and the false prophet had been thrown" (20:10; see 19:20) and where the unregenerate human host will be consigned immediately after the Great White Throne judgment (20:11–15).

Genesis 12:3; 18:18; 22:18. These prophetic promises to Abram (later Abraham), beginning with the Lord's call to him to leave his home country and his family to go to a land that God would show him, include the promise that all peoples on earth will be blessed through you." The third occurrence of this promise (22:18) followed Abraham's willingness to obey God in offering Isaac, his only son, as a sacrifice to Him. The author of the epistle to the Hebrews explains that "Abraham reasoned that God could raise the dead" (11:19), but God spared Abraham from the actual sacrifice, providing a ram caught in a thicket by its horns as a substitute (Gen. 22:12–13). For his obedience by faith God promised Abraham that "through your offspring all nations on earth will be blessed" (22:18).

Once again the prophetic promise as originally stated to Abraham seems vague, but the apostle Peter related it to the resurrected Christ (Acts 3:25). Then the apostle Paul clarified that the promise is specifically fulfilled in the Lord Jesus Christ: "The promises were spoken to Abraham and to his seed. The Scripture does not say 'and to seeds,' meaning many people, but 'and to your seed,' meaning one person, who is Christ" (Gal. 3:16). Earlier in that chapter Paul had pointed out that "the Scripture foresaw that God would justify the Gentiles by faith, and announced the gospel in advance to Abraham: 'All nations will be blessed through you'" (3:8).

Genesis 49:8–12. All the prophetic deathbed blessings of Jacob to his twelve sons are important. The most significant, however, is the blessing to Judah, which is identified as the regal tribe—"your brothers will praise you." Judah is called "a lion's cub" and is described as powerful and awesome, like a lion or lioness. He will be victorious over his enemies and "your brothers will praise you." These details of the blessing were fulfilled by David, who was of the tribe of Judah, and by Solomon, his son.

The remainder of Jacob's blessing of Judah had its beginning in David but continues in force today, though it is not completely fulfilled. It reads, "The scepter will not depart from Judah, nor the ruler's staff from between his feet, until he comes to whom it belongs and the obedience of nations is his" (49:10). The angel Gabriel in his message to the Virgin Mary concerning the birth of her Holy-Spirit-conceived son tied this prophecy to the Lord Jesus Christ, saying, "The Lord God will give him the throne of his father David, and he will reign over the house of Jacob forever; his kingdom will never end" (Luke 1:32b–33; see Ps. 2:7–9; Isa. 9:6–7).

Even though the Lord Jesus presented Himself in His ministry to the

Jewish people as the Messiah, the King of the Jews, and was crucified under that caption (John 19:19–22; see Matt. 27:37; Mark 15:26; Luke 23:38), it is obvious that these prophecies were not fulfilled at His first coming. Their fulfillment awaits His return to earth at His second coming in triumph and glory as "King of kings and Lord of lords" (Rev. 19:16) to establish His worldwide reign of righteousness and peace for a thousand years (20:4–6). The closing verses of Jacob's prophetic blessing on Judah (Gen. 49:11–12) poetically picture the abundance and prosperity that will characterize that millennial kingdom reign.

Deuteronomy 18:15–19. God had originally spoken directly to the assembly of Israel at Sinai out of the fire (Deut. 5:4). Out of fear, however, the elders of Israel asked Moses to be a mediator between God and them, receiving the message from God and delivering it to the people (see 18:16). This marked the beginning of the office of prophet, a person who receives God's message and delivers it to the people. Moses was the first, and in many respects, the preeminent prophet. Now in these verses, after forbidding Israel to use sorcery and divination as the heathen do, God promised to "raise up for them a prophet like you from among their brothers" (18:18; see v. 15).

Even though in both verses (18:15, 18) the singular—"a prophet"—is used, most commentators agree that this promise of God refers first to the procession of prophets who proclaimed His messages to Israel during the years after Moses, many of whom wrote the Old Testament prophetic books. In the general sense of being God's chosen instrument to deliver His message to the people, each of the prophets was like Moses. At the same time, however, Scripture makes it clear that Moses stood alone because "no prophet has risen in Israel like Moses, whom the LORD knew face to face" (34:10).

As a result, therefore, most Bible scholars recognize that the promise of a prophet like Moses ultimately is fulfilled in our Lord Jesus Christ. Even the people of Israel anticipated one who would fulfill this promise of a prophet like Moses in a final and ultimate sense, and they related His appearance to the coming of Elijah and the hope for Messiah. This is seen in the questions of the priests and Levites from the Jews of Jerusalem to John the Baptist, such as, "Are you the Prophet?" (John 1:21; see vv. 19–24).

Likewise, after He fed the five thousand, the people "began to say, 'Surely this is the Prophet who is come into the world'" (6:14). In his message to the people after the healing of the lame man in the temple gate Peter specifically identified Jesus as the fulfillment of this promise to Moses (Acts 3:17–23) and Stephen did the same (7:37).

1 Samuel 2:35. In conjunction with His judgment on Hophni and Phinehas, the ungodly sons of Eli the priest, God said, "I will raise up for myself a faithful priest, who will do according to what is in my heart and mind. I will firmly establish his house, and he will minister before my anointed one always." The short-range fulfillment of this prophecy came when King Solomon removed Abiathar, a descendant of Aaron's son Ithamar, as priest (1 Kings 2:26–27), replacing him with Zadok, a descendant of Aaron's son Eleazar. Even though Zadok's descendants proved unfaithful to God from time to time, they continued as high priests until service in the temple ended with its destruction by the Romans in A.D. 70 (see Mal. 2:1–9). In conjunction with the return of Christ to earth and the establishment of His millennial kingdom, however, the priesthood will be established with the descendants of Levi (3:3–4), and the descendants of Zadok will offer sacrifices (Ezek. 44:17–19). In the final sense the Lord Jesus Christ, "a priest forever, in the order of Melchizedek" (Ps. 110:4; see Heb. 4:14–5:7; 7:11–8:2)—is the fulfillment of God's promise of a "faithful priest, who will do according to what is in my [God's] heart and mind" (1 Sam. 2:35).

2 Samuel 7:11–13, 16 (see 1 Chron. 17:10b–11, 12b–14). Although not mentioned as such in these passages, these promises from God to David and his offspring are called "an everlasting covenant" by David (2 Sam. 23:5) as well as by others (Pss. 89:3, 28, 34, 39; 132:11–12). The immediate fulfillment was carried out by Solomon, David's son, who built the temple as the house of God in Jerusalem (1 Kings 6:1–38; 7:13–8:66). God's promise that "your house and your kingdom will endure forever before me; your throne will be established forever" (2 Sam. 7:16), however, extends far beyond Solomon. Ultimately it is fulfilled in our Lord Jesus Christ.

Even though the exercise of regal authority on the throne of David in Jerusalem has been interrupted because of sin, as God warned (7:14), prophets of Israel recognized an eschatological, messianic restoration and fulfillment of God's promise. Concerning the child to be born and the son given who will rule in the future, Isaiah prophesied, "He will reign on David's throne and over his kingdom, establishing and upholding it with justice and righteousness from that time on and forever," declaring, "The zeal of the Lord Almighty will accomplish this" (Isa. 9:7). Likewise Jeremiah prophesied, "'The days are coming,' declares the Lord, 'when I will raise up to David a righteous Branch, a King who will reign wisely and do what is just and right in the land. In his days Judah will be saved and Israel will live in safety. This is the name by which he will be called: The Lord Our Righteousness'" (Jer. 23:5–6; see 33:14–16). Amos also prophesied about a future day when the Lord "will restore David's fallen tent" (Amos 9:11), and Micah predicted that out of Bethlehem Ephrathah "will come for me one who will be ruler over Israel, whose origins are from of old, from ancient times" (Mic. 5:2). All these prophecies will be fulfilled in Jesus Christ, to whom "the Lord God will give . . . the throne of his father David" to "reign over the house of Jacob forever; his kingdom will never end" (Luke 1:32–33). This will be fulfilled when Christ returns to earth and establishes His millennial reign.

Psalm 2:7–9. The Lord's decree, mentioned in verse 7, "refers to the Davidic Covenant [2 Sam. 7:14a] in which God declared that He would be Father to the king, and the king would be His son."[1] The statement, "You are my Son; today I have become your Father," was an ancient Near Eastern formula used when kings were enthroned. This applies, as verses 8–9 reveal, to the establishment of Christ's millennial kingdom. The angel Gabriel, however, announced to the Virgin Mary that her son "will be called the Son of the Most High" (Luke 1:32) and "the Son of God" (1:35) and that "the Lord God will give him the throne of his father David, and he will reign over the house of Jacob forever; his kingdom will never end" (1:32–33). Furthermore, when the Holy Spirit descended on Jesus at His baptism "in bodily form like a dove," a "voice came from heaven: 'You are my Son, whom I love; with you I am well pleased'" (Luke 3:22; see Matt. 3:16–17; Mark 1:10–11; John 1:32–34). As a result the statement in Psalm 2:7 does have relevance to Jesus' incarnation and earthly ministry.

Psalm 16:8–10. These verses express David's confident faith in God, especially in God's protection and deliverance from death. God's shield of protection delivered Israel's warrior king in many battles, but finally in old age death overtook him (1 Kings 2:10). In a real sense, therefore, David's expressed hope that God will not "let your Holy One see decay" (Ps. 16:10) transcends his personal experience. The apostle Peter made this clear in his sermon on the Day of Pentecost when he quoted these verses of Psalm 16 and pointed out that David, a prophet, was predicting the resurrection of Jesus Christ from the tomb without His body having experienced decay (Acts 2:25–32). In his sermon at Antioch in Pisidia the apostle Paul also quoted the clause, "You will not let your Holy One see decay," and applied it to Jesus' resurrection (13:35–36). Concerning Psalm 16:10 Allen Ross wrote, "Preservation from the decaying grave is the idea behind both David's and Jesus' experiences, but with David it came through a *deliverance* from death, whereas with Jesus it came through a *resurrection* from death."[2]

Psalm 22:1, 6–8, 12–18. Evangelical Bible students have difficulty deciding when in David's life he experienced the mental and physical affliction and suffering expressed in this psalm, especially in verses 1–18. The majority place it during the time of King Saul's pursuit of David and his men, but the record in 1 Samuel does not reflect such mental, emotional, or physical suffering, nor a sense of being abandoned by God (Ps. 22:1). Others place it during David's flight from Jerusalem across the Jordan River to Mahanaim after his son Absalom's revolt (2 Sam. 15–18). Although this experience has some similarities, Ross rightly concludes, "No known incident in the life of David fits the details of this psalm."[3]

In the New Testament it is evident that Jesus Christ and the Gospel authors recognized and stated connections between this psalm and the crucifixion and death of Jesus. Shortly before Jesus "gave up his spirit" (Matt. 27:50; John 19:30) He "cried out in a loud voice, '*Eloi, Eloi, lama sabachthani?*'—which means, 'My God, my God, why have you forsaken me?'" (Matt. 27:46; Mark 15:34). This is a direct quotation of Psalm 22:1; it is most fitting because at that moment Jesus was bearing the judgment of God for the sin of the world (2 Cor. 5:21; see John 1:29, 35; Rom. 4:25).

Matthew recorded that "the chief priests, the teachers of the law and the elders mocked" Jesus on the cross (Matt. 27:41), taunting him to come down from the cross, and then they would believe. They quoted Psalm 22:8, saying "He trusts in God. Let God rescue him now if he wants him" (Matt. 27:43). The passersby also "hurled insults at him" (Matt. 27:39; Mark 15:19), "the soldiers also came up and mocked him" (Luke 23:36), and even "the robbers [at least one of them] who were crucified with him also heaped insults on him" (Matt. 27:44; Mark 15:32). The other robber, recognizing Jesus' innocence, asked to be remembered when Jesus came into His kingdom, a request Jesus promised to grant (Luke 23:39–43). These passages from the Gospels fulfill Psalm 22:6–8.

Concerning Psalm 22 Ross observed, "The expressions describe an execution, not an illness; yet that execution is more appropriate to Jesus' crucifixion than David's experience. . . . David used many poetic expressions to portray his immense sufferings, but these poetic words became literally true of the suffering of Jesus Christ at his enemies' hands."[4] This is especially true in Psalm 22:12–18, climaxing with the soldiers taking his clothes and "dividing them into four shares, one for each of them" and casting lots for his "undergarment" (tunic), which "was seamless, woven in one piece from top to bottom" (John 19:23; see Matt. 27:35; Mark 15:24; Luke 23:34). The apostle John observed that this "happened that the Scripture might be fulfilled" and quoted Psalm 22:16 (John 19:24).

Psalm 40:6–8. In these verses David, a man after God's own heart (Acts 13:22; see 1 Sam. 13:14), recognized that God desires a committed life of obedient service (Rom. 12:1) more than sacrifices and offerings, and so he dedicated himself to do God's will. Though David failed to fulfill this commitment totally, which is true of each of us as well, it was fulfilled perfectly in the incarnation and ministry of Jesus Christ. Jesus told the Jews, "I do nothing on my own but speak just what the Father has taught me. . . . I always do what pleases him" (John 8:28–29); the author of the epistle to the Hebrews quoted these verses from Psalm 40 as fulfilled "when Christ came into the world" (Heb. 10:5–7). The writer's words, "a body you prepared for me," are quoted from the Septuagint, an ancient Greek translation. These words pertaining to Jesus' body are appropriate to the context as well as to the Incarnation.

Many other statements in the Psalms are quoted in the New Testament as fulfilled in the life and ministry of our Lord (e.g., Pss. 45:6–7 [Heb. 1:8–9]; 68:18 [Eph. 4:8]; 110:1 [Heb. 1:13]). Numerous others are fulfilled by incidents in Jesus' life and ministry without the Gospel writer explicitly saying he was referring to the passages in the Psalms (e.g., [Matt. 26:14–16; Mark 14:10–11, 44; Luke 22:47–48]; 69:21 [Matt. 27:48; Mark 15:36; John 19:29]). These underscore the wealth of Old Testament prophecies that anticipate the incarnation and ministry of Christ.

Isaiah 7:14. This prophecy obviously had an imminent fulfillment because it was announced by Isaiah as a sign from the Lord to King Ahaz, who with false piety refused to "put the Lord to the test" by asking for a sign (7:12–13). To serve as a sign to Ahaz, the young virgin, her marriage, and the birth and naming of her son Immanuel would probably have to have been known to Ahaz. Within approximately three years of Isaiah's giving God's sign, the kingdoms of Syria and Israel in alliance against Judah were conquered and destroyed by Tiglath-Pileser, king of Assyria, in fulfillment of the sign.

Some Bible students believe this prophecy and the sign have only an immediate significance and fulfillment. According to this view, the angel's announcement to Joseph about Mary's conception (Matt. 1:22–23) was merely coincidental. A second view considers the prophecy applicable only to our Lord Jesus Christ, because it is addressed to the "house of David" (Isa. 7:13), not specifically to Ahaz, who was then the Davidic king. This view does not eliminate an immediate significance of the message, because approximately three years afterward the northern kingdom of Israel and Damascus would no longer be formidable foes of Judah. A third position combines these two views, recognizing both an immediate sign to Ahaz and the house of David and an ultimate fulfillment in the conception and birth of our Lord by the Virgin Mary.

Isaiah 9:6–7. This prophecy of Israel's Messiah is at least partially fulfilled with the incarnation of our Lord Jesus Christ in that He is described as a child and as a son. At the same time "he will be called Wonderful Counselor, Mighty God, Everlasting Father, Prince of Peace," titles and qualities that will be displayed in His rulership in peace, justice, and righteousness "on David's throne and over his kingdom . . . from that time on and forever" (9:6–7). The prophecy joins the birth of the Child with the rulership of the King without mentioning the obvious necessary lapse of time between them, that is, between Jesus' first advent and His still future second coming as "King of kings and Lord of lords" (Rev. 19:16). As John Walvoord observes, "In this passage, as in many passages in the Old Testament, the first and second comings of Christ were not distinguished."[5]

Isaiah 11:1–12:6. This extended passage predicts a coming "shoot . . . from the stump of Jesse," a prophecy fulfilled in the incarnation of Christ, who was in the line of descent legally through Joseph (Matt. 1:16) and physically through Mary (Luke 3:31–32). Part of the prophecy was fulfilled in Jesus' first coming because in His life and ministry He did enjoy the presence of the "Spirit of the Lord . . . the Spirit of wisdom and of understanding, the Spirit of counsel and of power, the Spirit of knowledge and of the fear of the LORD" (Isa. 11:2), and he did "delight in the fear of the LORD" (11:3). All this will also characterize our Lord Jesus Christ's second coming and millennial reign over the whole world as described in the rest of the passage. This event is identified as occurring "in that day" when "the Root of Jesse will stand as a banner for the peoples" (11:10; 12:1, 4).

Isaiah 40:3–5. This prophecy is related to Jesus' incarnation because it is identified with the ministry of John the Baptist, His forerunner. Verses 4 and 5 speak of events that will occur as part of Christ's second coming, but its identification with the ministry of John the Baptist shows that the Lord Jesus was presented then as Israel's Messiah and Savior and, had they recognized and received Him as such, the kingdom would have begun. John's message to Israel was, "Repent, for the kingdom of heaven is near"(Matt. 3:2; see Mark 1:4; Luke 1:17; 3:3; John 1:6-8). Matthew then wrote, "This is he who was spoken of through the prophet Isaiah" and he quoted Isaiah 40:3 (Matt. 3:3; see Mark 1:2–3; Luke 3:4–6; John 1:23).

Isaiah 49:1–7. This passage begins a section of Isaiah's prophetic book generally recognized as the prophecy concerning the Servant of the Lord (chaps. 49–57). Isaiah 49 begins with the servant speaking: "Before I was born the LORD called me; from my birth he has made mention of my name. . . . He said to me, 'You are my servant, Israel, in whom I will display my splendor'" (49:1, 3). To this the servant responded that He had accomplished nothing and His labor had been in vain but He would leave His reward with His God (49:4).

Because the Lord addressed His servant as Israel, the Jewish people consider themselves the servant charged with carrying the message of the one true God to everyone. As the passage continues, however, this conclusion cannot be supported. The servant said that the Lord "formed me in the womb to be his servant, to bring Jacob back to him and gather Israel to himself" (49:5), hardly possible if the servant is Israel. Later the servant described Himself as "him who was despised and abhorred by the nation," Israel (49:7). We must remember that the name Israel, meaning "a ruler with God," was given to Jacob when he wrestled with the Angel of the Lord at the Jabbok River the night before he met his brother Esau (Gen. 32:24–28). The name obviously was applied to the descendants of Jacob and to the nation they became, but it is applied here to God's Servant, who is and will be a Ruler with God.

This servant is Jesus Christ, called by the Lord before His birth to be God's Servant. He was indeed "despised and abhorred by the nation," the people of Israel, to the point that they cried to Pilate, "Crucify him!" (Matt. 27:22–23, 25; see Mark 15:12–14; Luke 23:21; John 19:6, 15). In God the Father's conversation with Him, God told Him, "'It is too small a thing for you to be my servant to restore the tribes of Jacob, and bring back those of Israel I have kept. I will also make you a light to the Gentiles, that you may bring my salvation to the ends of the earth'" (Isa. 49:6). This clarifies the identification of the Servant with Christ.

Isaiah 61:1–2. This passage, including the verses that follow in this chapter, are the proclamation of the Servant of the Lord about His ministry. Our Lord Jesus Christ read verse 1 and the first clause of verse 2 when He returned to His hometown of Nazareth and was asked to read the Scripture in the synagogue on the Sabbath (Luke 4:16–19). He deliberately ended his reading with the clause "to proclaim the year of the Lord's favor" in the middle of verse 2, because that ended the description of His ministry in His first coming. The remainder of verse 2 describes His ministry at His return to earth in "vengeance" and triumph. With the audience obviously expecting Him to continue reading the passage, Jesus said to them, "Today this scripture is fulfilled in your hearing" (Luke 4:21).

Jeremiah 23:5–6; 33:15–17. In Isaiah 11:1, 10 the Messiah is called a "shoot . . . from the stump of Jesse," David's father. But in Jeremiah He is called "a righteous Branch . . . from David's line" (33:15) because in the

New Testament He is said to fulfill promises to David (Luke 1:32–33; see 2 Tim. 2:8; Rev. 5:5; 22:18). Although Jesus is David's Branch from His conception, His ministry as such is identified primarily with His return to earth at His second coming and His millennial reign on David's throne. This is substantiated by the references to the Branch in Zechariah 3:8 and 6:12. However, during His ministry in His first coming the people Jesus healed frequently called Him the "Son of David" (Matt. 9:27; 12:23; 15:22; 20:30–31; Mark 10:47–48; Luke 18:38–39). Also, as He rode into Jerusalem on a donkey on the day now called Palm Sunday, His followers then called Him "the Son of David" (Matt. 21:9, 15). That incident is specifically predicted in Zechariah 9:9, where the "Daughter of Zion . . . Jerusalem" is called on to rejoice and shout because "your king comes to you, righteous and having salvation, gentle and riding on a donkey, on a colt, the foal of a donkey." Critics complain that this fulfillment was deliberately arranged by Jesus, which is undoubtedly true (Matt. 21:1–11; Mark 11:1–10; Luke 19:28–40; John 12:12–16); but it was done to confront the Jewish leaders and people one last time with the opportunity to recognize and accept Him as God's promised Messiah.

Zechariah 12:10; 13:7. These two prophecies of Zechariah relate to the incarnation and first-coming ministry of Jesus Christ, specifically His rejection and crucifixion. This is especially true of the call, "'Awake, O sword, against my shepherd, against the man who is close to me!' declares the LORD Almighty, 'Strike the shepherd, and the sheep will be scattered.'" Jesus quoted this latter statement in predicting the scattering of His disciples at His arrest and crucifixion (Matt. 26:31; Mark 14:27). Zechariah 12:10 describes the mourning and sorrow of the people of Israel when the Lord Jesus will return to be their King and they recognize Him as "the one they have pierced."

Once again numerous additional prophecies in the Old Testament prophetic books fulfilled in our Lord Jesus Christ could be mentioned. For example, Micah 5:2 (already mentioned) and Malachi 3:1 ("the messenger of the covenant, whom you desire, will come")relate to His incarnation and first-coming ministry. As Jesus told his disciples when He appeared to them after His resurrection, "Everything must be fulfilled that is written about me in the Law of Moses, the Prophets and the Psalms"

(Luke 24:44). Peter, after healing the lame man at the temple gate called Beautiful, said in his sermon to the people, "this is how God fulfilled what he had foretold through all the prophets, saying that his Christ would suffer. . . . Indeed, all the prophets from Samuel on, as many as have spoken, have foretold these days" (Acts 3:18, 24). The majority of the remaining Old Testament prophecies about the Messiah, however, predict His return to earth at His second coming and describe the establishing of His millennial kingdom and reign (discussed in chaps. 11–13).

OLD TESTAMENT ANTICIPATIONS IN TYPOLOGY

Typology is an aspect of biblical theology that deals with parallels between the Old and New Testaments involving Jesus Christ and His body, the church. The word *type* transliterates the Greek word *typos,* which, with its synonyms, provides the basis for this study. A "type" has been defined, then, as "an event, person, or object which by its very nature and significance prefigures or foreshadows some later event, person, or object."[6] The New Testament provides the basis for this study by identifying certain things as types. For example, the apostle Paul described Adam as "a pattern [*typos,* type] of the one to come [Jesus Christ]" (Rom. 5:14), and he spoke of the experiences of the Israelites in the wilderness "as examples *[typoi]* . . . written down as warnings for us" (1 Cor. 10:11; see v. 6).

The fact that types are identified as such in the New Testament shows that typology is a legitimate part of biblical and theological study. It also demonstrates that types are a part of God's eternal master plan with a definite purpose in His program and revelation in Scripture. They are not simply coincidental similarities between things in the Old Testament and aspects of Jesus' life and ministry that happened to be noticed by Him and the New Testament writers. Types correspond in many respects with Old Testament prophecies and constitute predictions and anticipations of what is to come as God's master plan unfolds. Also, like Old Testament prophecy (Rev. 19:10), types focus in their New Testament antitypes on the person and work of Christ.

In the study of typology two extremes have surfaced. On the one hand some writers tend to see more types in Scripture than can reasonably be justified. They also tend to force a comparison between every detail of the Old Testament type and its antitype. As Wick Broomall notes, "Sober exegesis must prevail over wild fancies. . . . At the other extreme are found those who refuse to see in OT history any typical meaning. The true view is found between these extremes."[7] Some Bible students restrict their identification of types to the things specifically identified as such in the New Testament; however, this seems too restrictive because Paul indicated that Israel's wilderness experiences, without mentioning specifics, "occurred as examples [typoi]" (1 Cor 10:6). The following are some of the types recognized by most evangelicals.

Adam (Rom. 5:14; 1 Cor. 15:22, 45–49). The typical relationship between the first man, Adam, and Jesus Christ is not surprising. But the relationship includes both a comparison or parallelism—Adam "was a pattern [typos] of the one to come" (Rom. 5:14)—and also contrasting (anti-thetical) connections. This latter aspect is stated in 1 Corinthians 15:22—"For as in Adam all die, so in Christ all will be made alive." The apostle discussed the contrast between Adam and Jesus Christ more fully in 1 Corinthians 15:45–49. Quoting Genesis 2:7, he wrote "So it is written, 'The first man Adam became a living being'; the last Adam, a life-giving spirit. The spiritual did not come first, but the natural, and after that the spiritual. The first man was of the dust of the earth, the second man from heaven. As was the earthly man, so are those who are of the earth; and as is the man from heaven, so also are those who are of heaven. And just as we have borne the likeness of the earthly man, so shall we bear the likeness of the man from heaven." As human beings we cannot avoid bearing the likeness of Adam and the sentence of physical and spiritual death for sin through him, but the choice of spiritual life and eternity with God through faith in Christ's redemptive death is available to every person.

Noah, the Ark, and the Flood. A number of Scriptures present Noah—his preparation of the ark in obedience to God for the deliverance of his family and the animals—as a type of present spiritual experiences and of future judgment. This is done simply by drawing a comparison between Noah and his experience and what it illustrates: "As it was in the days of Noah, so it will be in the coming of the Son of Man" (Matt. 24:37; Luke 17:26). Matthew then described how people were continuing on their daily routines without heeding Noah's message of impending judgment until the Flood suddenly overtook them (Matt. 24:38–39). Luke drew the same comparison with the rescue of Lot and God's judgment on Sodom and Gomorrah (17:28–29). The apostle Peter also used the experiences both of Noah and of Lot as examples of God's ability to rescue the godly from His judgment on the ungodly (2 Pet. 2:5–9).

The apostle Peter also stated that in the ark "only a few people, eight in all, were saved through water, and this water symbolizes baptism that now saves you also—not the removal of dirt from the body but the pledge of a good conscience toward God. It saves you by the resurrection of Jesus Christ, who has gone into heaven and is at God's right hand" (1 Pet. 3:20–22). Some churches teach that Peter's statements that Noah and his family "were saved through water" and that "this water . . . saves you" mean that water baptism is necessary for salvation. But, as A.T. Robertson explains, this "saving" by water is "only symbolic . . . not actual. Baptism, Peter explains, does not wash away the filth of the flesh either in a literal sense, as a bath for the body, or in a metaphorical sense of the filth of the soul. . . . Peter here expressly denies baptismal remission of sin."[8] Roger Raymer also comments on the significance of water baptism: "Baptism represents a complete break with one's past life. . . . The act of public baptism would 'save' them [Peter's readers] from the temptation to sacrifice their good consciences in order to avoid persecution. For a first-century Christian, baptism meant he was following through on his commitment to Christ, regardless of the consequences."[9]

Melchizedek. Identified as "king of Salem," Melchizedek was also a "priest of God Most High" (Gen. 14:18), who blessed Abraham after his defeat of Kedorlaomer and the rescue of Lot and his possessions (14:19–20), and to whom Abraham gave "a tenth of everything" (14:20). Melchizedek's priesthood preceded the Levitical priesthood of Aaron and his descendants in both time and significance. God's Messiah is as "a priest forever, in the order of Melchizedek" (Ps. 110:4) in the unchanging decree of God. This is the basis for Melchizedek's serving as a type of Christ both in His sacrifice of Himself on the cross as God's redemptive and propitiatory offering for sin, and in His present ministry for believers in the presence of God (Heb. 2:17; 4:14–5:10; 6:19–10:25).

Isaac. Without specifically being so identified, Isaac serves as a type of Christ because Scripture calls him Abraham's "one and only son" (Heb. 11:17), whom Abraham by faith offered as a sacrifice to God. Although God spared Isaac's life (Gen. 22:10–12), Abraham was committed to the sacrifice, reasoning "that God could raise the dead, and figuratively speaking, he did receive Isaac back from death" (Heb. 11:19). Jesus Christ is God's "one and only Son" (John 1:14; 3:16, 18; 1 John 4:9), whom God "did not spare . . . but gave him up for us all" (Rom. 8:32). As a result the Lord Jesus is typified in a sense by the "ram caught by its horns" that Abraham offered as a sacrifice in Isaac's place (Gen. 22:13), because Jesus is our Substitute who bore the judgment of God for our sins (2 Cor. 5:21; Gal. 3:13). In addition to serving as a type of Christ, Isaac, together with his brother Ishmael as well as their mothers Hagar and Sarah, serve as an allegorical illustration of two covenants—the Mosaic Covenant of law at Mount Sinai and the Abrahamic Covenant of promise fulfilled in Christ (Gal. 4:21–31).

David. Jesus Christ, as already discussed, is David's prophesied Offspring who will occupy his throne and "reign over the house of Jacob forever; his kingdom will never end" (Luke 1:32–33). David also, however, serves as a type of Christ, even though that is not specifically stated in Scripture. First, David illustrates Jesus in that, although he was guilty of grievous sins, God called him "a man after my own heart; he will do everything I want him to do" (Acts 13:22; see 1 Sam. 13:14). God called the Lord Jesus "my Son, whom I love; with him I am well pleased" (Matt. 3:17; see Mark 1:11; Luke 3:22), and Jesus said, "I always do what pleases him" (John 8:29; Rom. 15:3). In addition, when the Pharisees accused Jesus and His disciples of breaking the Sabbath because they plucked and ate some heads of grain when they were hungry, Jesus reminded them of David's action in entering "the house of God" and eating "the consecrated bread" when he was hungry (Matt. 12:3–4; Mark 2:25–26; Luke 6:3–4; see 1 Sam. 21:3–6). Then He said concerning Himself, "I tell you that one [lit., 'something'] greater than the temple is here. . . . For the Son of Man is Lord of the Sabbath" (Matt. 12:6, 8).

Jonah. Jesus Christ personally identified the prophet Jonah and his experience in the large fish as a type of His resurrection. When the Pharisees demanded of Him a miraculous sign to validate His messianic claims, Jesus said they would receive no sign "except the sign of the prophet Jonah. For as Jonah was three days and three nights in the belly of a huge fish, so the Son of Man will be three days and three nights in the heart of the earth" (Matt. 12:39–40; see Luke 11:29–30), thus predicting His resurrection. Explaining that the people of Nineveh repented at Jonah's message, He said, "And now one [lit., 'something'] greater than Jonah is here" (Matt. 12:41; Luke 11:32).

Many other valid types could be mentioned, ones specifically identified in Scripture as well as others that are not. For example, the Lord Jesus compared Himself to the bronze snake Moses lifted up on a pole to provide healing from the deadly venomous snakebites with a glance of faith (Num. 21:8–9). Jesus told Nicodemus, "Just as Moses lifted up the snake in the desert, so the Son of Man must be lifted up [referring to His death on the cross], that everyone who believes in him may have eternal life" (John 3:14–15). Other types include the mercy seat (Rom. 3:25) and the Passover (1 Cor. 5:7).

As mentioned before, Paul identified the experiences of the Israelites in the wilderness "as examples *[typoi]*, to keep us from setting our hearts on evil things as they did" (1 Cor. 10:6; see v. 11). In addition, the earthly tabernacle erected in the wilderness according to the specifications given to Moses corresponds to the heavenly tabernacle into which our Lord Jesus Christ has entered and where He ministers (Heb. 9:1–10:25); the Levitical priesthood is contrasted with Jesus' priesthood after the order of Melchizedek (7:11–28); and the Mosaic Covenant is contrasted with the New Covenant (8:1–13). Hebrews also compares and contrasts Moses, who "was faithful as a servant in all God's house"—with Christ, "who is faithful as a son over God's house" (3:2–6). In fact, in a true sense all those in Hebrews 11 who lived by faith serve as types and examples for believers today.

CONCLUSION

This study of Old Testament anticipations of the incarnation and ministry of our Lord Jesus Christ in His first coming, His present ministry, and His future return and ministry should strengthen our faith in the Lord and encourage us to worship and serve Him more zealously. Without question God is in control of His world and He is working out His master plan according to His schedule. Believers may not know what the future holds from day to day, but they know who holds the future and they can trust Him.

Part 2

THE INCARNATE
SON OF GOD

Four

THE NAMES AND TITLES
OF THE SON OF GOD

HE PRECEDING CHAPTERS discussed the Lord Jesus' identity
as the eternal Word of God, the second person of the triune
Godhead, and His preincarnate ministry as the Angel of the Lord in His
various manifestations. A discussion of the primary names and titles given
to Him is now appropriate.

THE LORD JESUS CHRIST

The title "the Lord Jesus Christ," the full Christian name of our Lord,
bears witness to His deity, His humanity, and His ministry of providing
salvation. The Gospels do not record this full title being addressed to Jesus
in His earthly ministry.

The first usage of it recorded in Scripture was by Peter when he was
explaining his ministry of the gospel to the Gentiles to the believers in
Jerusalem (Acts 11:17). The next recorded usage was also by Peter at the
council in Jerusalem (15:11; see v. 26). In the Epistles, beginning with
Romans 1:7 and ending with Jude 21, it is used frequently, as are variations of it. Interestingly, in the Book of Revelation neither it nor any
variation of it is recorded until the closing verses (22:20–21).

Lord

The Greek word translated "Lord" is *kyrios.* "Lord" also translates the Hebrew word *ʾAdōnāy.* Both the Greek and Hebrew words include the idea of power or authority and signify mastery or ownership (Matt. 20:8; Mark 13:35). As a result they were used as a title of respect in addressing masters (e.g., Matt. 13:27), public officials (27:63), and teachers (John 4:11), and are sometimes translated "Sir." When the disciples addressed Jesus as "Lord," they were recognizing His deity (e.g., Matt. 8:25; 14:30), but it was also a title of respect (e.g., 18:21). In the Old Testament the word *Lord* also translates the Hebrew word *Yahweh,* the personal name of God. In many English versions it is printed in capital letters, Lord (e.g., Gen. 2:4). In the Acts of the Apostles and the rest of the New Testament, when Jesus is spoken of or addressed as Lord, His deity clearly is in mind (e.g., Acts 9:5–6; Rom. 10:9; 1 Cor. 4:4–5; Heb. 1:10). Variations such as "the Lord" (Mark 11:3; John 21:7, 12), "my Lord" (John 20:13), and "Lord Jesus" (e.g., Acts 4:33; Rom. 14:14) also refer to His deity. In the Old Testament, Jeremiah referred to Christ as "the Lord [Yahweh] Our Righteousness" (Jer. 23:6; 33:16); that is, He is the Source of righteousness available to believers.

Jesus

For Christians the chorus correctly states that "Jesus is the sweetest name I know." It is the Lord's given name and is the English transliteration of the Greek *Iēsous.* This in turn transliterates the Hebrew *Yᵉhôšūaʿ* (shortened form *Yᵉšūaʿ*), translated "Joshua." It means "He whose salvation is Yahweh" or "Yahweh's salvation." It was the name of Moses' lieutenant (Num. 11:28) and successor (Deut. 31:14, 23; 34:9), who led the Israelites into Canaan and conquered it (Josh. 1:1–6). The name "Jesus" was assigned to Him by God in the angel's appearance to Joseph in a dream (Matt. 1:20) "because he will save his people from their sins" (1:21). Because it was a popular name as a result of Joshua's significance in Israel's history, our Lord was frequently called "Jesus of Nazareth" (26:71; Mark 1:24; Luke 18:37; John 1:45; Acts 2:22) to distinguish Him from others named Jesus (e.g., Col. 4:11).

Christ

This title for Jesus is a transliteration of the Greek word *Christos*, which translates the Hebrew word *mᵉšîah*, Messiah, the "Anointed One." In Judaism "the tabernacle and everything in it" (Lev. 8:10) were anointed, as were Aaron as high priest and his sons as priests (Lev. 8:12, 30). Later, when God provided kings for Israel in response to their desires, the kings were anointed (1 Sam. 10:1; 16:12–13). The word was used prophetically in the Old Testament to speak of a promised Deliverer, who was to fulfill God's plans for Israel and all mankind (Ps. 2:2–9; Isa. 61:1–3; Dan. 9:25–26). When Jesus was on earth people anticipated the coming of the Messiah, that is, the Anointed One (John 4:25; 7:27b), and Jesus claimed to be that Christ (John 4:26; Luke 4:17–21). Andrew referred to Jesus as the Messiah (John 1:41), who is variously called "Christ" (Matt. 1:16), "the Christ" (Matt. 16:16, 20), and "Jesus Christ" (Mark 1:1; Acts 3:6).

VARIATIONS OF THE TITLE "SON"

Numerous names and titles involving variations of the word "Son" are given to Jesus, almost exclusively in the New Testament. Many of them point to His relationship to humanity. For example, in tracing Jesus' genealogy as far as His legal father, Joseph, is concerned, Matthew called him "the son of David" and "the son of Abraham" (Matt. 1:1). As the ultimate Descendant of David, Jesus is called "a shoot . . . from the stump of Jesse" (Isa. 11:1), "the Root of Jesse" (11:10), "a Righteous Branch" (Jer. 23:5; 33:15), "the Root of David" (Rev. 5:5), and "the Root and the Offspring of David" (22:16).

Because of this legal family relationship Jesus was called "Joseph's son" (Luke 4:22) and "the carpenter's son" (Matt. 13:55). Luke began his genealogy by writing that Jesus "was the son, so it was thought, of Joseph" (Luke 3:23), and Matthew closed his genealogy by identifying Joseph as "the husband of Mary, of whom was born Jesus" (Matt. 1:16). So because of Jesus' virgin birth, Joseph was Jesus' legal father but not His physical father.

In His hometown of Nazareth people spoke of Him as "the carpenter" and "Mary's son" (Mark 6:3). This mother-son relationship is referred to several other times in the New Testament. The angel told Joseph to "take

Mary home as your wife, because what is conceived in her is from the Holy Spirit. She will give birth to a son" (Matt. 1:20–21). Joseph did, and he "had no union with her until she gave birth to a son" (1:25). Likewise the angel Gabriel told Mary, "you will be with child and give birth to a son" (Luke 1:31). In Bethlehem Mary "gave birth to her firstborn, a son" (2:7). Elizabeth told Mary, "Blessed is the child you will bear" (1:42), and called her "the mother of my Lord" (1:43). Mary is called "the mother of Jesus" (Acts 1:14), "Jesus' mother" (Luke 8:19; John 2:3), "your mother" (Luke 8:20), and frequently "his mother" (Matt. 2:11, 13–14, 20–21; 12:46–47; see Mark 3:31–35; Luke 2:48, 51).

Son of God

The title "Son of God" was first applied to Jesus by the angel Gabriel in his announcement to the Virgin Mary. Explaining that her conception would be by the Holy Spirit, he said that "the holy one to be born will be called the Son of God" (Luke 1:35; see v. 32). John the Baptist, after witnessing the descent of the Holy Spirit on Jesus at His baptism by John, said, "I testify that this is the Son of God" (John 1:34). This was also the confession of Nathanael (1:49); of Martha, the sister of Lazarus and Mary (11:27); and of Peter, spokesman for the disciples (Matt. 16:15–16; see 14:33). When the earthquake occurred at Jesus' crucifixion, the centurion and soldiers who carried out the execution "were terrified, and exclaimed, 'Surely he was the Son of God'" (27:54; see Mark 15:39; Luke 23:47).

Significantly the demons, minions of Satan, whom Jesus exorcised in numerous healing miracles, recognized and addressed Jesus as the "Son of God" (Matt. 8:29; Mark 3:11; Luke 4:41; see 8:28, "Jesus, Son of the Most High God"). Even Satan himself acknowledged Jesus as the Son of God when he said, "If you are the Son of God" (Matt. 4:3, 6). In Greek this word "if" introduces a condition that assumes the statement to be true, and therefore can be translated "Since [or, assuming] you are the Son of God." Only the Son of God could turn stones into bread or cast Himself down from the highest point of the temple and have God protect Him from injury.

The closest Jesus came to directly calling Himself the Son of God occurred when the Jewish Sanhedrin asked Him, "'Are you then the Son of God?'" and Jesus replied, "'You are right in saying I am'" (Luke 22:70; see Matt. 26:63–64; Mark 14:61–62). Jesus did claim a close, unique relationship with God as His Father that amounted to His saying, "'I am God's Son'" (John 10:36; see vv. 29–30, 37–38). The first declaration of this relationship came when Jesus as a lad of twelve told Joseph and Mary when they found Him in the temple, "Didn't you know I had to be in my Father's house?" (Luke 2:49).

In claiming identity as God's Son on earth, Jesus emphasized His submission to God the Father's will and work. He told the Jews who persecuted Him for healing on the Sabbath, "I tell you the truth, the Son can do nothing by himself; he can do only what he sees the Father doing, because whatever the Father does the Son also does" (John 5:19). At the same time, however, Jesus' relationship with God the Father involved their equality in nature (10:30). After Jesus healed a man on the Sabbath, He said to the Jews, "My Father is always at his work to this very day, and I, too, am working" (5:17). Then they "tried all the harder to kill him," because "he was even calling God his own Father, making himself equal with God" (5:18). Nothing could be a clearer statement of His affirmation of deity. True, Jesus and God the Father are one in purpose, but John 5:17–18 and 10:30 affirm more than that: Christ is also equal to the Father in that Jesus possesses deity, the very essence of the Godhead.

Jesus' unique relationship to God the Father is underscored by His speaking repeatedly of God as "my Father" (e.g., Matt. 7:21; 18:10, 19, 35; Luke 10:22; 22:29; 24:49; John 5:43; 12:26–28; 14:2, 20–21, 23, 31; 15:1, 10, 15, 23–24; 16:25, 32). By contrast Jesus told His disciples to address God as "Our Father" (Matt. 6:9; see Luke 11:2), and in speaking to them He called God "your Father" (Matt. 10:20; 18:14; Mark 11:25; Luke 12:30–32; John 20:17).

Peter affirmed that Jesus is "the Christ, the Son of the living God" (Matt. 16:16). Interestingly the high priest asked Jesus, "Are you the Christ, the Son of the Blessed One?" (Mark 14:61). This is especially noteworthy since "Blessed One" is a Jewish substitute term for "God" (see Mishnah Berak'ot 7.3).

My Son, Whom I Love

Jesus' claim to be the Son of God was confirmed in a unique way by God the Father Himself. At Jesus' baptism by John the Baptist, which marked the beginning of Jesus' messianic ministry, God spoke from heaven, saying, "You are my Son, whom I love; with you I am well pleased" (Mark 1:11; see Matt. 3:17; Luke 3:22). Similarly, at Jesus' transfiguration on the mountain, God spoke to Peter, James, and John, saying, "This is my Son, whom I love; with him I am well pleased." Then God added, for the three disciples and for us as well, "Listen to him!" (Matt. 17:5; see Luke 9:35). Because of this unique relationship confirmed by God from heaven, John called Jesus "the one and only Son" (John 1:14; 3:16, 18; see 1:18, "the only Son"). In Psalm 2:7, quoted in Hebrews 1:5, God the Father called Jesus "my Son," and the words "in whom I delight" are from Isaiah 42:1.

Some Bible teachers have suggested that Jesus *became* the Son of God in His incarnation. In other words, He was not God's Son in eternity past before He became incarnate. This view has several weaknesses. First, it ignores clear statements in the Scriptures about Jesus' existence as the Son of God before the Incarnation. Galatians 4:4, for example, states that the Incarnation occurred "when the time had fully come," implying that the "Actor" was waiting in the wings for the appropriate moment of His appearance. The verse continues, "God sent his Son." The verb translated "sent" is coupled with a preposition that more literally could be translated "sent out from," again implying that He was the Son of God before He was incarnated. The same exact form of that verb is used in verse 6, which says, "God sent the Spirit of his Son"; the Spirit obviously came from heaven. Other Scriptures also speak of God sending His Son (1 John 4:9–10, 14), using a compound verb that literally could be translated "sent away from," implying preexistence with God the Father. And dozens of times the Gospel of John records that God "sent" His Son from heaven. Not one verse in the Bible states that Jesus ever *became* God's Son. He always was His Son, from all eternity.

Jesus' own references to His relationship with God the Father prior to the Incarnation are also significant. In His high priestly prayer Jesus requested, "And now, Father, glorify me in your presence with the glory I had with you before the world began" (John 17:5). Later He prayed concerning the disciples, "They knew with certainty that I came from you, and they believed that you sent me" (17:8b). Still later He stated that God the Father had "loved me before the creation of the world" (17:24b).

Another affirmation of Jesus' eternal Sonship is His participation in creation. The writer to the Hebrews stated that through His Son, God "made the universe" (Heb. 1:2). The Son, whom the Father "loves" (Col. 1:13), "is the image of the invisible God, the firstborn over all creation. For by him all things were created . . . all things were created by him and for him" (1:15–16).

The teaching that Jesus' Sonship began at the Incarnation ignores and destroys the eternal relationship among the three Persons of the Trinity, whereas the Bible clearly teaches the eternal distinctions in the Trinity as Father, Son, and Holy Spirit.

Son of Man

The title "Son of Man" occurs ninety-four times in the New Testament, eighty-nine of them by Jesus with reference to Himself in the four Gospels. In the Gospels others used this title of Him only when they referred to His own use of it. For example, they asked, "Who is this 'Son of Man'?" (John 12:34). Outside of the Gospels Stephen used the term "the Son of Man" in referring to the ascended glorified Jesus whom he saw in his vision just before he was martyred (Acts 7:55–56). Also the title was used by the author of Hebrews in quoting Psalm 8:5 (Heb. 2:7), and by the apostle John in his vision of the glorified Jesus standing among the seven lampstands representing the seven churches ("among the lampstands was someone 'like a son of man,'" Rev. 1:13) and in his vision of the Crowned One seated on a cloud with "a sharp sickle in his hand" (14:14).

Jesus' self-designation as "the Son of Man" (the first occurrence is in Matt. 8:20) may reflect the Aramaic use of the phrase as a substitute for "I," but it also obviously speaks of His humanity and His identity with humankind. Since the title was used repeatedly by God in addressing the prophet Ezekiel (e.g., Ezek. 2:1, 3, 6, 8), Jesus' use of it may serve to identify Him as a prophet, a fact recognized by the people (Matt. 21:11, 46;

Mark 6:15; Luke 7:16; 24:19b; John 4:19; 9:17) and claimed by Jesus (Matt. 13:57; Mark 6:4; Luke 4:24).

Since the title had messianic significance as a result of its occurrence in Daniel 7:13 as interpreted by subsequent Jewish scholars, Jesus' use of it was a claim to His identity as Israel's promised Messiah. This involved His ministry as the Suffering Servant and redemptive sacrifice (Matt. 20:28) who provides eternal life (John 6:53–58), accomplished by His death and resurrection at the end of His first coming. Jesus' exercise of "authority, glory, and sovereign power," His being worshiped by "all peoples, nations and men of every language," and His eternal kingdom and "everlasting dominion" (Dan. 7:14) will not be realized until His return to earth to establish His messianic kingdom, but Jesus was conscious of and spoke of His possession of those future messianic prerogatives (Matt. 16:27–28; 24:30; 26:64). At least some of those messianic rights were exercised by Jesus in His first coming, including the authority to forgive sins (9:6) and His authority over the Sabbath (12:8).

NAMES AND TITLES USED BY JESUS OF HIMSELF

In addition to calling Himself "the Son of Man," Jesus applied a number of descriptive titles to Himself, most of which are found in the Gospel of John and begin with "I am." This is significant in view of His words "I am" in John 8:58, an assertion of eternality and deity. The day after He miraculously fed the five thousand, Jesus challenged the people to work "for food that endures to eternal life, which the Son of Man will give you" (6:27), declaring, "I am the bread of life" (6:35, 48) and "I am the living bread that came down from heaven" (6:51).

At the Feast of Tabernacles Jesus attended in Jerusalem (John 7:14), He said to the people, "I am the light of the world" (8:12). This related to the practice of "lighting giant lamps in the women's court in the temple. . . . The wicks were made from the priest's worn-out garments."[1] Later Jesus repeated that declaration in His response to His disciples' question about the man born blind (9:1–4). Still later Jesus said, "I have come into the world as a light" (12:46). The apostle John called Jesus "the true light" (1:9; see 1:4–8).

Another custom the Jews observed at the Feast of Tabernacles was to make "a solemn procession each day from the temple to the Gihon Spring. A priest filled a gold pitcher with water while the choir sang Isaiah 12:3. Then they returned to the altar and poured out the water."[2] Although Jesus never stated, "I am the living water," He did stand on the last day of the feast and proclaim loudly, "If any man is thirsty, let him come to me and drink" (John 7:37). Similarly at Jacob's well in Sychar Jesus told the Samaritan woman, "If you knew the gift of God and who it is that asks you for a drink, you would have asked him and he would have given you living water" (4:10).

In discussing with the Jews His care for them as sheep, Jesus declared, "I am the gate for the sheep" (John 10:7) and "I am the gate; whoever enters through me will be saved" (10:9). To carry the analogy forward, Jesus identified Himself not only as the gate into the sheepfold but also as "the good shepherd" (10:11, 14). Jesus said that as the Good Shepherd He would lay down his life for the sheep (10:11, 15, 17–18). He also knows and cares for His sheep, keeping them from harm and providing for their needs. The New Testament writers built on this claim, calling Him "that great Shepherd of the sheep" (Heb. 13:20) and "the Chief Shepherd" (1 Pet. 5:4; see 2:25).

When Jesus went to Bethany, a village adjoining Jerusalem, to restore Lazarus to life, He comforted Martha, one of Lazarus' sisters, by saying, "Your brother will rise again" (John 11:23). When she responded that she knew Lazarus would "rise again in the resurrection at the last day" (11:24), Jesus declared, "I am the resurrection and the life" (11:25). As Jesus went on to explain, He is the Source of eternal life, and as a result, the Source of resurrection for all who believe in Him (11:25–26; see 5:21, 24–26, 28).

Jesus' announcement to His disciples that He would be leaving them and returning to His "Father's house . . . to prepare a place" (14:2) for them disturbed the disciples. His statement that they knew "the way to the place" where He was going (14:4) brought Thomas's response, "Lord, we don't know where you are going, so how can we know the way?" (14:5). To this, Jesus replied, "I am the way and the truth and the life" (14:6). To emphasize His exclusiveness as the only way to God, Jesus continued, "No one comes to the Father except through me." Building on this declaration the author of Hebrews wrote, "We have confidence to enter the Most Holy Place by the blood of Jesus, by a new and living way opened for us through the curtain, that is, his body" (Heb. 10:19–20).

As Jesus continued His instructions to the disciples, He spoke of the coming ministry of the "the Spirit of truth" (14:17), whom He called "another Counselor" (14:16; see 14:26; 15:26; 16:7). The Greek word rendered "Counselor" means a person "called to one's aid" (in a judicial sense), and thus may be translated "an advocate, pleader, intercessor."[3] Jesus did not directly declare, "I am a Counselor." But when He called the Holy Spirit "another Counselor," He meant "another of the same kind." In effect, therefore, He was identifying Himself as the Counselor who would soon be replaced by the Holy Spirit. As a result the apostle John identified Jesus as the "one who speaks to the Father in our defense" (1 John 2:1) when a Christian sins. "Wonderful Counselor" is one of the titles Isaiah assigned to Jesus (Isa. 9:6).

To emphasize the spiritual intimacy that needed to exist between Himself and His disciples to ensure their effective ministry, Jesus declared, "I am the true vine" (John 15:1) and "I am the vine; you are the branches" (15:5). With this claim Jesus was contrasting Himself with Israel, which "yielded only bad fruit" (Isa. 5:2). In addition to these seven "I am" titles, Jesus also called Himself "the Lord of the Sabbath" (Matt. 12:8; Luke 6:5), "Master" (Matt. 23:8), and "Teacher" (23:10; Mark 14:14).

NAMES AND TITLES GIVEN TO JESUS BY OTHERS

Of all the names and titles given to Jesus by other persons perhaps one of the more significant is "Immanuel—which means, 'God with us'" (Matt. 1:23; see Isa. 7:14). This was mentioned by the angel in his announcement to Joseph of the son to be born to Mary. It identifies Him as the Promised One (Isa. 7:14; 8:8) and affirms His deity as well as His humanity and earthly ministry. In the angel Gabriel's announcement to Mary, he said her son would be called "the Son of the Most High" (Luke 1:32) and "the holy one" (1:35). In addressing the women at the tomb after the resurrection the angel called Him "Jesus the Nazarene" (Mark 16:6; see Matt. 2:23).

During His earthly ministry Jesus was addressed as "Rabbi" by His disciples as well as by some who sought His help. The first use of this title was by two disciples of John the Baptist—one of whom was Andrew (John 1:40). Leaving John to follow Jesus, they said, "Rabbi, where are you staying?" (John 1:38).

Later Nathanael also addressed Jesus as "Rabbi" as well as "the King of Israel" (John 1:49) in response to Jesus' demonstration of His divine omnipresence and omniscience (1:47–48). On several occasions the disciples as a group addressed Jesus as "Rabbi" (John 4:31; 9:2; 11:8). Others who also addressed Him this way include Peter (Mark 9:5; 11:21), Judas Iscariot (Matt. 26:25, 49: Mark 14:45), Nicodemus (John 3:2), and the crowd of people whom Jesus had fed (6:25). In addition Mary Magdalene called Jesus "Rabboni" ("my Rabbi") after His resurrection (20:16). Bartimaeus too addressed Him as "Rabboni" (Mark 10:51, NKJV), though some manuscripts read "Rabbi."

Titles similar to "Rabbi" applied to Jesus are "Teacher" ("Rabbi" is sometimes translated "Teacher") and "Master." The title "Teacher" is used by Jesus' disciples (Mark 4:38; 9:38; 10:35; 13:1; Luke 21:7); individuals seeking His help (Mark 5:35; 9:17) or advice (Mark 10:17, 20); individuals commending Him (Matt. 8:19; Mark 12:32); and Pharisees, Sadducees, and other Jewish leaders who opposed Him (Matt. 12:38; 22:36; Mark 12:14, 19; Luke 7:40; 10:25; 12:14; 19:39). The word "Master" is found exclusively in Luke and is used only by Jesus' disciples (5:5; 8:24, 45; 9:33, 49) except on one occasion (17:13) when ten lepers sought His healing. *Epistata*, the Greek word rendered "Master," means "a leader" and thus suggests Jesus' authority.[4]

A significant title applied to Jesus in the New Testament is that of "Servant," used by Peter in his message to the crowd after he healed the crippled man (Acts 3:13, 26), and in the prayer of the disciples after Peter and John's release by the Sanhedrin (4:27, 30). It was picked up by the apostle Paul in his description of the "emptying" of Christ Jesus (Phil. 2:7–8). The Servant concept lies behind John the Baptist's identification of Jesus as "the Lamb of God, who takes away the sin of the world!" (John 1:29, 36; see Isa. 52:13–53:12). Although the Lord Jesus never referred to Himself as God's Servant, that concept lay behind His several dozen references to His being sent by the Father to do the Father's will and the work the Father gave Him to do (e.g., John 4:34; 5:30, 36; 6:38; 8:28–29; 12:49–50; 17:4).

Although He never directly called Himself a prophet, Jesus implied that He was one when He spoke of His being rejected in Nazareth, His hometown: "only in his home town and in his own house is a prophet without honor" (Matt. 13:57; see Mark 6:4; Luke 4:24; John 4:44). And the common people clearly considered Him a prophet (Matt. 21:11, 46; see Mark 6:15; Luke 7:16; 24:19; John 4:19; 7:40; 9:17). When Jesus asked His disciples who the people said He was, one of their replies was "one of the prophets" (Matt. 16:14; Mark 8:28).

When people on two occasions called Him "the Prophet" (John 6:14; 7:40), they had in mind Moses' statement, "The Lord your God will raise up for you a prophet like me from among your own brothers. You must listen to him" (Deut. 18:15; see Acts 3:22; 7:37). When asked by the Jews from Jerusalem, "Are you the Prophet?" John the Baptist emphatically answered "No" (John 1:21), but he implied that the person coming after him whom he would announce—that is, Jesus—would be the Prophet.

Besides being called a prophet, Jesus also has several regal titles: "Prince of Peace" (Isa. 9:6), "King" (Jer. 23:5; Zech. 14:9), "Ruler over Israel" (Mic. 5:2), "the king of the Jews" (Matt. 27:37; Mark 15:26; Luke 23:3, 38; John 19:19), "the Deliverer" (Rom. 11:26; see Isa. 59:20), "the ruler of the kings of the earth" (Rev. 1:5), "the ruler of God's creation" (3:14); "King of the ages" (15:3), and "King of kings and Lord of lords" (17:14; 19:16).

In addition, Jesus is the believers' "high priest" (Heb. 2:17; 3:1; 4:15; 5:10; 6:20; 9:11), "great high priest" (4:14), "great priest" (10:21), and "priest" (5:6; 7:3, 17, 21; 10:12). In this priestly capacity, He is the "Mediator" between God and humanity (1 Tim. 2:5).

The title "Savior," often used of Christ, points to the purpose of His incarnation—to bring salvation to mankind. Hearing the Samaritan women's words about Jesus, the people of the town of Samaria said, "We know that this man really is the Savior of the world" (John 4:42). Later John wrote that Jesus is "the Savior of the world" (1 John 4:14). The title "Savior" is often combined with other titles: "the Savior Jesus" (Acts 13:23); "our Savior, Jesus Christ" (2 Tim. 1:10); "Christ Jesus our Savior" (Titus 1:4); "God and Savior Jesus Christ" (Titus 2:13; 2 Pet. 1:1); "Jesus Christ our Savior" (Titus 3:6); "our Lord and Savior Jesus Christ" (2 Pet. 2:20; 3:18); and "our Lord and Savior" (2 Pet. 3:2).

Just as lambs on the Jewish Passover were sacrificed to deal with the people's sins, so Jesus was sacrificed on the cross to atone for sin. As such He was called "the Lamb of God" (John 1:29, 36) and "our Passover Lamb" (1 Cor. 5:7).

As the Savior sent from God as the Father's representative, Jesus is called "the apostle," that is, the One sent from God the Father with delegated authority (Heb. 3:1).

Paul called Jesus Christ "the image of God" (2 Cor. 4:4) and "the image of the invisible God" (Col. 1:15), that is, the exact reflection and representation of God the Father (Heb. 1:3). Since the Father is invisible (John 1:18; 5:37; 6:46; 1 Tim. 1:17; 1 John 4:12), Jesus has revealed Him to humanity (John 1:18). He is God's "firstborn" (Rom. 8:29; Heb. 1:6; 12:23), and Paul said Jesus is "the firstborn over all creation" (Col. 1:15). This does not mean, as some cultists suggest, that He was created by God the Father, but that He, like the firstborn son in a family, holds the place of prominence as the "heir of all things" (Heb. 1:2).

As "the beginning" (Col. 1:18), He is the creative Origin of all things. And as "the Beginning and the End" (Rev. 21:6; 22:13), He is the Source and the culmination of all creation.

Because Christ is the first one ever to receive a resurrected body, Paul called Him "the firstborn from the dead" (Col. 1:18). The apostle John also spoke of Jesus as "the firstborn from the dead" (Rev. 1:5). In farming, the first crops to be harvested were called "firstfruits" (Lev. 23:10–11), an indication that more crops were to follow. Similarly in Jesus' resurrection He is "the firstfruits" of the dead (1 Cor. 15:20), which means His followers will also be resurrected. As "the firstborn from among the dead" (Col. 1:18), He is the Heir of all who will be resurrected to eternal life.

A clear, forthright affirmation of Jesus' deity is given in Hebrews 1:8. Speaking of Jesus, the writer quoted Psalm 45:6, "Your throne, O God, will last forever and ever." Another direct claim of His deity, in which Jesus is called God, is in Romans 9:5: "Christ, who is God over all." Another is in Titus 2:13, in which Jesus is called "our great God." And Isaiah titled Him "Mighty God" and "Everlasting Father" (Isa. 9:6). The title

"Everlasting Father" does not mean Jesus the Son is to be confused with God the Father. Instead the term refers to Jesus' fatherly compassion, protection, and provisions, similar to that of a caring earthly father.

Acknowledging His deity, Peter called Jesus "the Holy and Righteous One" (Acts 3:14), and Stephen, Ananias, and John spoke of Him as "the Righteous One" (7:52; 22:14; 1 John 2:1).

The apostle John used numerous titles of Jesus, including "the Word" (John 1:1, 14); "the Word of life" (1 John 1:1); "Advocate" (2:1, NKJV); "the Word of God" (Rev. 19:13); "the faithful witness" (1:5); "the Alpha and the Omega" (1:8; 21:6; 22:13, the first and last letters of the Greek alphabet, which express His fullness); "the First and the Last" (1:17; 2:8; 22:13); "the Beginning and the End" (21:6; 22:13); "the Faithful and True" (19:11); "the Lion of the tribe of Judah" (5:5); and "the Lamb" (5:8, 12–13; 6:1, 3, 5, 7, 16; 7:9–10, 14, 17; 12:11; 13:8; 14:1, 4 [twice], 10; 15:3; 17:14 [twice]; 19:7, 9; 21:9, 14, 22–23, 27; 22:1, 3).

A number of titles applied to Jesus relate Him to those who believe on Him, more particularly to the church. The first of these is "Author," also translated "Prince" (Acts 5:31). The Greek word *archēgos* means "one who begins or originates," or, with reference to a person, a "founder, author, prince, leader."[5] Peter told the Jews in the temple area that they "killed the author of life" (3:15), speaking of Jesus. The writer of Hebrews called Jesus "the author of their salvation" (Heb. 2:10) and "the author and perfecter of our faith" (12:2).

Another title that relates the Lord Jesus to the church is Bridegroom. John the Baptist applied this title to Jesus when he explained to his disciples, "The bride belongs to the bridegroom. The friend who attends the bridegroom waits and listens for him, and is full of joy when he hears the bridegroom's voice. That joy is mine, and it is now complete" (John 3:29). Jesus in effect applied the title to Himself when He explained why His disciples were not fasting. "How can the guests of the bridegroom fast while he is with them? They cannot, so long as they have him with them. But the time will come when the bridegroom will be taken from them, and on that day they will fast" (Mark 2:19–20). Jesus' parables of the wedding banquet (Matt. 22:1–10) and of the ten virgins and the wedding feast (25:1–13) also allude to His identity as the Bridegroom. Related to this picture are the references to Christ and His church as husband and wife (2 Cor. 11:2; Eph. 5:22–33; Rev. 19:7–9; 21:9; 22:17).

A graphic title that relates Jesus Christ to His church is that of "the head of the body, the church" (Col. 1:18). Paul stated that "God . . . appointed him to be head over everything for the church, which is his body" (Eph. 1:22–23). Believers are encouraged to "grow up into him who is the Head, that is Christ" (4:15; see Col. 2:19), and Christ as "the head of the church, his body" is the example for husbands as "head of the wife" (Eph. 5:23). Several passages refer to the church as Christ's body and to believers as members of that body (Rom. 7:4; 12:4–5; 1 Cor. 12:12–14, 27; Eph. 2:15b–16; 4:4; Col. 1:24; 3:15). This analogy portrays the intimacy of relationship between the Lord Jesus and believers and the relationship among believers.

Jesus Christ is also identified as the Stone. In relation to Israel, Jesus is "a stone that causes men to stumble and a rock that makes them fall" (Isa. 8:14). In discussing the Jews' unbelief Paul wrote, "They stumbled over the stumbling stone," and then he quoted Isaiah 8:14 (Rom. 9:33–34; see 1 Pet. 2:8). Psalm 118:22 is related to Israel's unbelief and God's building on it: "The stone the builders rejected has become the capstone." Jesus quoted this passage and related it to Himself in His discussion with the Jewish leaders in the temple courts shortly before His crucifixion (Matt. 21:42; see Mark 12:10; Luke 20:17). Also Peter quoted it when he addressed the Sanhedrin (Acts 4:11), and in his first epistle (1 Pet. 2:7).

Peter developed the picture of the Lord Jesus as a stone more fully than anyone else. He described Jesus as "the living Stone—rejected by men but chosen by God and precious to him" (1 Pet. 2:4). He continued the picture by describing believers as "living stones . . . being built into a spiritual house" (2:5), and then quoted Isaiah 28:16 loosely: "See, I lay in Zion, a chosen and precious cornerstone, and the one who trusts in him will never be put to shame" (2:6). Paul also referred to Jesus Christ "as the chief cornerstone" in whom "the whole building" of believers "is joined together and rises to become a holy temple in the Lord" (Eph. 2:20–21).

Peter also called Jesus an "Overseer of your souls" (1 Pet. 2:25). In this role He lovingly watches over and directs the lives of His own.

The fact that so many names and titles exist to describe the Lord Jesus underscores both the fullness and the complexity of His person. (The following table lists 108 titles discussed in this chapter.) Just as the multitude of facets in a diamond increases its brilliance, so the many names and titles of Christ reveal Him as "the radiance of God's glory" (Heb. 1:3).

Titles and Names of Jesus Christ*

Lord Jesus Christ	Son of Man
Lord	Bread of Life
My Lord	Light of the World
Lord Jesus	True Light
The LORD Our Righteousness	Gate
Jesus	Good Shepherd
Jesus of Nazareth	Great Shepherd
Christ	Chief Shepherd
Messiah ("the Anointed One")	Resurrection
Jesus Christ	Way
Son of David	Truth
Son of Abraham	Life
A Shoot	Wonderful Counselor
Root of Jesse	Vine
Righteous Branch	True Vine
Root of David	Lord of the Sabbath
Root and Offspring of David	Master
Joseph's son	Teacher
The Carpenter's son	Immanuel
Carpenter	Son of the Most High
Mary's son	Holy One
Son of God	Jesus the Nazarene
Son of the Most High God	Rabbi
Son of the Living God	King of Israel
Son of the Blessed One	Rabboni
My Son	Servant
One and Only Son	Lamb of God
Only Son	Prophet

Prince of Peace	God
King	Everlasting Father
Ruler over Israel	Holy and Righteous One
King of the Jews	Righteous One
Deliverer	Word
Ruler of the kings of the earth	Word of life
Ruler of God's creation	Advocate
King of the ages	Word of God
King of kings and Lord of lords	Faithful Witness
High Priest	Alpha
Great High Priest	Omega
Great Priest	First
Priest	Last
Mediator	Faithful and True
Savior of the world	Lion of the tribe of Judah
Savior	Lord
Our Passover Lamb	Author
Apostle	Prince
Image of God	Author and Perfector of our
Image of the invisible God	faith
Firstborn	Bridegroom
Firstborn of all creation	Head of the church
Heir	Stone
Beginning	Cornerstone
End	Chief Cornerstone
Firstborn from the dead	Overseer
Firstfruits	

*These titles are listed in the order in which they were discussed in this chapter.

Five

THE INCARNATION OF THE SON
OF GOD ANNOUNCED

———◈———

PEOPLE HAVE ALWAYS been intrigued, it seems, with the question of whether living beings inhabit other planets and have visited the earth. Half a century ago Orson Wells temporarily threw much of the United States into turmoil with his radio broadcast simulation of an invasion from Mars. As both the century and the millennium draw to a close, this fascination increases, and much of it is bizarre. The Bible makes it clear that God's hosts of angels inhabit the heavens (Mark 12:25; 13:32; Eph. 3:10) with access to the earth in ministry for God (Gen. 28:12–13; Luke 2:13–15; John 1:51). Angels, however, are spirit beings (Heb. 1:14) with powers to assume bodily form to appear and to minister to people (Gen. 18:1–19: 21; Matt. 28:2–7; Acts 1:10–11) but without an inherent bodily form. As a result, the incarnation of our Lord Jesus Christ is the first and only time someone has come from heaven and identified himself with humanity.

In *Mere Christianity* C. S. Lewis entitles his chapter on the Incarnation "The Invasion." Perhaps a more accurate description would be "the infiltration," because, as Lewis writes, "Enemy-occupied territory—that is what this world is. Christianity is the story of how the rightful king has landed, you might say landed in disguise, and is calling us to take part in a great campaign of sabotage."[1] God, nonetheless, has announced a number of times the incarnation of His Son and the birth of His Son's forerunner as well.

THE JESUS SEMINAR AND
THE SEARCH FOR THE HISTORICAL JESUS

Before discussing the biblical evidence concerning the incarnation of the eternal Son of God, His person as the God-Man, and His earthly life and ministry, it is important to discuss the search for the historical Jesus that has marked liberal biblical studies for the last couple of centuries. Of significance is the "Jesus Seminar," a continuing search since 1985 for what the historical Jesus said and did. This study is being carried on "under the auspices of the Westar Institute."[2] The primary leader of the Jesus Seminar is Robert W. Funk, assisted by cochairman John Dominic Crossan. The first meeting of thirty scholars was held March 21–24, 1985, at St. Meinrad School of Theology, a Roman Catholic seminary in southern Indiana. Since that time it has met semiannually at different locations with a total of two hundred individuals involved in one way or another. Its definitive production, *The Five Gospels: In Search of the Authentic Words of Jesus*, edited by Robert W. Funk, Roy W. Hoover, and the Jesus Seminar (New York: Macmillan, 1993) lists seventy Fellows.

In some respects the search for the historical Jesus is the product of the Reformation, which is in part the product of the Renaissance. More specifically the search for the historical Jesus is the product of the Enlightenment with its emphasis on rationalism and the scientific method. This involved the rejection of God's intervention in this world and human affairs—the denial of the miraculous—as represented by Deism. "In other words," as Robert Strimple points out, "the starting point of the modern quest of the historical Jesus is the assumption that the Jesus presented in our biblical gospels is not the Jesus of history."[3]

Hermann Samuel Reimarus (1694–1768) is generally acknowledged as the father of the "search" for the historical Jesus. Its beginning is pinpointed to 1778 with the posthumous publication of his Wolfbüttel Fragment entitled "Concerning the Aims of Jesus and His Disciples." Other leaders include David Friedrich Strauss, with the publication of his *Life of*

Jesus Critically Examined (1835), Johannes Weiss with his *Jesus' Procla-mation of the Kingdom of God* (1892), and Albert Schweitzer with *The Quest for the Historical Jesus* (1906).

The major difference between the older quest for the historical Jesus and the quest identified with the Jesus Seminar lies in their basic attitudes toward the study of the Gospels. The older critics were seeking to identify and eliminate what was not historical (i.e., the supernatural and miracu-lous) from what was basically considered a historical record of Jesus' ministry. The Jesus Seminar, on the contrary, is seeking to discover what is historical in what is assumed to be essentially unhistorical. It is not surprising, as a result, that "eighty-two percent of the words ascribed to Jesus in the gospels were not actually spoken by him, according to the Jesus Seminar."[4]

The rules of evidence formulated and adopted by the Jesus Seminar "to guide its assessment of gospel tradition"[5] lack substantiation from other sources and are therefore highly suspect. The first, for example, is that "the evidence provided by the written gospels is hearsay evidence . . . secondhand evidence," because none of the authors of the Gospels "was an ear or eyewitness of the words and events he records."[6] This assumes that Matthew and John did not write the Gospels attributed to them—a highly questionable conclusion. It also rejects the promise of Jesus to the Eleven that the Holy Spirit would "bring to your remembrance all things that I said to you" (John 14:26, NKJV). It also rejects as invalid Luke's as-sertion that he wrote his Gospel only after "having investigated everything carefully from the beginning" so that Theophilus "might know the exact truth about the things you have been taught" (Luke 1:3–4, NASB).

The other rules of written evidence adopted by the Jesus Seminar simi-larly are assumed without substantiation. These include the idea that sayings of Jesus were brought together in clusters or were provided with a narrative context by the Gospel writers. Furthermore, according to the Jesus Seminar, the Gospel writers expanded the sayings or parables, added interpretive ma-terial, or revised them to conform to their own viewpoints. These authors also allegedly attributed to Jesus statements from common wisdom or their own statements. Jesus is identified as the Galilean "Sage" who "is self-effacing, modest, unostentatious,"[7] and anything in the Gospels that contradicts that picture is simply eliminated as not part of the historical Jesus.

Criticism of the Jesus Seminar and its methodology has come not just from theologically conservative evangelicals but also from Roman Catholics and theologically liberal Protestants. In the preface to his book *The Real Jesus* Luke Timothy Johnson characterizes the work of the Jesus Seminar as "a kind of second-rate scholarship" and "ersatz scholarship."[8] Later he quotes a number of leading New Testament scholars with critical evaluations of the Seminar and its findings, including Howard Clark Kee, who "declared the Seminar 'an academic disgrace.'"[9]

Johnson explains why he draws this conclusion about the Seminar and its pronouncements. "Like a great deal of Gospel criticism," he wrote, "it began with the assumption that the Gospels are not accurate histories but are narratives constructed out of traditional materials with literary art and theological motives."[10] He continued, "From the start, then, we see that the agenda of the Seminar is not disinterested scholarship, but a social mission against the way in which the church controls the Bible, and the way in which the church is dominated by a form of evangelical and eschatological theology—that is, a theology focused both on the literal truth of the Gospels and the literal return of Jesus."[11] With justification Johnson concluded that "any pretense the Seminar has maintained with regard to scientific discovery was . . . merely pretense: the results were already determined ahead of time. The goal was the construction of a new Gospel that portrayed a noneschatological and 'nonmythical' Jesus."[12]

Johnson also criticizes the Jesus Seminar for its methodology. "The Jesus Seminar's promise to deliver, by means of historical methods, 'the real Jesus' is, we have seen, fraudulent on two counts. The first is that its historical methodology is flawed. The second is that even the best historical reconstruction cannot supply 'the real Jesus,' any more than it can supply "the real Socrates." Historians can make a number of important, indeed critical assertions about Jesus' ministry, but the evidence provided by the ancient sources does not enable a satisfying reconstruction of it."[13]

Careful analysis and study of the Gospel records of the life and ministry of Jesus Christ is always appropriate, but to reject their accuracy and authenticity, which is supported by strong external evidence, in an effort to reconstruct His person, life, and ministry, as the Jesus Seminar does, is wrongheaded.

THE BIRTH OF THE FORERUNNER ANNOUNCED

John the Baptist is identified in the Gospel of Mark as the forerunner of Jesus Christ. To confirm John's ministry Mark quoted from Malachi 3:1 and Isaiah 40:3—the latter verse also being quoted by Matthew (3:3) and Luke (3:4) and by John himself (John 1:23). By revelation the apostle John described John the Baptist "as a witness to testify concerning that light, so that through him all men might believe. He himself was not the light; he came only as a witness to the light" (1:7–8). A forerunner was a precursor who announced coming royalty; this was John's ministry. When John's disciples complained to him about Jesus that "everyone is going to him," John reminded them, "You yourselves can testify that I said, 'I am not the Christ but am sent ahead of him'" (3:28).

The incarnation of Christ is unquestionably the supreme miracle—God joining Himself with humanity forever as the God-Man. It is fitting, therefore, from the human perspective that His human forerunner's conception also be a miracle and be announced by an angelic messenger. It is also fitting that Jesus' forerunner be a descendant of Aaron, brother of Moses and first high priest in Israel, through both his father Zechariah of "the priestly division of Abijah" (Luke 1:5) and his mother Elizabeth, since he would set Jesus apart to His public messianic ministry on earth (Matt. 3:13–17; John 1:29–34). The name of John's father, Zechariah, is also appropriate. It means "God remembers," something God was certainly doing in the birth of John and the incarnation of Jesus.

On one occasion when Zechariah's priestly "division was on duty and he was serving as priest before God," Luke related that "he was chosen by lot ... to go into the temple of the Lord and burn incense" (Luke 1:8–9). The choice was by lot but it was not by chance; it is written of the lot that "its every decision is from the LORD" (Prov. 16:33). As Zechariah performed his duties, "an angel of the Lord appeared to him" (Luke 1:11), who later identified himself as Gabriel (1:19). The angel announced that, despite his wife Elizabeth's barrenness in her advanced age, his prayers for a son would be answered and she would conceive and bear a son, whose name was to be John (1:7, 13). This child was to be a Nazirite and would "be filled with the Holy Spirit even from birth" (1:15). In announcing John's birth, Gabriel in effect also announced the coming of God's Messiah, because he said that John "will go on before the Lord, in the spirit and power of Elijah [see Mal. 4:5; Matt. 11:14] . . . to make ready a people prepared for the Lord" (Luke 1:17).

Knowing of God's miraculous provision of Isaac to Abraham and Sarah when she was barren and beyond the age of conceiving and bearing a child (Gen. 18:9–15; 21:1–7), Zechariah should have trusted the angel's message; but, like many of us, he doubted God's revelation and asked, "How can I be sure of this? I am an old man and my wife is well along in years" (Luke 1:18). For his lack of faith Zechariah was struck dumb from that moment (1:20, 22, 62–65). In his song that followed his restored ability to speak, Zechariah understood and proclaimed the ministry of his son John as the forerunner of the Messiah (1:76).

THE VIRGIN CONCEPTION ANNOUNCED

Through the centuries Christians have spoken of the virgin birth of Jesus. This is part of the Roman Catholic Church's exaltation of Mary and its teaching that in Jesus' birth her virginity remained undisturbed and that she remained a virgin throughout her life even though she married Joseph. Actually the birth of Jesus was a completely normal human birth. It was His conception that was miraculous; He was conceived by God the Holy Spirit (Luke 1:35). It is because of this fact, not because Mary was "immaculate," that the angel Gabriel called Him "the holy one to be born" and "the Son of God" (1:35).

To Mary

The angel Gabriel, who told Zechariah of the birth of his son John, appeared next to a virgin named Mary who was "pledged to be married to a man named Joseph, a descendant of David" (Luke 1:27). This was in Nazareth, a town in Galilee, and occurred in the sixth month of the pregnancy of Zechariah's wife, Elizabeth. As with Zechariah, Gabriel told Mary, "Do not be afraid" (1:30; see v. 13), understandably a necessary statement when an angel appears! He also called Mary "highly favored" and told her, "The Lord is with you" (1:28) and "you have found favor with God" (1:30). Then he proceeded to tell her, "You will be with child and give birth to a son" to be named Jesus (1:31). This child would be called "the Son of the Most High" (1:32), the promised Messiah who would receive "the throne of his father David, and . . . reign over the house of Jacob forever" in an everlasting kingdom (1:32–33).

From Gabriel's opening statement it sounds as though Mary was being told what would happen without her having a choice to accept or reject the assignment. This is not true; human beings are not automatons, but God knew Mary's submissive spirit. Mary did ask, however, "How will this be . . . since I am a virgin?" (1:34). This question did not reflect lack of faith; it was simply a request for an explanation of the procedure. Gabriel explained that the child would be conceived by God the Holy Spirit and therefore He would be called "the Son of God" (1:35). To encourage Mary, Gabriel told her of her relative Elizabeth's divinely provided pregnancy. Mary undoubtedly was aware of the misunderstanding and accusation she would face, but her response to Gabriel and the Lord is a model for all believers—"I am the Lord's servant. . . . May it be to me as you have said" (1:38).

To Joseph

Although God loves and blesses godly single parents, He is the creator of marriage and the two-parent family (Gen. 1:27–28; 2:20–24). He needed, therefore, to inform Joseph, Mary's fiancé, of the nature of her situation. Joseph was also an integral part of the puzzle because he gave Jesus his legal right to the throne of David through Solomon (Matt. 1:6–16), while Mary, also a descendant of David through another son, Nathan, gave Jesus His physical right to the throne (Luke 3:23–31).

When Joseph first learned of Mary's pregnancy, he was not aware of its supernatural origin. As a result "he had a mind to divorce her quietly" because he "was a righteous man and did not want to expose her to public disgrace" (Matt. 1:19). This shows that Joseph genuinely loved Mary. At that point God sent an angel (whether Gabriel or not is not stated) to inform Joseph in a dream concerning Mary's part in the plan of God. He was instructed to "take Mary home as your wife" and to name her son

"Jesus, because he will save his people from their sins" (1:20–21). Like Mary, Joseph was obedient to the divine instructions and "took Mary home as his wife. But he had no union with her until she gave birth to a son" (1:24–25). This implies that Joseph and Mary enjoyed normal marital relations following the birth of Jesus, a fact supported by references to his brothers (Matt. 12:46–47; 13:55–56; John 2:12; 7:3; 5, 10; Acts 1:14). Thus the Bible does not support the Roman Catholic teaching of the perpetual virginity of Mary.

THE OCCURRENCE OF THE BIRTH OF JESUS

Joseph and Mary were living in Nazareth, a small town in Galilee, where Joseph worked as a carpenter (Luke 1:26–27). The Bible, however, had prophesied that Bethlehem, where David was born, would be the birth-place of "one who will be ruler over Israel" (Mic. 5:2), God's Messiah. God's control of the affairs of men and of nations to fulfill that predic-tion should encourage all believers to trust Him to carry out His program. Unaware of God's prompting, "Caesar Augustus issued a decree that a census should be taken of the entire Roman world.... And everyone went to his own town to register" (Luke 2:1, 3). As a result Joseph "went up from the town of Nazareth in Galilee to Judea, to Bethlehem the town of David, because he belonged to the house and line of David. He went there to register with Mary, who was pledged to be married to him and was expecting a child" (2:4–5). There in Bethlehem in exact fulfillment of God's prophecy "the time came for the baby to be born, and she gave birth to her firstborn, a son" (2:6–7).

Evidence that the incarnation of the Son of God was a quiet "infiltra-tion," not an open "invasion," includes the fact that Mary placed the infant Jesus "in a manger, because there was no room for them in the inn" (2:7). The apostle John wrote, "He came to that which was his own, but his own did not receive him" (John 1:11). When Jesus first returned to His home-town of Nazareth, He ministered in the synagogue. Amazed by His teaching, the people asked, "Isn't this Joseph's son?" (Luke 4:22). When He rebuked them for their lack of faith, "all the people in the synagogue were furious" and "got up, drove him out of the town, and took him to the brow of the hill on which the town was built, in order to throw him down the cliff. But he walked right through the crowd and went on his way" (4:28–30). When He returned to Nazareth later, the people dismissed Him as "the carpenter's son" (Matt. 13:55), and "they took offense at him" (Mark 6:3).

THE ANNOUNCEMENT OF THE BIRTH OF JESUS

Proud parents send birth announcements of their children, their first-born in particular, to their extended family members and their friends. Proud fathers place in their front yard wooden storks festooned with balloons and a placard announcing the details. Some fathers try to find an unusual way to announce their child's birth. When my firstborn daughter arrived, I reproduced in miniature the birth certificate with her photograph and footprints on it, and sent it as the announcement. No one, however, ever has or ever will top the birth announcement of God the Father at the birth of His Son, our Lord Jesus Christ.

To the Shepherds

God announced the birth of Jesus to shepherds in the fields near Bethlehem, who were "keeping watch over their flocks at night" (Luke 2:8). This is appropriate because David had been a shepherd (1 Sam. 16:11–12; 17:14) and Jesus Christ called Himself "the good shepherd" who "lays down his life for the sheep" (John 10:11; see vv. 14–16). He was also called "that great Shepherd of the sheep" (Heb. 13:20), "the Shepherd and Overseer of your souls" (1 Pet. 2:25), and "the Chief Shepherd" (5:4). Numerous commentators suggest that these shepherds were caring for the sacrificial sheep for the temple sacrifices in Jerusalem. If that is true, it is appropriate that the birth announcement of "the Lamb of God, who takes away the sin of the world" (John 1:29; see v. 36)—and who thus ended the need for those sacrifices—was made to these shepherds. It also demonstrates God's interest in and concern for lowly people in this world (1 Cor. 1:27–29).

Luke reported that the announcement was made by "an angel of the Lord" (Luke 2:9). This angel, whose identity is not stated reported, "Today in the town of David a Savior has been born to you; he is Christ the Lord" (2:11). The identifying sign would be "a baby wrapped in cloth and lying in a manger" (2:12). As soon as the angel's announcement was given, "a great company of the heavenly host appeared with the angel, praising God and saying, 'Glory to God in the highest, and on earth peace to men on whom his favor rests'" (2:13–14). That was a birth announcement that will never be matched. It announced the birth of the eternal Son of God as a person joined forever with the human race as its Messiah, Savior, Ruler, and Judge. This announcement to the shepherds constituted, in effect, an announcement to the people of Israel.

To the Magi

God the Father also made an announcement of the birth of His Son to the Gentiles. Centuries earlier through Isaiah, God had said to His preincarnate Son, "It is too small a thing for you to be my servant to restore the tribes of Jacob and bring back those of Israel I have kept. I will also make you a light for the Gentiles, that you may bring my salvation to the ends of the earth" (Isa. 49:6; see 42:6; 51:4). No announcement is stated as such, but the Magi, when they came to Jerusalem and asked concerning "the one who has been born king of the Jews," said, "We saw his star in the east and have come to worship him" (Matt. 2:2). These men, astrologers and philosophers from Parthia, were part of a class of soothsayers that extended back at least to Daniel and his three friends (Dan. 1:3–6, 17–20). As a result the Magi evidently knew the Old Testament passages mentioning a star and the coming King of Israel (Num. 24:17; Isa. 60:1–3).

No one knows what this star was except that it announced the birth of God's Son. Efforts to identify it with an astronomical phenomenon focus on "an unidentified comet . . . a supernova [or] several planets [that] converged with a brilliant star,"[14] but a natural explanation is fruitless. W. White appropriately wrote, "A more acceptable alternative seems to be that God provided a source of light which cannot now be determined."[15] Apparently the star did not lead the Magi from their homes to Jerusalem; but when they left Jerusalem for Bethlehem (Matt. 2:4–8), "the star they had seen in the east went ahead of them until it stopped over the place where the child was. When they saw the star, they were overjoyed" (2:9–10). This shows that it was a supernatural provision from God.

The star apparently had first appeared and had been seen by the Magi in conjunction with the actual birth of Jesus in Bethlehem. The consultation of the Magi (traditionally thought to be three because three kinds of gifts were given to Jesus), their preparation of their caravan to make the journey through bandit-infested territory and the journey itself took time. As a result Jesus was no longer a newborn infant lying in a manger, as often depicted in Christmas pageants. The family of Joseph, Mary, and Jesus was living in a house (2:11), and Jesus is called "the child," the Greek word *paidion* signifying "a young child," not an infant *(brephos)*. When King Herod realized the Magi had returned to their homes without informing him of the child's location, "he gave orders to kill all the boys in Bethlehem and its vicinity who were two years old and under" (2:16). So Jesus then was obviously in this age range.

THE PROCLAMATION OF THE BIRTH OF JESUS

The announcements of the birth of Jesus were essentially private affairs. The Magi saw the star and interpreted it in conjunction with predictions in Jewish Scriptures. Although they reported the news to Herod and the Jewish leaders in Jerusalem, the news was still localized. The angelic announcement to the shepherds was at night so that, even though it was a brilliant display, it was witnessed only by them. After they confirmed the angel's message by finding Mary, Joseph, "and the baby . . . lying in the manger" (Luke 2:16), Luke wrote that "they spread the word concerning what had been told them about this child" (2:17); but this was a comparatively small number of people in the town of Bethlehem. A need existed for a public proclamation of the good news of the birth of Israel's Messiah.

By Simeon

As faithful Jews, Joseph and Mary had Jesus circumcised the eighth day (Lev. 12:3), and they named Him Jesus as Gabriel told Mary (Luke 1:31) and the angel told Joseph (Matt. 1:21). After waiting thirty-three additional days for Mary's purification according to the Law of Moses (Lev. 12:4), Joseph and Mary went to Jerusalem to the temple to present Jesus, their firstborn son, to the Lord (Exod. 13:2) and to offer the sacrifice of redemption for Him according to the Law of Moses (13:12–13). This sacrifice was to be a lamb, but those who could not afford a lamb could substitute "two doves or two young pigeons" (Lev. 12:8; see Luke 2:24). The fact that they brought the latter reveals Joseph and Mary's low economic level.

Simeon, a "righteous and devout person," was "waiting for the consolation of Israel, and the Holy Spirit was upon him" (Luke 2:25). He represented a godly remnant in that era of apostasy and formalism. God had revealed to him that "he would not die before he had seen the Lord's Christ" (2:26). When Joseph and Mary came into the temple with Jesus, Simeon, led by the Holy Spirit (2:27), took Jesus "into his arms, and praised God" (2:28). He declared his readiness now to depart in death, "for my eyes have seen your salvation, which you have prepared in the sight of all people, a light for revelation to the Gentiles and for glory to your people Israel" (2:30–32).

Simeon, who is never mentioned before or afterward in the Bible, then blessed Joseph and Mary and, as a prophet, spoke the following message concerning Jesus' incarnate life and ministry and Mary's future heartache: "This child is destined to cause the falling and rising of many in Israel, and to be a sign that will be spoken against, so that the thoughts of many hearts will be revealed. And a sword will pierce your own soul too" (2:34–35). Undoubtedly Simeon's actions and words were observed and heard by many in the crowded temple courts.

By Anna

Described as "a prophetess" (Luke 2:36), Anna is identified by her family and personal history. Widowed after seven years of marriage, she was then eighty-four years of age (2:36–37). Luke reported that "she never left the temple but worshiped night and day, fasting and praying" (2:37), evidence of her devotion to God. Approaching Joseph and Mary and Jesus as Simeon left, Anna "spoke about the child to all who were looking forward to the redemption of Jerusalem" (2:38). Through Simeon and Anna, public proclamation of the birth of God's Messiah was made to the people of Israel, and in particular to the devout and godly ones who were looking and praying for His promised coming.

Six

THE PERSON OF THE
INCARNATE SON OF GOD

———◦❖◦———

O UR LORD JESUS CHRIST is a unique person, not in our contemporary watered-down sense of "unusual" but in the absolute
meaning of "one of a kind." He is the theanthropic person, the God-Man.
As such He is the permanent joining of the eternal Word, the second person of the triune Godhead, with humanity. As the revelatory person of
the Godhead, the Word was eternally destined to become incarnate. The
incarnation of the Word was not the result of the Trinity casting lots, with
the Word happening to draw the short straw, nor was it a case of His
being outvoted by God the Father and God the Holy Spirit; it was His
mission as the Word, the expression of God, to manifest and display God
in human form. The apostle John stated, "No one has ever seen God, but
God the One and Only, who is at the Father's side, has made him known"
(John 1:18). The Greek phrase translated "made him known" can in effect
be transliterated into English as "exegeted him."

During His ministry the Lord Jesus made the same affirmation concerning His person. In response to His disciple Philip's request, "Lord,
show us the Father and that will be enough for us" (John 14:8), Jesus
responded with a note of sadness in His heart, if not His voice. "Don't
you know me, Philip, even after I have been among you such a long time?
Anyone who has seen me has seen the Father. How can you say, 'Show us

the Father'?" (14:9). Philip's problem, despite his association with Jesus as a disciple from the beginning of Jesus' ministry (1:43), was that Jesus looked like any other person, such as one of the prophets of the Old Testament with divinely provided power to perform miracles. Philip recognized Jesus as the promised Messiah of the Old Testament (1:45), but he did not yet understand that Jesus is the God-Man, the union of deity and humanity in one person.

THE UNION OF GOD AND MAN IN ONE PERSON

The Council of Chalcedon (A.D. 451) provided a fairly lengthy and involved statement of the doctrine of the person of Christ incarnate. In brief it can be stated as the union of "full Deity and perfect humanity . . . without mixture, change, division, or separation in one Person forever."[1] This is called the hypostatic union. Like the doctrine of the Trinity, it "is one of the most intricate studies"[2] in the field of theology. This is because, again like the Trinity, the person of Jesus Christ is totally unique. Also, as in formulating the doctrine of the Trinity, we have only the testimony of Scripture in seeking to understand the doctrine of the person of Jesus Christ incarnate.

Formulating the doctrine of the incarnate person of Christ is complicated by Scripture that states the Incarnation involved a stepping down, a condescension. The apostle John wrote, "The Word became flesh and made his dwelling among us" (John 1:14). Speaking of Jesus' location and possibly His temporary position as well, the author of the epistle to the Hebrews stated that He "was made a little lower than the angels" (Heb. 2:9). If it involved position as well as location, it was only temporary, because elsewhere the author emphasized Jesus' superiority over the angels in His exaltation to "the right hand of the Majesty in heaven" (1:3; see vv. 4–13).

The difficulty in determining what the Incarnation involved in relation to Jesus' deity centers on the apostle Paul's statement that "being in very nature God, [He] did not consider equality with God something to be grasped, but made himself nothing" (Phil. 2:6–7). The Greek verb *kenoō*, rendered "emptied" in several translations (ASV, NASB), in transliteration provides the name for this step of condescension called "the kenosis." In another place Paul wrote concerning Christ, "though he was rich yet for your sakes he became poor" (2 Cor. 8:9). What this "emptying" or "becoming poor" meant is the crux of the problem.

The Full Deity of Jesus Christ

The kenosis did not involve the abandonment of any of the attributes or other elements of the nature of deity—something that God, being immutable, could not do. Otherwise Jesus would be less than God. In addition to Jesus' statement to Philip, He had stated earlier, "When a man believes in me, he does not believe in me only, but in the one who sent me. When he looks at me, he sees the one who sent me" (John 12:44–45). Even before that, in speaking to the Jews in the temple area at the Feast of Dedication, Jesus had declared, "I and the Father are one" (10:30). The neuter form of the Greek word translated "one" indicates that Jesus was speaking of a unity of nature with God the Father. The Jews picked up stones to stone Him for blasphemy, stating that "you, a mere man, claim to be God" (10:33). Still earlier Jesus had told the Jews, "I tell you the truth . . . before Abraham was born, I am" (8:58), applying to Himself the name by which God identified Himself to Moses and for Israel (Exod. 3:14). Here also the Jews recognized the significance of Jesus' claim and "picked up stones to stone him" (John 8:59).

If Jesus' claims to being God are not true, then either He was deluded or He was a deceiver; but His life, ministry, and teachings do not indicate Him to be either. Furthermore, other New Testament authors affirmed the deity of Jesus Christ. Before writing of Jesus' kenosis, Paul spoke of Jesus "being in very nature God" and His not considering "equality with God something to be grasped" (Phil. 2:6). Elsewhere Paul described Christ as "the image of the invisible God" (Col. 1:15; see 2 Cor. 4:4), and the author of the epistle to the Hebrews wrote that "in these last days he [God] has spoken to us by his Son" (Heb. 1:2), whom he described as "the radiance of God's glory and the exact representation of his being" (1:3). Paul called Jesus "God" (Rom. 5:2) and "our great God and Savior, Jesus Christ" (Titus 2:13).

Jesus exercised divine attributes. In His earthly life and ministry Jesus used numerous attributes possessed only by God. When Philip brought

Nathaniel to Jesus, the Lord said Nathanael was "a true Israelite, in whom there is nothing false" (John 1:47). This is more than human insight; it is divine omniscience (Ps. 139:1–6). When Nathaniel asked, "How do you know me?" Jesus answered, "I saw you while you were still under the fig tree before Philip called you" (John 1:48), thereby demonstrating divine omnipresence (Ps. 139:7–12). Jesus claimed divine eternality when He asked God the Father to "glorify me in your presence with the glory I had with you before the world began" (John 17:5). On several occasions Jesus demonstrated more than human knowledge of the thoughts of humans (Luke 6:8; 11:17; John 2:24–25); the most outstanding instance was when He told the Samaritan woman at the well of Sychar, "You are right when you say you have no husband. The fact is, you have had five husbands, and the man you now have is not your husband" (John 4:17–18). Jesus also demonstrated divine omnipotence in His control over the storm (Matt. 8:23–27; see Mark 4:36–39; Luke 8:23–24), His multiplication of the loaves and fish (Matt. 14:17–21; 15:34–38; 16:9–10; see Mark 6:38–44; 8:5–9), and His ability to restore life to the dead (Luke 7:12–15; Mark 5:22–24, 35–43; John 11:11–15, 21, 38–44).

Jesus exercised divine prerogatives. The exercise of divine prerogatives during His earthly ministry also demonstrates that Jesus did not lose any of His deity at His incarnation. One such prerogative is the forgiveness of sins, which Jesus exercised. On one occasion a paralyzed man in Capernaum was carried on a bed to Jesus by four friends. Unable to get to Jesus because of the crowd, they went to the roof, removed the tiles, and lowered their friend in front of Jesus (Mark 2:1–4; see Matt. 9:1–2, Luke 5:18-19). "When Jesus saw their faith, he said to the paralytic, 'Son, your sins are forgiven'" (Mark 2:5; see Matt. 9:2; Luke 5:20). Some of the "teachers of the law" mentally accused Jesus of blasphemy, correctly thinking to themselves, "Who can forgive sins but God alone?" (Mark 2:7; see Luke 5:21).

Knowing their thoughts (evidence of divine omniscience), Jesus said to them, "Which is easier; to say to the paralytic, 'Your sins are forgiven,' or to say, 'Get up, take your mat and walk'?" (Mark 2:9; see Matt. 9:5; Luke 5:23). Obviously it is easier to say "Your sins are forgiven," because who can tell outwardly whether they have been or not? Then Jesus said, "But that you may know that the Son of Man has authority on earth to forgive sins. . . . He said to the paralytic, 'I tell you, get up, take your mat and go home'" (Mark 2:10–11; see Matt. 9:6; Luke 5:24). Immediately the man "got up, took his mat and walked out in full view of them all" (Mark 2:12; see Matt. 9:7, Luke 5:25). By healing the paralytic Jesus demonstrated His divine prerogative to forgive sins.

On another occasion, when Jesus was eating dinner in a Pharisee's house, a "woman who had lived a sinful life in that town" (Luke 7:37) came and washed Jesus' "feet with her tears. Then she wiped them with her hair, kissed them and poured perfume on them" (7:38) as evidence of her repentance and faith. Jesus told her, "Your sins are forgiven. . . . Your faith has saved you; go in peace" (7:48, 50).

This sinful woman's ministry to Jesus was evidence of her faith in Him, for which she received forgiveness of her sins. But her washing His feet also expressed her worship of Him. The right to receive worship is another prerogative of the incarnate Lord Jesus. The Magi who came to Jerusalem looking for the "king of the Jews" said, "We have come to worship him" (Matt. 2:2). When they came to the house where Jesus was, "they bowed down and worshiped him" (2:11). After Jesus walked on the water, stilled the storm, and entered the boat, his disciples "worshiped him" (14:33). So did the man blind from birth whom Jesus healed (John 9:1, 38). It is not surprising that after Jesus' resurrection the women (Matt. 28:9) and the disciples (28:17) worshiped Him. And after His ascension the disciples worshiped the Lord as they returned to Jerusalem (Luke 24:52). Angels, too, worship Jesus, "the firstborn" (Heb. 1:6). He accepts worship because it is His prerogative as the incarnate Son of God.

A significant passage of Scripture that discusses Jesus' exercise of divine prerogatives is John 5:16–30. His basic affirmation to the Jews to whom He spoke was, "My Father is always at his work to this very day, and I, too, am working" (5:17). Later He said, "Whatever the Father does the Son also does" (5:19). Then Jesus claimed the authority to give "life to whom he is pleased to give it" (5:21), both physical life in resurrection and spiritual life in salvation. In addition Jesus said that God the Father "has entrusted all judgment to the Son, that all may honor the Son just as they honor the Father" (5:22–23). Jesus' authority over the resurrection of the dead and the judgment of everyone is stated more fully in verses 25–30.

The Perfect Humanity of Jesus Christ

The person of our Lord Jesus Christ involved the union of perfect humanity with full deity. This means that He was totally free of any taint of the Adamic sin nature. The angel Gabriel described the Virgin Mary's Holy-Spirit-conceived son as "the holy one" (Luke 1:35). This is not because Mary was "immaculate" as Roman Catholics believe. That only pushes the miracle back a generation and makes it more difficult to explain, because Mary was conceived normally by two parents with Adamic natures. Instead it was because God said to Mary, "The Holy Spirit will come upon you, and the power of the Most High will overshadow you" (1:35). Later in His ministry Jesus challenged the Jews who rejected His teaching; He asked, "Can any of you prove me guilty of sin?" (John 8:46).

Although He was free of sin by nature and by action, Jesus apparently lived a normal life. Luke reported that "the child grew and became strong; he was filled with wisdom, and the grace of God was upon him" (Luke 2:40). He displayed that wisdom when Joseph and Mary took Him to Jerusalem at the age of twelve and He was accidentally left behind. His parents found him "after three days . . . in the temple courts, sitting among the teachers, listening to them and asking them questions. Everyone who heard him was amazed at his understanding and his answers" (2:46–47). Luke wrote that he "was obedient to them. . . . And Jesus grew in wisdom and stature, and in favor with God and men" (2:51–52). What a shock it must have been to Mary when her next child showed the first evidence of his Adamic sin nature, which Jesus never displayed.

Jesus' human nature was perfect in the sense of His being free from sin. He was "without sin" (Heb. 4:15); He "had no sin" (2 Cor. 5:21), and "in him is no sin" (1 John 3:5). His human nature was also complete in that it included a soul and spirit and well as a body. As a result Jesus could feel the range of normal human emotions. He wept at the tomb of Lazarus (John 11:35) and the Jews said, "See how he loved him!" (11:36). He could feel righteous anger (Mark 3:5), which He displayed in driving the merchants and moneychangers out of the temple at His triumphal entry into Jerusalem (Matt. 21:12–13; see Mark 11:15–17; Luke 19:45–46). In the Garden of Gethsemane Jesus spoke of His soul being "overwhelmed with sorrow" (Matt. 26:38; see John 12:27).

Jesus learned the carpenter's trade from Joseph and was known as "the carpenter's son" (Matt. 13:55), and "the carpenter" (Mark 6:3). He became hungry (Matt. 4:2), thirsty (John 4:7; 19:28), and tired (4:6) like any human being. He was "tempted by the devil" (Matt. 4:1–11; see Mark 1:13; Luke 4:1–12). The author of the epistle to the Hebrews explained that "we have one who has been tempted in every way, just as we are—yet was without sin" (Heb. 4:15; see 2:18). By angelic instruction His parents named Him Jesus (Luke 1:31; 2:21; Matt. 1:21, 25), a meaningful name in Jewish history (Josh. 1:1), and Jesus delighted in calling Himself "the Son of Man" (Matt. 8:20, the first of eighty-nine times). Jesus truly lived as a Man among men.

THE RELATIONSHIP OF GOD AND MAN IN ONE PERSON

The Scriptures make it clear that Jesus is the union of full deity and perfect, complete humanity. Jesus is the God-Man. The Scriptures are not as clear, however, in delineating the relationship between the divine nature and the human nature in the person of Christ. They are clear that it is a hypostatic union, a union of natures to form one person. Jesus is the theanthropic person who feels and thinks and acts as one person. He is not a split personality with His divine and human natures in conflict. In Scripture Jesus never spoke of either His deity or His humanity as separate from Himself; He always spoke and acted as one person.

Errors concerning the Union

Nestorianism, named after Nestorius (died ca. A.D. 451), views Jesus as having a dual personality. This is only one of several errors advanced and rejected as the Christian church sought to understand the biblical teaching concerning the person of Jesus Christ. The earliest to be advanced is called "Docetism," derived from a transliteration of the Greek verb *dokeō*, which means "to seem." It taught that Jesus only seemed to be a man; His body was only an apparition. The apostle John refuted this view when he wrote, "Every spirit that acknowledges that Jesus Christ has come in the flesh is from God, but every spirit that does not acknowledge Jesus is not from God" (1 John 4:2–3). And John emphasized earlier, "That which was from the beginning, which we have heard, which we have seen with our eyes, which we have looked at and our hands have touched—this we proclaim concerning the Word of life" (1:1). Docetism is also mentioned in 2 John 7 ("deceivers, who do not acknowledge Jesus Christ as coming in the flesh") and refuted in Colossians 2:9 ("For in Christ all the fullness of the Deity lives in *bodily* form"). Ryrie accurately writes, "This heresy undermines not only the reality of the Incarnation but also the validity of the Atonement and bodily resurrection."[3]

Another early heresy concerning the person of Jesus is "Ebionism," named for a sect of Jewish Christians in the early centuries of the church. In effect it denied the virgin birth of Jesus, considering Him the natural son of Joseph and Mary. Ebionites taught that the eternal Christ was united with the human Jesus when John baptized Jesus. Some of them held that "the Christ" left Jesus on the cross, pointing to His cry, "My God, my God, why have you forsaken me?" (Matt. 27:46; Mark 15:34). According to this view Jesus died just as a man, not as the God-Man. Many Bible students believe 1 John 5:6–8 is a refutation of this heresy, which was advanced near the close of the apostolic era by Cerinthus and accepted by others. If Jesus was the natural son of Joseph and Mary, he was not "the holy one" (Luke 1:35), but received an Adamic sin nature from his parents. Furthermore, if He died as a man, His death could not be the infinite sacrifice for the sins of the world.

Still another heresy concerning the person of Christ in the early centuries of the church is Monarchianism. In an effort to preserve absolute monotheism in opposition to Trinitarianism, its adherents presented one of two points of view. The Adoptionist or Dynamic Monarchians "maintained that Jesus was God only in the sense that a power or influence from the Father rested upon His human person."[4] The Modalist Monarchians, also called Sabellians from Sabellius (third century A.D.), taught that "in the Godhead the only differentiation was a mere succession of modes or operations."[5] Modalism, however, is refuted by the separate presence of the three persons of the triune Godhead at Jesus' baptism by John the Baptist: "the Spirit of God [was] descending like a dove and resting on" Jesus (Matt. 3:16); God the Father in "a voice from heaven" identified Jesus as "my Son, whom I love" (3:17; see Mark 1:10–11; Luke 3:21–22). This group was also known as Patripassionists, because they taught that God the Father suffered and died as Jesus Christ, God the Son. A contemporary version of this error is the Jesus Only movement.

Arianism, named for its originator Arius (ca. A.D. 250–ca. 336), denied the eternality and full deity of the Word who became incarnate as Jesus Christ. Arianism taught that the Logos "was not eternal but was created by the Father from nothing as an instrument for the creation of the world; and that therefore he was not God by nature, but a changeable creature."[6] This heresy is promoted in our day by both the Jehovah's Witnesses and the Mormons (the Church of Jesus Christ of Latter-Day Saints). Charles Taze Russell, founder of the Watchtower Bible and Tract Society, which later became known as the Jehovah's Witnesses, described Jesus Christ as "the highest of all Jehovah's creation, so also he was the first, the direct creation of God, the 'only begotten,' and then, he, as Jehovah's power, and in his name, created all things—angels, principalities and powers, as well as the earthly creation."[7] The Mormon author James E. Talmadge affirmed the preexistence of Christ before His conception by Mary and birth in Bethlehem, but he taught that Jesus was not God, a member of the Trinity. Talmadge wrote, "He had lived with the Father as an unembodied spirit, the Firstborn of the Father's children."[8]

Another ancient error is called Eutychianism, named for its originator Eutychus (ca. A.D. 378–454). In opposition to Nestorianism, this view held that in the incarnate Christ deity and humanity were blended into one nature like the ingredients in a cake. As a result Jesus was not fully divine, and yet He was more than human; He had a theanthropic nature but was not the theanthropic person, the God-Man. This heresy is also known as Monophysitism, meaning "one nature," in the sense that He had *one* blended nature, not a divine nature and a human nature. A variation of this view is that, although Christ had two natures, He had only one will. This is known as Monothelitism. Even though Jesus could express His human will in the sense of wish or desire, as voiced in His prayer in the Garden of Gethsemane (Matt. 26:39, 42), His personal will in the sense of moral choice always followed the will of God the Father.

Since erroneous views of the relationship between the deity and humanity in the incarnate person of Christ arose before the close of the apostolic generation, it is understandable that the church of that time struggled to reach a position in accord with the biblical teaching. This was debated among church leaders and formulated in statements of church councils until the issue was more or less settled at the councils of Chalcedon (A.D. 451) and Constantinople (A.D. 680). Modern versions of these ancient heresies, however, underscore the need for constant vigilance to preserve the true biblical doctrine.

Describing the Union

The accounts of the incarnate life of Jesus in the Gospels help us draw accurate conclusions concerning the relationship between the divine and human natures in the person of Christ. A most important conclusion is that Jesus never used His deity to make life easier for Himself. When the devil challenged Him to prove He was the Son of God and satisfy His hunger by turning stones into bread (Matt. 4:3; Luke 4:3), something Jesus could do, He refused. His refusal was not just because it was the devil's challenge; it was also because He would not relieve His hunger through His divine powers. Similarly, Jesus never sent His disciples ahead of Him and then miraculously transported Himself there to meet them; He walked the dusty paths and grew weary along with the disciples. Before He walked on the water to meet His disciples in the boat after sending them ahead, He remained behind to pray (Matt. 14:23). He also wanted to teach impetuous and questioning Peter to keep looking to Jesus in faith instead of at the surrounding circumstances (14:15–33; see John 6:16–21).

On the other hand, the human nature of Jesus, although it was sinless at conception and birth (Luke 1:35), was subject to temptation and falling into sin in and of itself, just as the sinless human natures of Adam and Eve had been until they disobeyed God and sinned (Gen. 1:26–28: 2:15–18,

20–25; 3:6–13, 16–23). However, because Jesus' human nature was joined with His divine nature in one person, He not only did not sin when tempted by the devil or at any time later in His earthly life, but He could not sin. Theologically this is called the impeccability of Christ.

Some evangelical Christians, even though they state emphatically that Jesus never did sin, insist that He *could* have sinned. They base this belief in the peccability of Jesus on the reality and genuineness of His humanity. As stated by Charles Hodge, "If He was a true man, He must have been capable of sinning."[9] This argument, however, ignores the fact that the true humanity of Jesus was without a sin nature from conception (Luke 1:35). This view also overlooks the fact that His human nature was united with the divine nature of the eternal Son of God, the Word, into one Person. Though Jesus had a true human nature, He was more than a true man; He was the God-Man.

Christians who believe Jesus was capable of sinning (even though He never did sin) also base this belief on their understanding of temptation and the reality of Jesus' temptation. On this point Hodge wrote, "Temptation implies the possibility of sin. If from the constitution of his person it was impossible for Christ to sin, then his temptation was unreal and without effect, and He cannot sympathize with his people."[10]

However, this view misunderstands the meaning of temptation. The word in Hebrew, Greek, and English means primarily "to test" or "to prove by testing" and only secondarily "to solicit to do evil." The Old Testament states that Israel tempted "the LORD" (Exod. 17:2; Deut. 6:16; Mal. 3:15), and the New Testament speaks of tempting God (Acts 5:9; 15:10; 1 Cor. 10:9). Everyone would agree that God cannot sin because of "the constitution of his person," but God obviously can be and is tempted in the sense of being tested and proved by testing. But this is far different from Jesus having the ability to sin. A small tugboat attacking a huge ocean liner is unable to sink it; nonetheless it is still a real attack. In other words, for a temptation to be real, the one receiving the attack (Jesus) need not be susceptible to sin.

Also, when Hodge wrote that impeccability makes Christ's "temptation unreal and without effect," he misunderstood both the person of Christ and the character of His testing. After forty days of fasting, Jesus was hungry and humanly desirous of food to a degree few of us, if any, have ever known. Furthermore, through His divine nature He had the ability to turn stones into bread. However, the desires of Jesus' sinless human nature and the omnipotence of His divine nature were always controlled by the unified person and will of the God-Man, which always chose and acted in obedience to the will of God the Father (John 5:10; 8:59). Therefore it was impossible for Christ to sin.

Furthermore, He could and does "sympathize with his people" (Heb. 2:9–18; 4:14–16). This is true not only because Jesus experienced the normal human feelings and desires of His people apart from a sin nature, but also because His omniscience enables Him to know and sympathize with them.

We have already mentioned how Jesus displayed the omniscience, omnipotence, and omnipresence of God, but Scripture also reveals that He showed a lack of knowledge because of His human nature. As He walked along with Jairus, "a large crowd followed and pressed around him" (Mark 5:24). A woman who had suffered with a "bleeding for twelve years" (5:25) "touched His cloak" (5:27), thinking, "If I just touch his clothes, I will be healed" (5:28). Sensing that power had gone out from him, Jesus asked, "Who touched my clothes?" (5:30). Jesus may have known who she was and so He asked only to encourage the woman to respond, or His question may reflect ignorance from the standpoint of His human nature. When the healed woman came forward, Jesus told her, "Daughter, your faith has healed you. Go in peace and be freed from your suffering" (5:34). Later, in the Olivet Discourse, when speaking of the coming of the Son of Man (Matt. 24:27), Jesus said, "No one knows about that day or hour, not even the angels in heaven, not the Son, but only the Father" (Matt. 24:36; Mark 13:32; see Acts 1:7), again showing personal lack of knowledge in His human nature. This expression of the attributes of both His deity and His humanity in His single person is called the communion of attributes, the doctrine that "the attributes of both natures belong to the one Person without mixing the natures or dividing the Person."[11]

Our Lord Jesus' making "himself nothing"—perhaps more literally emptied himself—(Phil. 2:7, NASB), therefore, did not in any way constitute a laying aside of His deity or any of His divine attributes. It did involve voluntarily not using His divine attributes at times, as when He experienced human weariness and lack of knowledge, but Jesus always possessed a full divine nature. The glory of that divine nature was veiled, however, so that Christ Jesus was "made in human likeness" and was "found in appearance as a man" (2:7–8). At times that veil was removed, as when Jesus took Peter, James, and John "up a high mountain" where "he was transfigured before them. His face shone like the sun, and his clothes became as the light" (Matt. 17:1–2; Mark 9:2–3). His transfiguration explains why the apostle John could write, "We have seen his glory, the glory of the One and Only Son, who came from the Father, full of grace and truth" (John 1:14). Struck with the uniqueness of Jesus Christ, Napoleon Bonaparte wrote, "Everything in Christ astonishes me. His spirit overpowers men, and His will confounds me. Between Him and whoever else is in the world there is no comparison. He is truly a being by Himself."[12]

Phillips Brooks, a well-known nineteenth-century preacher, spoke of Jesus' humanity and deity in an interesting way:

Here is a man who was born in an obscure village, the child of a peasant woman. He grew up in another obscure village. He worked in a carpenter's shop until he was thirty, and then for three years He was an itinerant preacher. He never wrote a book. He never held an office. He never owned a home. He never had a family. He never went to college. He never traveled two hundred miles from the place where He was born. He never did one of the things that usually accompany greatness. He had no credentials but Himself. He had nothing to do with the world except the power of His divine manhood. While still a young man, the tide of popular opinion turned against Him. He was turned over to His enemies. He was nailed on a cross between two thieves. His executioners gambled for the only piece of property He had on earth while He was dying—His coat. When He was dead, He was taken down and laid in a borrowed grave through the pity of a friend. And on the third day He arose from the dead. Nineteen centuries have come and gone, and today He is the centerpiece of the human race and the leader of the column of progress. I am far within the mark when I say that all the armies that ever marched, and all the navies that ever were built, and all the parliaments that ever sat, and all the kings that ever reigned put together have not affected the life of man on earth as powerfully as has that One solitary life. The explanation? He is the Son of God, the risen Savior.[13]

Lewis Sperry Chafer made these comments about the incarnate Christ:

He was weary; yet He called the weary to Himself for rest. He was hungry; yet He was "the bread of life." He was thirsty; yet He was "the water of life." He was in agony; yet He healed all manner of sicknesses and soothed every pain. He "grew, and waxed strong in spirit"; yet He was from all eternity. He was tempted; yet He, as God, could not be tempted. He was self-limited in knowledge; yet He was the wisdom of God. He said, "My Father is greater than I" (with reference to His humiliation, being made for a little season lower than the angels); yet He also said, "He that hath seen me hath seen the Father," "I and my Father are one." He prayed, which is always human; yet He Himself answered prayer. He said, "This is your hour, and the power of darkness"; yet all power is given unto Him in heaven and in earth. He slept on a pillow in the boat; yet He arose and rebuked the storm. He was baptized, which was only a human act; yet at that time God declared Him to be His Son. He walked two long days' journey to Bethany; yet He knew the moment that Lazarus died. He wept at the tomb; yet He called the dead to arise. He confessed that He would be put to death; yet He had but a moment before received Peter's inspired declaration that He was the Christ, the Son of the living God. He said, "Whom do men say that I the Son of man am?"; yet John tells us, "He needed not that any should testify of man: for He knew what was in man." He was hungry; yet He could turn stones into bread. This He did not do; for had He done so, He would not have suffered as men suffer. He said, "My God, my God, why hast thou forsaken me?"; yet it was that very God to whom He cried who was "in Christ, reconciling the world unto himself." He dies; yet He is eternal life. He freely functioned in His earth-life within that which was perfectly human, and He as freely functioned in His earth-life within that which was perfectly divine. His earth-life, therefore, testifies as much to His humanity as to His Deity, and both of these revelations are equally true.[14]

Seven

THE EARTHLY LIFE AND MINISTRY
OF THE INCARNATE SON OF GOD

———◦◈◦———

HE LORD JESUS CHRIST was the union of the eternal Word,
the second person of the triune Godhead, and perfect and complete humanity, from the moment of His conception by the Holy Spirit (Luke 1:35). Although it is not stated, Jesus, like John the Baptist, was undoubtedly "filled with the Holy Spirit even from birth" (1:15). As a result of His conception by the Holy Spirit, Jesus was "the holy one" (1:35), free from an Adamic sin nature, and His divine nature kept Him from committing sin even as a child and an adolescent.

Little is said in the Gospels, however, concerning Jesus' childhood and youth—simply His circumcision and naming on the eighth day (2:21), Mary's purification and Jesus' redemption by sacrifice as the firstborn thirty-three days later (Lev. 12; Luke 2:22–24), the flight and sojourn in Egypt until Herod's death (Matt. 2:13–15) and the return to Joseph and Mary's original hometown, Nazareth in Galilee, after Herod's death (2:19–23). The only other incident mentioned in the Gospels concerning Jesus' life before His baptism by John was the journey to Jerusalem with His parents for the Feast of the Passover when He was twelve years old (Luke 2:41–42). Jesus may have gone with them on previous trips, "but at twelve a Jewish boy became a 'son of the law' and began to observe the ordinances, putting on the phylacteries as a reminder."[1] This custom is now observed by Jews in the bar mitzvah at age thirteen. Luke wrote that "the child grew and became strong; he was filled with wisdom, and the grace of God was upon him" (2:40). And after the incident in Jerusalem He "went down to Nazareth with them and was obedient to them. . . . And Jesus grew in wisdom and stature, and in favor with God and men" (2:51–52).

Whether Jesus as a child was conscious of His divine nature is not stated, but perhaps He was not. It would seem that Jesus' response to Mary when His parents found Him in the temple—"Why were you searching for me? . . . Didn't you know I had to be in my Father's house?" (2:49)—was the first indication of His awareness of His unique relationship to God. The apocryphal and pseudopigraphal Gospels, however, are filled with fanciful tales of young Jesus restoring dead playmates to life, healing wounds and broken bones, and touching play birds made of clay and having them come to life and fly away. But the simplicity and sobriety of the true Gospels show their genuineness in contrast to these bizarre stories.

JESUS' BAPTISM

John the Baptist, son of Zechariah, began his ministry "in the fifteenth year of the reign of Tiberias Caesar . . . during the high priesthood of Annas and Caiaphas" (Luke 3:1–2). Because of the difficulty in correlating biblical events with the calendar in use today, the beginning of John's ministry is viewed as having occurred at some time between A.D. 27 and A.D. 29. After discussing all the options, one specialist in biblical chronology places it "sometime in A.D. 29,"[2] which would make John the Baptist thirty years old, the age when priests and Levites began their temple service (Num. 3:2–3, 22–23, 29–30). This would have been appropriate since John was qualified to be a priest (Luke 1:5). Since Jesus was slightly more than six months younger than John (1:36–38), His coming to John for baptism and the beginning of His ministry also took place when he was thirty years old.

The phrase introducing John's ministry is significant—"the word of God came to John" (3:2). Essentially the same phrase introduced the prophecies of Haggai (1:1), Zechariah (1:1), and Malachi (1:1), the three postexilic prophets before the four centuries of "silence" from God to Israel. It may be said, therefore, that John's ministry continued the Old Testament prophetic tradition. When John had been thrown into prison by Herod the tetrarch (Matt. 14:3–12; 11:1–2), Jesus said of John, "Then what did you go out to see? A prophet? Yes, I tell you, and more than a prophet" (11:9; Luke 7:26).

At the same time John the Baptist marked the transition to a new epoch in the outworking of God's eternal plan. Jesus continued to identify John as the forerunner of Israel's Messiah, quoting Malachi 3:1 (Matt. 11:10), and as "Elijah, who was to come" if he was accepted by the Jewish people (Matt. 11:14; 17:10–13; Mark 9:11–13; Luke 1:17; John 1:21–23; see Mal. 4:5). Jesus praised John, saying, "I tell you the truth: Among those born of women there has not risen anyone greater than John the Baptist" (Matt. 11:11; Luke 7:28).

The fact that John the Baptist's ministry was "in the Desert of Judea" (Matt. 3:1), "on the other side of the Jordan" (John 1:28) instead of in Jerusalem, shows that he stood apart from the established Jewish religious hierarchy of priests, scribes, Pharisees, and Sadducees. Efforts to identify John the Baptist with the Dead Sea sect because of his ministry in the Judean desert are groundless. He was described by the angel Gabriel to his father Zechariah as coming "in the spirit and power of Elijah" (Luke 1:17) and living as a Nazirite, not taking "wine or other fermented drink" (1:15; Num. 6:1–4), from birth. John dressed like Elijah (Matt. 3:4; 2 Kings 1:8), his diet was similar to Elijah's (Matt. 3:4; 1 Kings 17:3), and his location also was similar (Mark 1:4; Luke 3:3; 1 Kings 17:3), in fulfillment of the prophecy of Isaiah 40:3–5.

As the forerunner of God's Messiah, John's ministry was to call the Jewish people to "Repent, for the kingdom of heaven is near" (Matt. 3:2), "preaching a baptism of repentance for the forgiveness of sins" (Mark 1:4; Luke 3:3). He exhorted the various groups who came to him—tax collectors, soldiers, ordinary people—to "produce fruit in keeping with repentance" (Luke 3:8), giving each group specific instructions (3:10–14). He denounced the Pharisees and Sadducees who came to him as a "brood of vipers" (Matt. 3:7) and warned them not to rest in being descendants of Abraham without bearing the fruit of genuine repentance (3:8–9).

John the Baptist also proclaimed that "after me will come one who is more powerful than I, whose sandals I am not fit to carry. He will baptize you with the Holy Spirit and with fire" (Matt. 3:11; Mark 1:7; Luke 3:16; John 1:15, 26, 30). John then explained that "the reason I came baptizing with water was that he might be revealed to Israel" (1:31), which was accomplished when Jesus was baptized by John. Jesus' baptism "with fire" probably refers to His judgment to come, in which He will purge, as if by fire, unbelievers from His kingdom (see Matt. 3:12). The apostle John wrote that John the Baptist also proclaimed Jesus as "the Lamb of God, who takes away the sin of the world!" (John 1:29; see v. 36). John recognized and accepted his part in God's program, telling his disciples when they complained about Jesus' growing popularity (3:26), "You yourselves can testify that I said, 'I am not the Christ but am sent ahead of him.'. . . He must become greater; I must become less" (3:28, 30).

As already noted, Jesus was approximately six months younger than John the Baptist (Luke 1:36); therefore He was thirty years old when He was baptized by John. When Jesus came to him, John demurred, saying, "I need to be baptized by you, and do you come to me?" (Matt. 3:14). Jesus responded, "Let it be so now; it is proper for us to do this to fulfill all righteousness" (3:15). Bible students have puzzled over His meaning. Jesus did not need to repent of sin, as did others whom John baptized. But He did need to identify with sinners for whom He would provide the redemptive sacrifice in His death. In a sense His baptism by John also constituted His induction into His messianic office and ministry, since it resulted in His anointing by the Holy Spirit and His approval by God the Father as "he went up out of the water" (3:16).

Although Jesus' anointing was of a more exalted kind, it followed the pattern of Israel's custom of anointing kings (1 Sam. 10:1; 1 Kings 1:34–35, 38–39; 19:16; 2 Kings 9:6; 11:12), priests (Exod. 28:41; 29:7; 30:30–33; 40:13–15), and on at least one occasion (and possibly more) prophets (1 Kings 19:16; see 1 Chron. 16:22; Ps. 105:15). This anointing marked their appointment to and/or induction into office.

Although Jesus most likely was filled with the Holy Spirit from birth as was John the Baptist (Luke 1:15), the descent of the Spirit on Him "as a dove" (John 1:32, 33; see Matt. 3:16; Mark 1:10; Luke 3:21) marked His identity as the promised Messiah and His induction into that office and ministry. This was also confirmed by an audible voice from heaven that said, "This is my Son, whom I love; with him I am well pleased" (Matt. 3:17; see Mark 1:11; Luke 3:22). God the Father repeated the same words of approval of Jesus at His transfiguration (Matt. 17:5; Mark 9:7; Luke 9:35). As stated before, at Jesus' baptism all three persons of the Godhead were present: Jesus, the incarnate Son of God, God the Holy Spirit, and God the Father.

JESUS' MESSAGE AND MINISTRY
AS GOD'S PROMISED MESSIAH

Although the eternal Word of God became incarnate as Jesus, to be "the Lamb of God, who takes away the sin of the world!" (John 1:29), He also came as the Messiah for God's people Israel, as promised in the Old Testament. This is stated in Gabriel's announcement to Mary (Luke 1:32–33) and in the angel's proclamation to the shepherds (2:11). To prepare the Jewish people for their Messiah was the point of John the Baptist's message and ministry. As a result, from the beginning of Jesus' earthly ministry to His crucifixion an important part of Jesus' message and ministry was presenting Himself to the Jewish people as their promised Messiah.

At the beginning of His ministry Jesus' message was the same as John's—"Repent, for the kingdom of heaven is at hand" (Matt. 4:17; see 3:2; Mark 1:14–15). As Jesus traveled "in all Galilee" He proclaimed "the good news of the kingdom" (Matt. 4:23; 9:35). When He returned to Nazareth, Jesus read in the synagogue the part of a messianic prophecy from Isaiah that applied to His earthly ministry (Luke 4:18–19; see Isa. 61:1–2a), and He said, "Today this scripture is fulfilled in your hearing" (Luke 4:21). Although Jesus did not "proclaim freedom to the prisoners" literally in His ministry on earth in His first coming, He did in the sense of providing freedom from physical bondage to disease (e.g., 5:12–13) and disability (John 5:3–8) and from mental bondage (Luke 8:2–3, 27–33, 35). In addition He certainly did "preach good news to the poor . . . recovery of sight to the blind" (e.g., John 9:1–7), released "the oppressed," and proclaimed "the year of the Lord's favor." Jesus told the twelve apostles,

"'Do not go among the Gentiles or enter any town of the Samaritans. Go rather to the lost sheep of Israel. As you go, preach this message: 'The kingdom of heaven is near'" (Matt. 10:5–7; see Luke 9:21).

When John the Baptist languished in Herod the tetrarch's prison and Jesus did nothing to set him free, he began to question if Jesus was the promised Messiah. So John sent two of his disciples to Jesus asking, "Are you the one who was to come, or should we expect someone else?" (Luke 7:19; Matt. 11:3). Jesus told them to tell John that they had seen the blind receive their sight, the lame walk, lepers cured, the deaf healed, and the dead raised, and that the good news was being preached to the poor (Luke 7:22; Matt. 11:4–5). At the close of His earthly ministry in His triumphal entry into Jerusalem Jesus was clearly presenting Himself to the Jewish people as their Messiah in fulfillment of Old Testament prophecies (Matt. 21:1–11; Mark 11:1–11; Luke 19:28–40; John 12:12–16; see Isa. 62:11; Zech. 9:9).

It is important to recognize, however, that Jesus' offer of Himself as the Messiah was rejected by both the Jewish leaders and the people. Before "the chief priests and the whole Sanhedrin" (Mark 14:55) Jesus responded "I am" to the high priest's question, "Are you the Christ, the Son of the Blessed One?" (14:61–62; see Matt. 26:63–64; Luke 22:66–70). But they condemned Him for blasphemy instead of accepting His testimony (Mark 14:63–64; see Matt. 26:65–66). Likewise, when "Pilate asked Jesus, 'Are you the king of the Jews?'" Jesus responded, "'Yes, it is as you say'" (Luke 23:3; John 18:33–37).

When Pilate presented Jesus to the Jewish leaders and people as "Christ" (Matt. 27:22) and "the king of the Jews" (Mark 15:12; John 19:14), they shouted, "Take him away! Take him away! Crucify him" (19:15; see Matt. 27:22–23; Mark 15:12–13). When Pilate asked the Jews, "Shall I crucify your king?" the chief priests answered, "We have no king but Caesar" (John 19:15). Similarly, when Pilate told the Jews that Jesus' death would be their responsibility, "All the people answered, 'Let his blood be on us and on our children'" (Matt. 27:25). This rejection of Jesus as Messiah and King by the Jewish leaders and people has implications for dispensationalism, which are discussed in chapter 8.

Jesus' earthly message and ministry identified Him as a prophet as well as the promised Messiah. Jesus spoke of Himself as a prophet when

He alluded to His death in Jerusalem by saying, "It cannot be that a prophet perish out of Jerusalem" (Luke 13:33, KJV). He was often called a prophet by others because of His miracles (Mark 6:15; Luke 7:16; John 6:14; 9:17), His teaching (7:40), and His knowledge of individuals' lives (4:19). His followers called Him "Jesus the prophet, from Nazareth in Galilee" (Matt. 21:11; see v. 46; Luke 24:19).

Jesus' prophetic ministry involved both His preaching and teaching and also His predictions of His death and resurrection (John 2:19, 21–22; Matt. 16:21), of the destruction of the temple (Matt. 24:2), and of the sign of His coming and "of the end of the age" (24:3), as well as other events. A great example of His teaching is the Sermon on the Mount (Matt. 5–7), which has been called "The Manifesto of the King." Lewis Sperry Chafer says that it "was given . . . as a feature of the kingdom proclamation which first occupied the ministry of Christ on earth. It constituted the authoritative edict of the King relative to the character of the kingdom, its requirements, and the conditions of admission into it."[3] Both John the Baptist and Jesus were preaching, "Repent, for the kingdom of heaven is near" (3:2; 4:17), so that, although the Sermon on the Mount had both immediate application to Jesus' audience and to readers today, it ultimately relates to the millennial kingdom of righteousness and peace. When Jesus finished it, "the crowds were amazed at his teaching, because he taught as one who had authority [which He did], and not as their teachers of the law" (7:28–29; see 13:54; 22:33; Mark 1:22; 6:2; 11:18; Luke 4:32; John 7:46).

JESUS' AUTHENTICATION AS MESSIAH BY HIS MIRACLES

Much of Jesus' ministry was occupied in the performance of a wide range of miracles. The Gospels record a total of thirty-five separate miracles.[4] The first one was the turning of water into wine, recorded in John 2:1–10. John wrote that His miracles were "miraculous signs" (2:11) or just "signs" (NKJV, ASV). In the New Testament four Greek nouns are used, all translated "miracle" in English at times. On the basis of those words Henry Thiessen defines a miracle as "a unique and extraordinary event awakening wonder (*teras*), wrought by divine power (*dynamis*), accomplishing some practical and benevolent work (*ergon*), and authenticating a messenger and his message as from God (*sēmeion*)."⁵ This definition certainly applies to the miracles of Christ, especially His authentication as God's promised Messiah.

Jesus' miracles identified Him as the Christ in accord with Old Testament prophecies (Isa. 35:5–6; 61:1). Jesus never performed miracles for His own gratification (Matt. 4:2–4) or exaltation (4:5–7), but for the benefit of others (e.g., feeding the five thousand [14:14–21] and the four thousand [15:32–39]) or as a testimony to others concerning His identity as God's Messiah, the Son of God (e.g., stilling a storm [8:23–27] and "walking on the lake" [14:25–33]). Jesus' miracles relieved physical suffering and hardship of various kinds (e.g., 8:2–4; 9:2–8; 12:9–13), even restoring life to the dead (9:18–19, 23–25; Luke 7:11–15; John 11:11–14, 17–44). He exorcised demons (Matt. 8:28–33; 9:32–33; 12:22; 17:14–18; Mark 1:21–28). Also He performed miracles pertaining to nature, such as an abundance of fish (Luke 5:1–11; John 21:1–11), locating the tribute money (Matt. 17:24–27), and causing a fruitless fig tree to wither (21:18–19). Jesus undoubtedly performed many other miracles as well, because on numerous occasions Matthew wrote of Jesus "healing every disease and sickness among the people" (4:23–24; see 8:16; 9:35; 11:21, 23; 12:15; 14:14, 36; 15:30–31; 19:2; 21:14) and the apostle John wrote, "Jesus did many other things as well" (John 21:25), which undoubtedly included miracles.

Since Jesus was primarily presenting Himself to the Jewish people as God's promised Messiah in His earthly life and ministry, He traveled mainly between Galilee and Judea. On some of His trips between Galilee and Jerusalem He avoided Samaria, where people of mixed ancestry lived, by going around it through Decapolis. Jesus also instructed the twelve apostles when He sent them out, "Do not go among the Gentiles or enter any town of the Samaritans. Go rather to the lost sheep of Israel" (Matt. 10:5–6). On one occasion when "Jesus withdrew to the region of Tyre and Sidon" (15:21), a woman with a demon-possessed daughter came to Him asking for His help (15:22, 25). Matthew identified her as a "Canaanite woman" and Mark stated she "was a Greek, born in Syrian Phoenicia" (Mark 7:26). Emphasizing His messianic ministry, Jesus said, "I am sent only to the lost sheep of Israel" (Matt. 15:24). In response to her plea,

"Lord, help me!" (15:25), Jesus said, "It is not right to take the children's bread and toss it to their dogs" (15:26), still emphasizing His messianic ministry to the Jewish people and undoubtedly also testing the genuineness of the woman's faith. "Yes, Lord," the woman replied, "but even the dogs eat the crumbs that fall from their masters' table" (15:27). "Then Jesus answered, 'Woman, you have great faith! Your request is granted.' And her daughter was healed from that very hour" (15:28).

It is important to point out that the Lord Jesus recognized the humanity-wide outreach of His messianic mission (see Isa. 42:6–7; 49:6) and that He ministered to Gentiles and Samaritans on numerous occasions. The centurion whose highly valued servant was sick was undoubtedly a Gentile, probably a Roman (Luke 7:2), a conclusion drawn from the fact that he "sent some of the elders of the Jews" to Jesus to seek help (7:3). They told Jesus, "This man deserves to have you do this, because he loves our nation and has built our synagogue" (7:4–5). When the man sent word that he trusted Jesus simply to say the word and his servant would be healed, Jesus told "the crowd following him . . . 'I have not found such great faith even in Israel'" (7:9), and he healed the servant.

When He rebuked the Jewish people for their failure to respond to His miracles and accept Him as their Messiah, Jesus referred to the ministry of the Old Testament prophets to Gentiles as examples of God's humanity-wide working. He reminded the people in Nazareth that Elijah ministered "to a widow in Zarephath, in the region of Sidon" (4:26) and Elisha healed "Naaman the Syrian" of leprosy (4:27). When Jesus reproached the people in the cities of Galilee for their failure to repent, He told them, "If the miracles that were performed in you had been performed in Tyre and Sidon, they would have repented long ago in sackcloth and ashes" (Matt. 11:21), and "if the miracles that were performed in you had been performed in Sodom, it would have remained to this day" (11:23). These statements are a display of Jesus' divine omniscience.

Jesus also ministered to Samaritans even though "Jews do not associate with Samaritans" (John 4:9). The animosity between these peoples goes back to the people of the land—ancestors of the Samaritans—who hindered the Jews' efforts to rebuild Jerusalem after their return from exile in Babylon (Ezra 4). On one occasion when Jesus and His disciples were passing through Samaria on the way to Jerusalem, the people in the village where He sent His disciples to make arrangements "did not welcome him, because He was heading for Jerusalem" (Luke 9:53). This animosity explains the Samaritan woman's surprise at the well of Sychar when Jesus asked, "Will you give me a drink?" (John 4:7). The conversation resulted in Jesus' spiritual ministry to her, His disclosure that He is the Messiah (4:25–26), and His spiritual ministry to many of the Samaritans of Sychar (4:29–30, 39–41).

Amazingly, Jesus held Samaritans up to the Jewish people as examples of gratitude and helpfulness. When Jesus healed ten lepers in a village "along the border between Samaria and Galilee" (Luke 17:11), the one who "came back, praising God . . . and [who] threw himself at Jesus' feet and thanked him . . . was a Samaritan" (17:15–16). Whether the parable of the Good Samaritan is a report of an actual incident or not, the Samaritan, not the priest or the Levite, was the one who had compassion on the victim of the robbers (10:30–37). When the Greeks who were Jewish proselytes at the Passover in Jerusalem came to Philip saying, "Sir, we wish to see Jesus" (John 12:20–21), Jesus rejoiced in the humanity-wide provision of redemption from sin and salvation to be accomplished through His death. He said, "But I, when I am lifted up from the earth"—a reference to His crucifixion, not His ascension—"will draw all men to myself" (12:32). He did not mean by this that everyone would be saved, but that all kinds of people would come to Him, including Greek Gentiles who were present then (12:20). He draws people to Himself without discrimination, without regard for their nationality or ethnic background.[6] As Jesus told Nicodemus, "God so loved the world that he gave his one and only Son, that whoever believes in him shall not perish but have eternal life" (3:16). The apostle John wrote, "Yet to all who received him, to those who believed in his name, he gave the right to become children of God" (1:12).

JESUS' MISSION TO DIE ON THE CROSS
AS THE REDEMPTIVE SACRIFICE

Not only was the Incarnation of the eternal Word a part of the triune Godhead's eternal plan but so also was His substitutionary redemptive sacrifice on the cross to provide salvation and eternal life for all who believe in Him. In the Book of the Revelation He is called "the Lamb that was slain from the creation of the world" (Rev.13:8). The epistle to the Hebrews states, "When Christ came into the world, he said: 'Sacrifice and offering you did not desire, but a body you prepared for me. . . . Then I said, . . . I have come to do your will, O God'" (Heb. 10:5, 7). A veiled prophecy of Jesus' death was made to Mary when Simeon told her, "A sword will pierce your own soul" (Luke 2:35). In addition, whether he was aware of its full significance or not, John the Baptist identified Jesus at His baptism as "the Lamb of God, who takes away the sin of the world!" (John 1:29–36).

A question to be considered, however, is, When was the incarnate Christ conscious that He would die on the cross as God's redemptive sacrifice for sin? Some theologians say He was not aware of His coming sacrificial death. However, He apparently lived with this consciousness from very early in His ministry. When He drove the merchants and moneychangers out of the temple at the Feast of Passover after turning the water into wine, "the Jews demanded of him, 'What miraculous sign can you show us to prove your authority to do all this?'" (John 2:18). Jesus' enigmatic response was, "Destroy this temple, and I will raise it again in three days" (2:19). John explained that "the temple he had spoken of was his body. After he was raised from the dead, his disciples recalled what he had said. Then they believed the Scripture and the words that Jesus had spoken" (2:21–22).

Jesus' interview with Nicodemus apparently occurred on that same trip to Jerusalem. He told Nicodemus, "Just as Moses lifted up the snake in the desert, so the Son of Man must be lifted up, that everyone who believes in him may have eternal life" (3:14). From these two statements it is obvious that our Lord was conscious both of the manner of His death and its significance and of His resurrection.

Jesus began to share the necessity of His death and the fact of His resurrection with His disciples after Peter declared—undoubtedly speaking for the group—"You are the Christ, the Son of the living God" (Matt. 16:16; Mark 8:29; Luke 9:20; see John 11:27). Jesus told them that "he must go to Jerusalem and suffer many things at the hands of the elders, chief priests and teachers of the law, and that he must be killed and on the third day be raised to life" (Matt. 16:21; Mark 8:31; Luke 9:22). Peter, again probably speaking for the group, "took him aside and began to rebuke him," saying, "Never, Lord! . . . This shall never happen to you" (Matt. 16:22). With their recognition of Jesus as the Messiah, Peter and the other disciples were anticipating the restoration of the kingdom to Israel and the reestablishment of His reign on David's throne, not the Messiah's rejection and death as the Suffering Servant of God (Isa. 52:13–53:12).

Somewhat earlier than His revelation to the apostles about His upcoming death and resurrection Jesus had responded to a request from "some of the Pharisees and teachers of the law" for "a miraculous sign" (Matt. 12:38; 16:1; Mark 8:11; Luke 11:16), by saying, "A wicked and adulterous generation asks for a miraculous sign! But none will be given it except the sign of the prophet Jonah. For as Jonah was three days and three nights in the belly of a huge fish, so the Son of Man will be three days and three nights in the heart of the earth" (Matt. 12:39-40; 16:4; Mark 8:12; Luke 11:29–30, 32). This not only predicted His death somewhat enigmatically but also confirmed His acceptance of the factual occurrence of the prophet Jonah's miraculous experience.

After His disclosure of the necessity of His death and resurrection to His apostles, "Jesus resolutely set out for Jerusalem" (Luke 9:51). Interestingly, Luke related this not to Jesus' awareness of His approaching death but to His glorification: "As the time approached for him to be taken up to heaven." Jesus' settled resolve to obey God's will, even though it involved death by crucifixion, is illustrated and underscored by what immediately follows. When one prospective disciple wanted first to go back and say goodbye to his family, Jesus responded, "No one who puts his hand to the plow and looks back is fit for service in the kingdom of God" (9:62). On this final journey to Jerusalem Jesus again told His apostles the trip would end in His arrest, suffering, death, and resurrection (18:31–34).

Despite His commitment to fulfill God's will as the sinless incarnate Son of God, Jesus' shrinking back from being made "sin for us" (2 Cor. 5:21; see Gal. 3:13) is understandable. This reluctance is displayed in Jesus' agonizing prayer in the Garden of Gethsemane the night of His arrest. When He asked Peter, James, and John to watch while He went on to pray,

He said, "My soul is overwhelmed with sorrow to the point of death" (Matt. 26:38; Mark 14:34). Then Jesus went "a little farther . . . fell with his face to the ground and prayed, 'My Father, if it be possible, may this cup be taken from me. Yet not as I will, but as you will'" (Matt. 26:39; Mark 14:35–36; Luke 22:41–42). In the Old Testament a "cup" sometimes symbolized wrath (Jer. 25:15), and so Jesus was aware that His coming death meant He would bear the wrath of God the Father against sin. Though Christ had no sin (2 Cor. 5:21), He bore the sins of the world on Himself (1 Pet. 2:24). Thus He was made "a curse for us" because of His being hanged on a tree (Gal. 3:13).

Luke reported that "an angel from heaven appeared to him and strengthened him. And being in anguish, he prayed more earnestly, and his sweat was like drops of blood falling to the ground" (Luke 22:43–44). After finding the disciples sleeping, Jesus left again and prayed, "My Father, if it is not possible for this cup to be taken away unless I drink it, may your will be done" (Matt. 26:42; Mark 14:36). Finding the disciples sleeping again, Jesus went a third time, repeating the same prayer (Matt. 26:44), which reveals the depths of His agony (see Heb. 5:7–8).

At Jesus' arrest, one of His disciples "reached for his sword, drew it out and struck the servant of the high priest, cutting off his ear" (Matt. 26:51). John revealed that this disciple was Simon Peter (John 18:10). Jesus then made two interesting statements. First He told Peter, "Do you think I cannot call on my Father, and he will at once put at my disposal more than twelve legions of angels? But how then would the Scriptures be fulfilled that say it must happen this way?" (Matt. 26:53–54). This shows His complete control of the situation. Then He also said, "Shall I not drink the cup the Father has given me?" (John 18:11), showing His complete submission to God's will. To the same point, when Pilate told Jesus, "Don't you realize I have power either to free you or to crucify you?" Jesus responded, "You would have no power over me if it were not given to you from above" (19:10–11).

The Jewish Sanhedrin condemned Jesus as "worthy of death" for what they believed was blasphemy (Matt. 26:65–67; Mark 14:63–64; Luke 22:70–71). They took Him to Pilate, the Roman governor, because, as they said, "we have no right to execute anyone" . . . so that the words Jesus had spoken indicating the kind of death he was going to die would be fulfilled" (John 18:31–32). Pilate told the Jews that Jesus' death was their responsibility (Matt. 27:24), to which they responded, "Let his blood be on us and on our children" (27:25). But along with the Jews, the Roman government and the Gentiles were also responsible for rejecting and crucifying Jesus.

The spiritual atmosphere of Jesus' crucifixion is seen in the fact that "from the sixth hour until the ninth hour darkness came over all the land" (27:45; Mark 15:33; Luke 23:44). "About the ninth hour Jesus cried out in a loud voice . . . 'My God, my God, why have you forsaken me'?" (Matt. 27:46; Mark 15:34). It was at this point, as Jesus bore the sin of the world, that God, the Judge of sin, turned away from Jesus Christ, His incarnate Son, the Sin-bearer, as far as the personal consciousness of Jesus was concerned. Jesus said, "My God, my God," not "my Father, my Father," because God the Father did not forsake His only Son. There never was, nor could there be, separation between the persons of the Godhead. Then "Jesus called out in a loud voice, 'Father, into your hands I commit my spirit'" (Luke 23:46). John recorded that Jesus said, "It is finished" (John 19:30), signifying the completion of His propitiatory, redemptive sacrifice for sin. "With that," John continued, Jesus "bowed his head and gave up his spirit" (19:30; Matt. 27:50).

By using B.C. and A.D. our calendars count the years from the incarnation of the eternal Word as Jesus Christ, but in a very significant sense His death, not his birth, is the fulcrum of cosmic history. One indication of that fact is that "at that moment the curtain of the temple was torn in two from top to bottom" (Matt. 27:51; Mark 15:38; Luke 23:45). This was the work of God to signify the end of the Mosaic Covenant and system with its countless offerings and sacrifices, because the one final, perfect sacrifice had now been made (see Heb. 7:26–28; 9:11–10:4, 9–12). The Jewish sacrifices undoubtedly continued until the destruction of the temple under the Roman general Titus in A.D. 70, and Jewish worship continues today, but the death of Jesus marked the end of the Mosaic Covenant and the establishment of the New Covenant based on the finished work of Christ.

The death of Jesus also marked the fulfillment of God's prophecy to the serpent in the Garden of Eden that he, that is, the devil, would strike the heel of the offspring of the woman (Gen. 3:15). At Jesus' death Satan and his forces of evil were seemingly victorious. In truth, however, the very opposite took place; Jesus Christ's death, followed as it was by His resurrection, marked Satan's defeat. Jesus shared in "humanity so that by his death he might destroy him who holds the power of death—that is, the devil" (Heb. 2:14; see John 12:31; 1 John 3:8). Satan has not yet been removed from this world, but he is a defeated foe, his final destiny is certain (Rev. 20:1–3, 7–10), and Christians can enjoy victory over him and his evil hosts (Eph. 6:10–17; 1 Pet. 5:8–9; 1 John 4:4).

The cross of Jesus Christ, God's incarnate Son, was God the Father's exclamation point—His declaration "It is finished" for the salvation of those who believe in Him.

Part 3

THE GLORIFIED
CHRIST OF GOD

Eight

CHRIST'S ASCENSION TO THE
RIGHT HAND OF GOD THE FATHER

———◈———

WHEN THE APOSTLE PAUL presented the Lord Jesus Christ as the example for the Christian's proper spiritual attitude, he moved directly from Jesus' humility and obedience to God in suffering and death ("he humbled himself and became obedient to death—even death on a cross!") to the height of His glorification ("Therefore God exalted him to the highest place and gave him the name that is above every name," Phil. 2:8–9). Our Lord did the same thing in His high priestly prayer when He asked, "Father, the time has come. Glorify your Son, that your Son may glorify you. . . . I have brought you glory on earth by completing the work you gave me to do. And now, Father, glorify me in your presence with the glory I had with you before the world began" (John 17:1, 4–5). Luke related Jesus' heading for Jerusalem to suffer and die to "the time . . . for him to be taken up to heaven" (Luke 9:51).

In this regard Jesus' encounter with Mary Magdala early on the morning of His resurrection is interesting. When Mary realized it was Jesus and not the gardener, she apparently embraced Him, because Jesus told her, "Do not hold on to me, for I have not yet returned to the Father" (John 20:17). Some writers teach that the resurrected Jesus was about to ascend to heaven at that moment to present His blood in the Most Holy Place of the heavenly tabernacle (Heb. 9:11–14, 23–26). They conclude that Mary's embrace would have contaminated Him and His blood and rendered His presentation of His blood in heaven ineffective. However, what Jesus was really telling Mary was that, though He appeared to her to be the same as He was before His crucifixion, He was a different person with an immortal body whose proper residence was in heaven at the right hand of God. From the divine perspective, moving from the tomb to the throne was one giant step. Jesus' resurrection appearances and ministry were only a temporary "stop-off" on His way to His rightful glorification.

GLORIFIED IN RESURRECTION

Since exaltation to the right hand of God the Father was the goal of Christ's glorification, why did He spend forty days (Acts 1:3) in resurrection appearances and ministry to His disciples? First, it gave them "many convincing proofs that he was alive" (1:3). The Jewish leaders bribed the soldiers who had guarded Jesus' tomb to spread the story that "His disciples came during the night and stole him away while we were asleep" (Matt. 28:13). While the disciples would know this was not true, without resurrection appearances by Jesus they would not know what had happened with His body.

Second, Jesus' disciples needed instruction from Jesus' appearances to prepare them for their ministry after His ascension. Luke wrote that during His resurrection ministry Jesus spoke to His disciples "about the kingdom of God" (Acts 1:3). He also told them, "Do not leave Jerusalem, but wait for the gift my Father promised, which you have heard me speak about. For John baptized with water, but in a few days you will be baptized with the Holy Spirit" (1:4–5).

During Jesus' ministry before His death, the disciples were so preoccupied with His identity as the Messiah and the prospect of the restoration of the kingdom to Israel that they could not grasp His revelation to them about His approaching death and resurrection (Matt. 16:22; Mark 8:31–32; 9:31–32; Luke 9:21–22, 44–45). The two disciples to whom Jesus appeared on the road to Emmaus illustrate this situation. Their faces were downcast (Luke 24:17), and they told Jesus, "We had hoped that he was the one who was going to redeem Israel" (24:21). Even after His resurrection, when the disciples met with the resurrected Jesus, the Eleven asked, "Lord, are you at this time going to restore the kingdom to Israel?" (Acts 1:6). This question shows that they expected the kingdom would come when the Holy Spirit came. Obviously Christ had a vital resurrection ministry in teaching His disciples, including His special instructions to Simon Peter (John 21:15–19) and His giving of the Great Commission to the eleven disciples (Matt. 28:18–20; see Acts 1:8).

The Lord's Immortal Body

It is important to remember that the Lord Jesus was the first person to experience resurrection and to occupy an immortal body. The apostle Paul affirmed, "Christ has indeed been raised from the dead, the firstfruits of those who have fallen asleep" (1 Cor. 15:20), and he revealed that "in Christ all will be made alive. But each in his own turn: Christ, the firstfruits" (15:22–23). All those whom He had restored to life, including Lazarus, who had been in the tomb "four days" (John 11:39), were restored to physical life, not resurrected to immortality. Presumably they died again. Apparently this also applies to those who "were raised to life" in conjunction with the earthquake that occurred when Jesus died on Mount Calvary (Matt. 27:52). However, since "after Jesus' resurrection they went into the holy city and appeared to many people" (27:53), their being "raised to life" may have occurred after Jesus' resurrection and was a true resurrection. If this is true, they were taken to heaven at the time of Jesus' ascension.

In his sermon on the Day of Pentecost Peter said, "God raised him [Jesus] from the dead, freeing him from the agony of death, because it was impossible for death to keep its hold on him" (Acts 2:24). Then he quoted from a psalm of David: "My body also will live in hope, because you will not abandon me to the grave, nor will you let your Holy One see decay" (2:26–27; Ps. 16:9–10). Peter pointed out that David was not speaking of himself, because he "died and was buried, and his tomb is here to this day" (Acts 2:29). Instead he was speaking prophetically "of the resurrection of the Christ, that he was not abandoned to the grave, nor did his body see decay. God has raised this Jesus to life, and we are all witnesses of the fact" (2:31–32).

The point is that the same body of Jesus that was physically abused (Isa. 52:14), nailed to the cross, and placed in Joseph of Arimathea's "own new tomb" (Matt. 27:60; see Luke 23:53; John 19:41) was resurrected to eternal life immortal and imperishable. The characteristics of His resurrection body are the pattern of the resurrection bodies believers will receive either when our Lord comes in the air to translate His body, the church, to heaven (1 Thess. 4:13–18) or when He returns to earth to establish His kingdom (Rev. 20:4–6). Paul explained to the Corinthians, "So will it be with the resurrection of the dead. The body that is sown is perishable, it is raised imperishable; it is sown in dishonor, it is raised in glory; it is sown in weakness, it is raised in power; it is sown a natural body, it is raised a spiritual body. . . . And just as we have borne the likeness of the earthly man, so shall we bear the likeness of the man from heaven" (1 Cor. 15:42–44, 49).

The fact that Jesus' resurrection body had identity with the body that was placed in the tomb is substantiated by His inviting the ones gathered the evening of His resurrection to look at "His hands and feet" (Luke 24:39–40). Obviously His body still bore the nail holes of His crucifixion. Thomas, who was not present then, declared, "Unless I see the nail marks in his hands and put my finger where the nails were, and put my hand in his side, I will not believe it" (John 20:25). When Jesus appeared to the group "a week later . . . and Thomas was with them" (20:26), He told Thomas, "Put your finger here; see my hands. Reach out your hand and put it into my side" (20:27). Jesus also had told His disciples earlier, "Touch me and see; a ghost does not have flesh and bones, as you see I have" (Luke 24:39). Earlier that resurrection morning Mary of Magdala had apparently embraced the resurrected Jesus (John 20:17), and when Jesus appeared to the women and greeted them, "they came to him, clasped his feet and worshiped him" (Matt. 28:9).

Further evidence of the physical reality of Jesus' resurrection body is the fact that He ate food. Luke reported that He ate broiled fish (Luke 24:42). Although Luke did not report that Jesus ate anything with the two disciples at Emmaus, "When he was at the table with them, he took bread, gave thanks, broke it and began to give it to them" (24:30). Likewise at Jesus' appearance to the disciples along the shore of the Sea of Galilee, the

Lord had prepared "a fire of burning coal there with fish on it, and some bread" (John 21:9). Then Jesus invited them, "Come and have breakfast," and He "took the bread and gave it to them, and did the same with the fish" (21:12–13). Though John did not say Jesus ate the food, it is likely that He did.

At the same time Jesus' resurrection body had characteristics that set it apart from the normal physical body. When John appeared to the woman near the empty tomb at that resurrection morning, Matthew wrote, "Suddenly Jesus met them" (28:9), suggesting He appeared out of nowhere. That evening, "when the disciples were together, with the doors locked for fear of the Jews, Jesus came and stood among them" (John 20:19; Luke 24:36), apparently having the ability to appear at will. This also involved the ability to disappear, because, when the eyes of the Emmaus disciples "were opened, and they recognized him, he disappeared from their sight" (Luke 24:31). The incident with these two disciples also reveals the resurrected Jesus' ability to hide His identity, for "they were kept from recognizing him" (24:16), which continued until "their eyes were opened, and they recognized him" (24:31). Mary of Magdala's inability to recognize the resurrected Jesus until He called her by name (John 20:16) was probably the result more of her distraught state and tears and passing glance at the figure who spoke to her than of a supernatural hindrance to her recognition (20:14–15).

The Empty Tomb

The strongest evidence for the genuineness of Jesus' resurrection is the fact of the empty tomb. The story spread by the bribed guards that His disciples stole Jesus' body while they slept had "been widely circulated among the Jews" (Matt. 28:15). This story was obviously false. If the disciples had stolen the body, why were they willing to suffer persecution and death for their proclamation of Jesus' resurrection?

Modern skeptics have insisted that Mary of Magdala and the other women in the early morning darkness simply went to the wrong tomb and had hallucinations of seeing angels and Jesus. But when Joseph of Arimathea placed Jesus' body "in his own new tomb" (27:60), "Mary

Magdalene and the other Mary were sitting there opposite the tomb" (27:61). Mark wrote, "Mary Magdalene and Mary the mother of Joses saw where he was laid" (Mark 15:47), and Luke said, "The women who had come with Jesus from Galilee followed Joseph and saw the tomb and how the body was laid in it" (Luke 23:15). So they certainly knew where He was buried.

That they went to the wrong tomb takes a long stretch of the imagination. If we accept that idea, Simon Peter and John also went to the wrong tomb (John 20:2–4). Not only that, but the "strips of linen" (20:5–7) and the "burial cloth" (20:7) also were at the wrong tomb. When the disciples began preaching Jesus' resurrection, all the Roman guards or authorities or Jewish leaders would need to have done was go to the correct tomb, open it, and show Jesus' body, easily identifiable by the wounds of His crucifixion. In fact, Joseph, the owner of the tomb, even though a secret disciple, could have done the same thing.

The Lord's Resurrection Appearances

Luke declared that Jesus "showed himself to these men [the apostles] and gave many convincing proofs that he was alive. He appeared to them over a period of forty days" (Acts 1:3). Ryrie lists ten separate resurrection appearances of Christ,[1] actually eleven if the appearance on the day of Ascension is counted separately. Five of these were on the day of resurrection and the rest in the forty days of resurrection ministry. The apostle Paul also included Jesus' appearance to him on the road to Damascus (Acts 9:3–7), even though it occurred after our Lord's ascension (1 Cor. 15:8–9). Another postascension appearance is the one to the first martyr Stephen (Acts 7:55–56). Ryrie concludes, "In all, 538 (549 if the eleven, Matt. 28:16, be distinct from the 500 [1 Cor. 15:6]) persons are *specified* as having seen the risen savior."[2] This implies that other appearances to still more persons may have occurred, which may well be true.

Modern skeptics dismiss the biblical accounts of the resurrection appearances of Jesus as hallucinations brought on psychologically by the disciples' intense desire and hope for Jesus to be still alive. According to Scripture the psychological mood of Jesus' followers was the exact opposite. After seeing "the tomb and how his body was laid in it," the women "went home and prepared spices and perfumes" (Luke 23:55–56). Mark reported that "when the Sabbath was over, Mary Magdalene, Mary the mother of James, and Salome bought spices so that they might go to anoint Jesus' body" (Mark 16:1), asking each other, "Who will roll the stone away from the entrance of the tomb?" (16:3; see Luke 24:1). Clearly they were not anticipating a resurrection.

On the resurrection morning when Mary Magdalene went "to the tomb and saw the stone had been removed from the entrance" (John 20:1), she ran to Simon Peter and the other disciple and told them, "They have taken the Lord out of the tomb, and we don't know where they have put him!" (20:2). She did not say, "Jesus has been raised from the dead." When she returned to the tomb, she stood outside it, crying (20:11). When the angels inside the tomb asked her why she was crying, she replied, "They have taken my Lord away . . . and I don't know where they have put him" (20:13). Then when Jesus appeared to her and asked the same question, she thought He was the gardener. So "she said, 'Sir, if you have carried him away, tell me where you have put him, and I will get him'" (20:15). At no time did she assume Jesus had been resurrected until she was convinced by His appearance to her.

The same attitude of sadness and despondency is seen in the two disciples on the Emmaus road. When Jesus approached them and asked what they were discussing (Luke 24:16–17), "they stood still, their faces downcast" (24:17). Even though they had heard reports that Jesus was alive (24:22–24), they obviously were not filled with hope of His resurrection. Even after the other apostles told Thomas of seeing the resurrected Jesus, Thomas doubted (John 20:24–28). Likewise, when "the eleven disciples went to Galilee, to the mountain where Jesus had told them to go" (Matt. 28:16; 28:7, 10), Matthew continued, "When they saw him, they worshiped him; but some doubted" (28:17). Rather than experiencing psychologically induced illusions of Jesus' resurrection, the disciples had to be convinced of its reality by "many convincing proofs that he was alive" (Acts 1:3).

The *coup de grace* to the skeptics' argument that Jesus' resurrection appearances were psychologically induced hallucinations is Paul's report that "he appeared to more than five hundred of the brothers at the same time, most of whom are still living" (1 Cor. 15:6). Hallucinations such as visions of the Virgin Mary are individual experiences, occurring to one person at a time, although possibly experienced by different individuals at different times. The resurrected Jesus' appearance to more than five hundred people at once cannot be explained as a hallucination; it must be true.

GLORIFIED IN ASCENSION

When Jesus' mission on earth was completed with His sacrificial death and resurrection (John 17:4; 19:30), He was glorified by His being ascended to the place of honor at the right hand of God the Father in heaven (John 17:5). When Luke wrote of Jesus going to Jerusalem to die, for example, he described it as "the time . . . for him to be taken up to heaven" (Luke 9:51). Jesus' resurrection appearances and ministry of instruction to His disciples (Matt. 28:18–20; Luke 24:25–27; John 21:15–19; Acts 1:3–8), necessary and important as they were, were only a temporary "interruption" on His journey from the cross to the crown.

A number of factors show the significance of the resurrected Jesus Christ making a public, visible ascension from earth to heaven. First, the disciples needed to know with certainty that He had left them. He had been with them for forty days since His resurrection, apparently appearing now and then to an individual or a group but not with them constantly as He was before His death. They needed to know that they would no longer have the Lord's personal presence, but would have the Holy Spirit's power for their witness and ministry as Christ's representatives (Matt. 28:18–20; John 14:16, 26; 16:7–15; Acts 1:4–5, 7–8).

Second, the disciples needed to see Jesus ascend to heaven in His immortal, resurrection body, because this is the way Christians as members of Christ's body, the church, will ascend to heaven in the Rapture (1 Cor. 15:51–58; 1 Thess. 4:16–18).

Third, the disciples needed to watch as Jesus "was taken up before their very eyes, and a cloud hid him from their sight" (Acts 1:9; see Mark 16:19; Luke 24:51), and to hear the words of the angels, "This same Jesus, who has been taken from you into heaven, will come back in the same way you have seen him go into heaven" (Acts 1:11). This promise of the ascended Lord Jesus' return to the earth relates to His second coming to establish His kingdom of righteousness and peace on David's throne. This promise does not refer to the Rapture, His coming in the air to take His church to be with Him; at His second coming, His bodily appearance will be evident to the world ("Behold, He is coming with the clouds, and every eye will see him," Rev. 1:7, NKJV), but at the Rapture only church age saints will see Him. With His ascension to the right hand of God the Father in heaven the first coming of the incarnate Son of God ended and His present session began.

Nine

CHRIST'S PRESENT MINISTRY AT
THE RIGHT HAND OF GOD THE FATHER

S A BOY of twelve, having trusted the Lord Jesus Christ as my Savior, I faced the problem of repeatedly yielding to temptation and falling into sin. I would be filled with guilt and remorse and would vow not to sin again, but invariably I would. It was frustrating and I wondered why the Lord did not help me resist. In my daily Bible reading I had learned that the glorified Jesus had been "exalted to the right hand of God" (Acts 2:33; 5:31; Eph. 1:20; Col. 3:1), where "he sat down at the right hand of God" (Heb. 10:12; 8:1; 12:2). In my childish mind I pictured Him sitting there at ease, twiddling His thumbs and doing nothing to help me in my dilemma. Fortunately, as my knowledge of the Bible expanded and I grew as a Christian, I learned of the Lord's provision of the Holy Spirit and of Christ's present ministry for His own at the right hand of God the Father. Yielding to the Holy Spirit's control and availing myself of the present ministry of my Lord have not made me free of sin, but they have helped me to live a victorious Christian life.

CHRIST'S POSITION AT GOD'S RIGHT HAND

In the ancient world the seat at the right hand of a monarch was the place of honor. It was given to a victorious general or to a wise and faithful counselor. It has been rightfully awarded to the Lord Jesus as the One who has completed the task God gave Him (John 17:4)—the One who by His death on Calvary's cross defeated Satan, sin, and death. David had written, "The LORD says to my Lord, 'Sit at my right hand until I make your enemies a footstool for your feet'" (Ps. 110:1). Jesus Himself referred to this passage when He debated with the Pharisees concerning His identity as the Christ. To His question, "Whose son is he?" they correctly responded, "The son of David" (Matt. 22:42; Mark 12:35). Seeking to show them that He was more than a human being, Jesus asked, "How is it then that David, speaking by the Spirit, calls him 'Lord'?" (Matt. 22:43). Then He quoted Psalm 110:1 and asked, "If then David calls him 'Lord,' how can he be his son?" (Matt. 22:44–45; Mark 12:36–37). Similarly, in his sermon on the Day of Pentecost, the apostle Peter pointed out that "David did not ascend to heaven," and then Peter quoted Psalm 110:1 as a prophecy of the exaltation of Jesus (Acts 2:34).

Of importance is the fact that the throne at God's right hand is the throne of God the Father, not Jesus' throne. The author of the epistle to the Hebrews wrote that Jesus "sat down at the right hand of the throne of God" (12:2; see 8:1; Matt. 5:34; 23:22; Acts 7:49). The glorified Christ in His messages to the seven churches through the apostle John said, "To him who overcomes, I will give the right to sit with me on my throne, just as I overcame and sat down with my Father on his throne" (Rev. 3:21). Furthermore, the exalted Jesus is to remain at God the Father's right hand as the honored One until God fulfills His promise to "make His enemies a footstool for His feet" (Pss. 110:1; see Matt. 22:44; Mark 12:36). Our Lord's present activity in building and ministering to His church is separate from and does not compromise His remaining at God's right hand until that promise is fulfilled.

The promoters of a position called progressive dispensationalism view Jesus' position at God's right hand differently. Its exponents are dispensationalists because "they view the church as a *new manifestation of grace,* a new dispensation in the history of redemption,"[1] and they affirm that "the church is a new institution, begun at Pentecost."[2] At the same time, however, they insist that "Jesus' rule from God's right hand initially yet decisively fulfills promises made to David."[3] They recognize a future millennial dispensation with Christ reigning visibly on earth in Jerusalem on David's throne with Israel as the head of the nations; but now, "As the Davidic heir, Jesus sits in and rules from heaven."[4] As a result they believe that both the dispensation of Christ's present ministry from heaven and the future millennial dispensation are "united as aspects of the messianic reign of Christ."[5] "*Both* dispensations are seen in the New Testament as fulfillments of the Davidic covenant."[6]

The difference of opinion begins in progressive dispensationalism's teaching concerning Jesus' presentation of Himself as the promised Messiah in His ministry on earth in the first Advent. According to this view, Jesus' presentation of Himself to the Jewish people inaugurated His messianic kingdom. "In the gospel of Luke, it is clear that with Jesus' presence, and especially in his Resurrection-Ascension, comes the beginning of Jesus' kingdom." And "first, there is an inauguration with Jesus' coming and particularly in his resurrection-ascension to [sic] God's right hand."[7]

In support of the position that Christ's presence marked the inauguration of His messianic kingdom, progressive dispensationalists point to Jesus' miracles of healing the sick, giving sight to the blind, enabling the lame to walk, and raising the dead. Jesus told John the Baptist's disciples to describe these miracles to John as confirming evidence that He was "the one who was to come" (Matt. 11:3), the Christ, the One whom John had announced (3:2, 11–12). No one questions the fact that such miracles demonstrate Jesus' identity as Israel's Messiah, but performing miracles is not the same as marking the inauguration of His messianic kingdom. Instead the miracles identified Him as the Messiah in His offer of Himself as such to the Jewish people.

As His ministry continued, the Jewish religious leaders increasingly opposed Jesus and rejected Him as their Messiah until Caiaphas, "high priest that year" (John 11:49), told the Sanhedrin, "it is better for you that one man die for the people than that the whole nation perish" (11:50). John continued, "So from that day on they plotted to take his life" (11:53). Speaking of the Jewish people at Jerusalem in particular, John later wrote, "Even after Jesus had done all these miraculous signs in their presence, they still would not believe in him" (12:37). This rejection, John noted, fulfilled Isaiah 53:1, which he quoted. The Jewish people's rejection of

Jesus as their Messiah was final when Pilate presented Jesus to the crowd as their King and the crowd shouted, "Take him away! Crucify him!" and the chief priests said, "We have no king but Caesar" (John 19:15). In the face of such rejection of the King by His subjects, the kingdom can hardly have been inaugurated.

Progressive dispensationalism makes much of Peter's statement that the miracle of the disciples speaking in tongues as a result of the filling of the Holy Spirit on the Day of Pentecost was "what was spoken by the prophet Joel" (Acts 2:16). They quote Joel 2:28–32, pointing out that the beginning of the present dispensation of the church is identified as part of "the last days" (Acts 2:17). This is not quite correct, however, because "the last days" are Peter's words, not Joel's, who said, "And afterward" (Joel 2:28). Progressive dispensationalists are partially correct, however, because the writer to the Hebrews used the phrase "in these last days" in relationship to Jesus' incarnation and first coming (Heb. 1:2). Although the outpouring of the Holy Spirit at Pentecost *corresponds* to what Joel prophesied, he was speaking about an outpouring in the dark days immediately preceding the second coming of Christ to earth (Joel 2:30–31), not the outpouring to begin the church.

Progressive dispensationalism also focuses on Peter's quotation at Pentecost from two of David's psalms (Pss. 16:8–11; 110:1) that speak prophetically of Jesus' resurrection in a body that did not experience decay. They draw the conclusion that since by resurrection and ascension "God has made this Jesus, whom you crucified, both Lord and Christ" (Acts 2:36), He is now fulfilling the Davidic Covenant and reigning in heaven. True, Jesus is David's greater Son (Luke 1:32), but the focus of the Davidic Covenant is God's promise to David that "your house [i.e., lineage] and your kingdom will endure forever before me; your throne will be established forever" (2 Sam. 7:16; see 7:13; Ps. 89:28–29, 34–37) on earth, and not in heaven. Christ is not now fulfilling the Davidic Covenant; instead He is now at God's right hand, waiting "for his enemies to be made his footstool" (Heb. 10:13; see Ps. 110:1). In the future He will return to earth to occupy David's throne and fulfill God's promises to David.

In a real sense what Peter did both in his message on the Day of Pentecost and more specifically in his sermon in Solomon's Colonnade (Acts

3:11–26) was to call the Jewish people to repent and to accept Jesus as their Messiah so that He could return and establish His messianic kingdom. In effect it was a reoffer of the kingdom. Peter said, "Repent, then, and turn to God, so that your sins may be wiped out, that times of refreshing may come from the Lord, and *that he may send the Christ, who has been appointed for you—even Jesus.* He must remain in heaven until the time comes for God to restore everything, as he promised long ago through his holy prophets" (3:19–21, italics added). Though many individual Jews responded to Peter's message ("about three thousand" on the Day of Pentecost; 2:41) and the apostles' witness ("the Lord added to their number daily those who were being saved"; 2:47), the Jewish religious leaders rejected His message and increasingly persecuted the apostles (4:3, 5–7, 18–21; 5:17–27, 41) and others, resulting in the martyrdom of Stephen (6:12; 7:54–60) and greatly increased persecution that dispersed all of the believers except the apostles (8:1, 3).

Progressive dispensationalists, together with the adherents of what they call "revised dispensationalism,"[8] accept a single New Covenant instituted by Christ with the Twelve at the Passover Feast the evening before His arrest and death (Matt. 26:17–20, 26–29; Mark 14:12–17, 22–25; Luke 22:7–20), and commemorated by His church in the Lord's Supper (1 Cor. 11:23–26) as a proclamation of "the Lord's death until he comes" (11:26). For the people of Israel, represented by the Twelve, the New Covenant will become effective with the establishment of the messianic kingdom at Christ's return to earth. Jesus told the Twelve, "I will not drink of this fruit of the vine from now on until the day when I drink it anew with you in my Father's kingdom" (Matt. 26:29; Mark 14:25; Luke 22:16, 18). At that future time the blessings of the New Covenant will be bestowed on the repentant, redeemed people of Israel as prophesied by Moses (Deut. 30:1–10) and the prophets (Isa. 11:10–12:6; 14:1–3; 25:6–9; 26:1–27:13; 59:20–60:22; Jer. 31:1–25, 37:1–23; Dan. 2:44–45; 7:15–18, 23–27; 12:1–2; Joel 2–3). Although some blessings of the New Covenant now enjoyed by members of Christ's body, His church, are the same as some to be bestowed on redeemed Israel in the messianic kingdom, Israel will also experience many different blessings then.

Also progressive dispensationalism identifies the spiritual blessings of the New Covenant with God's promises to David in the Davidic Covenant. However, nothing of a spiritual nature is mentioned in the promises of the Davidic Covenant; the promises deal only with a house (lineage), a kingdom, and a throne being established and enduring forever (2 Sam. 7:16; Ps. 89:28–29, 33–37). True, the spiritual blessings of the New Covenant will be poured out on the people of Israel in conjunction with the establishment of the messianic kingdom. But this is not because those blessings are part of the promises of the Davidic Covenant; rather, they will occur because of Israel's repentance and return in faith to the Lord.

Progressive dispensationalism makes the same mistake in tying the spiritual blessings of the New Covenant to the promises of the Abrahamic Covenant (Gen. 17:1–8; 15:18–20). God did tell Abram, "you will be a blessing . . . and all peoples on earth will be blessed through you" (12:2–3). Abraham also is a blessing as the stellar Old Testament example of justification by faith (15:4–6; Rom. 4:1–25; Gal. 3:6–9). God's specific promises to him in the covenant, however, were that his offspring would be as the stars of the heavens (Gen. 15:5) and that God would give "the whole land of Canaan . . . as an everlasting possession to you and your descendants after you" (17:8; see 15:18). When Israel returns to the land of Canaan and occupies it as an everlasting possession in the millennial kingdom age, they will experience the spiritual blessings of the New Covenant, blessings which are an outgrowth of the promises in the Abrahamic Covenant and, in particular the promise that "all peoples on earth will be blessed through you" (12:3).

In Hebrews 7:4–10:25 the New Covenant is contrasted with the Mosaic Covenant and the system of sacrifices, offerings, and Levitical priesthood related to that covenant. It is new as the replacement of the old Mosaic Covenant (8:8–13; Jer. 31:31–34). The New Covenant also is identified with a better high priest, one "in the order of Melchizedek" (Heb. 6:20). This new high priest is the Lord Jesus, of course, who "did not take upon himself the glory of becoming a high priest" (5:5) but "was designated by God to be high priest in the order of Melchizedek" (5:10). God the Father said to Him, "You are a priest forever, in the order of Melchizedek" (5:6; see 7:21; Ps. 110:4).

Since "Melchizedek was king of Salem and priest of God Most High" (Heb. 7:1; Gen. 14:18) and Christ is a priest "in the order of Melchizedek," progresssive dispensationalists tie Christ's priestly work of bestowing blessings together with His being the Davidic king and conclude that He is now bestowing those blessings as part of His reign as the Davidic king in heaven. They believe that "the Melchizedekian priesthood is part of the Davidic Covenant"[9] simply on the basis of the inclusion of the statement, "You are a priest forever, in the order of Melchizedek" (Ps. 110:4) in the same psalm as the statement, "The LORD says to my Lord; 'Sit at my right hand until I make your enemies a footstool for your feet'" (110:1). However, no reference to the Davidic Covenant is made in the psalm, nor is either statement a promise in the Davidic Covenant. They also believe that "the Melchizedekian priesthood is an office given to David's son as part of his inheritance."[10] But nowhere does the Bible state that the Melchizedekian priesthood is part of the inheritance of Christ, David's Descendant.

In addition, Melchizedek ministered to Abram as "priest of God Most High" approximately a thousand years before David's reign. Therefore instead of the Melchizedekian priesthood being an office given to David's Son as part of His inheritance, as progressive dispensationalism states, the reverse is true: Being David's Son is an honor given to Christ, the Melchizedekian Priest, as part of His inheritance. Progressive dispensationalism, however, says that Christ's bestowal of spiritual blessings now are part of His reign as the Davidic King in heaven. Further, although Melchizedek was "king of Salem," he ministered to Abram, blessed him and God Most High, and received "a tenth of everything" from Abram as priest of God Most High (Gen. 14:18–20). Since Abram was not a resident of Salem, Melchizedek had no real relationship to him. Also being a king does not necessarily mean functioning as a king. Christ is King now, but He is not now reigning as the Davidic King, fulfilling the Davidic Covenant. David was anointed as king of Israel by Samuel (1 Sam. 16:1, 12–13) more than fifteen years before he was publicly anointed as king over Judah and seven and a-half more years before he was publicly anointed as king of all Israel (2 Sam. 5:2–5; 1 Chron. 11:1–3; 12:38). Certainly, therefore, Jesus Christ as David's Son and Heir can now be the Davidic King without functioning as such until He returns to earth and establishes the kingdom.

In many respects the crux of the difference of opinion with progressive dispensationalism focuses on its interpretation of the statements in Psalm 110:1, 4, the quotation of Psalm 110:1 by Peter in Acts 2:34–35, and the relationship of those verses to the fulfillment of the Davidic Covenant. In an excellent article on the interpretation of Psalm 110, Elliott Johnson writes, "Is Jesus' present position at God's right hand one of royal, Davidic status? Several observations about Psalm 110:1 and Peter's quotation of it in Acts 2:34–35 help show that the answer to that question is no: *1. The Messiah's present seating awaits a future conquest. . . . 2. The Messiah's present position does not include the images of coronation. . . . 3. The Messiah's present seating involves what Yahweh decreed.*"[11] In contradiction to progressive dispensationalism Johnson concludes from Psalm 110 that "Messiah's present session does not involve His reigning on David's throne."[12]

CHRIST'S PRESENT MINISTRY THROUGH THE HOLY SPIRIT

Jesus had been announced by John the Baptist as the One who "will baptize you with the Holy Spirit and with fire" (Matt. 3:11; Mark 1:8; Luke 3:16). Jesus Himself instructed the apostles about the coming ministry of the Holy Spirit. The evening before His arrest and crucifixion He explained to them, "It is for your good that I am going away. Unless I go away, the Counselor [the Holy Spirit, John 14:16–17] will not come to you; but if I go, I will send him to you" (John 16:7). Later John recorded that in His appearance to the apostles the evening of His resurrection Jesus commissioned them, saying, "'As the Father has sent me, I am sending you.' And with that he breathed on them and said, 'Receive the Holy Spirit'" (20:21–22). This gift of the Holy Spirit before the Day of Pentecost apparently was to enable the apostles to understand Jesus' life, ministry, death, and resurrection and to relate these events to the Old Testament prophecies of them in preparation for Pentecost and what followed (see Luke 24:8; John 12:16; 2:17, 22).

During His postresurrection ministry Jesus instructed His disciples, "Do not leave Jerusalem, but wait for the gift my Father promised, which you have heard me speak about. For John baptized with water, but in a few days you will be baptized with the Holy Spirit" (Acts 1:4–5). Just before His ascension Jesus told the disciples in response to their question about restoring "the kingdom to Israel" (1:6), "But you will receive power when the Holy Spirit comes on you; and you will be my witnesses in Jerusalem, and in all Judea and Samaria, and to the ends of the earth" (1:8). This baptism with the Holy Spirit occurred on the Day of Pentecost and is described by Peter as "what was spoken by the prophet Joel" (2:16–21; see Joel 2:28–32).

The Beginning of Christ's Church

Although the outpouring of the Holy Spirit on the Day of Pentecost corresponds to part of Joel's prophecy, it also marks something totally unique in God's eternal plan, the beginning of the church of the Lord Jesus Christ made up of those who are joined with Him as members of His body by the baptism of the Holy Spirit (1 Cor. 12:13; Gal. 3:27–28; Eph. 4:4–5). The beginning of the church on Pentecost is symbolically significant, because that day in Israel marked the offering of firstfruits (Lev. 23:15–21). Although the baptism by the Holy Spirit into the body of Christ at the moment of saving faith is itself nonexperimental in the sense that it is not accompanied by any outward signs, on the Day of Pentecost it was accompanied by a "sound like the blowing of a violent wind came from heaven," "tongues of fire that separated and came to rest on each of them," the filling "with the Holy Spirit," and speaking "in other tongues as the Spirit enabled them" (Acts 2:1–4). These spectacular signs marked the beginning of the church and served as a witness to the Jewish people, as Peter explained in his sermon.

Jesus Himself had foretold the beginning of His church as a new thing when He responded to Peter's confession of Him as "the Christ, the Son of the living God" (Matt. 16:16) with the declaration, "on this rock I will build my church" (16:18). The use of the future tense "will build" indicates that Christ's church is something new, not just a continuation or variation of the nation of Israel as God's chosen people. This is why the church made up of Jews and Gentiles with equal standing as members of the body of

127

Christ (1 Cor. 12:13; Gal. 3:27–28) was described by the apostle Paul as a mystery (Eph. 3:3–12; 5:32; Col. 1:25–27)—something hidden and not known in the past but now clearly and fully revealed and proclaimed.

Although the church began on Pentecost, its true character came to be understood by its leaders only gradually, because at first it was composed only of Jews. Peter was introduced to the true nature of the church by his visit to Cornelius, a Gentile convert to Judaism (Acts 10:1–2), and his vision and instruction from God not to "call anything impure that God has made clean" (10:15). When "the Holy Spirit came on all who heard the message . . . while Peter was still speaking" (10:44), he "ordered that they be baptized in the name of Jesus Christ" (10:48), because, Peter said, "they have received the Holy Spirit just as we have" (10:47). Here again the baptism of the Holy Spirit was accompanied by "speaking in tongues and praising God" as outward evidence to Peter and his companions of its occurrence. When Peter was criticized when he returned to Jerusalem, he explained everything that had happened and said, "So if God gave them the same gift as he gave us, who believed in the Lord Jesus Christ, who was I to think that I could oppose God?" (11:17). The assembly agreed, saying, "So then, God has even granted the Gentiles repentance unto life" (11:18).

The next and final step in recognizing the unique character of Christ's church came when Paul and Barnabas returned to Antioch in Syria from their first missionary journey "and reported all that God had done through them and how he had opened the door of faith to the Gentiles" (14:27). This raised the issue of how the Gentile believers were to be received, because Cornelius, although a Gentile, had already become a proselyte to Judaism before receiving Christ. Some visitors to Antioch from Judea insisted, "Unless you are circumcised according to the custom taught by Moses, you cannot be saved" (15:1). But Paul and Barnabas disputed this position (15:2), because it meant that believers had to become identified with Judaism in order to be Christians. This would have made the church a branch of Judaism.

The issue was taken to Jerusalem, where "the apostles and elders met to consider this question" (15:6) of whether "the Gentiles must be circumcised and required to obey the law of Moses" (15:5). Peter reminded them of his experience with Cornelius and concluded, "Now then, why do you try to test God by putting on the necks of the disciples a yoke that neither we nor our fathers have been able to bear? No! We believe it is through the grace of our Lord Jesus that we are saved, just as they are" (15:10–11). Then, after Barnabas and Paul recounted their experiences, James indicated that Peter's experience was supported by the Old Testament prophets, in effect quoting Amos 9:11–12. James recommended that they "not make it difficult for the Gentiles who are turning to God" but should write them, "telling them to abstain from food polluted by idols, from sexual immorality, from meat of strangled animals and from blood" (15:19–20). In this way they would avoid offending Jews scattered throughout the Roman Empire (15:21).

This emphasis of Scripture on the uniqueness of the church, the body of Christ, as a mystery of God hidden from past ages—in the Old Testament—is why it is wrong for progressive dispensationalism to identify the ministry of the Holy Spirit and the present session of Christ with His reigning at God's right hand as the Davidic King in initial fulfillment of the Davidic Covenant. This blurs the uniqueness of the church, even though progressive dispensationalism insists that the church is a new institution begun at Pentecost.

Sending the Counselor

During His public ministry the Lord Jesus was almost the constant companion of His disciples, from His calling them to follow Him (John 1:43; Matt. 4:19–22; 9:9) to His ascension to God's right hand. This was in the pattern of the Jewish rabbi, "which means Teacher" (John 1:38), a title used of Jesus (1:49; 3:2; 4:31; 6:25; Matt. 23:7–10; see John 20:16) and of John the Baptist (John 3:26). As they traveled and preached the gospel of the kingdom of heaven, Jesus taught both the public and His disciples (Matt. 5:1–2; 7:28–29; 24:3; Luke 24:25–27; Acts 1:3).

While on earth, however, Jesus was limited by His physical body. To send His disciples to be His "witnesses . . . to the ends of the earth" (Acts 1:8; see Matt. 28:19; Luke 24:47–48) required His glorification to God's right hand and His empowerment of the disciples through the Holy Spirit. As Jesus told them, "I tell you the truth: It is for your good that I am going away. Unless I go away, the Counselor will not come to you; but if I go, I will send him to you" (John 16:7). Just before He ascended to heaven Jesus told them, "You will receive power when the Holy Spirit comes on you" (Acts 1:8).

In John's Gospel Jesus taught the apostles about His sending the Holy Spirit and the Spirit's ministry to them. The Greek noun for Counselor is *parakletos,* frequently simply transliterated Paraclete. It literally means "called to one's aid" (in a judicial sense) and therefore it is frequently translated "an advocate, pleader, intercessor,"[13] in which sense it is used of the Lord Jesus (1 John 2:1) with God the Father. Jesus called the Holy Spirit "another Counselor," whom He said the Father would give the disciples in response to His request to be with them forever (John 14:16). The word "another" is significant, because it means another of the same kind, in other words, one like Christ.

Jesus explained that the Holy Spirit would be not only the disciples' Companion and Intercessor but also their Teacher, reminding them of everything Jesus had said to them (14:26). Later Jesus told them, "When the Counselor comes, whom I will send to you from the Father, the Spirit of Truth who goes out from the Father, he will testify about me" (15:26). Still later He said, "I have much more to say to you, more than you can now bear. But when he, the Spirit of truth, comes, he will guide you into all truth. He will not speak on his own; he will speak only what he hears, and he will tell you what is yet to come. He will bring glory to me by taking from what is mine and making it known to you. All that belongs to the Father is mine. That is why I said the Spirit will take from what is mine and make it known to you" (16:12–15).

The Lord Jesus said He would send the Holy Spirit not only to minister both to and through His followers but also to minister to the unsaved. He told the apostles, "When he comes, he will convict the world of guilt in regard to sin and righteousness and judgment: in regard to sin, because men do not believe in me; in regard to righteousness, because I am going to the Father, where you can see me no longer; and in regard to judgment, because the prince of this world now stands condemned" (16:8–11). As Blum explains, "Conviction is not the same as conversion but is necessary to it. . . . The Spirit works on the minds of the unsaved to show them the truth of God for what it is. Normally this process includes human aid (see 15:26–27)."[14]

CHRIST'S MINISTRY AS HEAD OF HIS BODY, THE CHURCH

The spiritual relationship established between Jesus Christ and everyone who believes in Him—His church—through the ministry of the Holy Spirit is described biblically in several ways. One of the most graphic is that of a body, with Christ as its Head, because it portrays not only the relationship between Christ, the Head, and the members of the body but also among the members. Drawing the parallel to a physical body, Paul explained, "The body is a unit, though it is made up of many parts, and though all its parts are many, they form one body. So it is with Christ. For we were all baptized by one Spirit into one body—whether Jews or Greeks, slave or free—and we were all given the one Spirit to drink" (1 Cor. 12:12–13). As a result of the Holy Spirit's presence and ministry in believers as members of Christ's body, "There are different kinds of gifts, but the same Spirit. . . . Now to each one the manifestation of the Spirit is given for the common good. . . . All these are the work of one and the same Spirit, and he gives them to each man, just as he determines" (12:4, 7, 11).

Paul graphically described the interrelationship and interdependence of the parts of the body on each other. On the one hand, if all the members were only one part, how would it exercise the other functions of the body (12:14–20)? On the other hand, no part of the body can say to another part, "I don't need you!" because all are indispensable, especially the weaker (12:21–26). Paul concluded this illustration with the application, "Now you are the body of Christ, and each one of you is a part of it" (12:27). Elsewhere Paul wrote, "Just as each of us has one body with many members, and these members do not all have the same function, so in Christ we who are many form one body, and each member belongs to all the others" (Rom. 12:4–5), and "there is one body and one Spirit" (Eph. 4:4).

Lest undue emphasis be placed on the Holy Spirit and His ministry, however, we must always remember that He ministers as the Representative of and in the place of the glorified Christ at God's right hand. As Christ said

131

concerning the Spirit before He left the apostles, He "will testify about me" (John 15:26) and "He will bring glory to me" (16:14). The glorified Christ is always "the head of the body, the church" (Col. 1:18, 24; Eph. 4:15), and as a result He directs the growth of His body (Eph. 4:16; Col. 2:19) and distributes gifts to its members (Rom. 12:6–8; 1 Cor. 12:12–31; Eph. 4:7–8, 11–13; Col. 3:15). Our Lord distributes the gifts through the Holy Spirit (1 Cor. 12:4–11), but He Himself is the directing Head (Eph. 4:4–7).

The glorified Christ is concerned, as a result, about what happens to the members of the church, His body. When the members of the Sanhedrin were stung by Stephen's bold accusations and "were furious and gnashed their teeth as him" (Acts 7:54), he "looked up to heaven and saw the glory of God, and Jesus standing at the right hand of God" (7:55). When he described what he saw, "they covered their ears and, yelling at the top of their voices, they all rushed at him, dragged him out of the city and began to stone him" (7:57–58). Later, when Saul of Tarsus was on his way to Damascus "breathing out murderous threats against the Lord's disciples" (9:1), the glorified Christ stopped him on the road with "a light from heaven" (9:3) and asked, "Saul, Saul, why do you persecute me?" (9:4). To Saul's question, "Who are you, Lord?" Christ responded, "I am Jesus, whom you are persecuting" (9:5). Persecution and harm to a Christian is persecution and harm to our glorified Lord.

CHRIST'S MINISTRY AS THE GREAT HIGH PRIEST

As the promised Great High Priest "in the order of Melchizedek" (Ps. 110:4; Heb. 5:6, 10; 6:20; 7:11, 17, 21), the glorified Christ now carries out this priestly ministry at the right hand of God. Although Scripture indicates that Christ "became the source of eternal salvation for all who obey him and was designated by God to be the high priest in the order of Melchizedek" (5:9–10) and that "he has become a high priest forever, in the order of Melchizedek" (6:20), it also says that "when this priest had offered for all time one sacrifice for sins, he sat down at the right hand of God" (10:12; see 7:27; 9:26). This implies that He was ministering as a priest in His crucifixion.

If Jesus was not ministering as a priest during His earthly ministry, He was preparing for it, because the writer of Hebrews stated, "He had to be made like his brothers in every way, in order that he might become a merciful and faithful high priest in service to God, and that he might make atonement for the sins of the people. Because he himself suffered when he was tempted, he is able to help those who are being tempted" (Heb. 2:17–18). Later the writer added, "Therefore, since we have a great high priest who has gone through the heavens, Jesus the Son of God, let us hold firmly to the faith we profess. For we do not have a high priest who is unable to sympathize with our weaknesses, but we have one who has been tempted in every way, just as we are—yet was without sin" (4:14–15). Perhaps, like the Aaronic priests, Jesus was a priest from conception and birth, or at least from His anointing with the Holy Spirit and the beginning of His public ministry at His baptism by John.

The Intercessor

The supreme work of Christ as the Great High Priest, of course, is "to do away with sin by the sacrifice of himself" (Heb. 9:26; see 7:27). Another important present ministry, however, is His receiving believers' prayers and supplications for "mercy and find grace to help us in our time of need" (4:16). Furthermore, "he is able to save completely those who come to God through him, because he always lives to intercede for them" (7:25; see 9:24; Rom. 8:34). The classic illustration of that intercession is Jesus' prayer to God the Father, recorded in John 17.

The accessibility of our Lord Jesus as the Christian's Intercessor and the constancy of His intercession for believers with God the Father make the use of the Virgin Mary as well as a galaxy of saints not only unnecessary but actually an affront to the Lord and His ministry. Jesus Christ is the "one mediator between God and men" (1 Tim. 2:5), and He and the Holy Spirit (Rom. 8:26–27) are the only intercessors. Christians have the privilege as well as the responsibility to pray for others as well as themselves, but all our prayers are to be directed to God the Father in the name of the Lord Jesus (John 16:23–24).

The Advocate

In addition to being the Christians' heavenly Intercessor, the Lord Jesus is also our Advocate with God the Father. The apostle John wrote, "My dear children, I write this to you so that you will not sin. But if anybody does sin, we have one who speaks to the Father in our defense—Jesus Christ the Righteous One" (1 John 2:1). The phrase "one who speaks in our defense" translates the same Greek noun, *parakletos,* that was described earlier as applied to the Holy Spirit.

The first time I heard Lewis Sperry Chafer speak, his message was on this passage and its context. He pointed out that Christ was not the typical defense attorney, because, in exercising His office, He has the title "the Righteous One." Jesus has the perfect defense: "He is the atoning sacrifice for our sins, and not only for ours but also for the sins of the whole world" (2:2). As an entering student at Dallas Seminary, I was impressed by this truth, because this issue of my sin and how to deal with it had disturbed me as a youth and an immature Christian. From the context Chafer pointed out how to deal with sin. To "claim to be without sin" is to "deceive ourselves" (1:8). To "claim we have not sinned" is "to make him out to be a liar" (1:10). But, "If we confess our sins, he is faithful and just and will forgive us our sins and purify us from all unrighteousness" (1:9).

CHRIST'S OTHER PRESENT MINISTRIES AND RELATIONSHIPS

During His earthly ministry the Lord Jesus described Himself as a Shepherd, and the same imagery is used of Him in His present ministry. Jesus told a gathering of Pharisees, "I am the good shepherd. The good shepherd lays down his life for the sheep" (John 10:11). In the same discussion He told them, "I know my sheep and my sheep know me" (10:14). A bit later He said, "My sheep listen to my voice; I know them, and they follow me. I give them eternal life, and they shall never perish; no one can snatch them out of my hand" (10:27–28). To the Christian these are comforting and encouraging words. In the same general discussion Jesus called Himself "the gate for the sheep," adding that "whoever enters through me will be saved. He will come in and go out, and find pasture" (10:7, 9).

In Hebrews Jesus is called "that great Shepherd of the sheep" (Heb. 13:20). Peter described his readers as having been "like sheep going astray, but now you have returned to the Shepherd and Overseer of your souls" (1 Pet. 2:25). Likewise he urged the elders in the group to "be shepherds of God's flock" (5:2–3). If they carry out these duties, "when the Chief Shepherd appears, [they] will receive the crown of glory that will never fade away" (5:4).

In the Gospels Jesus also referred to Himself by quoting the Old Testament to the effect that "the stone the builders rejected has become the capstone; the Lord has done this, and it is marvelous in our eyes" (Matt. 21:42; Mark 12:10–11; Ps. 118:22–23; see Luke 20:17). Paul developed this relationship between Christ and His church when he wrote that we are "built on the foundation of the apostles and prophets, with Christ Jesus himself as the chief cornerstone. In him the whole building is joined together and rises to become a holy temple in the Lord. And in him you too are being built together to become a dwelling in which God lives by his Spirit" (Eph. 2:20–22). Peter used much the same figure when he wrote, "As you come to him, the living Stone—rejected by men but chosen by God and precious to him—you also, like living stones, are being built into a spiritual house to be a holy priesthood" (1 Pet. 2:4–5).

Another relationship between Christ and His church is that of the bride and her bridegroom, as well as a husband and his wife. When John the Baptist's disciples complained to him about Jesus that "everyone is going to him" (John 3:26), John explained, "The bride belongs to the bridegroom. The friend who attends the bridegroom waits and listens for him, and is full of joy when he hears the bridegroom's voice. That joy is mine, and it is now complete" (3:29). Paul said the relationship between the husband and wife is to be like that of the relationship between Christ and the church, a relationship of love and submission (Eph. 5:22–33). When Christ returns to earth in His second coming, He will be like a bridegroom who, having taken his bride (the church) to himself, will then celebrate with a wedding banquet. "For the wedding [feast] of the Lamb has come, and his bride has made herself ready" (Rev. 19:7). An angel told John to write, "Blessed are those who are invited to the wedding supper of the Lamb" (19:9).

One other relationship between Christ and His church that is connected with His present ministry at God's right hand is that of the vine and the branches. Jesus told the apostles, "I am the vine, you are the branches. If a man remains in me and I in him, he will bear much fruit; apart from me you can do nothing. . . . This is to my Father's glory, that you bear much fruit, showing yourselves to be my disciples" (John 15:5, 8). Earlier He had explained, "I am the true vine and my Father is the gardener" (15:1), and "every branch that does bear fruit he prunes so that it will be even more fruitful" (15:2). He told them, "Remain in me, and I will remain in you. No branch can bear fruit by itself; it must remain in the vine. Neither can you bear fruit unless you remain in me" (15:4). As believers abide in fellowship with Christ, they, like branches on a grapevine, can bear fruit, that is, they can produce the qualities of godly character.

Ten

CHRIST'S TRANSLATION
OF HIS CHURCH TO HEAVEN

———◆———

ESUS' ANNOUNCEMENT to His apostles that He would be leaving them (John 13:33, 36) greatly disturbed them. To calm their agitation He told them, "Do not let your hearts be troubled. . . . In my Father's house are many rooms; if it were not so, I would have told you. I am going there to prepare a place for you. And if I go and prepare a place for you, I will come back and take you to be with me that you also may be where I am" (14:1–3). This is not a promise to take believers to heaven at the moment of death, as many teach. As Merrill Tenney wrote, "'I will come back' is one of the few allusions in this gospel to Jesus' return. . . . His return is as certain as His departure, and he would take them with him to his Father's house."[1] A. T. Robertson explains that the Greek verb translated "I will come back" is a "futuristic present middle, [a] definite promise of the Second Coming of Christ."[2]

It is important, however, to distinguish this coming of Christ to take His church to be with Him in heaven from His return to the earth to establish His kingdom. The coming that Jesus referred to in John 14:3 is the Rapture, in which the glorified Christ will "take you to be with me that you may also be where I am," that is, to heaven. In His present ministry, He is preparing places in heaven for His own.

THE RAPTURE: THE RESURRECTION
AND TRANSFORMATION OF ALL CHRISTIANS

The event known as the Rapture of the church includes the physical resurrection of all dead Christians in immortal, spiritual bodies (1 Cor. 15:35–38, 42–50) together with the transformation of all living Christians (15:51–58), and Christ's transporting them to heaven. The word *Rapture* transliterates a Latin word that means "to seize, snatch." As a result, in older English the word meant "to be carried away in body or spirit," whereas in modern-day English the word is often used to speak of an ecstatic experience. But in the Rapture the church will be physically transported to join the glorified Christ in heaven.

Believers in Thessalonica had become concerned about fellow Christians who had died. The apostle Paul wrote to them, "Brothers, we do not want you to be ignorant about those who fall asleep, or grieve like the rest of men, who have no hope" (1 Thess. 4:13). He explained, "We believe that Jesus died and rose again and so we believe that God will bring with Jesus those who have fallen asleep in him" (4:14). He continued, "According to the Lord's own word, we tell you that we who are still alive, who are left till the coming of the Lord, will certainly not precede those who have fallen asleep" (4:15). He elaborated, "For the Lord himself will come down from heaven, with a loud command, with the voice of the archangel and with the trumpet call of God, and the dead in Christ will rise first" (4:16). Someone has jokingly noted that dead Christians will be resurrected before living believers are taken up, because the former will have to travel six more feet from their graves. "After that," Paul continued, "we who are still alive and are left will be caught up with them in the clouds to meet the Lord in the air. And so we will be with the Lord forever" (4:17). His final word was, "Therefore encourage each other with these words" (4:18). These are encouraging words and good reason why Paul called the coming of Christ for the translation of His church "the blessed hope—the glorious appearing of our great God and Savior, Jesus Christ" (Titus 2:13).

This coming of Christ in the air will be limited to His church, believers of the present church age. Some Bible teachers, however, include Old Testament saints among those who will be resurrected in the Rapture.

One reason they suggest this is Paul's reference to "the voice of the archangel and the trumpet call of God" (1 Thess. 4:16), both of which they identify with the people of Israel, especially the archangel, Michael (Dan. 10:13, 21; 12:1; Jude 9; Rev. 12:7). In 1 Corinthians, on the other hand, Paul stated, "We will not all sleep, but we will all be changed—in a flash, in the twinkling of an eye, at the last trumpet. For the trumpet will sound, the dead will be raised imperishable, and we will be changed" (15:51–52). Here the dead are obviously the ones whom he called "the dead in Christ" in 1 Thessalonians 4:16. Furthermore, Paul introduced the truth in 1 Corinthians as "a mystery" (1 Cor. 15:51), something hidden from past ages that is now revealed. It is not likely, therefore, that it would include the resurrection of Jewish Old Testament saints. When Christ returns to earth in His second coming to establish His millennial kingdom, another phase of the "first resurrection" will occur. This will most likely be the time when Old Testament saints will be resurrected (Rev. 20:4–6).

The glorious, imperishable, powerful, spiritual bodies all Christians will receive (1 Cor. 15:42–44) will be like the body with which our Lord Jesus rose from the tomb, ministered for forty days to His disciples, and then visibly ascended from their presence into heaven with the angelic promise that He would come back the same way. As Paul explained, "Just as we have borne the likeness of the earthly man, so shall we bear the likeness of the man from heaven" (15:49).

Another difference of interpretation exists over the time of the translation of all Christians in relation to other future events predicted in Scripture, particularly the time of great tribulation on the earth (Matt. 24:21). In the two major passages in which Paul discussed the Rapture (1 Cor. 15:50–58; 1 Thess. 4:13–18), no preceding event or anticipatory sign is mentioned. It is the next specific event in God's program. Therefore, believers are exhorted to live exemplary lives honoring to God, "while we wait for the blessed hope" (Titus 2:13). Christians are to remember that our "citizenship is in heaven. And we eagerly await a Savior from there, the Lord Jesus Christ" (Phil. 3:20; 1 Cor. 1:7). The belief that the glorified Christ could come for His church at any moment is called the imminent return of Christ. This is the belief that no predicted biblical event must precede it and that, as a result, it could occur at any moment. This has been the belief of many

Christians from New Testament days. This is why Christians are exhorted to "eagerly await" the Lord's coming (Phil. 3:20); their next step might take them heavenward to meet their Lord and Savior.

This teaching is also known as "pretribulationism," the belief that the translation of the church will occur before the Great Tribulation. In addition to being based on the imminency of Christ's coming for His church, however, pretribulationalism also rests on the biblical teaching that "God did not appoint us to suffer wrath but to receive salvation through our Lord Jesus Christ" (1 Thess. 5:9) and that Jesus has rescued us "from the coming wrath" (1:10). The tribulation is the outpouring of God's wrath on a Christ-rejecting world of mankind, designed at least in part to bring the Jewish people to repentance before God (Dan. 12:1; Joel 2:1–18). Thus it has no relationship to the church of Jesus Christ. Most of the other views of the relationship between the translation of the church and the tribulation—midtribulationalism, posttribulationalism, and the recent "pre-wrath rapture" view—compromise in some way or another the biblical teaching of the imminent coming of Christ and of the nature of the tribulation.

An additional view not in accord with the biblical teaching is the partial rapture position. This is a divergent position from pretribulationalism, but it insists that the Rapture is only for Christians "who are watching and waiting for Christ's return. . . . Thus, the *subjects*, not the *timing* of the Rapture is at issue. . . . The Rapture is viewed as a reward, not a privilege." As pretribulationist Paul Lee Tan explains, this position holds that "several groups will be raptured during the Tribulation—as they become spiritually prepared."[3] The Scriptures used to support this view are misinterpreted. For example, Paul's statement, "each in his own turn" (1 Cor. 15:23), in relation to their being resurrected does not indicate divisions in the ranks of believers. Instead it points to what Paul explained in the same verse: "Christ, the firstfruits; then, when he comes, those who belong to him." That is, the sequence is Christ's resurrection and then the resurrection of those who are His. Paul specifically affirmed that Christ "died for us so that, whether we are awake or asleep [spiritually], we may live together with him" (1 Thess. 5:10).

THE JUDGMENT SEAT OF CHRIST
TO REWARD ALL CHRISTIANS

In exhorting the Corinthian Christians to seek to live to please the Lord (2 Cor. 5:9), the apostle Paul reminded them, "For we must all appear before the judgment seat of Christ, that each one may receive what is due him for the things done while in the body, whether good or bad" (5:10). Elsewhere Paul warned the Corinthians about the importance of building properly on the foundation of Jesus Christ. "If any man builds on this foundation using gold, silver, costly stones, wood, hay or straw, his work will be shown for what it is, because the Day will bring it to light. It will be revealed with fire, and the fire will test the quality of each man's work. If what he has built survives, he will receive his reward. If it is burned up, he will suffer loss; he himself will be saved, but only as one escaping through the flames" (1 Cor. 3:12–15).

The Greek word rendered "judgment seat" in 2 Corinthians 5:10 is *bēma*. This is appropriate because in the Greco-Roman world *bēma* was the name for the seat where judges rendered decisions. It is used of Pilate's seat when he delivered Jesus to the Jews for crucifixion (John 19:13). It is translated "court" in Acts 18:12, 16, 17; 25:6, 10, 17. At the judgment seat of Christ He will make decisions or judgments concerning the actions of Christians. However, the *bēma* was also the seat from which awards for various Grecian races and games were distributed. It was in this sense that Paul used the word *bēma*. Earlier Paul had written, "It is the Lord who judges me. Therefore judge nothing before the appointed time; wait till the Lord comes. He will bring to light what is hidden in darkness and will expose the motives of men's hearts. At that time each will receive his praise from God" (1 Cor. 4:4–5). At the judgment seat of Christ no sins will be mentioned since they have been paid for by the death of Jesus, but believers' service will be dealt with on the basis of their motives. The last sentence in the above quotation points to the fact that at the judgment seat of Christ every Christian will receive some reward from the Lord.

THE MARRIAGE OF CHRIST, THE LAMB,
AND HIS BRIDE, THE CHURCH, IN HEAVEN

After the church is translated to heaven, she must pass before the judgment seat of Christ before her marriage to Christ, the Bridegroom. This is because the judgment seat deals with "the things done while in the body, whether good or bad" (2 Cor. 5:10), and at the marriage Christ's bride will have "made herself ready" with fine linen, which depicts "the righteous acts of the saints" (Rev. 19:7–8). The spiritual union between Christ Jesus and the members of His church individually and corporately is so intimate that it is illustrated by a physical body and its head and serves as a model for husbands and wives in Christian marriage (Eph. 5:22–33). This union however, will be consummated when the church is transported to heaven, prepared by the judgment seat, and then finally united forever with Christ, her glorified Lord.

In discussing the marriage of the Lamb it is important to distinguish this both in time and place from the "wedding supper." The angel told John, "Write: 'Blessed are those who are invited to the wedding supper of the Lamb!'" (Rev. 19:9). Jewish weddings normally included three stages. After the parents of the groom paid the dowry (stage one), the groom would go to the bride's home (sometime later, perhaps up to a year) to claim her and take her to his home (stage two; see Matt. 25:1–13). This would be followed by a wedding feast (stage three) that might last for several days (John 2:1–10). In Revelation 19:9 the wedding feast is stage three. The marriage of Christ and the church (stage two) will have already occurred before the feast. One reason for saying this is that in Revelation 19:7 the word "bride" is not the usual word, *nymphē* (John 3:29; Rev. 18:23), but *gynē* (literally, a wife, a married woman). The instruction in Revelation 19:9 for John to write blessings on those invited to the wedding supper suggests that it is a future event that will follow Christ's triumphant return to the earth described in 19:11–19. In the Rapture, Christ will take His bride to Himself. Then when He returns to the earth, He will celebrate this union at a wedding banquet to which saints of other ages will be invited. As John Walvoord observes, "The beginning of the Millennium itself will fulfill the symbolism of the wedding supper (*gamos*)" and "the wedding feast is an earthly feast . . . and thus will take place on earth at the beginning of the Millennium."[4]

The glorified Christ reminds all Christians, "Yes, I am coming soon." And all Christians should respond, "Amen. Come, Lord Jesus" (22:20).

Part 4

THE REIGNING

KING OF GOD

Eleven

THE ESTABLISHMENT OF THE REIGN
OF THE KING ON EARTH

———◦◉◦———

WHEN THE LORD JESUS' DISCIPLES during His earthly ministry became convinced He was the Messiah, they anticipated that His establishment of the messianic kingdom would occur momentarily. After all, both John the Baptist and Jesus preached, "Repent, for the kingdom of heaven is near" (Matt. 3:2; 4:17), and, indeed, it was offered to the Jewish people. The disciples' expectation is illustrated by the mother of Zebedee's sons asking Jesus to grant that "one of these two sons of mine may sit at your right and the other at your left in your kingdom" (20:20–21; Mark 10:35–37). As Jesus and His disciples drew near to Jerusalem from Jericho on His final journey, He had told them a number of times of His approaching suffering and death. But still "the people thought that the kingdom of God was going to appear at once" (Luke 19:11).

In an effort to inform His disciples that this was not the case Jesus told the parable of "a man of noble birth" who "went to a distant country to have himself appointed king and then to return" (19:12). The experience of Herod Archelaus, son of Herod the Great, was similar to this. Archelaus went to Rome to secure from Augustus Caesar permission to reign as a client king over a Roman territory.[1] Jesus' parable teaches, of course, the need for Him to suffer and die, to be resurrected and ascend to heaven, where He is now carrying on His ministry to His body, the church, until

God the Father will put His enemies under His feet and give Him the kingdom. Progressive dispensationalism, in insisting that Jesus is now reigning in heaven as the Davidic King, does not face the implications of this parable in its obvious application to Jesus in His present ministry in heaven and His return to earth when He will reign as King.

In Jesus' parable, as with Herod Archelaus, the nobleman's "subjects hated him and sent a delegation after him to say, 'We don't want this man to be our king'" (19:14). This paralleled the response of the Jewish leaders and mob when Pilate presented Jesus to them as their King. Not only did they reject Jesus as King but they pressured Pilate to have Him crucified. After His resurrection Jesus' disciples still anticipated the establishment of His messianic kingdom, as seen in their question, "Lord, are you at this time going to restore the kingdom to Israel?" (Acts 1:6). In His response Jesus made it clear God the Father is in charge of the kingdom plans and schedule (1:7; see Matt. 24:36; Mark 13:32). When Christ does return to earth to establish His messianic kingdom, He will take vengeance on His enemies (Rev. 19:11–21), just as Archelaus did when he returned to Judea to rule from 4 B.C. to A.D. 6.[2]

THE TRIBULATION JUDGMENT
OF ISRAEL AND THE GENTILES

In this discussion of the tribulation the focus is on the glorified Christ and His involvement in it. First, it is important to see that the judgments of the tribulation as set forth in the "scroll with writing on both sides and sealed with seven seals" (Rev. 5:1) are controlled by "him who sat on the throne." Second, the execution of the judgments is committed to the "Lamb, looking as if it had been slain" (5:6), also identified as "the Lion of the tribe of Judah, the Root of David" (5:5). This is the glorified Christ, who "came and took the scroll from the right hand of him who sat on the throne" (5:7). This is appropriate in view of Jesus' statement during His earthly ministry that "the Father judges no one, but has entrusted all judgment to the Son. . . . And he has given him authority to judge because he is the Son of Man" (John 5:22, 27; see v. 30).

Although the judgments of the tribulation will occur when the glorified Christ is still in heaven, they are discussed here under His future ministry because they relate to the preparation for His return to earth to establish His messianic rule. Responsibility for those judgments rests with Christ because He is the One who will open the scroll's seals (Rev. 5:5), but the judgments themselves will be carried out by angelic agents. The judgments progressively increase in severity, but they are a unitary outpouring of God's judgment on a Christ-rejecting world. No basis exists in the scriptural account to insert either a midtribulational or a so-called pre-wrath Rapture of the church, as some Bible teachers do.

With the opening of the first seal a rider on a white horse "was given a crown, and he rode out as a conqueror bent on conquest" (6:2). This rider may well be the Antichrist, seeking conquest of the world. His efforts will be resisted, so the opening of the second seal reveals a red horse whose rider "was given power to take peace from the earth and to make men slay each other" (6:4). The natural consequence of worldwide conflict was famine, portrayed by the "black horse," with its rider "holding a pair of scales in his hand" (6:5) when the third seal will be opened. This in turn will result in plague and death, represented by the "pale horse" (6:8), when the fourth seal will be opened.

All the conflict and turmoil involved in the opening of the first four seals will result in the death of many "who had been slain because of the word of God and the testimony they had maintained" (6:9). These are revealed with the opening of the fifth seal and are individuals martyred for their faith in God and Christ during the Tribulation (7:14). The results of the opening of the first five seals come from the activities of people with each other, but are all under the control of God and the glorified Christ. With the opening of the sixth seal, however, the judgments will come directly from the Lord through cosmic disturbances (6:12–14). However, instead of repenting and turning to God, unsaved people will hide in caves and will call on the mountains and rocks to fall on them and hide them "from the face of him who sits on the throne and from the wrath of the Lamb! For the great day of their wrath has come, and who can stand?" (6:16–17). Although these judgments will fall on Jews and Gentiles alike, "144,000 from all the tribes of Israel" (7:4–8) will be sealed as servants of God with "a seal on the foreheads" (7:3).

The Thessalonian believers had been enduring "persecutions and trials" (2 Thess. 1:4). These difficulties, coupled with "some prophecy, report or letter supposed to have come from us [Paul], saying that the Day of the Lord has already come" (2:2), alarmed them. Paul, however, indicated that "that day will not come until the rebellion [*apostasia*, apostasy] occurs and the man of lawlessness is revealed, the man doomed to destruction. He will oppose and will exalt himself over everything that is called God or is worshiped, and so that he sets himself up in God's temple, proclaiming himself to be God" (2:3–4). The Day of the Lord, as a result, is identified by specific events. But the Rapture, in which Christ will come to gather His church to Himself—to which Paul referred as a source of encouragement (1 Thess. 4:18)—is not identified by other contemporary happenings. Therefore the Day of the Lord must follow the translation of the church. That "day"[3] includes the "seven years of Tribulation" and, in fact, "the entire period from the beginning of the Tribulation to the end of the millennium."[4]

The opening of the seventh seal (Rev. 8:1) introduces in turn the blowing of seven trumpets by seven angels (8:6), the "seven angels with the seven last plagues" (15:1), and "the seven angels" with "the seven bowls of God's wrath" (16:1). All this marks the completion of God's wrath (15:1), which will be consummated with the destruction of "BABYLON THE GREAT THE MOTHER OF PROSTITUTES" (17:5; see 18:2), the epitome of human independence and opposition to God and Christ. The destruction of Babylon will complete the outpouring of God's wrath and the preparation on earth for the return of the glorified Christ to establish His kingdom.

THE RETURN OF THE KING TO EARTH
IN TRIUMPH OVER HIS ENEMIES

The apostle John described the glorified Christ as a rider "called Faithful and True" seated on "a white horse" (Rev. 19:11). He is not to be confused with the previous rider on "a white horse" (6:2), as some Bible students do; numerous details make the distinction obvious. As Walvoord explains, "the white horse is a symbol of victory. Roman generals after a victory in battle would ride a white horse in triumph with their captives following."[5] This one also is named "the Word of God" (19:13) and "KING OF KINGS AND LORD

OF LORDS" (19:16). He will wear "many crowns" (19:12), He will have "a sharp sword" coming "out of his mouth" (19:15; see 1:16), perhaps symbolizing judgment, and He will be followed by "the armies of heaven . . . riding on white horses and dressed in fine linen, white and clean" (19:14). He will judge "with justice," He will "strike down the nations," and He will tread "the winepress of the fury of God Almighty" (19:11, 15). The fact that "God is love" (1 John 4:16) does not eliminate the necessity for His judgment of His enemies, both angelic and human.

The Judgment of the Beast and the False Prophet

When Christ returns to earth, He will be opposed by "the beast and the kings of the earth and their armies" (Rev. 19:19). This beast is described in Revelation 13:1–8. The dragon, identified as "that ancient serpent called the devil or Satan" (12:9), will give the Beast, the Antichrist, power and authority (13:2), with the result that he will have "authority over every tribe, people, language and nation" (13:7) in the three and a-half years preceding the Second Coming. Paul called this world ruler "the man of lawlessness" (2 Thess. 2:3) and "the lawless one" (2:8–9). "The secret power of lawlessness" that this man will personify "is already at work," but it is now being restrained until "the one who now holds it back . . . is taken out of the way" (2:7). This is most likely the Holy Spirit working in and through the members of Christ's body, the church, whom He indwells and empowers. When the Holy Spirit departs with the church in the Rapture, the lawless one will be free to manifest himself. In the middle of the seven-year Tribulation his identity will be plainly revealed by his setting "himself up in God's temple, proclaiming himself to be God" (2:4).

The apostle John called this person "Antichrist," one who is yet to come (1 John 2:18; see 4:3). But anyone who "denies the Father and the Son" is "the antichrist" (2:22) in attitude. Denying the Godhead is "the spirit of the antichrist," who "is already in the world" (4:3). As a result John wrote, "even now many antichrists have come" (2:18; 2 John 7). Likewise in His Olivet Discourse the Lord Jesus warned the apostles that "many will come in my name, claiming, 'I am the Christ'" (Matt. 24:5) and that "false Christs and false prophets will appear and perform great signs and miracles"

(24:24). He also said "the abomination that causes desolation" will be seen "standing in the holy place" (Matt. 24:15; Mark 13:14; see Dan. 9:27; 11:31; 12:11). This is the Beast, the lawless one, the Antichrist, "whom the Lord Jesus will overthrow with the breath of his mouth and destroy by the splendor of his coming" (2 Thess. 2:8).

Associated with the Beast, who is the Antichrist, is "another beast, coming out of the earth. In John's vision this beast "had two horns like a lamb, but he spoke like a dragon" (Rev. 13:11). This beast will exercise "all the authority of the first beast on his behalf," and will make "the earth and its inhabitants worship the first beast" (13:12; see vv. 14–15). Called the false prophet (16:13), he will be captured by the triumphant Christ together with the Beast and "the two of them" will be thrown into "the fiery lake of burning sulfur" (19:20). The armies they lead will be "killed with the sword that came out of the mouth of the rider on the horse" (19:21).

The Judgment of Living Jews and Gentiles

Although many Jews and believing Gentiles will be martyred in the Great Tribulation during the reign of the Beast (Rev. 12:17; 13:15), a multitude of both groups will still be alive when Christ returns to earth to establish His kingdom. He will examine their qualification to enter the kingdom. This judgment of living Jews is presented by Jesus in two parables in His Olivet Discourse. The first is the parable of the "ten virgins who took their lamps and went out to meet the bridegroom" (Matt. 25:1). The five foolish virgins, who did not take any oil with them (25:3), were not able to welcome the bridegroom when he came or to go with him to the wedding banquet (25:10). When they sought entrance, the bridegroom replied, "I tell you the truth, I don't know you" (25:12).

The second parable is that of a "man going on a journey, who called his servants and entrusted his property to them" (25:14). When he returned, he demanded an accounting. The faithful servants were rewarded with increased responsibilities, but the "worthless servant" was thrown "outside, into the darkness, where there will be weeping and gnashing of teeth" (25:30). This judgment of the Jewish people is predicted in Ezekiel 20:32–44 and Zechariah 13:1.

Many Gentiles will also be alive when the triumphant Christ returns to earth to establish His kingdom. They will be judged on the basis of their faith in Christ, as demonstrated by their treatment of the hunted Jews during the Beast's reign. Just as the ten Boom family and many others, both Christian and non-Christian, befriended and protected Jews during Hitler's regime, Gentiles who in the Tribulation will be trusting Christ and anticipating His return will risk their own lives by befriending Jews. Gentiles will be allowed to enter the kingdom if they have treated Jesus favorably, as represented by their treatment of "the least of these brothers of mine" (Matt. 25:40), that is, "Jews," who are "physical brothers of the Lord."[6] These Gentiles will be invited to "take [their] inheritance, the kingdom prepared for [them] since the creation of the world" (25:34). Unbelieving Gentiles "will go away to eternal punishment, but the righteous to eternal life" (25:46).

The Binding of Satan

Following his victory over Adam and Eve in the Garden of Eden, Satan, represented by the serpent, was told by God that the offspring of the woman in the person of Jesus, the incarnate Son of God, "will crush your head" (Gen. 3:15), signifying total defeat. This was accomplished by Jesus' sacrificial death and resurrection, so that the Holy Spirit now convicts "in regard to judgment, because the prince of this world now stands condemned" (John 16:11). When the seventy-two reported to Jesus, "'Lord, even the demons submit to us in your name,' he replied, 'I saw Satan fall like lightning from heaven'" (Luke 10:17–18). Jesus' response undoubtedly looks ahead to Satan's being "hurled to the earth, and his angels with him" (Rev. 12:9). But it also refers to Satan's power being broken by Jesus' earthly ministry, with Satan being subject to Jesus. Paul encouraged the Roman Christians by writing, "The God of peace will soon crush Satan under your feet" (Rom. 16:20). At the middle of the seven-year Tribulation, there will be "war in heaven," in which Michael and his angels will fight against Satan, the dragon, and he will be "hurled to the earth, and his angels with him" (Rev. 12:7, 9). Then at the beginning of Christ's messianic reign, Satan's activity on the earth will end for a thousand years. When Christ returns to earth, an angel will come down from heaven, with "the key to the Abyss and holding in his hand a great chain." He will bind Satan for a thousand years in the Abyss, and the devil will not be able to deceive the nations any more, until the thousand years are ended (20:1–3). Freedom from demonic and Satanic influence will mark the Lord's millennial kingdom of righteousness and peace.

THE RESURRECTION OF BELIEVING JEWS AND GENTILES

A roster of Old Testament saints—believing Israelites who achieved great feats for God by faith—died without receiving "what had been promised" (Heb. 11:39). Reasons they will not be resurrected with Christians at the return of Christ in the air for the resurrection and translation of church saints have already been discussed. Instead, Old Testament believers will be resurrected at the beginning of the messianic, millennial kingdom of Jesus Christ. Also included in this resurrection will be the Jewish and Gentile martyrs of the Tribulation. John wrote, "I saw the souls of those who had been beheaded because of their testimony for Jesus and because of the word of God. They had not worshiped the beast or his image and had not received his mark on their foreheads or their hands. They came to life and reigned with Christ a thousand years" (Rev. 20:4). When Christ returns to earth the citizens of the messianic kingdom will consist of (a) the church, which will return with Christ from heaven in glorified bodies, (b) resurrected saints from the Old Testament and the Tribulation in glorified bodies, and (c) redeemed Jews and Gentiles who will enter the Millennium in their mortal bodies because of their faith in Christ. All unbelievers and rebels will have been removed, as well as the Beast and the False Prophet, and Satan will have been cast into the Abyss bound in a great chain for the thousand years of the messianic kingdom.

Some Bible teachers believe that a good portion of the thousand years will be occupied in the judgment of living Jews and Gentiles. Divine judgment and justice, however, do not move as slowly nor as imperfectly as some human judicial systems. Christ's judgment may occupy a brief period of time as an interlude between His return to earth and the establishment of the kingdom itself, but the kingdom will include only glorified and living believers in the Lord Jesus Christ.

Twelve

THE ONE-THOUSAND-YEAR REIGN
OF THE KING ON EARTH

———◈———

HE CONSISTENT TEACHING of Scripture is that the Lord Jesus will return from heaven to establish His messianic kingdom on earth in fulfillment of God's promises to Abraham, David, and the people of Israel. The Lord Himself told His apostles that cosmic disturbances will follow the Tribulation and "at that time men will see the Son of Man coming in clouds with great power and glory. And he will send his angels and gather his elect from the four winds, from the ends of the earth to the ends of the heavens" (Mark 13:26–27; see Matt. 24:30–31). The apostles asked the resurrected Jesus if He would "restore the kingdom to Israel" (Acts 1:6), and Peter urged the Jews, "Repent, then, and turn to God . . . that he may send the Christ, who has been appointed for you—even Jesus. He must remain in heaven until the time comes for God to restore everything, as he promised long ago through his holy prophets" (3:19–21). This belief that Christ will return to earth to establish His messianic kingdom on the throne of David for one thousand years is known as premillennialism.

Two other points of view regarding the Millennium are amillennialism and postmillennialism. Amillennialism, which can be traced back at least as far as Augustine, if not to Origen, "holds that the kingdom promises in the Old Testament are fulfilled spiritually rather than literally in the New

Testament church." It holds that Christ will literally return to the earth, but it does not believe in His thousand-year reign on the earth. According to amillennarians "the kingdom of God is present in the church age," at the end of which "the second coming of Christ inaugurates the eternal state."[1]

In some respects postmillennialism is a development from amillennialism. Although elements of this view appear earlier, its systematic development is attributed to Daniel Whitby (1638–1725), a Unitarian. Simply stated, it teaches that "Christ's return to earth will occur at the end of the Millennium."[2] The older form of postmillennialism taught that the spread of the gospel of Christ would transform the world system and usher in an era of righteousness and peace, at the end of which Christ will return to inaugurate the eternal state. This view became fairly dominant during the optimistic period of social and industrial progress during the eighteenth, nineteenth, and early twentieth centuries. It was largely abandoned with the worldwide turmoil beginning with World War I. A more contemporary variation is known as "theonomic postmillennialism," which promotes "progress through the church's preaching of the gospel and application of the Mosaic Law" and affirms "the total transformation of culture through the application of biblical law."[3]

ITS FULFILLMENT OF THE OLD TESTAMENT
PROMISES TO ISRAEL

The crux of the difference between premillennialism and other points of view is the consistent literal interpretation of Scripture, including Old Testament prophecy. Premillennialism also takes literally the six references to one thousand years in Revelation 20:2–4, 6–7, which both amillennialism and postmillennialism spiritualize. Premillennialism interprets the covenantal promises God made to Abraham, David, and the Jewish people, as well as prophecies related to their fulfillment, as literal promises and prophecies referring to Israel's land and restoration, and an heir, throne, and kingdom.

God's Covenant with Abraham

God's promises to Abraham for his obedience in leaving his country, people, and father's household to go to a land God would show him (Gen. 12:2–3) were certainly fulfilled literally. Later, in a covenant confirmed with animal sacrifices, the Lord said, "To your descendants I give this land, from the river of Egypt to the great river, the Euphrates" (15:18). Still later God confirmed His covenant, changing Abram's name to Abraham and saying, "I will establish my covenant as an everlasting covenant between me and you. . . . The whole land of Canaan, where you are now an alien, I will give as an everlasting possession to you and your descendants after you; and I will be their God" (17:7–8). The sign of circumcision was given as "the sign of the covenant between me and you" (17:11). This covenant was later confirmed with Isaac (26:2–4) and Jacob (28:13–15), and its understanding by the people of Israel is stated in Psalm 105:8–11 and referred to by John the Baptist's mother, Elizabeth (Luke 1:55).

The Palestinian Covenant

Although the term "Palestinian Covenant" is the traditional name for the covenant recorded in Deuteronomy 29–30, perhaps a better title would be Land Covenant, because it deals with the land promised to Abraham and his descendants.[4] After listing "eight specific provisions" of this covenant, Fruchtenbaum concluded, "The special importance of this covenant is that it reaffirmed Israel's title deed to the land. Although Israel would prove unfaithful and disobedient, the right to the land would never be taken from Israel. While her enjoyment of the land is conditioned on obedience, ownership of the land is unconditional. Furthermore, it shows that the conditional Mosaic covenant did not lay aside the unconditional Abrahamic covenant."[5]

Israel's disobedience to the Lord in turning to idols would result in the land being judged (Deut. 29:22–27) and the people dispersed from the land (29:28; 28:64–65). Ezekiel described how God chose Israel to be His child (Ezek. 16:6–7) and later took her to be his cherished wife (16:8–14). Israel, however, was like a spiritual prostitute in that she forsook God to worship idols (16:15–34). As a result God would punish Israel with severe judgments and worldwide dispersion, both of which have occurred since the destruction of the temple and Jerusalem in A.D. 70. The LORD said, however, "Yet I will remember the covenant I made with you in the days of your youth, and I will establish an everlasting covenant with you. . . . So I will establish my covenant with you, and you will know that I am the LORD" (16:59–60, 62).

In view of Ezekiel's prophecy, this land covenant was not fulfilled by the entrance into and conquest of the land under Joshua nor in Israel's time of greatest expansion during Solomon's reign. Yet the covenant assures Israel that when she returns to the Lord and obeys Him wholeheartedly, then the Lord "will restore your fortunes and have compassion on you and gather you again from all the nations where he scattered you. . . . He will bring you to the land that belonged to your fathers, and you will take possession of it" (Deut. 30:2–3, 5). The Old Testament prophets frequently predicted this restoration of Israel to her land (Isa. 11:11–16; 43:5–7; Jer. 16:14–15; 23:3, 7–8; 31:7–11; Ezek. 11:16–17; 36:24, 28; Amos 9:14–15; Zeph. 3:19–20; Zech. 10:8–12). The Lord Jesus confirmed the fulfillment of this land covenant when He told the apostles that at His return the Son of Man "will send his angels with a loud trumpet call, and they will gather his elect from the four winds, from one end of the heavens to the other" (Matt. 24:31; see Mark 13:27). This apparently has begun to occur in the return of Jews to the land and the establishment of the nation of Israel, but the prophecies await complete fulfillment as part of Christ's second coming.

God's Covenant with David

This covenant was announced to David by the prophet Nathan in response to David's desire to build a temple for God in Jerusalem (2 Sam. 7:1–3). God promised that He would "raise up your offspring to succeed you" (7:12), a promise fulfilled in Solomon, who would build a house for God (7:13). God would discipline Solomon for doing wrong, but He would never take His love away from him as He did from Saul (7:14–15). God promised David, "Your house [i.e., lineage] and your kingdom will endure forever before me; your throne will be established forever" (7:16). The account also is found in 1 Chronicles 17:1–15. David described this as "an everlasting covenant, arranged and secured in every part" (2 Sam. 23:5). In addition it is affirmed in Psalm 89:3, 20–37.

Old Testament prophecies identify the fulfillment of this covenant with a future Descendant of David, Israel's Messiah. Isaiah spoke of the Child to be born and the Son to be given, who was obviously a divine person and would "reign on David's throne and over his kingdom, establishing and upholding it with justice and righteousness from that time on and forever" (Isa. 9:6–7; see 11:1–5). Jeremiah spoke of God making "a righteous Branch sprout from David's line" (Jer. 33:15) and indicated that God's covenant with David was as secure as His covenant with day and night (33:17–22; see 23:5–6). The angel Gabriel identified the Virgin Mary's Spirit-conceived Son, Jesus, as the One to whom "the Lord God will give . . . the throne of his father David, and he will reign over the house of Jacob forever; his kingdom will never end" (Luke 1:32–33). This will be fulfilled when Christ returns to earth in triumph and great glory.

Promises to the People of Israel

The promises to the people of Israel concerning restoration to fellowship with God in the messianic kingdom obviously are related to the fulfillment of the Abrahamic, Land, and Davidic covenants, but they also are directly related to the people. God told Israel through Moses, "For you are a people holy to the Lord your God. The Lord your God has chosen you out of all the peoples on the face of the earth to be his people, his treasured possession" (Deut. 7:6; 14:2; see Ps. 135:4). After calling the "sons of Jacob" God's "chosen ones" (Ps. 105:6), the psalmist stated that God "remembers his covenant forever, the word he commanded, for a thousand generations" (105:8).

Because Israel has turned away from God in disobedience and rebellion, God has had to discipline His chosen people with dispersion throughout the world and with severe hardships and trials. However, He declared to Israel, "I have chosen you and have not rejected you. So do not fear, for I am with you; do not be dismayed, for I am your God" (Isa. 41:9–10; see 43:1; 44:1–2). The apostle Paul emphasized the permanence of God's choice of the Israelites when he wrote, "Did God reject his people?

By no means! . . . God did not reject his people, whom he foreknew" (Rom. 11:1–2). Paul proved this by stating that God is now saving Israelites like Paul by having them respond to the gospel of Christ and become members of His body, the church, and by stating that in the future messianic kingdom "all Israel will be saved" (11:26; see Dan. 12:1). All this is true because "God's gifts and his call are irrevocable" (Rom. 11:29).

THE INHABITANTS OF THE MILLENNIAL KINGDOM

After the Lord judges the Israelites at the beginning of the Millennium to purge "those who revolt and rebel" against Him (Ezek. 20:38), the believing remnant of Israel will be brought "into the bond of the covenant" (20:37). They will be living citizens of the millennial, messianic kingdom of the Lord Jesus Christ. In addition the saints of the Old Testament will be resurrected to be citizens of the kingdom (Isa. 26:19; Ezek. 37:12–14). So also the tribulation martyrs, both Jews and Gentiles, will be resurrected to enter the millennial kingdom as the Lord's citizens. The kingdom inhabitants will also include the body and bride of Christ, His church resurrected and transformed before the Tribulation, which will return with Him. Thus at the beginning of the messianic kingdom every inhabitant will be a redeemed, believing person, either perfected through resurrection or transformation, or a living believer among the Jews or Gentiles.

Since the Lord Jesus Christ will be reigning as Israel's Messiah on the throne of David, the people of Israel will be "the head, not the tail" (Deut. 28:13) among the nations. Furthermore, Israel will be a united nation once again instead of being divided into Judah and Israel (Ezek. 37:15–28). Jerusalem will be the political capital of the world as the city from which Christ will reign on David's throne (Jer. 33:14–18); it will also be the spiritual center with a rebuilt temple for the worship of God (Isa. 2:1–3; 62:1–7; Mic. 4:1–3; Zech. 14:10–11, 16–17, 20–21). The redeemed people of Israel "will be called the priests of the LORD . . . ministers of our God" (Isa. 61:6).

The general teaching of the Old Testament (Ps. 132:10–11; Isa. 9:6–7; Jer. 33:17, 20–21) and the belief of the Jews was that the Messiah would fulfill God's promise to David that one of his descendants would restore his kingdom and sit on his throne. This was the angel Gabriel's promise to Mary concerning Jesus (Luke 1:31–33), it is what Jesus taught (Matt. 19:28), and it is what the disciples believed (Matt. 20:21; Acts 1:6). A question arises, however, concerning the place in the millennial kingdom of the resurrected David, especially in light of some prophecies that speak of him as a millennial ruler (Jer. 30:9; Ezek. 34:23–24; 37:24–25; Hos. 3:5). Some Bible students conclude that David will be the actual ruler, but others correctly teach that he will be a co-regent with the glorified Lord Jesus Christ. This is supported by Ezekiel's calling him a "prince" (Ezek. 34:24; 37:25).

THE WORLDWIDE EXTENT
OF THE MILLENNIAL KINGDOM

Although the land that was promised to Israel to be occupied during the millennium was said to be "from the river of Egypt to the great river, the Euphrates—the land of the Kenites, Kenizzites, Kadmonites, Hittites, Perizzites, Rephaites, Amorites, Canaanites, Girgashites and Jebusites" (Gen. 15:18–21), the dominion of the messianic kingdom will be worldwide over all the inhabitants of the earth. This is stated by Isaiah. "In the last days the mountain of the LORD's temple will be established as chief among the mountains; it will be raised above the hills, and all nations will stream to it" (Isa. 2:2). And "the nations will rally to [the Root of Jesse]" (11:10; see 24:14–16; 42:10–13). This worldwide rule is also demonstrated by the Lord's ability to "gather the exiles of Israel" and to "assemble the scattered people of Judah from the four quarters of the earth" (11:12; see v. 11; 66:20; Matt. 24:30–33), for this will be possible only if His authority is worldwide. All other efforts at a worldwide government throughout history have failed and will fail. This includes the United Nations of our present time and the tyrannical reign of the Beast during the Tribulation.

THE CHARACTER OF THE MILLENNIAL KINGDOM

Scripture indicates that Christ's millennial reign will be marked by the worship of God and the qualities of peace, justice, and righteousness. In that time, "Many peoples will come and say, 'Come, let us go up to the mountain of the LORD, to the house of the God of Jacob. He will teach us his ways, so that we may walk in his paths.' The law will go out from Zion, the word of the LORD from Jerusalem" (Isa. 2:3; Mic. 4:2; see Zech. 14:16–21).

If one thing has marked the recorded history of the world, it is the almost continuous pattern of warfare, bloodshed, and death. In the messianic kingdom, however, "They will beat their swords into plowshares and their spears into pruning hooks. Nation will not take up sword against nation, nor will they train for war anymore" (Isa. 2:4; Mic. 4:3). Isaiah also wrote, "They will neither harm nor destroy on all my holy mountain, for the earth will be full of the knowledge of the LORD as the waters cover the sea" (Isa. 11:9). This cessation of conflict and warfare will be because Messiah "will judge between the nations, and will settle disputes for many peoples" (2:4).

The Messiah's judgments and decisions will be carried out, resulting in peace not only because He has the power to enforce His decisions but also because they are equitable and just. His "reign on David's throne and over his kingdom" will be marked by "establishing and upholding it with justice and righteousness from that time on and forever" (9:7). This is because "the Spirit of the LORD will rest on him—the Spirit of wisdom and understanding, the Spirit of counsel and of power, the Spirit of knowledge and of the fear of the LORD" (11:2). As a result, "He will not judge by what he sees with his eyes, or decide by what he hears with his ears; but with righteousness he will judge the needy, with justice he will give decisions for the poor of the earth" (11:3–4). Righteousness and faithfulness will so thoroughly characterize His reign that those qualities are likened to a belt and sash (11:5). As a result, each family will enjoy peace and prosperity, for each one will have his own vineyard and fig tree (Mic. 4:4; Zech. 3:10).

Satan will be bound and cast into the Abyss at the beginning of the Millennium (Rev. 20:1–3), so that the evil influences of him and his demonic forces will no longer impact the living believers entering the kingdom. But those individuals without resurrected bodies, and children born to them, will be mortal human beings with an Adamic nature and the need to trust the Lord Jesus Christ as their Savior. Though the prospects of those children trusting the Lord and being saved will be greater than today, undoubtedly some will remain unsaved, especially as the thousand years go on. As a result, some will rebel against Messiah's rule and will require the punitive judgment of the Lord (Isa. 11:4).

THE TRANSFORMED NATURAL WORLD
OF THE MILLENNIAL KINGDOM

When Adam and Eve succumbed to the temptation of the serpent and sinned by eating the fruit of "the tree of knowledge of good and evil" (Gen. 2:16–17; 3:1–7), God judged the natural order of creation (3:17–19) as well as the serpent (3:14–15), Eve (3:16), and Adam. Everything God had created originally "was very good" (1:31), and the Garden of Eden in which Adam and Eve were placed as custodians was a paradise (2:8–9, 15, 20–25), but it was cursed by their sin. Paul stated, "We know that the whole creation has been groaning as in the pains of childbirth right up to the present time" (Rom. 8:22). It is appropriate, therefore, that the redemption of the human race in the millennial kingdom will also involve, at least in part, the restoration of the pristine state of the created world. Paul declared, "The creation waits in eager expectation for the sons of God to be revealed. For the creation was subjected to frustration, not by its own choice, but by the will of the one who subjected it, in hope that the creation itself will be liberated from its bondage to decay and brought into the glorious freedom of the children of God" (8:19–21). Although the total restoration of God's original creation will not occur until God creates "new heavens and a new earth" (Isa. 65:17; 66:22; 2 Pet. 3:13; Rev. 21:1), Scripture predicts great improvements will be made on the earth in the millennial kingdom of the Messiah.

The first step in the transformation of the natural world will occur with the return of Jesus Christ to the earth. Just as He ascended to God's right hand in heaven from the Mount of Olives (Acts 1:11–12), so He will return to earth to the same spot. "It will be split in two from east to west, forming a great valley, with half of the mountain moving north and half moving south" (Zech. 14:4). Furthermore, "On that day living water will flow out from Jerusalem, half to the eastern sea [the Euphrates River] and half to the western sea [the Mediterranean Sea], in summer and in winter" (14:8; see Ezek. 47:1–12).

In the millennial kingdom the land of Israel will experience greatly increased fertility and productivity of crops. As Amos predicted, "The days are coming . . . when the reaper will be overtaken by the plowman and the planter by the one treading grapes. New wine will drip from the mountains and flow from all the hills" (Amos 9:13; see Isa. 35:1–2, 6–7; 51:3; 55:12–13; Ezek. 34:27; 36:29–30, 34–35; Joel 3:18). To some degree this will be the result of ample rainfall at needed times (Isa. 30:23–26), but it will also result from altered topography of the land of Israel at the beginning of the millennial kingdom, as indicated by the "forming [of] a great valley" (Zech. 14:4) when Mount Olivet divides (see Isa. 35:1–2, 6–7; 41:18–20; 65:12–13). The most complete description of these changes is found in Ezekiel 47:1–12.

Another significant facet of the millennial kingdom will be a greatly increased human lifespan. Isaiah wrote, "Never again will there be in it an infant who lives but a few days, or an old man who does not live out his years; he who dies at a hundred will be thought a mere youth; he who fails to reach a hundred will be considered accursed" (Isa. 65:20). "For as the days of a tree, so will be the days of my people; my chosen ones will long enjoy the works of their hands" (65:22). Although Isaiah opened this section with the words, "I will create new heavens and a new earth" (65:17), he must have been talking about the millennial kingdom, because he spoke of death, which will not occur in the eternal state (1 Cor. 15:21; Rev. 21:4).

A final evidence of the transformation of the natural order will be the removal of the carnivorous and poisonous natures from all wild animals. Isaiah predicted, "The wolf will live with the lamb, the leopard will lie down with the goat, the calf and the lion and the yearling together; and a little child will lead them. The cow will feed with the bear, their young will lie down together, and the lion will eat straw like the ox. The infant will play near the hole of the cobra, and the young child put his hand into the viper's nest" (Isa. 11:6–8). God promised at that time to "make a covenant of peace with them and rid the land of wild beasts" (Ezek. 34:25; see Hos. 2:18).

Truly the earth will enjoy millennial peace, beauty, and productivity. At least in a partial sense the world will be redeemed when Jesus Christ, the Messiah, rules on earth as the sovereign King in the millennial kingdom.

Thirteen

THE CONSUMMATION OF THE
REIGN OF THE KING ON EARTH

———◈———

THE OBJECTIVE OF THIS BOOK has been to point out that the eternal plan of the triune Godhead has been to exalt the eternal Word, the Lord Jesus Christ, as the member of the Godhead who became incarnate to carry out God's program of redemption and salvation (Col. 1:18). This exaltation will be manifested in the messianic millennial kingdom but will not reach its climax until that reign ends and Christ "has destroyed all dominion, authority and power. For he must reign until he has put all his enemies under his feet" (1 Cor. 15:24–25). When God the Father "has put everything under his [Christ's] feet" (15:27), then Christ will hand "over the kingdom to God the Father" (15:24).

The fact that "the last enemy to be destroyed is death" (15:26) demonstrates that the millennial kingdom itself is not the consummation of God's program, because physical death will occur during the millennium (Isa. 65:20). The living believers who will enter the messianic kingdom will be saved because of their faith in Christ, but they will not be perfected. Therefore they will be subject to physical death. Furthermore, during the millennium children born to them will have the Adamic sin nature and will need to exercise faith in the reigning Christ. Undoubtedly many will do so, but those who do not will be judged with the sentence of death, because Christ will rule "with an iron scepter" (Rev. 2:27; 12:5; 19:15).

Physical death, therefore, which will continue through the Millennium, will be eliminated only at the end of the Millennium. This is also why the millennial kingdom is only a partial restoration of the pristine conditions of both humanity and the natural order in the Garden of Eden before the fall of Adam and Eve.

SATAN'S FINAL REBELLION AND JUDGMENT

Throughout the millennial kingdom Satan will be bound and imprisoned in the Abyss "to keep him from deceiving the nations," but at the end of the thousand years he will be "set free for a short time to deceive the nations" (Rev. 20:3, 7–8). This rebellion will serve two purposes. First, it will identify those human beings who will remain unregenerate and will merely be conforming outwardly to the Messiah's authority. After all, people will never have enjoyed such prosperity, abundance of food, and absence of violence and warfare. Satan's deception will lead them to reveal their true character. Second, the rebellion will demonstrate Satan's continued desire to "make myself like the Most High" (Isa. 14:14; see 2 Thess. 2:4). This lay behind the serpent's temptation of Eve, the devil's temptation of Jesus in the desert, and Satan's empowerment and motivation of the "man of lawlessness" (2:3–4, 9). His release from the Abyss to lead the unregenerate at the end of the Millennium into rebellion against Messiah, God's people, and Jerusalem (the city God loves, Rev. 20:9) will be his final effort to achieve his goal. It is doomed to fail as have all his other efforts, for fire will devour his human followers and he will be "thrown into the lake of burning sulfur, where the beast and false prophet," his Tribulation accomplices, "had been thrown" (20:9–10; see 19:20–21). There "they will be tormented day and night for ever and ever" (20:10).

The fact that the millennial kingdom will end in a revolt of citizens who have not responded in saving faith to the reigning Messiah has a tremendous lesson for political and social leaders today. Important as education, environment, and example are in directing young people to becoming productive and successful adults, those factors are not the ultimate criteria. What is important is what is in the heart of the individual. In the Millennium "the earth will be full of the knowledge of the LORD as the waters cover the sea" (Isa. 11:9). All satanic and demonic temptation will be eliminated, and crime and violence will not exist. The environment will be almost perfect and the advantages abundant. The Savior Himself will reign as Messiah, and perfected and living saints will inhabit the earth. In spite of all these positive motivations, multitudes will remain unregenerate, refusing to believe in Christ, and will follow Satan's deception in rebellion against the Messiah.

THE RESURRECTION AND GREAT WHITE THRONE JUDGMENT OF ALL UNBELIEVING DEAD

"Since death came through a man, the resurrection of the dead comes also through a man" (1 Cor. 15:21). This is physical resurrection to physical life, whether as a saved individual in an eternal, spiritual body (15:42–45) or as an unregenerate person subject to judgment and eternal separation from God in torment (2 Pet. 3:7). Both physical and spiritual death came to the human race as a result of sin, specifically disobedience to God's command not to eat the fruit of "the tree of the knowledge of good and evil" (Gen. 2:16–17; 3:6). Adam and Eve's spiritual death is seen in their hiding from God's presence in the Garden (3:8), and in due time they died physically. As Paul claimed, "As in Adam all die, so in Christ all will be made alive" (1 Cor. 15:22), that is, physically alive.

Paul also stated the order of resurrection: "Christ, the firstfruits; then, when he comes, those who belong to him" (15:23). This "first resurrection" (Rev. 20:5–6) consists of two parts: the resurrection of dead Christians at the translation of Christ's body, the church (1 Thess. 4:14–17), and the resurrection of all remaining believers (Old Testament saints and Tribulation martyrs) when Christ returns to earth to establish His millennial kingdom. The last step in the order of resurrection is "the second resurrection," when "the end will come" (1 Cor. 15:24). This is the resurrection of all unbelieving dead. John recorded that "the sea gave up the dead that were in it, and death and Hades gave up the dead that were in them" (Rev. 20:13).

This resurrection is to judgment. John saw "the dead, great and small, standing before the throne," and "the dead were judged according to what they had done as recorded in the books" (20:12). This would suggest that there are degrees of eternal torment for unbelievers, but there is no escape. Together with the books out of which the unbelievers will be judged in this Great White Throne judgment, another book will be opened, "which is the book of life" (20:12). Apparently this book is opened to prove that all the unbelieving dead properly belong before this tribunal, because "if anyone's name was not found written in the book of life, he [will be] thrown into the lake of fire" (20:15). The book of life records only the names of believers (21:27; 13:8; Phil. 4:3).

The Judge who sits on the Great White Throne to pronounce judgment on the resurrected unbelievers is the Lord Jesus Christ. Jesus told the Jews, "Moreover, the Father judges no one, but has entrusted all judgment to the Son, that all may honor the Son just as they honor the Father" (John 5:22–23). God has "given him authority to judge because he is the Son of Man" (5:27). Jesus also said His "judgment is just, for I seek not to please myself but him who sent me" (5:30). What regret and remorse will fill the hearts of unbelievers who stand before the One whose provision of salvation and eternal life they spurned to be condemned to separation from God in the lake of fire for eternity.

THE TRANSFER OF AUTHORITY
TO GOD THE FATHER

With the completion of Christ's ministry with the resurrection and judgment of the unbelieving dead and the consignment of death and Hades to the lake of fire (Rev. 20:14), Christ will hand over "the kingdom to God the Father" (1 Cor. 15:24). When this is accomplished, "then the Son himself will be made subject to him [God the Father] who put everything under him, so that God [the triune Godhead] may be all in all" (15:28). The objective of all that the eternal Word has done in carrying out the eternal plan of God for mankind and the world is expressed in the angel's command to John, "Worship God!" (Rev. 19:10; 22:9).

THE NEW HEAVENS AND NEW
EARTH IN THE ETERNAL STATE

A number of Scriptures state that the present heavens and earth will be removed and new heavens and a new earth created. In His Olivet Discourse the Lord Jesus said, "Heaven and earth will pass away, but my words will never pass away" (Matt. 24:35). The psalmist wrote, "In the beginning you laid the foundations of the earth, and the heavens are the work of your hands. They will perish, but you remain; they will all wear out like a garment. Like clothing you will change them and they will be discarded. But you remain the same, and your years will never end" (Ps. 102:25–27; see Heb. 1:10–12). Also Peter predicted, "The heavens will disappear with a roar; the elements will be destroyed by fire, and the earth and everything in it will be laid bare" (2 Pet. 3:10; see vv. 7, 12). Peter also wrote, "But in keeping with his promise we are looking forward to a new heaven and a new earth, the home of righteousness" (3:13; see Isa. 66:22). This is described in Revelation 21:1–22:5. While some scholars say the heavens and the earth will be renovated, Peter's words seem to suggest that they will be completely destroyed and then replaced with newly created heavens and earth.

The eternal state will include the provision of a new city of Jerusalem for redeemed people (21:9–27). In the eternal state "the dwelling of God is with men, and he will live with them. They will be his people, and God himself will be with them and be their God" (21:3). No temple will be in the New Jerusalem "because the Lord God Almighty and the Lamb are its temple" (21:22). Its citizens will be "only those whose names are written in the Lamb's book of life" (21:27).

CONCLUSION

In view of what the Lord Jesus has done, is doing, and will do, as presented in the Scriptures and discussed in this book, how should we as Christians respond? First, we should praise God for His grace in providing salvation and eternal life through faith in the sacrificial death of the Lord Jesus. Second, because of our position in Christ as members of His body, we should set our minds "on things above, not on earthly things" (Col. 3:2), because our "citizenship is in heaven" (Phil. 3:20). Third, we ought to lead holy lives. When Peter asked, "What kind of people ought you to be?" (2 Pet. 3:11), he responded, "You ought to live holy and godly lives," and he exhorted believers to "make every effort to be found spotless, blameless and at peace with him" (3:14). Fourth, we should live in the hope of our Lord's imminent coming to translate us into His presence (1 Thess. 4:13–18) and after that to return to earth to establish His messianic kingdom. He has promised, "Yes, I am coming soon," and the believer's response should be "Amen. Come, Lord Jesus" (Rev. 22:20).

Endnotes

———◦❦◦———

**CHAPTER 1—THE WORD OF GOD AS A MEMBER OF THE
TRIUNE GODHEAD**

1. G. W. Bromiley, "Word, Word of the Lord," in *Zondervan Pictorial Encyclopedia of the Bible,* ed. Merrill C. Tenney and Steven Barabas (Grand Rapids: Zondervan, 1975), 5:959.

2. Gordon H. Clark, *Thales to Dewey* (Boston: Houghton Mifflin Co., 1957), 19.

3. Ibid., 161.

4. Philip Schaff, *Apostolic Christianity A.D. 1–100,* vol. 1 of *History of the Christian Church* (New York: Scribner's Sons, 1882), 553–54.

5. Marvin R. Vincent, *Word Studies in the New Testament* (New York: Scribner's Sons, 1871), 1:458.

6. E. C. Colwell, "A Definite Rule for the Use of the Article in the Greek New Testament," *Journal of Biblical Literature* 52 (1933): 20.

7. A. T. Robertson, *A Grammar of the Greek New Testament in Light of Historical Research,* 5th ed. (New York: Harper & Brothers, 1923), 417.

8. Merrill C. Tenney, "John," in *Zondervan NIV Bible Commentary,* ed. Kenneth L. Barker and John Kohlenberger III (Grand Rapids: Zondervan, 1994), 2:296.

9. Quoted by Charles Hodge, *Systematic Theology* (New York: Scribner's, 1871; reprint, Grand Rapids: Baker, 1970), 1:458.

10. Ralph L. Woods, ed., *The World Treasury of Religious Quotations* (New York: Hawthorn, 1966), 1000.

11. Quoted in *Quotations for the Christian World,* ed. Edythe Draper (Wheaton, Ill.: Tyndale, 1992), 623.

12. A. T. Robertson, *Word Pictures in the New Testament* (New York: Harper & Brothers, 1930), 4:478–79.

CHAPTER 2—THE PREINCARNATE MINISTRY OF THE WORD OF GOD

1. John F. Walvoord, *Jesus Christ Our Lord* (Chicago: Moody, 1969), 52.

2. Ibid., 54.

CHAPTER 3—THE OLD TESTAMENT ANTICIPATION OF THE INCARNATION OF THE WORD OF GOD

1. Allen P. Ross, "Psalms," in *The Bible Knowledge Commentary, Old Testament,* ed. John F. Walvoord and Roy B. Zuck (Wheaton, Ill.: Victor, 1985), 792.

2. Ibid., 804 (italics his).

3. Ibid., 809.

4. Ibid.

5. John F. Walvoord, *The Prophecy Knowledge Handbook* (Wheaton, Ill.: Victor, 1990), 96.

6. D. F. Payne, "Typology, Biblical," in *New International Dictionary of the Christian Church,* ed. J. D. Douglas (Grand Rapids: Zondervan, 1974), 990.

7. Wick Broomall, "Type, Typology," in *Baker's Dictionary of Theology,* ed. Everett F. Harrison (Grand Rapids: Baker, 1960), 534.

8. Robertson, *Word Pictures* 6:119–20.

9. Roger M. Raymer, "1 Peter," in *The Bible Knowledge Commentary, New Testament,* ed. John F. Walvoord and Roy B. Zuck (Wheaton, Ill.: Victor, 1983), 852.

CHAPTER 4—THE NAMES AND TITLES OF THE SON OF GOD

1. Edwin C. Blum, "John," in *The Bible Knowledge Commentary, New Testament,* 303.
2. Ibid., 301.
3. G. Abbott-Smith, *A Manual Greek Lexicon of the New Testament* (Edinburgh: Clark, 1937), 340 (italics his).
4. Roy B. Zuck, *Teaching as Jesus Taught* (Grand Rapids: Baker, 1995), 42–43.
5. Abbott-Smith, *A Manual Greek Lexicon,* 62.

CHAPTER 5—THE INCARNATION OF THE SON OF GOD ANNOUNCED

1. C. S. Lewis, *Mere Christianity,* rev. and enlarged ed. (New York: Macmillan, 1952), 36.
2. Luke Timothy Johnson, *The Real Jesus* (San Francisco: Harper, 1996), 1.
3. Robert B. Strimple, *The Modern Search for the Real Jesus* (Phillipsburg, N.J.: P & R, 1995), 9.
4. Robert W. Funk, Roy W. Hoover, Jesus Seminar, eds., *The Five Gospels: In Search of the Authentic Jesus* (New York: Macmillan, 1993), 5.
5. Ibid., 16.
6. Ibid.
7. Ibid., 32.
8. Johnson, *The Real Jesus,* v.
9. Ibid., 18.
10. Ibid., 4.
11. Ibid., 6.
12. Ibid., 8.
13. Ibid., 141.
14. W. White, Jr., "Star of the Magi," in *Zondervan Pictorial Encyclopedia of the Bible,* 5:513.
15. Ibid.

CHAPTER 6—THE PERSON OF THE INCARNATE SON OF GOD

1. Charles C. Ryrie, *Basic Theology* (Wheaton, Ill.: Victor, 1986), 247.
2. John F. Walvoord, *Jesus Christ Our Lord* (Chicago: Moody, 1969), 106.
3. Ryrie, *Basic Theology*, 252.
4. "Monarchianism," in *Oxford Dictionary of the Christian Church*, ed. F. L. Cross (London: Oxford University Press, 1957), 914.
5. Ibid.
6. "Arianism," in *Oxford Dictionary of the Christian Church*, 80.
7. Charles Taze Russell, *Studies in the Scriptures* (Brooklyn, N. Y.: Watchtower Bible and Tract Society, 1886), 5:84.
8. James E. Talmadge, *The Philosophical Basis of Mormonism* (Independence, Mo.: Zion's Printing and Publishing, 1915), 7.
9. Hodge, *Systematic Theology*, 2:457.
10. Ibid.
11. Ryrie, *Basic Theology*, 250.
12. Source unknown.
13. Source unknown.
14. Lewis Sperry Chafer, *Systematic Theology* (Dallas: Dallas Seminary Press, 1948; reprint [8 vols. in 4], Grand Rapids: Kregel, 1993), 1:369.

CHAPTER 7—THE EARTHLY LIFE AND MINISTRY OF THE SON OF GOD

1. Robertson, *Word Pictures, 2:32.*
2. Harold W. Hoehner, *Chronological Aspects of the Life of Christ* (Grand Rapids: Zondervan, 1977), 37.
3. Chafer, *Systematic Theology*, 5:101.
4. Charles C. Ryrie, *The Ryrie Study Bible (NASV)* (Chicago: Moody, 1978), 1973.
5. Henry C. Thiessen, "An Outline of Lectures in Systematic Theology," 3d ed. (unpublished class notes, Wheaton College, 1942).
6. *The NIV Study Bible* (Grand Rapids: Zondervan, 1985), 1621.

ENDNOTES

CHAPTER 8—CHRIST'S ASCENSION TO THE RIGHT HAND OF GOD THE FATHER

1. Ryrie, *The Ryrie Study Bible (NASB)*, 1932.
2. Ibid.

CHAPTER 9—CHRIST'S PRESENT MINISTRY AT THE RIGHT HAND OF GOD THE FATHER

1. Craig A. Blaising and Darrell L. Bock, *Progressive Dispensationalism* (Wheaton, Ill.: Victor, 1993), 49 (italics theirs).
2. Darrell L. Bock, "The Reign of the Lord Christ," in *Dispensationalism, Israel and the Church,* ed. Craig A. Blaising and Darrell L. Bock (Grand Rapids: Zondervan, 1992), 65.
3. Ibid.
4. Ibid., 50.
5. Craig A. Blaising and Darrell L. Bock, "Dispensationalism, Israel and the Church: Assessment and Dialogue," in *Dispensationalism, Israel and the Church,* 381.
6. Ibid. (italics theirs).
7. Ibid., 65.
8. Blaising and Bock, *Progressive Dispensationalism,* 31.
9. Ibid., 152.
10. Ibid.
11. Elliott E. Johnson, "Hermeneutical Principles and the Interpretation of Psalm 110," *Bibliotheca Sacra* 149 (October–December 1992): 433–34 (italics his).
12. Ibid., 436.
13. Abbott-Smith, *A Manual Greek Lexicon,* 340 (italics his).
14. Edwin A. Blum, "John" in *The Bible Knowledge Commentary, New Testament,* 328.

CHAPTER 10—CHRIST'S TRANSLATION OF HIS CHURCH TO HEAVEN

1. Merrill C. Tenney, "John," in *Zondervan NIV Bible Commentary,* 345.
2. Robertson, *Word Pictures,* 5:249.

3. Paul Lee Tan, "Rapture, Partial," in *Dictionary of Premillennial Theology*, ed. Mal Couch (Grand Rapids: Kregel, 1996), 347–48 (italics his).

4. John F. Walvoord, "Revelation," in *The Bible Knowledge Commentary, New Testament*, 975.

CHAPTER 11—THE ESTABLISHMENT OF THE REIGN OF THE KING ON EARTH

1. Walter L. Liefeld, "Luke," in *Zondervan NIV Bible Commentary, New Testament*, ed. Kenneth L. Barker and John Kohlengberger III (Grand Rapids: Zondervan, 1994), 272.

2. Harold W. Hoehner, "Herod," in *Zondervan Pictorial Encyclopedia of the Bible*, 3:138.

3. Arnold G. Fruchtenbaum, "Day of the Lord," in *Dictionary of Premillennial Theology*, 87.

4. Paul Enns, *The Moody Handbook of Theology* (Chicago: Moody, 1986), 633; see 129.

5. John F. Walvoord, "Revelation," in *The Bible Knowledge Commentary, New Testament*, 947; see 976.

6. Louis A. Barbieri, Jr., "Matthew," in *The Bible Knowledge Commentary, New Testament*, 81.

CHAPTER 12—THE ONE-THOUSAND-YEAR REIGN OF THE KING ON EARTH

1. Rick Bowman and Russell L. Penney, "Amillennialism," in *Dictionary of Premillennial Theology*, 37.

2. Thomas D. Ice, "Postmillennialism," in *Dictionary of Premillennial Theology*, 307.

3. Ibid.

4. Arnold Fruchtenbaum, "Palestinian Covenant," in *Dictionary of Premillennial Theology*, 291.

5. Ibid., 291–92.

Bibliography

Berkouwer, G. C. *The Person of Christ.* Grand Rapids: Wm. B. Eerdmans Publishing Co., 1947.

Briner, Bob. *The Management Methods of Jesus.* Nashville: Thomas Nelson, 1996.

Chafer, Lewis Sperry. *Systematic Theology.* Dallas: Dallas Seminary Press, 1948; reprint (8 vols. in 4), Grand Rapids: Kregel Publications, 1993.

Couch, Mal, ed. *Dictionary of Premillennial Theology.* Grand Rapids: Kregel Publications, 1996.

Elwell, Walter A., ed. *A Topical Analysis of the Bible.* Grand Rapids: Baker Books, 1991.

Enns, Paul. *The Moody Handbook of Theology.* Chicago: Moody Press, 1989.

Gariepy, Henry. *100 Portraits of Christ.* Wheaton, Ill.: Victor Books, 1987.

Henry, Carl F. H. *God, Revelation, and Authority.* Vols. 2 and 3. Waco, Tex.: Word Books, 1976, 1979.

Hodge, Charles. *Systematic Theology.* 3 vols. New York: Charles Scribner's, 1911.

Hoehner, Harold W. *Chronological Aspects of the Life of Christ.* Grand Rapids: Zondervan Publishing House, 1977.

Ice, Thomas, and Timothy Demy, eds. *When the Trumpet Sounds.* Eugene, Oreg.: Harvest House Publications, 1995.

Lucado, Max. *No Wonder They Call Him Savior.* Portland, Oreg.: Multnomah Press, 1986.

Morgan, G. Campbell. *The Crises of the Christ.* Westwood, N.J.: Fleming H. Revell Co., 1936.

Pentecost, J. Dwight. *The Words and Works of Jesus Christ.* Grand Rapids: Zondervan Publishing House, 1961.

Ryrie, Charles C. *Basic Theology.* Wheaton, Ill.: Victor Books, 1986.

Schilder, K. *Christ in His Suffering.* Translated by Henry Zylstra. Grand Rapids: Wm. B. Eerdmans Publishing Co., 1938.

_____. *Christ on Trial.* Grand Rapids: Wm. B. Eerdmans Publishing Co., 1939.

_____. *Christ on the Cross.* Grand Rapids: Wm. B. Eerdmans Publishing Co., 1940.

Showers, Renald E. *There Really Is a Difference: A Comparison of Covenant and Dispensational Theology.* Bellmawr, N.J.: Friends of Israel Gospel Ministry, 1990.

Walvoord, John F. *Jesus Christ Our Lord.* Chicago: Moody Press, 1969.

_____. *The Prophecy Knowledge Handbook.* Wheaton, Ill.: Victor Books, 1990.

_____, and Zuck, Roy B., eds. *The Bible Knowledge Commentary.* 2 vols. Wheaton, Ill.: Victor Books, 1983, 1985.

Wells, David F. *The Person of Christ.* Westchester, Ill.: Crossway Books, 1984.

Zuck, Roy B., ed. *Vital Christology Issues.* Grand Rapids: Kregel Publications, 1997.

_____. *Vital Prophecy Issues.* Grand Rapids: Kregel Publications, 1995.

Scripture Index

Subject Index

Simeon, 73–74, 75, 101
Simon Peter. *See Peter*
Sodom and Gomorrah, 26, 39
Solomon, 29, 158
Son, Jesus Christ as, 47–48
    of David, 36, 40
    of Man, 51–52
    of the Most High, 54
    to be Given, 159
Source, Jesus Christ as, 57
Star of Bethlehem, 72–73
Stephen, 51, 58
Stoics, on logos, 2
Stone, Jesus Christ as, 59, 135
Strauss, David Friedrich, 64
Strimple, Robert, 64
Suffering servant, Jesus Christ as, 52
    of God, 102

—T—

Talmadge, James E., 85
Talmud, 16
Tan, Paul Lee, 140
Teacher, Jesus Christ as, 55
Tenney, Merrill C., 7, 137
Tetragrammaton, 14
Theonomic postmillennialism, 156
Theophilus, 65
Thiessen, Henry, 97
Thomas, 112
Thousand–year reign, 155–64
Throne of Jesus, 119–20
Tiglath–Pileser, 33
Titles of Jesus Christ, 60–61
Titus, 104
Tribulation, 148–50, 151, 153, 154.
    See also Great Tribulation
Tribulation martyrs, 149
Trinitarianism, 84
Trinity, as biblical doctrine, 7–8
Triune Godhead, Jesus Christ as
    member, 1–12
Typology, in Old Testament, 37–42

—UV—

Unbelievers, judgment of, 167–68
United Nations, 161
Vine, Jesus Christ as, 54, 136
Virgin birth.
    *See Jesus Christ, conception
    announced*

—WXYZ—

Walvoord, John F., 34, 142–43, 150
Watchtower Bible and Tract Society,
    85
Weiss, Johannes, 65
Wells, Orson, 63
Whitby, Daniel, 156
White, W., 72
Wisdom of Jesus ben Sirach, 2
Wisdom of Solomon, 2
Word of God, 150
    as equal with God, 5–9
    as wisdom of God, 1–2
    creating world, 12
    in Old Testament, 23–42
    Jesus Christ as, 1–3, 58.
        See also Preincarnate Word of God
Yahweh, 14, 46
Zadok, 29
Zechariah, 17, 18, 67–68